THE MUDPUDDLE MANUAL OF NATURAL MAGIC

CIARA BLUME

Storm
PUBLISHING

This is a work of fiction. Names, characters, businesses, places, events and incidents are either the products of the author's imagination or used in a fictitious manner. Any resemblance to actual persons, living or dead, or actual events is purely coincidental.

Previously published in 2024.

Ebook ISBN: 978-1-83700-603-8
Paperback ISBN: 978-1-83700-604-5

Cover design: Sara Murtas
Cover images: Sara Murtas

Published by Storm Publishing.
For further information, visit:
www.stormpublishing.co

This book is dedicated to the little girl who spent long summer days reading eighty-year-old novels while sitting in an apple tree.
It's for Inez Haynes Irwin, whose sunny orange Maida books I still search for at antique bookstores and estate sales because I can still taste the apples and remember the delight.
Inez was a pretty cool character herself. You should check her out.
The Mudpuddle Manual is for my family and friends, who have had infinite patience with me while I write.
I promise I'll make dinner all next week.
And lastly, it's for HK, my beautiful odd-eyed feline editor who tried so hard to make it to the last chapter with me!
She was the most magical.

Picture a meadow dappled with sunlight where a kaleidoscope of butterflies flutters. These ethereal creatures have a peculiar gathering ritual known as "Mud Puddling."

With dainty feet and a reverence for the soil, the butterflies crowd around damp depressions of fecund earth. They take turns sipping at a muddy potion of decayed and fermented materials, minerals, and elemental magic.

This phenomenon is not merely about seeking sustenance. It is a ritual where the magical creatures gather to process, transform, and release beneficial earth energy. Their colorful wings shimmer with added brilliance after partaking. You should count yourself fortunate if you witness this bewitching behavior.

-EXCERPT FROM THE MUDPUDDLE MANUAL OF NATURAL MAGIC

ONE

STRANGE BEDFELLOWS

Guardianship of arcane items and magical artifacts is a role that should only be entrusted to pure blood witches and wizards.

In order to ensure they are neither misused nor diminished, these relics require carefully vetted caretakers. A curator's magic must be untainted.

To place our history in the hands of the impure is to risk irreparable harm to our magical heritage. It is the duty of the pureblooded to safeguard the power and legacy that our kind has maintained for generations.

-EXCERPT FROM THE ARCANE ELITE: PRESERVING THE SANCTITY OF WITCH BLOODLINES

The night before the Mudpuddle Bookshop and Cafe mysteriously vanished, Minerva Lathrop threaded her way past a rusted, green dumpster and into the narrow brick alley that hid the entrance to Primrose Court. The fog was so thick she could barely see past the end of her long, pointed nose, upon which a pair of round wire spectacles balanced. The glasses looked charming on her, lending a sweet granny effect to her pink apple cheeks. But they were just part of her costume. Her vision was still as sharp as her mind.

The fog blurred the texture of the brick-and-mortar walls that loomed close on either side. The gloomy, wet mist nearly extinguished the limited light in the alley. Ominous shadows crawled into every crevice, like pill bugs nestling under rocks.

None of this bothered Minerva one bit. She was familiar with the repelling wards in this alley and didn't spook easily. The shadows, creaks, and howls didn't faze her. She could have found her way home with her eyes closed.

She desperately wanted to close her eyes. Her lids were heavy after a long day of travel.

Over one arm, Minerva carried a handwoven straw bag. It contained her passport and a shiny new T-watch Minerva was determined never to use. If she was being honest, fear kept her from turning it on. She had no desire to take a dip in the well of collective consciousness. Keeping track of her own thoughts was plenty. Struggling with an external device that all the young folk seemed to wield like an extension of their own selves was unsettling. It made her feel incompetent. So she simply avoided it, carrying it only because she was told she must. For emergencies. Though she could hardly imagine what emergency might be that dire.

She was also dragging a simple, brown, mid-size leather suitcase, strapped to a metal trolley. The heavy bag wobbled and thumped along behind her in the alley, trolley wheels catching on the cobblestones. Minerva grimaced as the bag toppled. Wrestling with it reminded her that witches are flesh, like all mortals. She lived with the indignity of arthritis. It was worse when she left home and couldn't simply pop by the apothecary to pester her niece Lucretia for a remedy.

Minerva used to anticipate international travel eagerly, but it was getting harder and harder to bounce back from her annual procurement tour of the continent. Several times on this trip, she'd wondered whether it might be the last one. And what a shame if it was! This trip wasn't the victory lap she'd envisioned for her final mission. This trip had been nothing but an exhausting waste of her time. She'd failed to locate a single item to add to the Arcane Archives. She was returning home empty-handed and baffled.

Abandoned grimoires and discarded supernatural artifacts weren't tricky for conservationist witches to come by if they knew where to look. And even if they didn't know where to look. Those sorts of things were always turning up at auctions and estate sales. She'd also had great luck in lost luggage warehouses, flea markets, and thrift shops. Minerva knew all the best and worst places to find enchanted items. She'd had a knack for it even before she'd accepted the critical duty of securing objects for safekeeping. She'd never failed before.

She wasn't sure if it was her or something else. It made little sense. The sudden dearth of magical relics at home and abroad was disturbing.

Minerva now regretted subjecting herself to commercial transportation. Moving through Logan and Heathrow Airports, blending in with the ordinaries, was no way for a witch of her vintage to travel. She should have sprung for a private porter to take her directly to her destination.

At least she hadn't had to resort to an elaborate disguise. Her age did have some advantages. She did not need to waste any of her precious energy conjuring glamors. Older women were naturally invisible in modern Ordinary society.

Reaching the final stretch of the long, lonesome alley, Minerva dropped the pretense of being an Ordinary elderly tourist and released the handle to her roller bag. She breathed a sigh of relief as the suitcase continued to trail behind her, much like a pet. It paused obediently and hovered just above the cobblestones when she stopped to shake the broken cracker bits out of her pocket. The mice would appreciate the airline snacks far more than she had. The crumbs the Ordinaries had to make do with! Barely fit for her rodent friends.

Finally, Minerva turned sideways and shimmied behind a rusted metal sign hiding the arched entry to Primrose Court.

As soon as she stepped into the tunnel-like brick passage, she could see the moonlight streaming in from the other side of the bricked passageway, not more than ten feet away. She couldn't wait to return to the Mudpuddle bookshop, head upstairs, and crawl into bed.

The night sounds in Primrose Court were gentle as she emerged at the center of a large urban park. Pitch pine needles were tapping out a gentle rhythm. Ruffled oak and elm leaves danced in the wind. In the distance, she heard the distinctive trilling warble of an eastern screech owl singing along. The night sky was clear and bright. The silvery light from the full moon bathed the path ahead. The fog was gone.

Home at last. It could have been another world.

Exiting the park onto a wide tree-lined street, Minerva drank in the sight of the Mudpuddle, a three-story Queen Anne-style house comprising architectural bits and whimsy. It included a round turret, a widow's walk, and a wraparound covered porch. All the railings and posts were elaborately carved and detailed. The house greeted her with a wink from one of the two eyebrow windows set into the sloping shingled roof.

A sign, illuminated by a streetlamp, was posted near the front gate. It welcomed shoppers to the Mudpuddle Bookstore and Cafe. The Arcane Archives, hidden in the vault below the house, warranted no advertising. Visitors were few and far between and required special clearance from the Society for the Protection of Natural Magic.

As it was the wee small hours the house was completely dark and silent.

Minerva snapped her fingers at her roller bag. She smiled indulgently as it flew ahead of her, rushing down the path and up the front stairs to land with a soft thunk on the porch.

Hopefully, the sound wouldn't wake Zephyr. He wasn't expecting her home till tomorrow, but she'd switched to an earlier flight. There was no point in disturbing Zephyr's rest. She didn't need him to let her back in. The Mudpuddle never failed to unlock itself for her, its caretaker.

Minerva had known Zephyr since they were childhood sweethearts. Once upon a time, she'd been confident they'd have a future together. And then he'd been called away on a special mission for the Société pour la Protection de la Magie in Quebec. That decades-long mission had kept him away from Primrose Court ever since, with only the briefest of exceptions.

The Society, as the agency was known in the United States, had appointed Zephyr as the secondary guardian of the Arcane Archives. This meant that Zephyr minded the Mudpuddle Bookshop and protected the relics whenever Minerva traveled. It was an awkward, bittersweet arrangement that kept him in her life while ensuring they could never really be together. It would have been much simpler if the Society had let her niece Lucretia be the guardian. But the Mudpuddle tended to disapparate whenever Minerva left Primrose Court. Lucretia wasn't about to risk being inside the shop when this happened. The Mudpuddle only stayed put for her or Zephyr. And Zephyr only stayed put for the duration of his assignments.

He'd be gone first thing in the morning, probably before she woke.

Minerva let herself in and shuffled wearily past the dusty, cluttered shelves in the foyer gift shop. How quickly the dust gathered in her absence! She paused briefly to cast a cleaning spell and slipped in an overnight baking charm. The clock on the mantel chimed a reminder of how late—or early—it was. Four a.m. It would be nice to wake up to familiar smells and to replenish the bakery case in the morning. She didn't have to check to see that Zephyr had barely kept the place in cookies while she was away. Baking charms were not his forte.

Her bedroom was on the third floor of the turret. It was at the front corner of the house, aligned with the street corner, and boasted the best view possible, save for the widow's walk. Minerva accessed this private chamber via the spiral staircase hidden behind a revolving bookcase in the corner of the coffee shop.

Absent-mindedly, Minerva kicked off her pointed boots in the vestibule at the top of the stairs. She placed her hat and traveling cloak on the coat rack. Moonbeams streamed through the large, curved glass windows. They bounced off the mirrored glass ball on her nightstand and sparkled like stolen starlight when they hit the many mirrored shapes embedded in the midnight blue plaster walls. At the center of the circular room, a round cloud-like bed beckoned. Her bedroom really was the perfect peaceful, celestial dream space.

Minerva was startled as an unexpected exhalation ripped through the silence. She wasn't alone in the room! She felt the floorboards shake gently beneath her feet, humming along with the solid, even brushstroke of Zephyr's raspy snoring.

He was sleeping in her bed. Not in the guest room that she kept ready for him. Her bed. In her room. Whatever for?

He looked so peaceful. Once again, Minerva thought it would be a pity to wake him.

It was late, and Minerva was tired. Too tired to kick Zephyr out. So she unpinned her long braids, shook out her wavy gray hair, and crawled beside him fully clothed. Who cares anymore? We're both too old to worry about silly things like etiquette.

It wasn't just the cold that made Minerva shiver as she pressed closer to the ambient warmth of the old but solid man in her bed. She had to admit that for once in her life it was nice not to go to bed alone.

TWO

BISCUITS AND CHEESE

In matters of courtship and marriage, the preservation of witch bloodlines should always be top of mind.

While the heart may flutter at the sly charms of a fae, or the bestial beauty of a shifter, such unions are beneath the pure blood witch or wizard.

One must seek a match that honors the sanctity of one's lineage, ensuring that future generations remain unstained by untoward influences.

-EXCERPT FROM THE ARCANE ELITE: PRESERVING THE SANCTITY OF WITCH BLOODLINES

Zephyr was gone when Minerva woke to the patter of raindrops against her window. But someone had snuck a warm patchwork quilt around her and placed a hot water bottle near her feet.

She was almost ashamed to acknowledge her delight when she found a note on her pillow.

That was a delicious surprise.

Zephyr's loose, scrawling handwriting had always taken up too much space on the page, much the way he had always taken up too much space in her heart. She blushed and flipped the note over, smiling at how his letters got smaller towards the end of the note. He'd reached the halfway point before realizing that he'd have to downsize to fit it all in.

"Come down when you're awake. There's something I'd love to talk to you about."

She could hear her own heart racing. He was still here. He wanted to talk. Why now? After all these years?

Minerva shut the thought down before she could even tentatively explore it. As the mousy sister and spinster aunt, she knew the folly of dreaming impossible dreams. She was who she was, and that's what made her the perfect caretaker for the Mudpuddle. There had been no one in her life after Zephyr, and she couldn't afford to get her hopes up again at her age. It was a ridiculous notion.

Besides, she hadn't been unhappy all these years. Running the bookstore and tending to the Arcane Archives was her whole life. She loved it.

She thought Zephyr probably wanted her help with a rally or a fundraiser. He frequently sent over flyers for some cause or another to be posted in the Mudpuddle. She'd allowed it, even though she was loath to let anyone else advertise there.

Minerva considered the Mudpuddle Bookshop and Cafe hers even though she did not technically own it. Her great-grandniece, Maida Lathrop Westabrook, an Ordinary girl who had never once set foot in Primrose Court, was still the legal owner.

This was a very troubling situation indeed.

It was not troubling because Minerva feared being usurped by the girl. Even though Maida Westabrook was the legal heir, the Mudpuddle required a magical caretaker. No Ordinary girl would do.

She was acutely aware that all good things come to an end, eventually. This included her life and tenure as caretaker. She often worried about what would happen to the Mudpuddle when she passed.

Perhaps it was time for the family to consult with a solicitor again.

Minerva carefully set a steaming floral teapot down on an ornate silver trivet. She liked to drink her morning tea at a table tucked into the shop's round reading nook. Not far from the cafe counter, the reading nook was snuggled into the turret beneath her bedroom.

It had the perfect street-view observation angle. She had a clear view of the passersby and their activities from her window seat. In the summer, when she cracked the windows, she enjoyed doing a bit of eavesdropping on their neighbors as well.

Two delicate bone china teacups were already on the table, set steadily in their saucers, patiently awaiting her pour. She closed her eyes and inhaled the vaguely floral scent of the tea, mingling with the scent of old books, ink, baked goods, and a savory sandwich Zephyr had concocted for them to share.

Onions, and pickled herring? She sighed contentedly. It was so good to be back home. More than that. Everything felt extra homey with Zephyr here to share the morning with her.

Zephyr sat in a chair by the leaded glass window. He was leaning forward with his elbows on the burnished oak table, reading a newspaper as if this were a regular morning ritual for the two of them. He would have looked very dignified if not for the cookie crumbs strewn all down the front of his woolly blazer and scattered in his gray beard.

"Zephyr! You could have at least waited until I finished brewing the tea!" Minerva chastised, noting the empty plate where her freshly baked cookies had been sitting moments before.

"Minerva, how can you honestly expect any man to resist your lemon drizzle biscuits for that long?" Zephyr protested. Despite his overgrown gray brows, the twinkle in his bright blue eyes was still visible. It belied his actual age. One hundred and eleven years old. He was three years older than Minerva, which made both of them elderly, but hardly ancient, for witches.

Minerva huffed half-heartedly and sat down. At least he hadn't started in on their sandwiches yet. She stared out the window as she waited for the tea to finish brewing and tried not to think about what he wanted to talk about.

Outside, the morning was gray and still—a sleepy Sunday. All was quiet now, but it wouldn't be long before customers streamed into the shop. Steam from the teapot gathered on the inside of the pane. It tempted Minerva to write her name on it, just like a child.

Reading her mind, Zephyr licked a finger, scrawled Z+M, and winked at her.

"It's been far too long since I woke up with a woman in my bed, Minnie. I wouldn't mind making it a regular thing." Zephyr got straight to the point.

"I'm not sure I could keep enough cookies in the shop, Zippy." She couldn't deny that his words gave her a thrill. She'd enjoyed sleeping next to him as well.

What was that feeling she was feeling? Vindication? Relief? Disbelief? There had to be a catch. It couldn't be this simple.

"I'm afraid we're too old to change our ways now," Minerva said.

"Nonsense. It's never too late to right a wrong," Zephyr countered.

"Hush. Someone will walk in and hear you," Minerva argued.

"I'm not sure I care if they do. I had an odd feeling last night, waiting for you to return, Minnie. I didn't want to go home today."

"Why would you when you had all the best books and magical baked goods at your disposal in my shop?" Minnie raised a brow.

"I didn't want to go home because I wanted to stay here. With you," Zephyr said. "I can't help but think what might have happened if I hadn't signed my life over to the Society. We could have run this place together."

"Stop." Minerva shook her head, hoping to clear her thoughts.

"There's no changing the past. Besides, I can't even think before tea."

"Can we talk about our future after the tea, then?" Zephyr asked.

"Maybe." Minerva shrugged, playing it cool. Maybe? Of course she would! Didn't she deserve a little happiness as well? She had quietly toiled for decades in this shop, accepting her fate, never even dreaming of anything more.

Her skin prickled with something. Hope? Excitement? Fear? She was glad there was nobody else in the shop. She needed a moment to process.

Zephyr shook out his paper and resumed reading. Minerva continued to look out the window at the empty sidewalk beyond the gate.

The residents of Primrose Court were all probably enjoying a good lie-in, but Minerva felt restless. She stole sidelong glances at Zephyr while waiting for the tea to brew. Impatiently, she tapped her spoon. She could have sped it up with magic, but that always affected the flavor.

There was no rushing a good brew.

Finally, after what felt like ages, Minerva lifted the lid of the pot to check. Honey brown and sweet smelling from the orange blossoms. She'd added in a pinch of lavender for her nerves.

"It's done," she announced. Zephyr folded his paper and squeezed her free hand as she poured.

"Thank you for letting me leave my flyers in the shop again," he said, pointing to a stack of leaflets on the counter. "It's vitally important that we get the word out about Nocturnaturals. I hate to think of the junior members of our community being harmed by that synthetic junk. Such dangerous times we live in, Minerva."

She didn't bother to argue with him about that. All times were dangerous to someone, somewhere. Ebb and flow. But things had been more tense than usual in Primrose Court lately, and the recent virality of Nocturnaturals "magical" products in the Ordinary world was only making the usual underlying tensions worse.

Zephyr sighed, his brow becoming ridged with imagined troubles. He was clearly thinking similar thoughts. But as she finished filling both cups, he met her eyes. "Not to worry, dear. We will weather this storm like all the others."

He held the teacup below his nose, inhaling deeply, his entire expression changing. "Perfection, as always. You don't have any more biscuits that I might dunk, do you?" His eyes sparkled, and when they met hers, she felt like she'd just been asked to dance.

"For you?" Minerva shook her head. "Fine. But only if you call them cookies. You were born and raised on this side of the pond. No need for such an affectation!" She pushed back her chair and stood to fetch a few more cookies.

But the tinkle of the bell on the door interrupted Minerva's mission. The first customer of the day had arrived.

THREE

UNEXPECTED COMPANY

As it is necessary to interact with lesser beings in the course of daily life, one must always maintain a veil of decorum.

Courtesy should not be mistaken for camaraderie.

Just as one would treat a servant with kindness but never as an equal, so too should one interact with shifters, fae, and other such creatures.

They have their place in the world, but it is not by our side.

—EXCERPT FROM THE ARCANE ELITE: UPHOLDING THE SANCTITY OF WITCH BLOODLINES

Minerva didn't recognize the cloaked customer. This was unusual, as Primrose Court was such a cloistered community by design. Newcomers were a rarity but not unheard of.

She smiled and was about to offer help, but the shopper waved to dismiss her before diving straight into the stacks and stacks of books that filled the converted bedrooms toward the back of the house. Most of the customers didn't stray far from the home's capacious parlor, which was now the heart of the bookshop cafe. But there were always others who preferred to wander off alone while perusing in the bookshop.

Minerva peered back at Zephyr. The old wizard was unabashedly grinning at her, his eyes growing starrier by the moment. Meanwhile, she'd forgotten why she was standing.

"So you'll let me have some more of your biscuits, then?" Zephyr raised an eyebrow, hopefully.

"Cookies! Do you even hear yourself? So pretentious." She rolled her eyes at him.

"Biscuits, cookies. I'll take whatever crumbs you care to toss my way." Zephyr sipped his tea without breaking eye contact.

Minerva felt a kaleidoscope of butterflies awakening in her belly. She wiggled her fingers as if the motion could release the fluttery feeling, but she just couldn't shake it. It was best to keep moving.

"You just reminded me," she said, busying herself behind the counter. "Would you like a marvelous piece of cheese with your breakfast?" She piled more cookies on an antique toile-patterned plate, leaving space to one side. Then she unlocked the small glass-fronted cheese fridge beside the counter and removed a precious parcel. Carefully, she unwrapped a small wheel of handcrafted white Stilton.

"I wondered about the dairy case. It's new, isn't it?" Zephyr nodded his approval at the display.

"Yes," she explained. "Lucretia tried to talk me out of it, but you know how much I enjoy an excellent cheddar." Her niece Lucretia had indeed argued against the addition, but it was difficult to take advice from someone who was lactose intolerant. Lactose and everything else. Lucretia was not known for being tolerant.

"Well, I'd say adding a petite fromagerie case was a gouda idea." Zephyr chuckled, and Minerva groaned.

"That's how you plan to woo me? With terrible dad jokes?"

"What's a dad joke?" Zephyr asked. He was genuinely curious, without guile.

"Oh, it's just a term that Ordinaries use for punny humor and pitiful jokes." Minerva placed the plate back on the table and sat down. Despite Zephyr's renowned intellect, this was one area where she had more cross-cultural expertise. Her travels had brought her into closer contact with the Ordinaries. She also had a vast collection of video cartridges and a small smuggled television stashed in her bedroom.

Watching Ordinary sitcoms was her guilty pleasure. That, and eating extraordinary cheeses. In fact, the two pursuits paired well.

Minerva sighed happily as she bit into a crisp, sweet lemon cookie topped with a bit of the Stilton. The flavors paired perfectly. She washed it all down with a sip of her aromatic tea.

Zephyr was still stealing glances at her. She noticed he hadn't turned the page of his newspaper since they'd started talking. The headline on the article he kept returning to read: "Langour Epidemic Worsens: Experts Question the Effects of Ordinary Products on Magical Folk."

She looked away. She didn't want to think about it, much less talk about it. Now that she was finally home and safe, she just wanted to relax. She topped off Zephyr's teacup.

"This is so nice," Zephyr said, taking her hand in his after she set the teapot down.

"Yes, it is," she admitted, making no move to pull her hand away.

The bells jangled once again as an unusually tall and brawny young man propelled the front door open with a rough shoulder thrust. Clearly, he didn't know his own strength. The doorknob hit the rubber bumper that was placed on the wall, precisely for this purpose, and stuck there a moment as if to regain its composure before closing again in a much slower and more dignified fashion.

Minerva studied the boy. He wasn't a regular here, but she'd seen him around town. He had high cheekbones and long, shaggy, dark hair that fell into his eyes. His large, wide-set brown eyes had a glossy, bestial sheen. One of his nostrils twitched, mid-flare. His lips pressed together, forming a tight, resentful seal. Despite the angst that oozed from every pore, there was something devastatingly beautiful about him.

Now that he was inside the shop, he seemed confused about why he'd come in. He glanced around as if he had lost his way, then looked back at the front door. Two rough-looking boys, presumably his friends, were waiting for him outside. They sat astride their kinetic bikes, hovering near the stairs.

"I'm looking for my friend Rosie, have you seen her?" he demanded bluntly.

Of course Minerva knew Rosie. She was a regular in the cafe, always there for game night and slam poetry readings. Even though the vivacious teen lived outside the neighborhood, she seemed to spend most of her free time in the shop.

The boy sneezed loudly, blowing dust clouds off the curio cabinet in the entry. She was too short to see the top, so she always forgot to spell away the dust there.

"Is everything old in this place?" he sneered at Minerva. He wasn't sure what his chief complaint was, but judging by the belligerent tone, he would not let that stop him from picking a fight.

Minerva hoped there wouldn't be trouble. Petty theft and pranks were par for the course, but on the whole, things were peaceful in Primrose Court.

"Is there anything else that I might help you with, young man?" She beamed her sweetest shopkeeper smile at him. It wasn't entirely his fault that he was so broody. Teen hormones could be akin to a curse. He was only sixteen or seventeen. Barely more than a child.

"Rosie was supposed to meet me here," the boy repeated. "I need to get a book from her. Are you sure she didn't leave it here for me?"

"Afraid not. Do you want to take a seat and wait for her? I can make you a sandwich and some tea if you like?" She didn't care whether he could pay for it. She could always spare a sandwich.

"No," he muttered, crossing to the counter and sweeping the

surface with his eyes. As if he expected his book to materialize there. "I just want my book."

"I don't have your book," Minerva said.

"You sure?" The boy raised a suspicious eyebrow. He continued to look around, pulling open stock drawers beneath the bookshelves, and nearly toppling a display in his haste. He eyed her skeptically and spoke to her like she was the child. "You didn't sell it to someone else by accident? Or maybe it slipped your mind?"

Now he was getting on her nerves. Normally, she would have more to say to such a rude teenager, but noting the colorful Nocturnaturals "performance patch" on the boy's bare bicep, she chose her words cautiously. She didn't want to rile him up further. She didn't know the circumstances that had driven him to dabble with that stuff.

"Yes, I'm sure. I haven't seen Rosie, and she hasn't left any books for...What did you say your name was?" Minerva kept her head high and jutted her chin out just a touch.

The boy pounded a fist on the counter and glanced back at his friends waiting outside. "I can't believe she didn't come!"

"What kind of book did you say it was? What's the title? Perhaps we have another in stock?" Minerva ducked behind the counter, sweeping up the stack of flyers Zephyr had placed there and hiding them on a lower shelf.

"You know what? Since you're here already, try the biscuits. They're really scrumptious," Zephyr called out from the reading nook. He'd folded his paper, concealing the disturbing headline.

The boy slowly pivoted towards Zephyr, noticing for the first time that someone else was sitting in the coffee shop. He shook his head with a shudder. Minerva smelled the strong animal scent clinging to him. He smelled gamey. Wet wool, with an unsubtle note of barn.

He must have shifted recently. Thick fuzz clung to his jawline and the backs of his hands.

Suddenly, the boy drew his brows together and lowered his

head at her, almost like a bull about to charge at the counter. Minerva's heart skipped a beat, and her hand flew to her wand pocket. But before she could wrap five fingers around the slender, polished bit of ash, Zephyr was on his feet, standing by her side.

Thunderbolts and lightning! He was still fast. Far quicker than one might have thought possible for a one-hundred-and-eleven-year-old wizard.

Zephyr drew himself to his full height, which was still close to six feet tall. But he barely reached the boy's chin.

"Easy there..." Zephyr spoke in soothing tones. "How about we all sit down for a nice cup of tea and cookies?"

The boy ignored him, swatting away the suggestion with a flick of his hand like a beast of burden swats flies with its tail.

Not a bull, she thought. A bull would have charged already. Once again, the boy tossed his head. He exhaled into a pouty lower lip, blowing the hair out of his eyes. Minerva smelled the not-unpleasant scents of wet grass and earth emanating from him, and suddenly she remembered him. Bardo Chan. He lived with his grandmother Pearl in an apartment on the edge of town. At least he had until recently. Pearl had passed away last month. All of Pearl's sons had been yak shifters. And so, apparently, was Bardo. A big gorgeous one from the looks of it. She allowed herself a small sigh of relief and loosened the grip on the wand in her pocket. Yaks were rarely violent in either their human or animal forms. He probably wasn't all that much of a threat.

Although, with that Nocturnaturals patch on his arm, who knew? The effects of synthetic magic on shifters was unpredictable. It could be lethal.

Minerva glanced outside, checking on the other two boys. They were shifters as well, though she wasn't sure what type. She wondered if their parents had bought the kinetic bikes for them or if they'd stolen them from local witches. Not her most charitable thought. But magical bikes were preposterously dear, and the boys were both dressed shabbily.

Zephyr approached the youth warily. Foolishly, she thought.

"So how long have you been using those patches, son?" Zephyr asked, keeping his voice steady, his tone neutral.

"I'm hardly your 'son', am I?" the boy scoffed and snorted. "You witches are the reason we need this stuff. We've endured decades of oppression because of your mind-controlling, prejudicial witch ways. Otherwise, we'd have just as much money and power as you. Possibly more."

"Do I look like I'm rich and powerful?" Zephyr asked. "Want to know a secret? I was just trying to convince this woman to take me back into her bed." He laughed self-deprecatingly as he brushed the rest of the cookie crumbs from his beard. "She probably thinks I'm too old, but I've still got some sparks left in the fireplace. If you hadn't just walked in, I might have tried to convince her to shut the place down for the day." He stopped just short of wagging his eyebrows.

Minerva glared at Zephyr, mortified. He was laying it on too thick, but she had to admit it was working on the boy. The sudden change of subject took all the wind out of the young shifter's sails. She watched as the boy's eyes darted from Zephyr to herself and back to her. Horrified understanding dawned across his features. He took a step back, flinching a bit.

"Ugh! Yuck! Gross." He grimaced. "Can you fossils still *do* that?" He touched the patch on his arm, rubbing two fingers across it like a child checking in on their lovey.

"Of course we can. And we don't need any of that synthetic Nocturnaturals garbage." Zephyr pointed to the patch, changing tack again now that the situation seemed less volatile. "That company isn't helping any of us. That's the one thing we should all be agreeing on. I'd like to invite you and your friends to a public meeting on Wednesday to learn a bit more about and discuss the problems with synthetic magic. It's an open meeting for all to attend. Fetch him a flyer, Minerva?" Zephyr smiled hopefully. "There will even be free snacks!"

"Do I look like I can't afford to buy my own snacks?" The

youth stomped his foot and narrowed his eyes at Zephyr. "Back off, graybeard."

Zephyr's hands went up, and he shrugged. "I mean you no harm..."

"Excuse me?" The unfamiliar customer who'd wandered in earlier called out from the next room. Minerva had almost forgotten he was there.

"I was hoping to retrieve a book from the Arcane Archives." The customer poked his head around the corner. "Is there someone here who might help me?" His accent had a hint of Creole.

"I'm sorry," Minerva spoke over her shoulder to him. "The Archives are closed on weekends. You'll also need to show your reference letter from the Society in order to access the book. Do you have that with you?" She turned to face him and was a bit startled by how attractive he was.

"Oh dear," the customer made a show of patting the pockets of his cloak. "I'm afraid I don't. But I don't think it should be necessary. It's my great-grandmother's grimoire. It never should have ended up here. Terrible mix-up. I was hoping we could sort it out ourselves."

Minerva frowned. As much as she enjoyed helping younger witches to reconnect with their roots, there were protocols. She could hardly hand things over to anyone who asked. There was something slightly off about this one as well. Not a witch, she thought. Possibly a powerful mage, though.

Mages were the rare exception to Primrose Court's ban on Ordinaries. Most of them were descended from witches whose bloodlines became too diluted to pass on their powers.

"Surely there's a way. My poor maman is heartsick at the thought of her grandmere's wisdom being mislaid, possibly falling into the wrong hands..."

"That is precisely the reason we have such strict protocols," Minerva cut him off. Zephyr gave her an approving nod. She didn't need his approval! But it still felt nice. And simultaneously, annoying.

The yak shifter cleared his throat and glanced sidelong at the stranger. They seemed to size each other up.

"It doesn't seem you have the book I was looking for in stock. But I was just thinking I was in the mood for a bite. Allow me to buy you some lunch?" The stranger crossed into the parlor, stopping to stand close beside the shifter. He gestured magnanimously at the bakery case. "What looks good to you?"

"Are you kidding me? I'm famished, but nothing here looks good. It's all old people's stuff. You wouldn't have to have a spare Nocturnaturals bar on you?" The boy held out his hand like a beggar.

"Actually, I do." The stranger slid a foil-wrapped package out from the folds of his cloak, taking his time, like a county fair magician doing a big reveal. "You're in luck! I picked these up on the Ordinary side last night. Brand new flavor—dragon fruit and mangosteen."

Zephyr's eyes bugged out at the sight of the Nocturnaturals bar. His face flashed with a beetroot incandescence as he raised his wand. He was so incensed that he didn't even notice the stray sparks leaping off the tip of his wand. Tiny white-hot bolts of agitation fired off in every direction, threatening to wreak havoc in the cafe.

"Absolutely not. No synthetic magic, and nobody but me uses a wand in my shop!" Minerva had her wand out now, too. She waved it about, eliminating the threat of tiny fires.

So much for a peaceful morning; she'd had quite enough already and hadn't even finished her cup of tea. It would be cold now.

Her eyes met Zephyr's for an instant. He was unrepentant.

"Whatever! Thanks for the bar!" The shifter boy snatched the snack from the stranger's hand and bolted out of the shop before anyone could stop him. He and his friends whooped victoriously as they sped off on their bikes.

Minerva's breath caught in her throat when she turned her

attention back to the shop's interior. Gone was the kind-eyed old man with cookie crumbs in his beard.

Zephyr's blue eyes blazed with a righteous fury that reminded her of the man who'd left her behind all those years ago. He'd been passionate about her but ultimately more passionate about fighting battles for the Society.

"What the Hecate do you think you're doing here?" Zephyr growled at the stranger. He had lowered his wand, but it was still conspicuously present, held tight in his hand.

Considering this, the stranger was remarkably unperturbed. He replied calmly.

"I don't see what the fuss is about. It's just a candy bar. One hundred percent organic. Loaded with vitamins and minerals. It's healthy! It's not like I stole a sale from the shop. We all know that shifter kid was only here to stir up trouble. He might even have tried to rob you. I did you a favor. I defused the situation. You can thank me now by showing me down to the Archives to retrieve my book."

"Nocturnaturals products are banned in Primrose Court and all magical territories!" Zephyr spat out, unable to back down. "That bar you just gave to those boys is illegal."

"Illegal to sell, but not to possess." The stranger shrugged coolly, also refusing to back down. "I sold nothing to that kid."

"As if that makes any difference? Do you have any idea what this stuff does to our kind?" Zephyr sputtered. "Have you even read the studies?"

"Those studies are biased. You can't believe everything you read. Here, why don't you try one? Might do you a world of good." When the stranger produced a second bar and shook it at Zephyr, Zephyr responded by raising his wand arm, chanting a curse.

But Minerva was faster. She froze the pair in place with a cool flick of her compact wand.

What an unfortunate turn of events. She didn't need Zephyr's protection. What she needed was some peace. A little comfort.

Perhaps she'd been foolish to think it possible. Zephyr's causes would always come first.

"That's enough. From both of you," Minerva said.

She walked over to the mage first.

"You're not from around here and you are clearly unfamiliar with the Mudpuddle. I do not allow Nocturnatural products for sale, consumption, or trade in my store. I am well within my rights to kick you out and ban you from returning, but...I believe in second chances."

Next, she stood before Zephyr and stared meaningfully into his unblinking eyes. "It's never too late to focus on what really matters."

She used her wand to summon his stack of flyers from behind the counter, neatly rolling them up and stuffing them into his coat pocket. "I shouldn't have to remind you that this is a bookshop, Zippy. A refuge. I know you mean well, but I'd prefer to keep politics out of the Mudpuddle. Please be sure to be rid of these flyers when you come back."

There was a tear in Zephyr's eye, but it was impossible to tell whether it was for her or for his lost cause.

Minerva turned back to the stranger now, wishing she'd gotten a name to put to the face. She noticed the unusual iridescent fabric of his cloak, which resembled fish scales. It changed color with the light, appearing green from one direction and black from the other. So flashy. It reeked of new magic and smelled as synthetic as the bars in his pocket.

She addressed him again.

"I'm sorry I didn't catch your name, but you're welcome to check back in with me tomorrow about the grimoire. I can help you contact someone at the Society if necessary. They're quite committed to keeping families together with their grimoires. Even when those families' bloodlines are compromised."

Minerva had mixed feelings about this policy.

There was no point in waiting for a reaction from either man because they were both still completely frozen in place.

"Anyway, I always find a brisk walk is helpful to clear my mind when I get fired up. So I will bid you both adieu for now and send you both on your way. I intend to finish my tea in peace."

Minerva flicked her wand again, and the heavy front door opened wide. Then a powerful, purpose-built wind lifted Zephyr and the stranger, swept them both out the door and carried them down the path. It deposited them both in the street, half a block away. They ought to thank her. She'd had the good grace to drop them upright on their feet, and not flat on their bottoms.

She stood in the doorway only for long enough to reanimate them before locking the shop and flipping the sign on the door to "Closed."

And in almost no time at all, she was back in her window seat, sipping hot tea alone.

FOUR

HIDDEN IN PLAIN SIGHT

One of the most closely kept secrets of natural magic is the art of camouflage. Many animals, plants, and insects exhibit this ability to blend almost seamlessly with their surroundings.

From an Ordinary perspective, natural camouflage seems like a gift. A beautiful invisibility cloak woven by nature herself. But fashion is notoriously fickle.

Magical naturalists know well that invisibility, like beauty, lies in the beholder's eye. The disguise is not the only thing that matters. Just as frequently, what keeps the unseen hidden is the viewer's inability to see.

—EXCERPT FROM THE MUDPUDDLE MANUAL OF NATURAL MAGIC

The angry customer slammed the candle down on the cafe counter so hard that Maida worried the glass container would shatter. Despite being seated at a small metal bistro table a few feet away, Maida bent forward to clutch her open notebook and shield the locket she was sketching.

"I demand a full refund." The woman's voice had the traumatized tones of a tea kettle whistle. "This candle didn't work."

Maida resumed her detailed sketch of the locket she'd found during her morning walk on the beach. She went out most mornings, but as a naturalist, rainy days like today were her favorite. The coast seemed most alive just after a storm.

"First my beach yoga class gets canceled for bad weather, and now you're going to give me a hard time?" the customer complained loudly. Her left eyelid twitched.

Maida couldn't focus. She considered moving to a table outside on the deck, but it was still quite windy and the space heaters weren't on in the rain. She'd been lucky to get one of the few spots inside. With the windows cracked, she could still smell the ocean air, but she didn't have to freeze. She was grateful for the cozy warmth of the coffee shop after spending the whole morning outdoors.

"I should have known better than to buy a candle from a cafe," the woman confided loudly to the disinterested jogger who was waiting for his post-run drink. She was wearing expensive workout clothing and a watch that Maida recognized as costing more than some people's cars. Maida's father had a similar watch. And he wasn't so happy either.

"What's wrong with the candle?" Addy, the pretty young barista, asked.

Addy lived in the same apartment complex as Maida, but the two women were barely acquaintances. Maida was thirty-five and a recluse and Addy was a twenty-three-year-old socialite. They had nothing in common besides their address. But in that moment, it was enough. Addy was desperately seeking some solidarity. She shot Maida an unmistakably exasperated look that said, "Can you believe this wench?"

Naturally, the angry customer clocked the silent exchange. The older woman's gaze swept over Maida like a rough, bristled broom.

Maida knew how the woman saw her. She sensed the stocktaking. The woman could forgive the messy bun at this hour. But no makeup? No manicure? No jewelry? No obvious brand names on her shapeless greige clothing? She sneered at Maida's tide-pool-friendly foam clogs before dismissing her.

Objectively, Maida knew there wasn't anything wrong with the way she looked. She wasn't ugly. Some might even call her striking. Her unusual violet-gray eyes and the bright fluffy mass of wavy platinum hair lent her an almost ethereal effect. Her hair and eyes caught people's attention. But not for long. She was like the shiny colorful rocks at the shoreline, which, upon closer inspection, turned out to be nothing special after all. That was just fine with her. She was happy to blend in. Not everyone needed to be a rock star.

Maida squirmed in her seat. Gritty sand was still lingering between her toes. She gave her right foot a little shake, pretending she'd noticed nothing. That woman and her problems were none of Maida's business. She went back to her drawing, adding in subtle shading to the bit of kelp she'd sketched on the beach.

A shocking amount of trash, plastic, plant matter, and other debris had washed ashore after last night's squall. Fall storms did a lot of damage. Maida had tried to help clean up the mess, taking photos of interesting bits of driftwood and natural debris along the way.

As a reward, the ocean had surprised her with an unexpected gift.

She might have missed the vintage locket hidden inside a clump of kelp if a sneaker wave hadn't intervened. The unlikely wave had swept the bundle up the beach, dragging and tumbling it until it tangled itself around her ankles.

If it hadn't been for that random wave, Maida would never have found it. That made it feel a little less random, actually. Like fate. She liked to tell herself these sorts of stories when strange things like this happened. Which was often. She was constantly finding lost items and reading people's minds. Sometimes she thought she saw things in the shadows that really shouldn't be there. Her father had always said she had an overactive imagination when she was growing up.

This had always felt more like an accusation than a compliment.

At first, as she unwrapped the kelp, Maida thought she was looking at a silvery shard of abalone. People talk about people finding lost jewelry at the beach all the time. But it had never happened to her. She almost couldn't believe it when she turned the freed locket over in her hand. It had the same greenish-black color as the seaweed that had concealed it. The chain had tarnished. Sea scale and crusty buildup coated the exterior. But it was still beautiful.

"Am I getting my money back or not?"

Maida was trying to concentrate on her sketch, but the scuffle at the counter wasn't over, and it was too big of a distraction.

"What exactly is the problem with it?" Addy examined the candle skeptically. "You've obviously used it, so...it works?" Addy's voice trailed off in a question that was not really a question.

"But not as advertised." The older woman glared at the pretty, blond, young barista. "I lit that thing every night for a week. Zero dates. Nada love!"

"I don't know what to say. It's an intention candle." Addy shrugged. "It doesn't work like ordering a pizza."

"Obviously." The woman rolled her eyes. "When I order a pizza, nine times out of ten, I get a man ringing my doorbell."

Maida bit her lip, trying not to laugh.

"There were directions on the box for performing a ritual," Addy spoke in a bored monotone. She turned to stir some steamed milk into another customer's drink. "Did you remember to set your intention before you lit the candle?"

"Are you kidding me?" The woman blinked more rapidly as her ire increased. "Do you think I need help with lighting a candle?"

Addy refused to be intimidated. She spoke slowly, as if she were addressing a small child. "I don't know? Do you remember to plug your toaster in before you try to make toast? How can you expect an intention candle to work if you don't set an intention?" Addy leaned back, brows raised, arms folded across her chest.

Maida was pretty sure this was only going to make matters worse.

"I'm pretty sure you set the intention for me when you ran my credit card. What I intended was for that candle to work. I certainly didn't intend for it to make my whole cottage stink like a whorehouse." She pursed her artificially plumped lips at Addy, who was barely paying attention now. She'd gone back to putting the finishing touches on a drink.

"White Chocolate Latte for Todd?" Addy called out.

The angry woman's sour expression vanished when a middle-aged man stepped forward to fetch his drink. She smiled alluringly and cheerfully handed his drink to him. But as soon as he departed, she resumed her campaign.

"So, do I need to speak to your manager?" She glanced around hopefully, waiting to see who might rush to her aid. "I'm not going anywhere till you give me my money back."

"Whatever. It's cool. I'll get you a refund." Addy sighed, capitulating as quickly and completely as she'd resisted. "I believe you. Between you and me, next time you should invest in Nocturnatural candles. I don't know what they put in their products, but I swear they are the only ones that work for me." She leaned in conspiratorially. "They aren't sold in stores, but I can hook you up. I'm a rep and I just got a big shipment in."

This was bold of Addy. Reckless too, given the recent rash of break-ins attributed to the theft of coveted products. It was all over the news. Locals were blaming immigrant gangs for the robberies. Supposedly, many Nocturnaturals products fetched more money on the black market than street drugs.

"No thanks." The woman sniffed. "I think I'll stick with pizza." She waited while Addy reversed the charge and then ordered an iced tea to go.

Finally, Maida could complete her sketch of the locket in

peace. After she was done, she took out a small camera to take a photo of the drawing. She would send one copy of the image to her agent, in order to add it to her portfolio. Most of the art she was commissioned to do was bespoke, but the items in the portfolio inspired clients.

She'd send a second copy of the picture, along with a photo of the locket itself, to her friend Zani. Zani traveled the world sourcing curious objects for whimsical museums and private collectors. If anyone had ideas where this locket might have come from, it would be her. She was a whiz at unearthing the provenance of almost anything.

She owed Zani a phone call. In the game of international phone tag, she had been "it" far too many times. She knew she was remiss but she was waiting for something remarkable to happen and nothing ever did. Meanwhile, every call and letter Maida received from Zani was jam-packed full of epic adventures. Their conversations had started to feel so one-sided. Maida thought her quiet life probably seemed quite banal to her old college roommate.

It wasn't only Zani she'd been putting off. Maida owed her father a call back too. She'd been stalling for a couple of days now, letting her answering machine handle his queries about her well-being. She had very different reasons for avoiding her father's calls. She simply wasn't in the mood for another one of his lectures. He never stopped pestering her to come back to the East Coast and get a proper job, preferably at Westabrook Enterprises.

She closed the notebook.

"Can I get another latte?" Maida asked Addy.

"No problemo," Addy said.

"Thanks." Maida stood to pay. She noticed the discarded candle that was still sitting on the counter next to the register. "What are you going to do with that candle?" she asked.

"Toss it in the trash." Addy shrugged. "Why? Do you want it?"

Maida studied the hand-poured candle. The wooden wick had been lit and half of the wax was gone. A chunk of pink quartz stuck out from the remaining wax like a tiny island. The rose petals had all sunk to the bottom. But there was nothing overtly wrong with it.

"If you were really just going to throw it away, I'd rather use it up and recycle the glass when it's done. One less thing in the landfill," Maida confessed.

"Then it's all yours." Addy nodded congenially.

"Are you sure?" Maida felt a little awkward accepting it now.

"Totally!"

"Thank you, Addy." Maida lifted the candle off the counter. She inhaled and closed her eyes. Rose, jasmine, and sandalwood. It smelled divine, if a bit strong.

"Let's just check if it still works." Addy pulled a matchbook from her apron and handed it over to Maida. "Go on, give it a go."

Maida struck a match, but just as she was about to light the candle, Addy blew it out.

"Wait!" she exclaimed. Maida looked at her quizzically. "Did you set your intention?" Addy pursed her lips and raised her eyebrows.

"Are you for real?" Maida squinted at her. She couldn't tell whether she was joking.

"I only use Nocturnaturals products in my practice," Addy admitted. "But it seems to me, if you're going to do a love summoning spell, you may as well do it right."

"I'm not interested in summoning a man." Maida saw Addy's brows fly up again and answered the unasked question. "Or a woman, or anyone. I'm perfectly content on my own."

Though she could do with some companionship, she thought.

Maida struck another match and lit the candle.

"Weird. But whatever floats your boat." Addy turned back to the espresso machine. "Did you want almond or oat milk in that latte?"

"Almond," Maida replied. "Can you watch my table while I use the restroom?"

"Sure thing." Addy gave her the thumbs-up sign. "Great chatting with you, Maida!"

This brief conversation was the most words they'd exchanged in the entire two years they'd been neighbors.

Maida wasn't particularly worried about anyone stealing her sketchbook. She'd stashed her wallet in her pocket. But as she passed by her table again, she set the candle down and slipped the necklace over her head. It looked much better now that she'd dried it off and brushed away the loose sand.

As she stood washing her hands in the tiny restroom, a silvery flash in the mirror caught her eye. Every time she looked at the locket, it seemed to get shinier. Impulsively, she reached for a paper towel and pumped some soap onto it. Cautiously she dabbed at the tarnish on the chain, careful not to rub too hard lest she damage the finish. The tarnish seemed to melt away. In a matter of moments, the thick chain was a chrome-bright, shiny silver.

She studied the sinuous rope-like design. It was unique, unlike any chain she had seen before.

Encouraged by her success with the chain, Maida went to work on the locket next. The scaly material that had seemed like cement earlier this morning dissolved like sugar. After only a few swipes and a rinse with plain tap water, she could see the engraved detail on the front of the locket. An old-fashioned loopy script letter "L" encircled by butterflies and flowers. Maida turned the locket over. The back was blank.

She cleared the last tiny bits of debris and sand from the hinge, using the corner of a paper towel. It still took several attempts of pressing the latch before the mechanism released. With the tiniest creak that sounded almost like a sigh, the locket sprang open, revealing the image inside.

Much to Maida's surprise, the locket did not contain an image of a person. It contained a painting of a house. An extraordinarily tiny, perfectly preserved, wonderfully detailed house. Not a real one, she thought. The house in the image was too fanciful, too magical, to exist in real life. It was more like something out of a storybook, a fairy tale, or perhaps a dream. Her curiosity was piqued.

As she made her way back to the table, Maida studied the house some more. It seemed familiar, yet foreign, and she couldn't shake the feeling of having seen it before.

A towering turret stood watch in one corner and a large wraparound porch hugged the whole facade. An especially peculiar feature was the eye-shaped window placed in the eaves. When Maida tilted the locket, the eye appeared to wink at her. And when she angled it in another direction, a wisp of smoke seemed to waft out of the stone-faced chimney. It looked so real she could almost smell it. What an artistic coup! The craftsmanship was spectacular.

Undoubtedly, the owner was missing it.

Maida was so lost in thought that she almost tripped over the outstretched legs of the man now seated in her chair at her table. He was flipping idly through her sketchbook.

She shot an accusatory look at Addy, who smiled and fanned herself lustily.

"He's hot!" Addy mouthed.

Maida rested a hand on her hip and frowned.

The man looked up. "Hi there. Care to join me?" His voice was deep and silky, seasoned with a southern drawl. Not the lowbrow type. His was the voice of a man who went sailing and wore tennis whites in expensive country clubs. That voice ordered an Old Fashioned cocktail, and she hoped, tipped well for a good pour.

She couldn't deny that his voice was appealing, even if Southern gentlemen were not her usual cup of tea.

She hadn't had tea in a long, long time.

She looked at him for real now. Technically, Addy was correct. The man was handsome. Not just ordinarily handsome. There was something almost unnatural about how good-looking this guy was. She almost couldn't make herself stop staring at him.

"Excuse me? That's my seat and my notebook."

"Oh. I'm sorry." The man gestured to Addy. "Your friend said I could sit here." He turned his attention back to her sketchbook. "These pictures are fantastic. Did you draw them?"

Maida stared at his hand still resting on her notebook. "Please stop touching my things?"

"Right. I'm sorry. That was rude. It's just that you left the book open. It was so tantalizing, who could resist?" The man pushed his seat back. He stood quickly and repositioned the chair, holding it out for her. She felt compelled to sit down, if only to reclaim her space. The seat was cool, considering how recently it had been vacated.

"I'm Cormac," the man said affably. He helped himself to the chair opposite hers. "Do you come here often?"

His attention ought to feel flattering, but something about it just didn't feel real. Men like Cormac usually looked right through women like her. He had to know how handsome he was.

She attempted to observe him as if he was just another specimen to sketch in the naturalist's notebook she brought along on her morning walks. An object composed of shadow and light.

Cormac had long-ish, streaky blond hair, and deep-set sapphire blue eyes. His sharp jawline contrasted with soft, full lips. There was something almost mathematical about the composition of his face. The cleft stamped in the dead center of his chin highlighted the unusual, improbable symmetry of it. It reminded her of those mirror effect pictures that showed you what you'd look like with two "good" sides. An optical illusion.

He was fit, too. Maida could also tell that the framework beneath his clothing enviably combined lean and muscular traits. He was lithe, like a surfer or a skateboarder. But his sleek black hoodie, pre-faded jeans, and immaculate sneakers all looked brand new. Far more expensive than the worn-out, sun-bleached hand-me-downs the local groms wore. She imagined he'd move like he was on wheels. Step, step, glide.

"Now it's your turn to tell me your name." Cormac directed a megawatt smile at her. Klieg lights. The whiteout effect washed all the other thoughts from her mind.

She blinked and had to look away. He was far too much for her. Perhaps he was an actor. Or a movie star. But not one she'd ever seen before.

"Can I...help you with something?" Maida was still seeing solar spots when she stared down at her sketchbook on the table. She closed it with one finger.

"Well, I'm not from around here." Cormac leaned towards her. "And I was hoping you could tell me a good place to get dinner. Or better yet, maybe you could show me?"

"That depends on what you like to eat," Maida answered. Truth be told, she didn't dine out much, but she got takeout frequently. Perhaps if she rattled off a few suggestions, he'd leave her in peace. That's what she wanted, right?

"Well, what do you like to eat?" He smiled a bit more hungrily at her now. The look gave her goosebumps. Not the pleasant kind. It reminded her of when she was a little girl, being warned not to venture off her father's estate. Watch your back, Maida. Don't talk to strangers, Maida. These were the rules drilled into her as the only daughter of a billionaire. *Don't trust anyone, Maida.*

That was the cardinal one.

But all that, of course, was in the past. Those rules were necessary to protect a weak, gullible child. Maida could take care of herself now. She was taking care of herself. She had an ordinary life. Nobody in Laguna Beach knew she was Maida Westabrook, the cosseted clean-energy heiress from Boston. In California, people knew her as Maida Lathrop, the quirky, reclusive artist.

She fiddled anxiously with the locket, index finger tracing the serendipitous letter L. It felt so warm and reassuring in her hand.

"Why did you sit down at my table? Is this some sort of prank?" Maida glanced around the quiet coffee shop.

Cormac tilted his head back, studied her, and smiled. "Why can't I simply be interested in getting to know you? Is it so impossible to believe that I glanced in the window, saw you sitting there sketching, and came in because I wanted to meet you?"

"Yes." Maida sneezed. The candle's scent was powerful. Almost overpowering. She shoved it towards the window.

"Here are your drinks." Addy gave Maida a sly smile as she approached the table.

She'd written their names on the side of the two paper cups in bubbly letters and had even drawn dreamy nested hearts in the foam. As she set the cups down on the table, she gazed meaningfully at the candle. "I hope this is what you intended."

Cormac studied Addy curiously for a moment, then picked up the candle to look at it.

"Wait a minute." He chuckled. "Is this some kind of love charm?" His smile was almost smug. He set the candle back down at the center of the table. "I'm all yours."

"It's just a silly candle that someone else returned, and it stinks." Maida blew the candle out. "And you don't strike me as the type to believe in love charms."

"Oh, I think you'll find I'm exactly the type!" he beamed. "There are too many things in the natural world that defy explanation. I one hundred percent believe in magic. In fact, I believe in the precision application of it."

This was the first thing he said that surprised her. Most of the men she met were much more skeptical about these things—more like her father.

"Come on. Have dinner with me. Please?" Cormac asked again. "What could it hurt?"

He got points for persistence but his flattering attention had to be some kind of ruse. Maida was growing uncomfortable. She couldn't imagine spending a whole evening with this beautiful creature when she'd already run out of things to say before her coffee got cold.

"Sorry, I already have plans."

She was looking forward to a quiet night in, as usual. She intended to enjoy some homemade tomato-basil soup with a grilled cheddar and gruyere sandwich. After that, she'd swaddle herself in a hand-knitted afghan, and curl up on the couch to read. Lovely and safe.

"I get where you're coming from." Cormac's overly earnest expression was beguiling, his words relatable. "You don't know me yet. I just really see something in you, Maida. I sense a connection between us."

"How do you know my name?" Maida's eyes narrowed warily and her heart pounded again. She was pretty sure she hadn't told him her name earlier.

"It's written on the cup." Cormac pointed at her coffee.

"Oh. Right." Maida exhaled and willed her pulse to slow down. She was overreacting. Why couldn't she act normal for once?

"Maida Lathrop," she said, holding out her hand to shake his.

"Of the Primrose Court Lathrops?" Cormac leaned forward excitedly.

"No." Maida shook her head. "I grew up in Boston."

A shadow crossed Cormac's face, and just as quickly his expression went blank. She had no idea what he was thinking. He pushed his chair away from the table.

"Listen, I didn't mean to freak you out. I've got to get back to work, so I'll just leave you alone," Cormac said. Before she realized what he meant to do, he flipped the sketchbook over and tore out a blank page from the back.

Maida clenched her fist and curled her toes. He should have at least asked before defacing her notebook!

He snatched up her pencil to scribble his name and a number on the torn sheet. "If you change your mind about dinner, just call me." He proceeded to score the paper and make several folds. "It doesn't have to be something fancy. We could even grab some takeout and have a picnic. Your place or mine."

Cormac revealed the origami masterpiece in the palm of his hand, then placed it on the edge of the table.

He pressed down on the back legs of the tiny paper frog. It

soared through the air in a perfect arc, landing in Maida's tote bag on the floor.

"Ball's in your court now," he said.

"Wow! Cool trick! How'd you do that?" Addy leaned across the counter, gawping at him with stars in her eyes.

"Magic." Cormac winked, standing to go. He tossed his empty cup in the trash and gave them both a little wave behind his back before gliding out the door.

Maida felt oddly disappointed by the way he rushed off. Like she'd missed the opportunity to say or do something she ought to have said or done. But, more than that she was relieved. She was rusty at flirting. This encounter had completely unsettled her.

It did not surprise Maida one bit, when Addy rushed over to her table a moment later.

"Do you know who that was?"

"He said his name was Cormac," Maida said. "Do you know him?"

"I wish! That was Cormac Vorador." Addy's tone was reverential. "He's the genius who founded Nocturnaturals. I can't believe he's here in California. What did he say to you? Did he ask you out?"

"He gave me his number, but I'm not interested," Maida said flatly. She examined her notebook, turning to the last page. It didn't appear to be damaged. The page had torn out cleanly. It still bothered her. She closed it again and wrapped the attached leather cord around the book tightly.

"So he's rich?" Maida asked.

"Richer than sin," Addy confirmed.

"Cool." Maida placed her tote on the table and tossed the notebook inside. She was relieved to hear this. Whatever Cormac wanted, it wasn't likely to be her father's money. He probably had no clue who she really was.

She removed the locket and wrapped it in a vintage floral silk handkerchief that she kept in her tote to polish her sunglasses.

Then she carefully placed the bundle into a zippered compartment where it would be safe.

"Why wouldn't you go out with him? That man is the modern-day equivalent of Prince Charming. I can't believe a real-life prince just asked you out and you're not going to go." Addy was incredulous.

"What can I say?" Maida tapped a little more sand out of her clogs. "I'm just an ordinary girl. I know that not all princes are really princes. Some of them turn out to be frogs." She pulled a soft, tan woolen wrap off the back of her chair and draped it around herself.

"In that case," Addy said tentatively, "could I get his number?"

"Sure, why not?" Maida reached into the tote to retrieve the paper frog. But both she and Addy startled and jumped back when an actual, living, tiny green tree frog suddenly shimmied out of the bag and onto the leather handle. Before either of them could react, it hopped across the table, onto the windowsill, and right out the window.

"Whoa! Did you see that? That was weird." Addy gaped.

"Just a coincidence," Maida reassured her calmly. "Storms always bring the critters out of the crevices. I was outdoors all morning. I must have picked up a stowaway."

Just the sort of thing that always seems to happen to me.

She retrieved the paper frog from her bag and handed it to Addy, along with the candle. "I think you should probably keep this, too. It made me sneeze. I think I might be allergic."

Before heading home, Maida used the pay phone to check her answering machine. There was another message from her father that she ignored, and one from his PA, Will, as well.

"Your dad's on his way to Kenya for a climate summit. There's something he's asked me to discuss with you. I'll be in Laguna tomorrow. Call me."

Maida frowned. She liked Will, but he didn't come to California all that often. The message sounded a bit ominous. Something was definitely up. She'd call him back as soon as she got home.

FIVE

AN UNUSUAL CASE

Dressing one's human self is about more than just fashion—it's a balance of comfort, style, and the occasional need for discretion.

Natural fibers such as cotton and wool are ideal, as they breathe and won't tear during near-shifts. Avoid tight clothing and opt for pieces with stretch, offering flexibility when your instincts take over.

Neutral tones help you blend in, while bold colors add a confident flair. A well-dressed shifter adapts to every form without losing his gentlemanly charm.

–EXCERPT FROM THE METAMORPHIC MAN: A GENTLEMAN SHAPESHIFTER'S GUIDE TO CULTURED CONDUCT

Arthur Hart set his brown leather briefcase down on the polished walnut dining room table of his modest Boston row house. The table, which also served as Arthur Hart's home office, was the scene of a crime. An empty pizza container lay open, grease stains soaking through the ridged cardboard. Two unwashed goblets with the dried remains of what looked like wine sat on the surface sans coasters. There were at least three half-drunk water bottles scattered about as well. Some of these had surely left rings. There was also a half-consumed bag of popcorn, some sticky candy wrappers, and a stack of hot-sauce smeared plates. It was hard to put a time stamp on any of it. It was all recent. He'd been gone less than twenty-four hours.

Typical teen carnage.

There were worse things than pizza boxes and dirty dishes, though. Arthur was acutely aware that coming home to a spotless but empty house every single night was what he had to look forward to in the not-too-distant future. The anticipation of this loneliness made him so much more tolerant of Rosie's mess.

Gemini, his daughter's oversized white Persian cat, jumped up onto the table, contributing some cat fur to the chaos. He still wasn't used to keeping a pet. Keeping a pet just wasn't a common practice in shifter homes. But the cat had been a birthday gift to his daughter from Pearl Chan, Rosie's former babysitter. Both she and Rosie had insisted that this particular cat was special and "meant for her." Pearl had wisely stopped just short of using the term "familiar" which would have been offensive, as well as a deal breaker. Only witches and Ordinaries enslaved animals that way.

Arthur hadn't been able to say no to either of them. Perhaps he was too permissive of a parent. He frequently vacillated between the certainty that he was too permissive, or too strict. Since he didn't have any other single dad friends to compare notes with, it was impossible to say. He simply tried his best and prayed it would be enough.

That had better not be wine in those glasses

Arthur lifted one of the goblets to his nose and sniffed. Berry juice. Non-alcoholic. Thank the gods for that.

Gemini meowed plaintively at him. He could see that her food bowl needed to be replenished. This worried him a bit. It wasn't like Rosie to neglect her cat.

"Rosie? Are you home?"

No answer. All the lights were off. She wasn't there. And she hadn't left a note. He'd also had no phone messages from Rosie during his quick trip to Baltimore. His answering machine was empty save for two missed calls from Buffalo Westabrook. Arthur assumed that the calls were related to the case he had just argued in the Maryland courts.

Even though the wealthy philanthropist had completely cut magic out of his own life and moved away from the magical community, Buffalo still looked after those in need. Arthur hated the term "benefactor" so he usually told people the Buffalo was "an old friend of the family" when asked about their personal connection.

Today, Buffalo had paid Arthur to defend an innocent shifter accused of stealing expensive car parts from an Ordinary auto shop. Things had gone well. The court dismissed the case after Arthur provided evidence of fraud committed by the owner.

Although Buffalo's charity cases added to Arthur's workload, he never turned them down. The extra cash was also helpful. He loved being a public defender, but the pay was never enough. Some months, he could barely make ends meet. His work left him no time for a social life. It was just work, sleep, defending Buffalo's innocents, and Rosie.

Arthur decided he would listen to Buffalo's messages later. After he caught up with Rosie. Wherever she was.

It wasn't that late yet. He'd wait for her to come home in her own due time. Rosie was headstrong and could be a slob, but she wasn't stupid. He would not be that overbearing dad.

He deposited the dirty dishes in the sink and immediately reconsidered. It was quickly growing dark outside. He'd feel so much better if he knew where she was.

Finally he settled on a compromise with himself. If she wasn't home in an hour, he'd let himself worry. Perhaps he'd even head over to Primrose Court himself. For now, though, he'd choose to have faith that all was well. If he knew his daughter, she was probably hanging around at the Mudpuddle Bookshop and Cafe, three dungeon levels deep into a role playing game with her magical friends. Without a doubt, her friends would be assisting her in coming up with arguments about why she should be permitted to go to school in the magical neighborhood. Life was so unfair. Particularly for teenage girls.

Arthur pulled a bottle of red wine out from the small wooden rack beneath the kitchen counter, uncorked it, and poured himself a glass. He'd earned it.

He sat down on his worn green corduroy sofa and closed his eyes. It had been a long day, full of uncertainties, but in the end he'd prevailed. He imagined the cozy homecoming scene back in Baltimore—the young fox shifter celebrating with his pretty wife and their triplet kits.

Arthur loosened his foulard-print tie and unlinked his cufflinks. He removed his jacket and slung it over the back of the couch. He bent forward to untie his wing-tipped oxfords before slipping them off. It felt nice to remove his uniform.

As a shifter, Arthur was an outlier.

Most shifters dressed in janitorial gray or security guard blues. A fair number wore prison jumpsuit orange. What those shifters had in common was that they wore uniforms to avoid being noticed. They used clothing as camouflage, hoping to disappear. Arthur was the opposite. He was unapologetically impossible to ignore. In both human and stag form, he always presented himself as a noble, handsome beast. He always dressed for success.

He wasn't vain or foppish. Fashion was just another weapon in his arsenal. He deployed it out of a sense of duty to his clients. Arthur knew his clients needed all the help they could get. His striking appearance worked to his client's advantage in both magical and Ordinary courtrooms. Unlike many of his peers, Arthur Hart also had no shame about being a shifter. He was just as proud of his magical heritage as he was of his own academic accomplishments. He wasn't afraid of being seen.

Today was no exception. Even though he'd had to scramble to accommodate Buffalo's request, Arthur had taken the time to pack a fresh razor so he could shave before court. He'd dressed in a clean, pressed, and flawlessly tailored suit. He took the time to polish his shoes and organize his briefcase. The only indications of his feral nature were the amber shards of firelight in his eyes and the curly forelock of hair that flopped forward in his face at present. Even after several months without a shift, these two features refused to be tamed.

He swirled his wine in the glass and considered what he wanted to do. Pretty soon, all his evenings would be like this. Would he try dating again? He dismissed the thought immediately. Dating services for shifters didn't exist, and even if they did, he wasn't sure he'd be interested. He'd had a terrible experience with Rosie's mom. Dating an Ordinary, or worse, a witch, was out of the question. This left nothing but fae, who everyone knew were fine for passionate flings, but terrible at long-term relationships.

Just as he raised the wine to his lips, the oversized watch on Arthur's right wrist began to vibrate and glow like the sun. Orange alerts were extremely uncommon. He set the wine glass down on the rustic iron and glass coffee table, not even bothering to use a coaster. Carefully, Arthur rotated the device to rest against his pulse point.

Telepathic watches, or T-watches as they were called in magical circles, were a recent development. They looked similar to the oversized watches that Ordinaries wore. But instead of simple Ordinary technology, T-watches used magical algorithms to harness the power of telepathy. Regardless of inborn abilities, this allowed the wearers to share their thoughts or feelings, simply by touching the screen. It was ingenious, but not without issues. The most problematic being the lack of privacy.

Private thoughts and feelings were constantly being broadcast to the entire local network by accident. Usually by older members of the community who were less adept with new technology.

For this reason, Arthur thought it prudent to stick to more Ordinary forms of communication. He used the watch infrequently. He only wore it in case Rosie wanted to reach him this way.

The orange alert hadn't come from his daughter, though. It was a public announcement, a warning about a generalized threat. The T-watch flashed blue, then green, as he unlocked it with his left thumb against the screen.

"This is not a test. This is a message from the magical emergency broadcast network."

"What's going on?" Arthur wondered. And then he concentrated on the most important question on his mind. "Rosie, where are you right now?"

If something was seriously wrong, he didn't care who read his thoughts. Perhaps they would help him find Rosie.

"I'm fine, Dad," she answered immediately. Arthur could tangibly feel her concern for him through the watch, which was quite heartwarming, actually. He could see why these things were so popular. "You're probably about to get bombarded with messages about the Mudpuddle. I didn't want you to worry. I'll—"

Another public broadcast abruptly interrupted her caring thoughts.

"The Mudpuddle Bookstore and Cafe remains missing after close to twenty-four hours. Authorities have confirmed that the body found on the property is that of one-hundred-and-eleven-year-old Zephyr Nightshade. Zephyr is a prominent wizard from the Primrose community. For this reason, the disappearance is now being investigated as a crime. The whereabouts of proprietress Minerva Lathrop are unknown. Reports are unclear whether she was inside the Mudpuddle when it vanished. If you have any additional information, we urge you to come forward or share it on a private channel. The Lathrop family has requested that we respect their privacy. Efforts are underway to investigate the scene and locate the Mudpuddle Bookshop. Local Authorities have requested that you avoid the area until further notice."

"You're there at the scene right now, aren't you, Rosie?" The thought slipped out before Arthur had a chance to censor it. Of course she was. She'd probably rushed right over. Just like he would have at her age. Foolish.

"Yes, but I'm just leaving. I'm on my way home now. We can talk more when I get—"

"Shame on you, girlie! You should be safe at home. What kind of father lets his daughter roam the streets after dark with a murderer on the loose?" This time Rosie's transmitted thoughts were interrupted by what felt like eavesdroppers.

"It was shifters, I tell you. I saw three hoodlums leaving the Mudpuddle yesterday, including that giant Ox Bardo Chan." Another thinker's thought intruded.

"Bardo Chan is not an Ox Shifter. He's a yak. And he has nothing to do with the Mudpuddle disappearing. Mind your own business!"

That response was definitely Rosie.

"Lover's quarrel, if you ask me. Minerva and Zephyr have always had a rocky relationship."

"I'll tell you what I think. I think it was—"

Arthur jerked his thumb away from the hot screen, breaking the connection and silencing the chorus of theories.

It did nothing to slow the roll of his own thoughts. Information tumbled and clattered in his head like stones. He stood and paced around the room twice. Then he dropped back onto the couch. He drank some more wine and slid a cork coaster under the glass.

A moment later, his telephone rang. It was Rosie, calling him from the pay phone in the alley.

"I just came through the passage, Dad. I'll be home in fifteen minutes." She was breathless. "I'll tell you everything I saw. I still can't believe it. Some people say that Minerva did it, and others say that it was Bardo. You'll defend him if he's in trouble, won't you? I told him you wouldn't let them pin it on him!"

Arthur pinched the bridge of his nose and took a deep breath. On her deathbed, Pearl Chan had warned Rosie to stay away from her grandson Bardo. And yet, his daughter still insisted on defending the Chan kid even after his own grandmother had disinherited him.

Arthur could already hear Rosie's argument. She would say that Bardo didn't have anyone else. That people have the wrong idea about him, but he's not actually that bad. Arthur would listen, while considering whether the rumors about the kid using synthetic magic were true. He cared about Bardo, but keeping his daughter safe was his top priority.

"Just come home safe, Rosie," Arthur said. "We can talk more when you get here."

"But, Dad, what if they never get the Mudpuddle to come back? It's the only place where shifters and witches all hang out together and get along."

"The Mudpuddle has vanished before," Arthur said. "And it's always come back."

"That was years ago. And it's never been gone this long!" Rosie insisted. "Minerva could always get it to come right back. What if something happened to her? How will they get it back?" Rosie was near tears now. Arthur could hear the desperation in her voice.

"I'm sure someone's working on it," Arthur said confidently and reassuringly. "They'll get it sorted. If anything has happened to Minerva, they'll find the rightful owner and get them to summon the house back. Enchanted properties might appear to have a mind of their own, but ultimately they have to answer to their owners."

He wanted to soothe her with stories that had happy endings, like he did when she was a little girl. But he didn't want to lie to her. There might be no simple way to bring the house back. Especially if the Mudpuddle's legal affairs weren't in perfect order. Who knew what kinds of contingencies and codicils the Lathrop witches had placed on that property? He had enough legal experience to imagine all the ways this could end badly. He pitied the poor soul who'd have to sort it out.

Losing the Mudpuddle wouldn't just be sad for Rosie, it would be devastating for the entire community.

"Can you imagine getting a phone call from someone telling

you that you've just inherited a magical bookshop?" Arthur attempted to change tack.

"Actually," a vaguely familiar male voice rang out from behind him, "I was thinking we should tell Maida Westabrook in person."

Arthur froze and glanced at his wrist. The voice wasn't coming from the T-watch. He hadn't even heard Rosie's response.

"Dad?" she asked. "You still there?"

He was on his feet in an instant, facing the red-haired man in his kitchen. He had frequently met Buffalo Westabrook's personal assistant in passing. There was no forgetting him. Will Porter was such a colorful, memorable character. Arthur suspected he was at least half fae. But other than that, he didn't know the man from Prometheus.

"You know what, Rosie?" Arthur replied to his daughter. "Could you pick up some cereal on your way home? I just remembered we're all out. Thanks, honey. See you soon." Arthur hung the phone receiver back on the wall.

"I wouldn't mind having a glass of what you're having," Will said, foraging through Arthur's cabinets, looking for a wine glass.

"What are you doing in my house, Will? How did you even get in?" Arthur asked.

"Oh, come on." Will cocked his head and pulled a disbelieving face. "You didn't ever suspect?"

"Suspect what?" Arthur's brows drew in and he raised himself to his full height, which was just shy of six foot five. "That you're some sort of cat burglar?"

"As if there's anything here worth stealing!" Will snorted. "Although...I do like that tie," he pointed to the expensive silk-print necktie draped over the back of the sofa.

Arthur stepped forward, looming over Will.

"Okay! Okay! I'll tell you how I got in. It's in my name. Say my name!" Will held his arms over his head.

"William?" Arthur said. He took another step forward. He was significantly larger than Will, which was highlighted by the close quarters of the cramped kitchen.

"My full name." Will cringed backward, leaning into the open cabinet. He helped himself to a fortuitously placed wine glass.

"William Porter," Arthur said.

"Mmm hmmm." Will nodded encouragingly. "Anything click with that?"

"Should it? Do I know you from somewhere? I don't think we've met outside of my dealings with Buffalo..."

"PORTER?" Will said it louder now, rolling his eyes.

Finally, Arthur understood. He almost couldn't believe it.

"For real? That's still a thing?"

Of course, there was no shortage of charlatans claiming to be porters. But the only thing they transported was cash. They left their gullible marks stranded. Usually in compromising positions in unsavory locations. The stories about their bold scams were legendary. But real porters were so rare that some shifters questioned whether they ever existed at all, and if they had, whether they might be extinct. Will might as well have claimed to be a unicorn, or a dragon.

As far as Arthur knew, the handful of real porters that remained worked exclusively for the Society and a few of the wealthiest witch dynasties. He wouldn't put it past Buffalo Westabrook to have a porter on staff, though. Certainly Buffalo wasn't someone to be trifled with.

Suddenly, the quirky PA made sense.

"FYI, I came in through your pantry, which could really use a restocking. Good call on the cereal run," Will said. His tone turned more serious. "Buffalo sent me for you."

Maida Westabrook. Arthur's mind had been playing catch up. Only now did the name register.

"What does Buffalo's Ordinary daughter have to do with the Mudpuddle?" Arthur asked.

"She's the rightful heir." Will threaded his way past Arthur and into the living room. He examined the tie. "Seems like the whole situation is a half-brined pickle. The Society wants it sorted ASAP, because of the sensitive nature of the Arcane Archives below the house. Without Minerva there to watch over the property, another caretaker needs to be assigned immediately. Only the owner can do that."

"But she's Ordinary. How are they going to get around that?" Arthur knew how protective Buffalo was of his Ordinary daughter. He was curious to hear Will's solution.

"We'll have to tell her some version of the truth."

"Isn't her father worried that will damage her?" Arthur raised an eyebrow. Sudden exposure to the magical world never ended well for Ordinaries. Even when they didn't lose it immediately, they often went mad over time.

"Maybe not the whole truth," Will amended. "It's a delicate situation. That's why we need a crack lawyer who's familiar with witch, shifter, and Ordinary laws. We're hoping to keep it simple. If we can quickly get her to sign over power of attorney and then get someone from the Society to muddle the memory, she should be okay. Buffalo's been trying to reach you all day. Do you even listen to your voicemail?"

Will picked up the bottle of wine and poured himself a glass.

Arthur sunk back into the couch. "So that's why you're here? To offer me a job?" He topped off his glass and set out another coaster for Will.

"Not exactly. Buffalo recommended you, but he's not the one in charge. I have your mission summons here." Will pulled a small parchment scroll from his pocket and tossed it towards Arthur. It drifted just above the coffee table, languidly unfurling itself. The signature line bore the official Society for the Protection of Natural Magic seal. Arthur read the short notice below.

They expected him to report to the West Coast headquarters by seven thirty a.m. local time the following day for a full debrief.

"This is crazy." Arthur stared at the notice in disbelief. The Society had never summoned him before. "How can they expect me to be in Los Angeles tomorrow morning? I'm not even sure I can get a flight with such short notice."

"Not a problem. I'm going with you!" Will held up his wine

glass, as if to invite a toast. "To an epic mission, partner! Are you ready?"

"You mean now?" Arthur set his glass down.

"I do. Technically, I'm not supposed to drink port and port, but between you and me it would not be the first time. I'm sure it will be fine!" Will smiled impishly.

"Absolutely not," Arthur shook his head. "I have a daughter. I have to make arrangements."

"But time is of the essence!" Will objected.

"How long does it take you to port to LA?" Arthur asked.

"Sixty seconds or less, depending on the weather." Will puffed out his chest a bit.

"Then there's no problem. We'll go first thing in the morning," Arthur said.

Will's chest deflated. He drained his wine glass.

"The thing is, I'm not that much of a morning person." Will pouted.

"Figure it out." Arthur stood and crossed to the front door to hold it open. The icy night air blew in through the door, chilling him and making him long for his other, thicker skin. "I'll meet you in Primrose Alley tomorrow at ten a.m. But right now, you need to go."

"Fine." Will stood and placed his empty glass beside the coaster. "Ten a.m. it is. But I'm not leaving that way." He turned towards the pantry. "Be sure to pack light. Nothing bigger than that thing." He pointed to Arthur's briefcase on the dining table.

And with that, Will stifled a small burp and stepped into the pantry. A moment later, the front and pantry doors slammed forcefully, as if sucked shut by a powerful vacuum. By the time Arthur reached the pantry to check inside, there was nothing left to see except half-empty shelves.

SIX

INCONSEQUENTIAL

Though lesser beings may lack our savior faire, they are not without cunning or ambition.

Underestimating one's foe due to their compromised bloodline is dangerous folly. Vigilance must be maintained, for even the weakest creatures can pose a threat when left unchecked.

The art of true superiority lies not only in quiet confidence but in the constant awareness that, though we are above them, the unworthy are ever seeking to pull us down.

-EXCERPT FROM THE ARCANE ELITE: UPHOLDING THE SANCTITY OF WITCH BLOODLINES

Minerva couldn't forget about the squirrels. She'd promised to drop off the books for their book club by the end of the weekend. Naturally, she despised disappointing anyone, but it was particularly dreadful to let down the squirrels. She knew how vindictive they could be. Failing to deliver their order promptly would result in her gutters being full of acorns. She'd planned to deliver their books as soon as she'd finished her morning tea. That part, she remembered clearly.

Minerva blinked, trying to get her eyes to focus. Everything was so blurry. And she wasn't in her bed. Where was she, exactly? The side hall? For heaven's sake! She could just barely make out one of her blue willow baskets on the side table beside the door. It was still full of colorful books meant for the squirrels. So she had not made the delivery.

The squirrels were reading the latest buzz-worthy bestseller to make a splash on the Ordinary charts. Same as always. They were a lot like lemmings in that regard. Minerva thought the book was mediocre, but that hardly mattered to them. They never actually read the books. They just liked to accessorize with fashionable novels and hear themselves chatter. And they loved tea parties.

Minerva liked clean gutters.

She had stashed some hazelnut shortbread, marmalade tea cakes, and a hunk of coastal cheddar in the oversized basket, as well as the books. She recalled setting the basket down on the bench by the side door and wrapping a hand-knit gray woolen shawl around her shoulders. It was cold enough for a proper coat outside, but she was just popping next door. The squirrels held their book club meetings in the neighbor's attic. Minerva had planned to leave the basket on the porch like she always did.

And then she'd heard...something? Hadn't she? Something had made her leave without the basket.

Only now did Minerva realize she was lying on the bare floor. The planks seemed wider than usual, and the wood grain expanded. She sat up and smoothed her calico skirt, desperately trying to catch her train of thought. Her memories felt foggy, like a dream you've already started to forget.

She'd been angry. She still felt angry. Minerva redoubled her efforts to concentrate. Why was she so angry? Because of Zephyr? That old nutter was going to break her heart again, wasn't he?

All at once, she remembered.

Zephyr had been there. She'd heard him shouting outside. He

hadn't been alone. She'd heard two voices coming from the side yard. The men had still been arguing, even after she'd ejected them like schoolboys. They had some nerve coming back onto her property for round two.

That wouldn't do. She'd had more than enough and wasn't about to have her entire day ruined by a ridiculous argument over an outlawed Ordinary candy bar. Or had they moved on to something more substantive? The men were still shouting loud enough for her to hear them. But she hadn't been able to make out what they were saying. She'd thrown open the door, leaving the basket behind.

It was all coming back to her now. In bits, pieces, and larger chunks. She remembered going outside. But she was less sure how she'd gotten back in.

When she'd stepped out the door that led to the side yard, the argument had seemed to end. She'd been hopeful. Perhaps she wouldn't have to have words with them after all. Maybe they had already resolved the argument. She'd almost turned back, just before she reached the garden shed.

But then she had felt the first crackling of dark magic. Colorful, breathtaking, and dangerous. It stung her eyes and burned her throat like smoke. Her skin prickled with the spark of it. It was like being surrounded by poisonous fireworks. It had seemed to originate inside the shed.

"Zephyr?" Bright blue burst of stars had exploded around her as she called out his name. Shimmery trails floated to the ground before disappearing into gray dust.

Minerva had cracked open the creaky shed door, squinting as she peered into the darkness. "Zephyr? Enough already. What's going on here?"

She'd almost tripped over him. His flyers were flapping on the concrete floor, edges singed. A few of them were burning. Zephyr hadn't looked like himself, crumpled on the ground like this. Shrunken. Shriveled.

"Zephyr! Get up!" Minerva had commanded, waving her small

wooden wand frantically to put out the flames before the entire shed caught fire. She hadn't even stopped when the key to the Mudpuddle dropped from her pocket. She had been so determined to save Zephyr's life that she didn't care.

"He's not getting up." The man's tone was callous. Almost bored. "It's too late."

How could it be too late?

Minerva's tiny heart pounded as it all came flooding back. Her body felt too small for her heart. Like it might beat right out of her chest. Her vision was still so fuzzy. And so was her face! Fine, silky fur covered her face from chin to forehead. And so were the tops of her hands! She blinked down, staring at them with disbelief. They were more like...paws?

When she jumped to her feet and spun around, Minerva was stunned to see a long piebald tail trailing behind her. Her long braids were gone. In their place were a pair of small velvety ears.

"Apollo's arrow!" When Minerva tried to speak, she squeaked. She sounded exactly like her rodent friends from the alley.

That mage! He had done this to her. She hadn't been able to stop him. She should have been able to stop him. But she'd been in shock, seeing Zephyr that way. He'd still had cookie crumbs in his clothes. Her cookie crumbs.

"What have you done?!" Minerva had cried out, whirling to face the mysterious mage who'd wandered into her shop earlier, her wand still drawn.

"Nothing, really. He was old and so worked up. I tried to get him to calm down, and then I tried to save him. I don't know. Must have done it wrong. He just collapsed. I guess it was just his time. Sorry, Minerva is it? Terribly tragic."

The words of sympathy had rung hollow as he bent to retrieve her key, slipping it into his own pocket. "The sad bit is that we could have avoided all of this if you'd just fetched my family's grimoire for me." He'd eyed her with pity as if she were a doddering old twit. "You should probably put down your wand. You seem confused. Is there someone we can call?"

"You're lying," Minerva had said, holding her position.

"Minerva, please, stand down. You might hurt yourself." The mage had taken a step towards her and just then she'd spotted the tiny tattoo on the inside of his wrist. A small lotus flower blooming inside a crescent moon. She recognized the Nocturnaturals logo.

"Who told you about the Archives?" Minerva had asked. Then she'd sneezed.

Something had smelled wrong. The burning smell. Dark magic was always acrid. But it rarely smelled like melted plastic.

That mage had worn the stench of synthetic magic, like it was his signature fragrance.

"Does it matter?" He'd shrugged, finally giving up the act. He pulled the key from his pocket and dangled it from an extended finger. "Now that I've got the key, I can just show myself in."

The Hecate he would! "You'll not get past the front door without my permission," Minerva had scoffed. Key or no key, the Mudpuddle wasn't unlocking for anyone whom its caretaker perceived as a threat.

"Then I guess I'll have to get someone else to help me. Perhaps I need to talk to the *owner*?"

He knew. He knew she was not the Mudpuddle's owner.

She'd pointed her wand at him, but she wasn't fast enough. He'd effortlessly dodged her fire and laughed coldly.

"Silly old witch!" he'd fired back. "You're like a little mouse. I'm guessing that if you disappeared, nobody would even miss you. How does it feel to be so inconsequential?"

Minerva had cast again, a disarming charm that focused all her remaining energy. But it hadn't worked. Her spell slid off him in small balls, like water beads rolling off waxed canvas. The magic regrouped on the ground, only to ricochet drunkenly off the shed wall. She'd watched in dismay as her weakened spell bounced off the wizard again. It splashed as it hit the ground, bursting like a spent water balloon.

The wizard had quirked a smug half-smile and leaned forward like a ravenous scavenger to suck up whatever dregs of magic were left. Her magic had gathered like mercury at the tip of his ridiculous-looking wand.

Minerva's tiny mouse nose wrinkled and her whiskers twitched in distaste. She was not normally one to criticize a wizard's wand, but that thing had been an abomination. Like a dime store disco ball or a child's toy. She was ashamed to admit that she'd been so gobsmacked by the absurd instrument that she'd failed to dodge the rather pedestrian curse he'd cast with it.

All at once, she'd felt the world whizzing away from her. Or perhaps it was her whizzing away from the world?

It had been impossible to know what was happening. She'd been so dizzy and disoriented as she shrank and changed. The only thing Minerva had known for certain was that she needed to get back to safety. She had to get back inside the Mudpuddle.

The open side door had seemed like it was getting farther and farther away. And it was swinging shut. She'd known what was coming next. The Mudpuddle, sensing danger, was getting ready to pull a disappearing act.

Minerva turned tail and sprinted for all she was worth. She'd run as if her life depended on it, which she was sure it did. The gap was barely a sliver by the time she got there. No human could have fit through. But Minerva wasn't a human anymore. She was a mouse.

She'd squeaked through the door a millisecond before it had slammed shut.

Which was how she ended up passed out on the floor, with dust in her fur. Safe inside her home. Safe and alone. Grief stabbed at her soft parts.

Oh, Zephyr. He was never quite her Zephyr. But that wouldn't stop her from avenging his death. She would put an end to that synthetic magic-wielding wizard, or she would die trying.

A terrible thought occurred to Minerva as she recalled the wizard's words. He intended to speak to the owner. Did he know the Mudpuddle was owned by Maida Westabrook, an Ordinary? If so, she could be in terrible danger!

She needed to send a message to the Society. Just as soon as she reversed the curse he'd cast on her.

Minerva patted her tiny pockets, feeling for her wand. Surely it was still there? Her clothing was intact. She had her needle and thimble. Her tiny coin purse held a few minuscule pennies. But there was no wand in her wand pocket. She must have dropped it. It was unthinkable to be without her wand. Horrifying. She hadn't been separated from it since her mother had made it for her when she was a child.

What was she going to do? She was a highly skilled senior witch, but she couldn't do complex magic without her wand. She definitely couldn't undo a spell of this size. Particularly in mouse form. For the first time in Minerva Lathrop's one hundred and eight years she was going to have to make do without magic.

Fear, frustration, grief, and the rumblings of an empty tummy assaulted her all at once. A tiny tear slid down her furry mouse face. She chased it away with the tip of her tail, which, having grown on her, was starting to grow on her. She could tell it was going to be a useful appendage.

Minerva filled her tiny mouse lungs with air, and exhaled. There was no point in wallowing. She'd simply have to figure out some other options. She started by helping herself to some treats in the blue basket.

The squirrels were going to have to make do without them.

SEVEN

INVASIVE SPECIES

Invasive species are those non-native organisms that disrupt the natural equilibrium. They often come bearing irresistible gifts. Take, for instance, the Black Swallow-wort, also known as Dog Strangling Vine. If not for its bewitching purple flowers, millions of acres of ancient woodlands might still be standing.

One must be sensitive to ferret out invaders. Carefully observe and record any changes in the energy that flows through your environment. You may perceive these changes with any or all of your senses. You may recognize them as a diminished aura or a strange, unpleasant smell. Some say that they can even hear the dissonance caused by invasive species.

-EXCERPT FROM THE MUDPUDDLE MANUAL OF NATURAL MAGIC

It wasn't a long walk home from the coffee shop. Maida's apartment complex was a short ways down the beach. The sunshine had already melted away the marine layer, making the sand along the water's edge sparkle.

Naturally, all the clever flirtatious things that Maida might have said to Cormac Vorador came to her now, when it was too late. Not that she would have said them, even if they had occurred to her. She wasn't looking for that kind of relationship.

She reviewed the encounter in her mind, anyway. She wondered what Addy might say if she called him. *When* she called him. Maida suspected the younger woman possessed enough confidence for the both of them.

It still didn't add up. The knowledge of his wealth and success only eased some of Maida's concerns. It implied that he wasn't interested in her family's fortune. But it did nothing to quell her impression that he was after something, and whatever it was, he didn't seem the type to accept no for an answer. She shivered and pulled her wrap closed as the breeze picked up again. It sent a chill through her.

Maida's thoughts circled back to her father. She'd put him off for far too long. She could phone him back now, from the payphone by the beach, but of course she wouldn't. There were too many other people around. She couldn't call home from a public phone. Someone might overhear something and figure out who she really was. Maida wasn't willing to take a risk like that. She'd finally gotten exactly what she wanted: a simple life in the real world. She'd fought hard to escape the airtight bubble her father had constructed for her. Granted, her world was lonely. But so was the alternative.

Her childhood had not been terrible. It had just been strict, solitary, and devoid of freedom. Breaking the rules was never an option.

From the time Maida was very small, her father had left her in the care of a diminutive Irish nanny, whom she'd affectionately called "Granny" Luna. Although Granny Luna wasn't truly Maida's grandmother, it often felt like she was. Instead of smuggling treats for Maida, she'd smuggled stories. Granny Luna had been full of ghost stories, enchanting folktales, and bewitching fables. These types of tales were forbidden, of course, but that didn't stop Granny from sneaking them. Most of the tales were of a cautionary nature.

For example, if Maida expressed a desire to explore the quaint old neighborhoods of Boston, Granny Luna might caution, "Careful. You never know what you moight be findin' when you go knocking about those old walls, child...Have I ever told you about the Boggarts?"

She had to wonder now if these frightening stories were part of her overall plan to shelter and protect the eager, inquisitive child Maida had been.

But as fanciful and fabulous as the tales Granny told were, she'd insisted that they were all just "made up malarky." Granny Luna drew a wide line between fact and fiction in Maida's daily life. She always had a logical explanation ready for the curious coincidences and strange events that seemed to rain down in Maida's wake. Once, when Maida was seven, she'd randomly plucked thirteen four-leaf clovers in a row. Granny Luna attributed this to a genetic mutation in that clover patch. When thousands of crows followed her home from school on her twelfth birthday, Granny pointed out she'd put freshly roasted peanuts into Maida's backpack.

And when Maida mentioned that she sometimes felt she was reading people's minds, Granny told her to stop being silly. She was just imagining things. Her father would never abide such nonsense.

Some might have described Buffalo Westabrook's aversion to magic as puritanical. But there was no religious basis for his intolerance, unless you counted science as a religion. Buffalo insisted on sticking to the facts.

"The truth! Nothing but the truth!"

Just not the whole truth, she'd often thought to herself. Maida felt sure that there was more mystery, magic and wonder in the world. Science was constantly playing catch up and falling short. There were no logical explanations for things like the origin of DNA or human consciousness.

She pictured her father's fist slamming on the table, determination in his deep-set eyes as he shut down any such musings. There was no arguing with him. The more Maida tried to discuss these sorts of things with her father, the more intransigent he became. He'd even suggested that her free spirited mother's predilection for such esotericism had led to her death. By this, Maida assumed he meant drugs. They almost never spoke of Larkspur Lathrop, and when they did, it was always in hushed tones.

"I almost lost you too, Maida...I cannot accept that kind of risk in my life ever again. That's the end of this discussion." After this, her father would pour himself a whiskey and retreat to his study.

Even as an adult, living on the opposite coast, Maida still felt the weight of her father's disapproval. She was sure Buffalo would have been happier with a more practical daughter. One who was down to earth like him. He should have had a daughter with a PhD in engineering or statistics. He deserved a daughter who was more outgoing, interested in the environment, and willing to help with his business.

Instead, he was stuck with her—a whimsical, artistic, magical-reality loving loner who didn't share his passion for saving the planet. She'd had no choice other than to distance herself from his disappointment. It was too heartbreaking for both of them to experience it on a near daily basis. He would never approve of her and her offensively woo-woo "lifestyle choices."

This didn't mean she didn't love her father. She desperately wished there was a way to mend their relationship, that didn't require her to hide her essential nature. After all, they only had each other. Maida recalled Buffalo's last two messages as she climbed the weathered wooden stairs from the beach, back up to street level.

"Blasted boulders! Why aren't you picking up, Maida? I'm going to be out of pocket for a couple of days and I really wanted to speak with you."

This was followed by another message.

"Fine. If you won't pick up my calls, I guess I'll have to send Will to pound down your door."

And then there was that last message from Will.

"Your dad's on his way to Kenya. There's something he's asked me to discuss with you. I'll be in Laguna tomorrow. Call me."

Was Will really coming all the way to Laguna Beach?

Guilt settled around her neck like a yoke. What if her father was sick? She swiftly dismissed that idea. Buffalo would never send his personal assistant to deliver serious news like that. Yet, his voice carried a subtle sharpness. Whatever it was, it wasn't trivial. What was so dire that he had to foist his PA on her?

If Maida was whimsical, Will Porter was wacky.

She didn't have any problems with Will, per se. She simply couldn't reconcile the fact that her father had no problem working intimately with someone who openly celebrated solstices and equinoxes. Not to mention the way her father pandered to Will's many superstitions. Will had insisted they renovate the elevators in the corporate HQ to make sure there were no mirrors facing each other.

Will Porter enjoyed his own special set of rules and exceptions, ones that applied to him, and him alone.

"Will Porter can light sage in your office, yet I can't even cross my fingers behind my back?" a teenaged Maida had once objected.

"Will is an employee. He's not my daughter." Buffalo had been unapologetic about the double standard. "But for the record, that poor kid has no family to speak of, Maida. He has a real knack for getting doors to open. Everyone loves him. It seemed like a harmless gesture to indulge him."

Her father had been right. Once Will wormed his way into your heart, there was no turning back. It was impossible to dislike him. He was like the older brother she never had, the one who got away with everything. As infuriating as that was, somehow, she didn't hold it against him.

It could be something simple. Perhaps her father wanted her to attend some party on his behalf? It wouldn't be the first time someone requested her presence at a West Coast gala event. That was out of the question, though. She'd sooner pose naked for a figure drawing class.

A block later, she was standing in front of her apartment building. Maida hitched her bag up to her shoulder and began climbing the spiral metal staircase snaking up the side. She lived on the fourth story but rarely used the ancient, slow elevator.

There were three units on each level, all facing the ocean, with spectacular views from inside, as well as from the communal breezeway out front. Each resident had decorated their section of the breezeway as they wished. Maida had turned hers into a small garden. It kept getting bigger and bigger. The bougainvillea, clematis, and trumpet vines threatened to take over the entire facade of the building, but no one had complained about it, to date. She never bought new plants. She didn't have to. Her neighbors made a habit of ditching their greenery on her doorstep the moment it drooped. She didn't mind. It gave her more subjects to sketch. She'd always make the plants look perkier in their portraits. She believed in the power of positive thinking. And it worked. Just a little water and tender loving care, and they always began to thrive again.

When she reached the third-story landing, Maida suddenly had the distinct feeling that something was wrong. She took the remaining steps two at a time, feeling anxious, without any idea of what the cause might be. Something was missing. Some sound or essential vibration. Similar to background music that you don't notice until someone abruptly shuts it off. It was too quiet.

Tripping in her lightweight clogs that weren't built for speed, Maida finally reached the corridor in front of her unit and gasped.

Someone had ransacked her small garden. They'd dumped

several pots out on the ground. Her precious plants' pale exposed roots looked as fragile as bird bones.

Her apartment door swung ajar, open just enough to see that the path of destruction had not stopped at her threshold.

Maida cradled the rosemary plant that she'd kept her spare key hidden in since moving in. The sturdy little bush had grown up and out of the pot, its thick, fragrant leaves creeping down the sides of its colorful Talavera planter. It had done a fine job of concealing the small plastic capsule that held her spare key. Until today. The capsule was discarded on the ground, melted and misshapen, as if the burglar hadn't even had the patience to figure out the latch, choosing instead to torch it with a lighter.

Her poor plant didn't just look beat up. It looked beaten. Its twiggy leaves were stripped. One clot of dirt still clung tenaciously to the inside of the smashed pot. Whatever was left of the remaining branches hung limp with shame. The scent of rosemary and burnt plastic that lingered in the air was almost overpowering. Maida was livid that someone had done this to her beloved rosemary.

"You can't blame yourself for this," Maida comforted the plant. "This wasn't your fault. I'm sure you put up quite the fight."

Before entering the apartment, Maida reached for the canister of pepper spray that she carried in her bag. Some wild, reckless part of her hoped the intruder was still there. They'd messed with the wrong plant mom.

But instead of the pepper spray, her fist closed around the lump of silk with the locket. Hastily, she tossed it back in the bag and located the canister.

Holding the tiny aerosol can aloft in front of her, she gave the door a shove with her shoe. The burnt plastic smell was even worse inside.

"Hello?" she called out. "Anyone home?"

The apartment was a small studio, with few places to hide, other than the bathroom and the closet. Adrenaline surging, she kicked both doors open, fully prepared to blind a perp. But that wasn't necessary. It didn't take long to verify that nobody was hiding inside.

Maida shut the front door, fastened the deadbolt and chain, and wedged a chair under the doorknob. Only then did she survey the damage. She was careful not to touch anything in case she needed to call the police, though she'd prefer to avoid that if she could. These types of incidents had a way of making it to the papers.

The intruder had dumped her jewelry box out on her nightstand, but all her things were still there. They had also gone through her closet, pulling complete outfits off their hangers. A trail of dresses, pants, and sweaters wound its way across the bed and onto the floor, all the way to the door. It was like her clothing had come alive and tried to make a run for it. The awkward poses where they fell resembled the taped out outlines of crime victims.

Even her bookshelves were breached. Her storybooks and reference texts were scattered. Thick vintage tomes were doing the splits on the hand woven kilim carpet. Maida suspected someone had shaken them out in search of cash. What had fallen out had been even more valuable, to Maida at least. For decades, she had been pressing and preserving leaves and flowers in the pages of those books. The invader had pulverized her precious flowers into a fine powder. Some of those blooms and buds went back as far as her childhood. She felt her temperature rising. Who would do this? Her skin crawled with disgust at the thought of someone else creeping around in her space. Her safe, private, space.

In the kitchen they'd spilled out her spice crocks. A plastic yogurt container that she'd been using for propagating plant cuttings was melted in her sink. All that was left of the tender cuttings were slimy smears of green on the linoleum floor. Maida dropped a kitchen towel over the wreckage. It hurt her heart to see it.

In the bathroom she found her shampoo and conditioner spilled out. Every jar of face cream and bottle of aspirin in the medicine cabinet was open. Had they been looking for drugs?

Maida didn't do any. Not even the faddish natural kinds that were so trendy.

The "Come to my Nocturnaturals House Party" flyers that had been slipped under her door in the last six months could have papered an entire wall of her apartment. Half the building's residents were trying to cash in as reps. Including Addy.

Suddenly, it all made sense. She wasn't the mark. Someone was targeting one of her Nocturnaturals peddling neighbors. That had to be it. When they didn't find what they were looking for here, they'd probably moved on. Like locusts. It was an awful thought, but at least she had an explanation for the invasion now.

It was going to take her the rest of the day to clean up. She'd have to order a new pot for the rosemary plant, and she'd also have to find a better place to stash her spare key. She chided herself. The plant pot was obvious, in retrospect. She'd just fooled herself into believing it was best to hide things in plain sight.

So much for a quiet night in finishing her book.

Maida picked her way back to the kitchen to make a calming cup of lavender tea before attempting to tackle the mess. She considered calling the police again, but what was the point? It wouldn't bring her plants back. She'd warn Addy, of course, but she didn't need the scrutiny, the records, or the hassle of filing a formal report. From the kitchen phone, Maida made a quick call to a locksmith who said he could be there within the hour.

She was still walking around with her bag tucked under her arm.

Placing it on the Formica covered breakfast bar, she went to fill the teakettle on the petite vintage stove. Then she sat down at the minuscule round table she'd wedged into the corner. Her father had dinner plates that were larger than her kitchen table, but it did just fine for her. It was covered with a cheerful yellow Provençal tablecloth.

Maida did a double take.

Much to her surprise, the square of silk with the locket inside was sitting out on the tabletop, right next to the wooden salt and pepper mill.

Had she set it down there? She had no memory of it but perhaps she couldn't recall doing it, in all the confusion. She got distracted when she was stressed. She'd been known to scour the apartment for a pair of glasses that were already on her head.

Maida unwrapped the silk handkerchief and looked at the locket again. She opened the locket and peeked at the picture inside once more. She could have sworn the house was depicted in full daylight when she looked at it earlier. But now the sun was setting in the little painting inside. Once again the window winked at her as she tilted the pendant in her hand.

She set the locket back down on the table and went to fetch the kettle to prepare some tea. What an unusual day this had turned into.

For once she had something to tell her friend about! She wanted to phone Zani immediately to help unpack and review all the strangeness. But a glance at the clock on the stove told her that wasn't going to happen now. Zani was working on an archaeological dig somewhere deep in the Carpathians. The family she was boarding with probably wouldn't appreciate being woken in the middle of the night. It would have to wait till later.

Then, with a pang of guilt about her own distractedness, Maida remembered the other calls she still needed to make. She could see the red light blinking on her answering machine.

Will Porter.

For a moment she considered confiding in her father's PA, but instantly wiped the thought away. There was no way she was sharing the news of the break-in with Will. He'd call her father and they would have a private security crew parked outside her door before she even finished her cup of tea. She didn't want that. But she still owed him a return call.

Maida carried the mug over to her comfy, tufted green leather wing chair. This was her favorite place to read, besides her bed. There was a hideous afghan spread across the back. One of

Granny Luna's many dubious attempts at learning how to crochet. Maida cherished it all the more because it was such a monstrosity of love.

She had to shove the pile of jewelry aside to make room for her cup of tea on the nightstand. It was no surprise that the burglar had stolen none of it. All of her pieces were from craft fairs and flea markets. The simple natural stone and crystal pieces she adored were only precious to her. Her homemade amethyst and quartz concoctions gave her more happiness than any solid gold watch ever could.

Maida sifted through the pile, looking for the aquamarine bracelet she'd made in a beading class last summer. Aquamarine engendered a sense of calm and peace. As she sorted, her hand closed around the vintage silver locket again.

What the hill and dale?

This time, she was certain she had not carried the locket over with her. Or had she? The square of printed silk was still sitting on the kitchen table, right where she had left it.

The locket felt warm and smooth in her hand. It vibrated gently against her skin, humming like the purr of a kitten. That was crazy. Maida slipped the chain over her head again, and let the locket settle against her chest, close to her heart. She stroked the L with her forefinger, pondering how it was possible that this locket felt so alive?

There was probably some clever clockwork mechanism hidden beneath the image. Perhaps it was one of those perpetual motion types that wound themselves with movement.

How on earth had something like that survived for so long in the ocean?

She was just about to take another peek inside when the phone on the nightstand sprang to life in a burst of bells. She knew exactly who it was, even before she picked up, plucking the receiver from its cradle on the second ring.

"What's up, Will?" she asked. He'd beaten her to the call.

"Oh, thank Juno you answered! We've been trying to reach you all day, Maida Lathrop Westabrook!" Will was only seven years older than Maida but he scolded as if he were her parent, and not a near peer.

"I'm sorry, it's just been a bit crazy here today," Maida apologized. "I was just about to call you back. I swear, I was holding the phone."

"Crazy how?" Will's tone pivoted to protective concern, faster than you could snap a rubber band. "What's going on? Is everything okay with you?"

"Of course!" Maida lied. "Everything is fine, Will. You just had me worried that something is wrong with my father. Is he okay?"

"Oh yeah, he's great. Keynote speaker at the big energy summit this year," Will confirmed.

"Shouldn't you be there with him, then?" Maida asked.

"Not this time," Will said. "He's asked me to stay behind and go over a bit of paperwork with you, having to do with an inheritance from your mother's estate."

"What inheritance?" Maida's brow furrowed. As far as she knew, her mother's family had cut her mother off when she became pregnant and dropped out of school. They'd never reached out to Maida. Not once.

"It's a historic house, actually. Funny story. It's been yours all along. How about I tell you about it tomorrow?"

"An entire house? Why hasn't anyone ever mentioned this to me before?" Maida was wary. Before her move to California, she'd carefully assessed her assets and liquidated quite a few. There were no houses listed in her portfolio.

"It's a complicated matter, legally speaking. Apparently, the estate was tied up in some sort of trust, overseen by a caretaker, and you know local codes, contingencies, codicils, blah, blah, blah...They've only just contacted your dad about it in order to get in touch with you." Will tutted. "That's why I'm bringing one of your dad's solicitors with me. Arthur Hart can explain it all to you tomorrow. Best we get the whole thing squared away ASAP."

That name was vaguely familiar. The groundskeeper at her father's house had been a Hart.

"Arthur Hart, as in Reginald Hart?" Maida asked.

"Yes, I believe that Reggie was his father," Will confirmed.

"Huh," Maida said. She did not recall the groundskeeper having a son. Reggie had lived in a small cottage on the grounds for years, and nobody ever visited him.

"So you'll meet up with us tomorrow? We have a bit of business to handle in LA first, but we can meet you at ten a.m. if that works."

Maida checked her calendar. She'd have to skip a lecture about monarch butterfly conservation and native milkweed species. But she didn't mind. She was sure she could get the same info elsewhere. Legal formalities aside, it would be nice to see Will's familiar face. She didn't get many visitors.

"Okay. Where do you want to meet?" Maida asked.

"How about that cute donut place near you?" Will asked.

"Do you mean The Bunny Hole?" Maida smiled. The fanciful donut shop was right up Will's alley, and it was also one of her favorite places to go for a treat.

"Yes! How about we meet there? They have the most stunning selection of donuts. It changes every week!"

"How would you know?" Maida asked suspiciously. "Have you been spying on me again for my dad?" She would not be surprised if he were. But she would be angry.

"The Bunny Hole is legendary." Will evaded the question. "I can't come to Laguna and miss it. You know how bad my FOMO gets around trendy local eateries."

"I thought you were coming here to see me," Maida teased.

"Both things can be true," Will replied.

"Okay then," Maida said. "Ten a.m. it is. But, Will, what if I don't want the house?" She hesitated, thinking about how much hassle a house could be, particularly a historic house. How old was it? What if it needed repairs? It sounded like the exact opposite of simple.

Just thinking about cleaning up her studio apartment exhausted her. She wasn't sure she wanted to take on any more projects.

"Oh, I think you'll want it," Will said. "But your dad and Arthur thought you might pass on the property, so they've drawn up some papers that will allow it to be reassigned."

"Phew," Maida exhaled.

"Between you and me, I really don't think you should do that!" Will blurted. He spoke so fast that his words almost ran together.

"Oh? Why not?" Maida asked. She wasn't accustomed to Will offering advice.

"It's just a feeling." He paused. "It's special, Maida. It's not an ordinary house."

"Well, that could be a problem, Will. I'm a very ordinary woman."

"But are you? Are you really?" Will asked. "I'm not sure I buy that. I see you, Maida. I think you're far more extraordinary than anyone gives you credit for. There's something different about you. Always has been."

Maida couldn't believe the words he was saying. It brought tears to her eyes. Too bad her father didn't see her the same way.

"Thank you, Will," she choked out.

"Well, don't go all maple syrupy on me now, Mayday. Just promise me you'll think about it? I'm not sure how else to say it, except that I think this house is magical. It's *chosen* you. You shouldn't turn your back on that." Will sounded oddly sage for a moment, before sighing dramatically and reverting to his usual flippant style. "Whatever. Take it or leave it. Makes no diff to me. Either way, I'm getting donuts and a day off from the deal. That's also magic."

Maida shook her head. Classic Will.

"See you tomorrow, bro." Maida used the affectionate term she reserved for him.

"See ya, sis."

She ended the call and reached down to grasp the locket again.

It fell open in her hand. An ink-dark sky full of twinkling stars swaddled the house in the picture. On the porch, a single lamp light was lit beside the front door. The rest of the rooms inside were dark, save for one room in the turret and the eyes in the eaves. They blinked at her lovingly, like a satisfied pet cat.

It was precisely the sort of place she'd always dreamed of living in. If only she could inherit an imaginary house exactly like this one.

EIGHT

PORTS IN A STORM

When traveling, especially on public transportation, preventing unexpected shifts is essential. Use calming techniques like controlled breathing, meditation, or subtle exercises, such as curling your toes, to keep instincts in check.

With private transportation, you have more freedom but should still stay prepared. Keep snacks and calming objects nearby, and always ensure your vehicle has enough space to safely accommodate any unexpected changes.

Whether public or private, the key to smooth travel is staying composed and discreet, so you reach your destination in the form you intended.

–EXCERPT FROM THE METAMORPHIC MAN: A GENTLEMAN SHAPESHIFTER'S GUIDE TO CULTURED CONDUCT

Arthur knew two things. One was that Minerva Lathrop would never abandon the Mudpuddle Bookshop, and the other was that there was definitely something strange about the way Zephyr Nightshade had been felled.

He'd gone to Primrose Court as soon as he awoke. Standing in the empty yard where the Mudpuddle used to be, he hoped to gather as much information as he could. It was necessary for him to do this before his meeting with Buffalo's daughter. How else could he advise her?

Arthur wasn't even sure what he was looking for. He'd heard all the theories about what had made the bookshop disappear, but none of them made sense. This was why he had to examine the property himself. Arthur was inclined to trust his own instincts.

The small garden shed was the only structure left on the corner lot. It reeked of melted machinery and synthetic magic. Arthur stooped to retrieve a singed flyer that had gotten stuck in the tines of a rake. The flyer advertised a town hall meeting to discuss the dangers of Nocturnaturals products. He'd been aware of the meeting. Arthur had intended to attend with Rosie.

She was still insisting her yak shifter friend had nothing to do with the Mudpuddle's disappearance, but Arthur was less sure. He certainly would be keeping a much closer eye on his daughter now.

When he reached the morgue, a coroner from the local coven was waiting outside for him. The balding wizard was fiddling with a memento mori themed ring. Arthur expected to be rebuffed, but the wizard shook Arthur's hand without hesitation when the shifter approached. In fact he seemed almost relieved to see him.

"Thanks for meeting with me," Arthur said. "I was hoping you might be able to tell me something about the condition of Zephyr's remains when he was found?"

He was going out on a limb here, but if he was to advise his client about the house, he needed to assess any threats.

"I actually think I have to show you something," the coroner said, leading him inside. "In all my years, I've seen nothing like this."

The coroner removed his ring and pocketed it in his lab coat. He donned a pair of rubber gloves as he directed Arthur towards the refrigerated rooms in the back.

"He's still here?" Arthur was taken aback.

Witches were adamant about having the speediest of burials in the simplest of vessels. Once the sacred essence of a witch's life was extracted, their flesh dehydrated and decomposed at preternatural speeds. You had to act very quickly to bury them whole, before their dust scattered to the wind.

"Very much so." The coroner nodded, pointing to the marble slab where the elder wizard was laid out, still dressed in his tweed morning jacket. Aside from a morbid pallor, a certain shrunkeness, and the absence of breath or a heartbeat, he might have been sleeping. Zephyr was as perfectly preserved as a pickle. But he didn't smell like one. Even in the climate controlled room, the acrid odor of burnt rubber and bubbling plastic was overwhelmingly strong. The smell was coming from the wizard's clothing and shoes, Arthur realized, and not the wizard himself. Mostly his shoes.

"Do you mind if I remove these?" Arthur asked.

"Not at all." The coroner shook his head. "It's not like he needs them for anything now."

Arthur unlaced and pulled off the wizard's tooled leather shoes and placed them in the hallway. He took a deep breath. That was so much better. He'd been right. The shoes had been the primary source of the smell. Now that they were gone he could breathe again.

"I believe you're pretty well versed in our laws, young man?" The coroner raised an eyebrow at Arthur. "What does your gut tell you? What do you suppose we should do with him?"

Seven years of studying the witches' legal system, and they still wanted to know what his gut told him.

Because he was a shifter.

Arthur tried not to bristle. It wasn't necessarily an insult. His "gut," aka his animal nature, told him many things. For instance, he was pretty sure that whoever had attacked Zephyr was a lousy shot. How else could you explain so much synthetic magic landing in his shoes.

"My gut tells me that Zephyr didn't die an entirely natural

death." Arthur's nose wrinkled. "His shoes reeked of synthetic magic."

"I thought I smelled something, but I couldn't be sure," the coroner agreed. "Your type certainly is more perceptive when it comes to that sort of thing. Do you think synthetic magic was the cause of death?"

The coroner looked anxious, and Arthur wondered if this was a trick question. They both knew that if he said yes, there'd be more paperwork. Lots more paperwork. And to what end? Witches loved their records. Every last thing needed to be written down.

"I couldn't say." Arthur shrugged. "But whatever happened, doesn't he need to be buried immediately?" Arthur asked. "The law is very specific about that. Burials need to take place within forty-eight hours."

"That's what the council decided as well. But when the burial committee went to prepare his body, they found this." The coroner lifted the sheet to expose Zephyr's tightly clenched left fist. A tiny nub of wood protruded from the cleft between his thumb and forefinger.

"Is that...?" Arthur bent closer to get a look.

"It is. It's a wand. And it's not his." The coroner pulled the sheet back further to show the wand resting beside Zephyr's right hand. "It's small, but it's definitely a wand. We think it's Minerva's. There's no removing it, not without desecrating his body."

Arthur didn't need to be told that desecrating the corpse of a witch was an extremely taboo act.

"He can't be buried with someone else's wand," Arthur acknowledged the other issue. And what if that was Minerva's wand? He couldn't help but consider the implications. "Perhaps a local member of the Society can advise?"

"That's the problem," the coroner confided. "The member of the Society we would normally ask for advice in such cases was Zephyr himself."

"There's no next of kin?" Arthur asked, already suspecting

what the answer would be. Zephyr was childless and had no siblings.

The coroner shook his head mournfully. "It's not really up to you or me, but it's nice to hear a fresh perspective. I suppose we'll just have to wait and see what the council decides. I'm just glad he hasn't disintegrated on us while they deliberate."

Arthur wished he could have stayed longer to discuss this conundrum with the coroner, but the Society had already assigned another job to him. He only hoped that bringing the bookstore back might somehow lead to justice for Zephyr. Arthur shook hands with the coroner, excused himself, and headed back outside.

Time was of the essence. It was already half past nine. Time to head back to the alley where he would be meeting Will, who would be taking him to meet with Buffalo Westabrook's daughter Maida.

Maida Westabrook. How long had it been? Almost thirty years? There was no way she would remember him. But he certainly remembered her. He hadn't expected to ever see her again, and certainly not in a tricky situation like this.

Arthur hated the idea of dragging an Ordinary into these magical matters. But the law was the law so what choice did they have? Technically, the Mudpuddle belonged to her, which meant only she could assign a caretaker, or bring it back herself. The sooner the matter was settled, the better. Even her overprotective father had recognized the necessity.

Arthur strode quickly into the park. Long, lithe legs gave him a steady, loping gait. He wasted no time navigating back through the passage and into the alley. He really had no idea what to expect from his alliance with Will. While Arthur would have preferred this to be a solo mission, he was excited about the opportunity to travel with a porter. Never in all his dreams had he imagined he'd have a chance to travel that way.

It was hard to believe that Arthur and Will would travel to Los Angeles on foot in a matter of minutes. Even one of Westabrook's fastest private jets would take hours.

He'd be home in plenty of time to make dinner for Rosie.

It was ten minutes before ten a.m. when Arthur emerged into the long gloomy alley. This gave him a few minutes to review the contracts he'd prepared last night. As advised by Will, he was traveling light. He had limited his baggage to one personal item—his briefcase. He'd loaded it up with the most important papers pertaining to Maida's inheritance.

A late night of research had paid off. Arthur had found an ancient exclusion that he believed might solve all their problems. Ordinaries could not be owners of magical properties without the assignment of an active caretaker. Therefore, if Maida was willing to assign power of attorney over to him, he could pass the property on to another member of the Lathrop family.

It was the simplest solution. The one that got him home the quickest.

Arthur briefly considered what he might pick up for dinner tonight after the matter was sorted, but his stomach soon went sour. Thanks to the malodorous protective wards in the transitional alley, it stank of old mackerel and putrid papayas. Horrible, but not nearly as awful as Zephyr's shoes.

Breathing was slightly better with his scarf over his nose, but his eyes still watered badly. He couldn't possibly reread the contracts here. Instead, he paced back and forth near the alley's entrance to the Ordinary street, stepping out every so often to gasp and fill his lungs with unobjectionable air.

When Will still had not shown up by ten a.m. Arthur was regretting the decision to arrive early. Admittedly, he'd been curious to see if Will would port in. Now he was getting concerned that the porter might ghost him.

Finally, at five past ten, an unmarked van pulled into the alley. The side door slid open with a whoosh and Will stuck his head out, jerking it sideways to indicate Arthur should get in.

"You're late," Arthur grumbled.

"Sorry, I stopped for coffee. I told you I'm not a morning

person." Will shrugged. He held out his hand to Arthur, who refused it. He didn't need anyone's help to climb into a van.

The van was opulent inside, appointed with exotic hardwood flooring and button tufted velvet walls. Although the center area was an open space, free of furnishings, four leather upholstered captain's chairs beckoned invitingly towards the back. The ceiling was high enough that Will could stand upright. Arthur still had to hunch over a bit, though. After Will slammed the door shut, Arthur reached back to set his bag down on a chair.

"Not so fast." Will shook his head at Arthur. "You'll need to hang on to that. And you'll need to climb onto my back."

"Pardon?" Arthur raised his eyebrows in disbelief. "Is this some sort of joke?"

Will rolled his eyes.

"Unless you'd prefer a firefighter's carry. I think you're just too big for me to cradle like a baby." Will sized Arthur up. "But I can try if you're into it." He took a nimble step forward and bent to hook an arm behind Arthur's knees.

Arthur gave him a swift shove, causing Will to lose his balance, but only for the briefest of instants. The smaller man promptly righted himself, like one of those irritating magnetic toys that cannot be toppled.

"What do you think you're doing?" Arthur stared at Will with the wilting horror he usually reserved for people who tried to ambush him with fragrance samples in the mall.

"Porting you?" Will looked amused. "Don't tell me you've never been with anyone like me before."

"Why would I have been?" Arthur was defensive now. "My lifestyle is simple. Creatures like me can't afford the likes of you."

"Hermes' heels! I can't believe it! I'm your first!" Will clapped with glee. "It won't hurt one bit, I promise." Then he turned to fling the door on the opposite side of the van open.

Arthur was expecting to see the exposed brick wall on the other side of the alley, but he found himself facing a sort of bright nothingness. The white light was blinding, and it was moving, breathing like a living thing. Clouds spun towards the center like the interior of a cyclone. His tie blew forward, and he felt himself being sucked towards the open door.

Crackles of rainbow colored lightning in the distance gave the swirling vortex a discotheque aesthetic, minus the thumping bass. Arthur was not a fan of nightclubs. He felt dizzy. His ears were plugged as if the van were an airplane in rapid descent.

"Climb aboard." Will bent down on one knee, presenting his back to Arthur. "And you should probably close your eyes after. There's less of a chance you'll lose consciousness if you keep them closed."

"Are you sure? I'm not...too big?" Arthur's heart was pounding even harder than the first time he'd ridden Cú Chulainn Coaster in Emerald Park. At least the roller coaster had been outfitted with a safety harness.

"I'm much stronger than I look," Will shouted. The wind was picking up now. "I promise I'll have you there in under sixty seconds. There's just one really important rule."

"What's that?" Arthur twisted the metal toggle to secure the flap of his briefcase and tightened the long strap across his body. Tentatively, he climbed onto the smaller man's back. He draped his arms around Will's neck and shoulders and closed his eyes.

"Don't fall off," Will shouted. And then he lurched forward into the void. Not down. Forward. That was surprising. Arthur's brain had been expecting Will to step down upon exiting, because he'd stepped up into the van on the other side. He scrambled to get a better hold of Will as he felt himself slipping.

He was tempted to open his eyes, but he recalled Will's warning about passing out.

"What happens if I lose consciousness?" Arthur was shouting as loud as he could, but his voice was barely audible.

"You might fall off," Will shouted back. His voice sounded so distant.

Will took another step, and then another. His strides were long and somewhat laborious, as if he were walking on loose sand or through deep snow. Arthur didn't dare look down to see. When he began to slip again, Will froze.

"Hang ON," Will commanded sternly.

"What happens if I fall off?" Arthur yelled.

"You don't want to know," Will barked back.

"I kind of do..." Arthur locked his knees tighter around Will's torso.

"It's bad..." Will hollered back.

"How bad?" Arthur clenched his fists around his own elbows, tightening his grip.

"Ow!" Will protested. "Ease up just a bit, would you? I have to breathe."

"How bad?" Arthur asked again.

"Infinity bad," Will yelled.

"Which means?" Arthur was getting frustrated. He was a dad. At the very least, Will should have informed him of the risks before they left the van.

Wind whipped them from every direction. The pressure in his ears intensified. He heard the rushing sounds of water, or perhaps that was his own blood coursing more quickly through his veins.

"Oblivion. Lost in the void." Will roared with effort as he took one last step onto what felt like solid ground. With a sort of ripple and a hollow pop, the wind, and the rushing in Arthur's ears, stopped. The air was noticeably warmer and there was birdsong in the distance.

"Oblivion?" Arthur bellowed. The sudden volume of his own voice startled him, echoing throughout this new chamber.

"Easy there, big guy. It almost never happens. Porting is perfectly safe. Safer than flying."

Arthur risked cracking one eye open, just wide enough to see that they were now standing in a large sunlit hall. There was black-and-white marble tile beneath Will's feet. Paintings of gods, goddesses, and mythological creatures lined the walls, extending to the vaulted ceilings. He glanced over his shoulder.

A ridiculous sight greeted Arthur in the oversized mirror they must have just passed through. He saw himself astride the smaller man, still holding on for dear life. Even more embarrassing, he realized his antlers were exposed. He'd started to shift.

It wasn't like him to lose control like that. No wonder Will had advised him to keep his eyes shut. He squeezed them closed again, just in case.

"Are we there yet?" Arthur asked.

"Welcome to the Museum of Natural Magic, Mr. Hart. The local time is seven-oh-six a.m. We hope you've enjoyed our sixty-second trip." Will affected the manner of a bored flight attendant.

"So...is it safe?" Arthur asked.

"Yes, we've arrived, Arthur." Will reached around to pat Arthur tenderly on the cheek. "You did just great. And you can get off me now."

NINE

A CONVERSATION AT THE MUSEUM

Being a good listener is essential for any gentleman, but shapeshifters face unique challenges. With heightened senses, it's difficult to focus on the person speaking. The key is learning to filter distractions and tune in with intention. Practice maintaining steady eye contact and concentrate on isolating a single voice. This allows you to use your sharp senses to enhance rather than hinder communication.

Equally important is managing your body language. A flicking tail, twitching ears, or restless movements can suggest impatience, even if you're fully engaged. Whether human or otherwise, ensure your posture is open and responsive. Listening isn't just hearing—it's making the speaker feel valued, even when instincts urge action. A true gentleman balances attentiveness with his natural instincts.

-EXCERPT FROM THE METAMORPHIC MAN: A GENTLEMAN SHAPESHIFTER'S GUIDE TO CULTURED CONDUCT

"Should we try to find the Director?" Arthur asked. His hands were still shaking, but his breathing had steadied.

"That's a formal portal." Will gestured back to the mirror. "I'm sure the Director's been made aware we've come through it. Someone should be out to fetch us soon. Just relax. We can just wait here in the gallery," Will said patiently. He was giving Arthur space to regain his composure, for which Arthur was grateful.

The art gallery was located in the second story central atrium of the stately mansion that housed the Museum of Natural Magic. The small private museum was, like many other similar establishments around the world, a cover for The Society for the Protection of Natural Magic.

Will and Arthur had entered through a large gilt-framed mirror at the top of the stairs. Just opposite, twin staircases descended into a ballroom filled with tantalizing exhibits. Arthur glimpsed fangs, claws, and exquisite flora.

On this level, the white walls were adorned with framed paintings that extended from the chair rail to the crown molding. A domed ceiling soared above them, wearing its golden celestial mosaic like a tiara. It was a quiet space, for now.

Arthur stared out the tall windows in front of the stairs, watching the palm trees swaying in the warm morning breeze. The sun was still low on the horizon. It was just after seven a.m. in California and the world was still waking. The Museum of Natural Magic would not be open to visitors for another three hours.

Through the windows, Arthur could see the entrance to the museum below them. There weren't any special flags flown outside the museum's doors, such as you'd expect to see at an official Ordinary outpost or embassy. The Society wasn't that obvious. But Arthur still questioned whether the witches who ran this outpost were being prudent enough.

Any magical creature could sense there was more to the place than met the eye. Magic lingered in the air, sparkling like dust motes. Things didn't behave as they should in the Ordinary world.

Every time Arthur looked up at the art on the walls, the images changed. The paintings were continually rearranging and refreshing themselves. He recognized several of the artworks, painted by some of the most famous artists from the past three centuries. It begged the question, were the originals truly here? Or had the resident witches cast a spell making blank walls appear to be full of art?

That was the thing with mental magic. Witches were fond of their mirror mazes and mind games. You never knew for sure what you were looking at. Arthur stared down at his own polished wingtips instead.

"Are you feeling more steady now?" Will asked. "The first time is always a kick in the pants. A significant number of first timers even pee themselves."

As infuriating as Will could be, Arthur could tell he was genuinely concerned about his welfare.

"All good. No leaks," Arthur reassured him.

"I never know how anyone is going to react." Will cracked his neck and stretched his shoulders. "You weren't too uncomfortable?" He adjusted his turquoise blue brocade jacket and straightened his tie in the gilt-framed mirror.

Even in a gallery full of vivid paintings, Will stood out. Everything about him was supersaturated and bold.

"It was awkward," Arthur acknowledged. "I wasn't expecting to be carried." He thought about it for a moment and went on. "But I suppose it's no more undignified than being crammed into a small seat for six hours on an Ordinary economy flight. And I didn't have to go through their security machines." The X-rays always made Arthur nervous. "So that was a win. How about you? How's your back?"

"I'm fine." Will waved away any concern. "People think of most fae as weaklings, but porters are uncommonly strong."

Arthur reappraised Will, noting that his earlier assumptions about Will being fae, and therefore weak, were unfounded.

"You'd have to be strong, to carry Buffalo," Arthur said. Buffalo was at least as tall as Arthur and twice as broad. People described him as a tank.

Will looked horrified at the suggestion.

"Why would you even say that? Buffalo never ports!" He imitated spitting three times in rapid succession to ward away the evil eye. Then he shook his finger at Arthur. "No magic for Buffalo, remember?"

"Right..." Arthur studied Will. "But then how on earth did he come to hire you as his PA? And why?" Arthur took a seat on the red velvet upholstered bench next to the mirror. "What is the point of hiring a porter if you don't intend to port?"

"Just because Buffalo doesn't use my porting abilities to travel, doesn't mean I'm not a useful asset to the company. I doubt you can find a PA who can run errands faster than I can." Will winked. He sat down beside Arthur and leaned back against the wall. "Buffalo started working with me, similar to how he started working with you. He took a special interest in me."

"Did your parents work for him as well, then?" Arthur was curious now. Will seemed to be about the same age as Arthur. But Arthur didn't recall any fae working on the Westabrook estate besides Maida's nanny, who'd come by to visit his father from time to time. They'd loved to trade tales about their lives back in Ireland.

"No such luck. I never knew my parents. A witch and a fae, most likely. I grew up in an orphanage for half-breeds. Buffalo visited occasionally. His donations were probably the only thing that kept that place running."

"I'm so sorry," Arthur said. He'd heard of such places. Full of sadness, squalor, and the unwanted results of forbidden affairs. Few of the orphans survived to adulthood.

"There were mostly shifter hybrids in my group." Will gazed straight ahead as he spoke, staring at nothing in particular. "None of them were born with significant abilities. They looked too different to pass as Ordinaries, trapped as they were in mid-morphic forms. And they were mean."

Arthur glanced sidelong at Will, raising his eyebrows.

"Not because they were shifters! Because their parents abandoned them. Abandonment will do that to you. We *all* had wounds," Will clarified. He turned to face Arthur as he went on with his story. "There were only a handful of us fae mixes. We were smaller and had a tendency to talk back, which meant we got pummeled quite often."

"That sounds terrible, Will." Arthur turned to face the other man. He was both surprised and touched by Will's candor. "I'm so sorry. I didn't know."

"Thanks for that." Will nodded, acknowledging the sympathy. "I think the only thing that kept those other kids from killing me was that Buffalo came down hard on the bullies when he visited. I really looked forward to his visits." Will studied his own hand for a moment. "Sometimes I even fantasized that one day he'd come back there and adopt me," he revealed.

"I can recall having similar wishful thoughts as a child," Arthur admitted. "And I wasn't even an orphan."

Will smiled wryly. "Pretty soon, it wasn't only a wish I made when I was awake. When I hit puberty, I started sleep-porting into Buffalo's house. It was embarrassing for me. I'd wake up in his pantry or his home theater, clueless how I got there. I couldn't explain it. I had no idea what was happening."

"Was Buffalo angry?" Arthur asked.

"A little. He didn't know how I was getting in, and neither did I but it obviously wasn't through the front door. You know how he feels about magic in his household. By the fairy moonlight, I'm just thankful that Granny Luna recognized me for what I was," Will said. "Have you met her? She was Maida's nanny. Full fae. Still works as a housekeeper for Buffalo."

"I remember her." Arthur nodded. "So that's how you found out you were a porter?"

"Yes," Will agreed. "It could have been a lot worse. I could have sleep-ported into a brothel, or time traveled, or woken in a lion's den."

"But you never ported into Maida's room?" Arthur asked. He could only imagine how that would have ended.

"Thankfully! There's a reason so few porters make it to adulthood." Will laughed. "Maida is pretty amazing, by the way. I would have loved to have a sister like her. She's rather extraordinary for a woman who's supposed to be an Ordinary."

Arthur wondered what she looked like now. He hated to interrupt Will's tale to ask for a photo. He'd see her soon enough, anyway.

"So what happened next?" Arthur urged Will to go on.

"Buffalo arranged for me to study in Japan for my formal porter training and apprenticeship. When I finished there, he hired me to work for his company. Not exactly the same as adopting me, but I'm still grateful. I owe him everything."

"What about Maida?" Arthur asked. "Do you think she ever suspected anything was unusual about you?"

Will looked sad for a moment. "I don't think so. Buffalo told her I was his intern, and then eventually he told her I got promoted."

Will jumped to his feet and strode a few feet down the hall to admire a painting. "But you know what? I'm not about to hide who and what I am—not for her or anyone. She's just never asked."

"Good for you," Arthur said. But he thought the opposite. He knew exactly what was likely to happen if Maida suspected something. Will would be sent far, far away.

"Hey, do you think that is a Picasso?" Will gestured at a painting that looked like a collection of squiggly lines to Arthur.

"You're correct. It is indeed a Picasso." A perky blond college-aged witch stepped into the hall from a side door and strolled confidently toward them. She wore a blue blazer bearing the museum's crest. "I'm Marigold. I'm an intern here. Welcome to the Museum of Natural Magic. I see you had no issue accessing the museum's portal. Director Berman will be with you shortly. She's just finishing a call."

"Excellent." Will clapped his hands. "Do we have time to have a look around, then? I've always wanted to tour the museum. I understand you have quite a few werewolf teeth in your collection?"

"I don't think we should, Will," Arthur protested. "Some other time, perhaps?" What was Will thinking? They were on a mission, not a pleasure trip.

"Have you never visited this museum?" Marigold seemed surprised. "I'd be happy to give you a quick tour."

Arthur shook his head again. "No thanks, we'll wait here," he said.

But Will ignored Arthur, linking his arm with Marigold's and marching her toward the stairs.

"Hurray! I'd love a tour!" he exclaimed giddily. "You and Director Berman can get started without me," Will called over his shoulder. "I really want to check out the fairy garden. You never know—it might work for a Westabrook event."

Arthur's jaw dropped.

He couldn't keep up with Will's whims. Porter or no, the man was prone to behaving like a child.

TEN

MORE THAN MEETS THE EYE

Diversity among shapeshifters is our greatest strength. Whether one dons feathers, fur, or scales, each gentleman brings a wealth of unique talents to the table—or the treetops, should that be more to one's liking.

The secret to fostering an atmosphere of inclusion lies in the art of respecting our differences while embracing what unites us all: the remarkable ability to shift between forms with grace and aplomb.

A true gentleman understands that every shifter, regardless of form, enriches the collective wisdom of our community. After all, variety is the spice of life, and a little variety in forms keeps things delightfully interesting.

-EXCERPT FROM THE METAMORPHIC MAN: A GENTLEMAN SHAPESHIFTER'S GUIDE TO CULTURED CONDUCT

"I'm sorry to have kept you waiting, Mr. Hart."

Amrita Berman's petite size was in stark contrast to the considerable power she wielded as the North American Director of the

Society. Arthur thought her striking elegance in her prime of fifty-seven years was no less notable than it must have been in her youthful thirties. There was nothing artificial about her beauty. No glamors to conceal her age. This was a witch whose appearance might change over time, but whose grace would remain commanding at any age.

The Director's dark eyes were shrewd, but not unkind, as she approached the bench where Arthur was waiting. "Call me Amrita. I've been looking forward to meeting you for a while, Arthur Hart," she said.

"It's an honor to meet you, Director Berman." Arthur stood quickly and bowed his head deferentially to the powerful witch.

He'd been expecting a hard, petty bureaucrat who leaned into her mental magic. He'd expected that he would have to prove himself today—that she would want to probe his mind and question his legal qualifications. But Amrita's energy was nothing like that. Her attention washed over him like the flattering light of the golden hour.

Arthur followed her down the hallway and into a side door that led to her private office suite.

"Please have a seat." Amrita pointed to a vintage, overstuffed chenille chair across from her desk. She crossed the room to prepare some tea. Thankfully, he knew what to expect next.

The Director would make him the tea of her choosing and serve it without asking how he liked it. Then he would accept and drink it without comment, other than to thank her. This common witch ritual was an acknowledgement of his trust and her trustworthiness.

His sensitive nose could detect notes of persimmon, rose, and clover as she meticulously dissected the leaves, twigs, and petals, crumbling the best parts into an ornate silver teapot. It was a relief, as these were some of his favorites. He could have been forced to imbibe wormwood and licorice root. Or poison, if she was so inclined.

A moment later, Amrita set the pot in front of him. She took her seat at the desk and reached into a drawer to retrieve a cup and saucer.

"Isn't Will Porter joining us?" Amrita paused before reaching for a second cup. A tiny wrinkle appeared between her brows.

"Will is currently walking the grounds with your intern. He should be here shortly, but he advised us to start without him," Arthur explained, trying to hide his annoyance with Will. There was no reason the porter had needed to take a tour of the museum right now. Arthur was irritated that Will might be making both of them look bad.

Amrita smiled enigmatically and clasped her hands together, resting her chin on steepled index fingers. "I certainly hope Will finds the museum as enchanting as I do. And I'm glad for the chance to chat privately with you."

"Will thought the museum might be an ideal spot for Westabrook Enterprises to host an event in the future." Arthur was relieved that the Director didn't seem upset as he offered the lame excuse for Will's absence.

Amrita rocked back in her seat, raising an eyebrow. Her lips twitched, failing to hide the hint of a smirk. "I highly doubt that would fly with Buffalo. In fact, this is probably the last place he'd want to be seen."

Of course, the Director would know that Buffalo didn't publicly align himself or his company with any organizations that were so open about magical beliefs.

"I'm sure you're correct," Arthur agreed, biting back his own smile. The charismatic witch's charm was infectious. He could see why she'd been chosen.

"You're familiar with the Westabrook family?" Amrita studied Arthur as she stirred the tea. "Your father was their groundskeeper, I believe?" Amrita wasn't really asking. She was establishing the facts, much as he would in a courtroom, when preparing to make a case. She wanted to make sure they were starting on the same page.

"Yes, and Buffalo paid for my education." Arthur spared

Amrita the need to ask the next question. "He's always been good to my family and a great supporter of the shifter community."

"So then, you've also heard the story about how Buffalo swore off his own magic?"

"I have," Arthur said. It had been a favorite cautionary tale of his father's, usually told after one too many pints. It went like this:

On the very night his daughter was born, and his witch wife was lost forever, Buffalo Westabrook was forced to make a terrible choice. Give up his magic, or give his newborn Ordinary daughter away. No Ordinary child could be allowed to remain in a magical home.

It was a sad tale, to be sure. But what Arthur still, to this day, thought was sadder was that his own father had scoffed at Buffalo's decision. There was no way Reginald would have given up his gifts for a "sickly, defective dud" like Maida Westabrook.

"Buffalo is a remarkable man. He sacrificed so much for his daughter." Amrita gazed out the window, her face unreadable.

"I'm a father too." Arthur nodded, thinking of his own daughter, knowing for certain he would make the same choice as Buffalo, if forced to choose. "I understand. There's nothing I wouldn't give up for my daughter, Rosie."

"I'm sure. But it's never that simple, is it? Many other people have also paid the price of Buffalo's decision, including you, Mr. Hart. One cost of Maida staying with her father was you being separated from yours." Poker faced, she turned back to stare at him, gauging his reaction.

Arthur's heart stuttered, missing a beat and then making up for it triple time.

"What do you know about that?" he asked, his face heating. Even now, decades later, the tatty edges of this memory were still fringed with shame. How did this witch know what he'd done?

Rationally, Arthur was aware he had done nothing wrong. He'd only been ten years old. But that didn't change the way the memory felt. He still blamed himself, because even as a child, Arthur had been schooled about the dangers of exposing himself to an Ordinary. His father had delivered countless lectures on the topic. Reginald Hart had usually paired these lectures with lengthy complaints about the hardship of being a single parent. He'd finished with a diatribe about the burden of raising a shifter on an Ordinary estate.

Similar to any Ordinary estate, the Westabrook estate did not allow the overt use of magic. But Buffalo's rules were even more stringent than most. He'd banned anyone from even *mentioning* magic. Even simple superstitions, like knocking on wood or throwing salt over your shoulder, were firing offenses.

"You must never, *ever* let anyone see what you really are when you're here on this estate, son," Reginald had cautioned. "I don't know that I could do anything to help you out if you did happen to slip."

It wasn't difficult for Arthur to mind his father. He spent his days at a shifter school in Primrose Court and only came home to his father's cottage at night. During the holidays he went to stay with friends or had a minder come to keep him company in the cottage. But on one particular swelteringly hot midsummer day, his father failed to make arrangements. Reggie had to bring his son to work with him.

"Go play in the garden and keep out of trouble while I tend the rose bushes," Reggie had instructed.

Arthur had kicked a stone along the path, chasing it till it landed with a plop in a small frog pond beside a willow tree. When he glanced up, he was startled to see a shy little girl. She appeared to be four or five years old. Why hadn't his father mentioned there were other children joining their parents at work? He'd wondered whose daughter she was.

It had never occurred to him that this little girl might be Maida Westabrook, the same child from his father's drunken tales.

The girl was spinning in circles on her rope swing beneath the willow tree.

"Want me to push you?" Arthur had offered.

The girl hadn't said a word, but her eyes had grown wider. Then she nodded, ever so slightly.

So he'd pushed her. A gentle, tiny nudge at first, as if she might break. He wasn't used to playing with little girls. Although she seemed quite sturdy, she was a pale little thing, with the oddest gray eyes and clouds of fine white-blond hair. She could be a heron, or a llama, or an arctic fox. He couldn't guess what she might eventually shift into, but that wasn't unusual. Many kids didn't start showing signs of shifting till well past puberty. He was just precocious.

The girl tipped her head back to look at him, and the corners of her mouth curled into a tiny smile.

He pushed her again, a little harder, and this time she pumped her legs.

"Higher!" she'd cried out breathlessly, after two more hearty shoves.

Arthur had complied. Her laughter was like shop bells. It opened doors and freed animals from their cages. It released him from the tedious boredom of having to come to work with his father. It made him forget everything. He was having fun!

"I can fly! I'm a bird!" The soaring girl's hair fanned out around her, floating as if she might take flight at any moment. A kaleidoscope of blue butterflies gathered in the tree branches above, flapping to cheer for her as she swung high into the branches, toes pointed. He wanted to bellow, and bray and kick up his own heels.

"Yes! Yes! And I'm a—"

Reginald had snuck up soundlessly on his son and grabbed him by the collar, choking the words right out of him.

"Shadow of a serpent! What do you think you're doing, lad? Get away from Maida Westabrook this instant!" Reginald Hart had then grabbed Arthur roughly and thrown him over his shoulder to carry him away. But it was too late. The incriminating crown of his developing antlers had already emerged.

Despite countless warnings and threats from his father, Arthur had done the one thing he was most forbidden to do. He had revealed himself to an Ordinary girl. And not just any Ordinary girl. He'd shown himself to Maida Westabrook, the daughter of his father's boss.

He still remembered how hard he'd fought not to be sick when her swing plummeted and veered sideways as she stared over her shoulder at him. Her gray eyes were wide with shock and disbelief. For a moment, he'd thought she would fall.

"Don't go!" she cried out, but he wasn't sure if anyone else had heard. He hadn't seen her lips move.

"Put me down." Arthur had kicked and strained, trying to see if the girl was okay. But he was no match for a full grown stag shifter like his father. Reggie had placed a burlap sack over Arthur's head.

It was the first, last, and only time Arthur had met Maida.

Amrita stirred the tea once again. "Imagine how different your life might have been if Buffalo had given up his daughter? You never would have been sent away to boarding school in Ireland."

"What do you know about my father's reasons for sending me away?"

"Everything, actually. Maida is my goddaughter," Amrita confessed. "I'm the one who suggested to Buffalo and your father that you'd probably be better off in a different environment. I can't take full credit for the idea, though. The fairy who cared for Maida —you may recall Beryl Luna—put a bee in my ear about Ireland. She knew you had kin there."

Amrita scrutinized him as she finally poured his tea. He felt little like drinking it now but he lifted the cup anyways, inhaling the pungent steam as he tried to assimilate all this new information.

"I'm also the one who muddled Maida's memory of meeting you in case you were wondering about that."

"Muddled?" Arthur was unfamiliar with the term as it applied to mental magic.

"It's not quite the same thing as erasing a memory. Muddling blurs the edges, making a memory seem more like a dream. She was still so young. Young Ordinaries have such fantastic imaginations. But..." She tapped her fingertips together, glancing up at the woodwork as she pondered. "This means there's a slight chance she might remember you."

Arthur set down his cup a bit carelessly, splattering the saucer. By the stars! His emotions were getting away from him. He'd thought he was here on a legal matter, but now they were discussing his personal history. It made him extremely uncomfortable, but there was nothing he could do about it. One didn't walk out of the Director's office. There was nothing to be done except face the topic head on.

"Is this why I'm really here—for the chance to redeem myself for something I did when I was ten years old?"

Amrita blinked, a bit taken aback. "Of course not, Arthur. There's absolutely nothing you have done that you need to redeem yourself for. You were just a child when you met Maida."

Arthur swallowed and scowled. "It wasn't as if I hadn't been warned. Especially as a shifter. Everyone always expects us to slip."

"You were a *child*," Amrita reassured him. "It had nothing to do with that." She waved a hand and the saucer was spotless again. "You don't trust witches, do you?"

Arthur massaged his forehead. "Look, Director Berman, I'm a simple creature. I don't like playing mind games. Please don't muddle anything or use your mental magic to read my mind. I thought I was here on a business matter."

"I don't need to use mental magic to read your mind," Amrita said. She shook her head sadly. "Your distrust of me is worn quite plainly. You're going to have to get past that if we're going to work together successfully. We both have vested interests in Primrose Court and we're not as different as you might think."

Without comment, Amrita suddenly unpinned and shook out her raven-colored hair. It fell to her shoulders, slowly separating into distinct sections that appeared to stiffen and shine. Within moments, her hair had transformed into a diadem of black and cobalt feathers, shimmering with green, purple, and pink highlights.

Arthur sucked in a deep breath, startled by what his eyes were showing him.

"Many progressive members of the Society recognize that most of us comprise many parts. My own great-grandmother identified as a crow." Amrita plucked a tiny black feather and handed it to him. "Keep this for luck," she said. But he knew it was more than that. It was proof that she hadn't merely tricked him with a glamor. This magic was physical, the same as his own.

"The ongoing strife between magical communities is a pity. You know, I'm hardly the only witch with shifter blood. And I'd venture to guess the reverse is true as well. Have you looked into your own genealogy?" She met his eye. "You might find some surprises."

Arthur shook his head. He knew who his father was, and his father's father before him. Such an inquiry seemed pointless. "I have not."

"I'm not saying the Society is without its flaws, but I'll have you know I am here to preserve and protect the *entire* magical community. I'm far more interested in our similarities than our differences." Amrita smoothed her hair back into strands and twisted it back up into a simple knot. She pinned it with a bit of polished bone. "Now that's settled. Let's focus on the task at hand. Tell me what you think should be done from a legal perspective."

Arthur was relieved to be back in safe territory as he reached for his briefcase. He had prepared for this part of the conversation. "I assume that the Society is seeking to ensure a smooth transition of ownership back to the Lathrops. So I did some research and drew the papers up."

"You already drew papers up?" Amrita looked surprised. "What for?"

"Will and I are meeting with Miss Westabrook after we finish here," Arthur explained. "Once she assigns power of attorney over to me, I will return to Primrose Court and handle the transfer of the property to another party on her behalf."

"Wouldn't it be nice if things could be that simple?" Amrita rocked back in her seat again and sighed. "What makes you think she'll go along with this?"

"Will seems to think Maida doesn't have any interest in the Mudpuddle." Arthur felt the first faint traces of worry as Amrita questioned him.

"Just because Maida doesn't think she's interested in the Mudpuddle, doesn't mean the Mudpuddle isn't interested in her." Amrita closed her eyes for a moment, as if she were considering her words carefully. "I know you have a degree in creature law and are familiar with witch magic as it pertains to property law. But that's not the same as understanding how certain domestic enchantments work, and the long-term effects of such powerful spells. All the centuries of magic poured into the Mudpuddle have created a third party with a valid interest in the proceedings."

"You're not suggesting that the house itself is a sentient entity?" Arthur scoffed. "That's preposterous."

"Is it really?" Amrita posed the question like a teacher, patiently urging a student to reconsider an incorrect answer.

"Fine," Arthur said, begrudgingly. "I won't deny that I am unfamiliar with such magic, and I don't doubt that such things are possible. But there is no place for anthropomorphism within the law."

"Perhaps there should be." Amrita stood to gaze out the window. Once again, she paused before going on. "I'm afraid it will not be possible for Maida to transfer ownership of the property in its present state. She may need the Mudpuddle's consent. In order to get that, she'd need to visit Primrose Court and coax the property back."

"You really want me to bring an unordained Ordinary into Primrose Court? We both know that's strictly forbidden. Not to mention the risks that would pose to Maida's mental health," Arthur challenged. Technically, she wouldn't be the first Ordinary to make it past the warded alley. They regularly made exceptions for Ordinary mages and mediums. But these were trained professionals who'd already seen past the veil. Maida was not one of them.

He shouldn't have to tell the Director that bringing Maida to Primrose Court so suddenly could drive Maida mad. They were going in circles.

"The Mudpuddle doesn't care what kind of mortal Maida is. All she knows is that it's Minerva who keeps the place running and that Maida's name is on her deed. She won't come back unless she feels it's safe to do so." Amrita paused to think for a moment. "I won't deny that bringing Maida to Primrose Court is risky. But we may not have a choice. The Mudpuddle is what keeps Primrose Court stable. Without it, I'm afraid relations between the witches, shifters and other magical folk who live there will deteriorate rapidly."

"She? Now the house has pronouns?" Arthur ran a hand through his hair. He was at a rare loss for words, questioning why they'd chosen him at all. "What am I actually doing here?" he asked. "I know how to draw up legal documents, Director Berman. But making a skittish domicile feel safe is well outside my wheelhouse. And if it's all the same to you, I'd rather not have to enlighten Ms. Westabrook about magic. Once was more than enough."

"You know what I've learned during my tenure here at the museum, Mr. Hart? Most Ordinaries have much more of a capacity for embracing natural magic than we give them credit for," Amrita said. "I believe you have untapped abilities that will see you through this mission as well. Otherwise, we never would have selected you." Amrita turned over her teacup, indicating that their meeting was over. "Just try to keep an open mind, Arthur."

ELEVEN

IF WALLS COULD TALK

The public areas of a pure-blooded witch's home should reflect the grace, heritage, and refinement of her magical lineage. Decorative items featuring the family crest proudly remind guests of the home's noble ancestry, while portraits of esteemed ancestors and heirlooms take places of prominence.

Velvet, brocade, and silk are ideal for upholstery, drapery, and tapestries, with fur pelts and leather accents subtly reminding bestial visitors of their place. Every aspect should blend luxurious elegance and subtle confidence, leaving visitors with no doubt about the owner's impeccable breeding.

-EXCERPT FROM THE ARCANE ELITE: UPHOLDING THE SANCTITY OF WITCH BLOODLINES

Minerva was dreaming about Zephyr.

"There's still sparks in the fireplace!" he joked.

In the dream, Zephyr was lecturing the shifter teenager one moment, and the next they were both gone. All that was left were Zephyr's flyers, burning in her empty hearth. They curled into long flaming ribbons, sending cinders up the chimney. She felt like someone was tapping on her shoulder.

When she awoke with a start, it surprised Minerva to find she was still in the mudroom off the side entrance. Examining her hands, she was surprised to find she was still a mouse. This should have been obvious because she was napping in her knitting basket, but she was always a little foggy before that first cup of tea.

Oh dear. How was she ever going to make tea?

Things could be worse. She stretched out, appreciating the warmth and luxury of her cashmere bedding. The guilt she once felt for abandoning the dull project was gone. She was just glad she remembered it was up here when she got cold. In order to reach the high shelf, she'd had to claw her way up a long scratchy mohair overcoat that was hanging on the wrought-iron coat rack. A precarious journey, but well worth it in the end.

The single striped mitten she'd swaddled herself into was the perfect size and shape for a mouse's impromptu camp out. Soft balls of unused hand spun yarn padded out the rest of her nest. She'd been comfortable enough to fall asleep, and she felt much better for the rest.

Minerva disliked many aspects of being a mouse, but it surprised her to find two things that brought her joy. One was having a tail. Who hadn't wished for an extra appendage on occasion? The other was her much improved senses of smell and taste.

Oh, the glory of that English cheddar! Nutty, buttery and bold, with a burst of peppery zing in the crispy crystals that melted on the tip of her tiny tongue like sparklers. She could smell it from here. Her whiskers twitched and her mouth watered. She felt sorry for the squirrels now. They would never get to taste the delicacy. Although, in retrospect, the squirrels had never once thanked her for the snacks she packed for them each month. This made her think they were ungrateful wretches.

Much as she wanted to eat more of the stash now, she knew she had to be frugal to make the supply last. She did not know how long she might be here, in this state or any other. In fact, she did not know how much time had passed since she'd made it back into the Mudpuddle. Her senses had been quite addled. But now, after eating and sleeping a bit, she felt more like her usual self. Just smaller, and with whiskers.

She was pretty sure the house had disappeared with her inside of it. There was no mistaking the sudden absence of the windows and lack of light coming from under the doors. The power must be off as well, otherwise the light in the hallway leading to the Archives would still be visible. She always left the hall light on.

The mudroom wasn't entirely dark, thanks to the emergency lighting system that was magically spelled into the house. An intricate celestial pattern of stars glowed all around her. It was almost as if the light were coming from tiny pinpricks on the walls. She'd only seen this enchantment unfold a handful of times, during magical power outages. Such events were rare, usually because of a full eclipse. She'd always assumed the enchantments were there to keep the customers safe.

It never crossed Minerva's mind that the backup lighting system might have been created for other kinds of disasters as well. The house hadn't come with a caretaker's manual. Only a children's storybook, penned by her great, great grandmother Flora Lathrop.

As far as Minerva knew, the Mudpuddle had never gone missing for more than a day. But she couldn't tell how much time she'd lost since her encounter with the mage. It could have been minutes, or it could have been hours. He could still be out there somewhere, which meant that time was of the essence!

She decided her first order of business would be to navigate back to the bookshop to check on the time and date. Papa Lathrop's cleverly carved mantel clock would still be keeping time. She was certain of it. The mantel clock guarded the time, even when the house disappeared. If she listened attentively, she could hear it even now—a faint distant ticking. Superior hearing was another benefit of being a mouse, apparently. But not one that would help her return things to normal. How was she to care for her home in this state? The house was clearly unhappy, and so was she.

Oh, how she longed to soothe the Mudpuddle with a warm fire in the foyer hearth. Surely it was missing her tender touch along its bookshelves, longing for the familiar aromas of sweet milky tea and biscuits baking. She'd only just returned from her travels. She knew the Mudpuddle had missed her. It always did. So it had already been out of sorts. And now, she worried that the poor place was traumatized. That made two of them.

Minerva couldn't let herself succumb to the overwhelming sense of despair that was threatening to sweep her away. She had to be brave—for herself, for the house, and for all of Primrose Court. If she could have done so at this moment, Minerva would have read a storybook aloud to the house, preferably its own. The Mudpuddle, like most pampered children, adored hearing its origin story over and over. And like most proud parents, Minerva never grew weary of the telling.

She would have loved to remind the Mudpuddle how Papa and Grandmere Lathrop had built their home as a refuge. It had been a haven not only for the Lathrops, but for the entire community. For almost three centuries, the house had served as a safe space for magical creatures of all sorts to gather, seek solace, share and learn. There was so much history here. Minerva could sing the Mudpuddle's praises all night long, if only she could sing.

But in her present state, Minerva couldn't even lift a book, let alone read it. The best she could do was squeak the story out from her memory. Did the Mudpuddle understand mouse language? It was worth a try.

"Once upon a time there was a magical house. A house that was more than a house. She was a special house because she was so full of stories. Some of them were her own, and thousands more from all over the world."

Minerva climbed out of the basket and surveyed the familiar space of the mudroom, from her unfamiliar angle. Everything felt strange. Her mouse eyes made everything look blurry. The tears welling up in them didn't help with that. This was just a temporary challenge, Minerva reminded herself. A situation that she would eventually triumph over. She was clever, and she was a Lathrop. Lathrops did not give up. They studied, they learned, they kept their wits about them, and they adapted their practice to fit their challenges.

This was the biggest secret about mental magic. It wasn't always so magical. Sometimes magic was just a matter of paying close attention to the tiniest of details. Minerva could do this. Even as a mouse. And even without her wand.

"The family that built this special home poured so much love into it. And all the creatures who came to gather under its eaves heaped on extra helpings. They all knew a secret, and the house knew it too..."

The mudroom was a small, simple space with wide wooden floorboards and paneled wood walls. From where Minerva stood perched on the shelf, there was no practical route back down to the floor. She could easily make the jump back over to the coat rack, but getting down the coat was going to be far more challenging and dangerous than getting up had been. Why hadn't that occurred to her before?

The floor was clean and bare, except for the basket full of books and treats by the door, and a rack for drying muddy shoes and boots. There was also a broom leaned against the wall in the corner beside the door. Minerva's broom. No fancy K-bikes for her. If she was going to ride out into the night, she'd be doing it the old-fashioned way. Nevermind that it had been decades since she'd flown. She always kept her wooden handled broom clean, polished, and at the ready. A witch never knew when she might need to summon a lift.

Now, for example.

Minerva closed her eyes and waved her hands in front of her in a well-practiced sweeping pattern, willing the broom to rise to her aid. Cautiously, she cracked one eye open.

Nothing.

Once again, she performed the motions, taking greater care to be sure her movements were precise. The results were the same.

After the third attempt, she dropped to all four paws, hanging her head over the edge of the shelf in defeat. This was torture. She'd lost the ability to perform even the simplest of spells.

"The secret of the house was that magic shared is magic multiplied. We're better together. We need each other to survive. The house understood that secret, and her very special role."

Minerva continued to recite the story, as much for herself as for the house.

Minerva's broom was barely seven feet away, its pearl inlaid monogram sparkling in the artificial starlight. It practically mocked her, sitting stationary in the corner like that. It was wrong in so many ways. Suddenly, it dawned on her. It wasn't only wrong that the broom wasn't responding. The broom shouldn't have been there in the first place.

She would never have left it beside the door like that! That was a reckless place to leave such a precious item. Minerva's broom belonged on the broom stand in the hall closet, not leaning against the wall bristles down!

Had she summoned the broom whilst running from the wizard? Or perhaps the broom had come to her aid, holding the door for her, and blocking anyone else from coming in? She wished she could recall.

Minerva crept down to the other end of the shelf, squinting to get a look at the broom from a better, closer angle. Her movement activated the glittering lights in the wall and the motion lit her path as she crawled to the end closest to the door. Once again, she flattened her body on the shelf and hung her head over the edge.

There was a bit of something silver and shiny caught in the broom's bristles. Too hard to tell what it was from up here, with her lousy eyesight. She would have to get closer to see. But, of course, this would require navigating a path back down to the floor and she was back to her original dilemma. She still did not know how she was going to get down. The ground was looking farther and farther away by the moment. Minerva tried not to panic. She had to stay on task.

Get to the clock.

"The house sheltered and cared for her creatures. And in return, her creatures cared for her as well. They kept her clean and well fed with fairy tales and folklore. Over time, the house grew and expanded, and her capacity for magic grew as well. She learned discretion and the importance of keeping some secrets—that not all stories were meant to be shared with everyone. She could be trusted with this important task."

Minerva had no way of knowing if the Mudpuddle heard her, but reciting the story was helping her to stay calm.

She could see into the hallway from this end of the shelf. How simple it would be to walk back to the bookshop in her human form. It was just three steps up, down the hall, and through the foyer.

Three steps up.

She'd almost forgotten about the stairs. She'd need a plan for climbing the stairs. Those steps represented mountains to a mouse. Sheer cliffs. But this was a problem for later. First, she would need to get down from this blasted shelf.

"Some people say that a house can't have feelings. But those people have never lived in a magical house like the Mudpuddle, and I feel so sorry for them."

Frustrated, Minerva retraced her steps back to the basket.

Perhaps she could use the yarn to fashion some sort of harness and rappel her way down to the floor? If only there was something to attach it to. But of course there was nothing, except the basket itself, and she had no confidence it would hold her.

Foiled again, she sat still at the edge of the shelf, thinking and wishing she had a parachute or a paper airplane to glide down upon. The lights began to fade.

"No. No. No. No. No! Stop that!" Minerva leapt to her feet and hopped in place. She flapped her mouse arms frantically. She was very grateful for the extra bit of balance afforded by her tail.

"Don't you dare go dim on me now, house! I need your help to show me the way!"

All at once the lights in the wall above the crown molding pulsed, illuminating the top edge of the crown molding.

"Are you trying to tell me something?" Minerva squeaked. "Do you understand me?"

In response, the entire room lit up in a dramatic burst of pulsating starlight that traveled up from the floor in a wave. When the wave broke on the ceiling, there was a bright flash, like lightning. Then the room settled back into semi-darkness. Minerva blinked to clear the spots from her vision. The room was dark now, except for a single track of lights tracing a path along the white crown molding. She looked up. Curiously, the light seemed to come from behind the molding.

Cautiously, Minerva climbed up the handle of the basket to get a better look. She rose up on two legs, standing on her tiptoes to edge closer to the wall. From here she could see that the top ledge of the crown molding didn't quite meet the ceiling. There was a small gap there. Too small to notice from the floor, but not too small for a tiny mouse, such as herself, to squeeze into. This was where the light was coming from.

Taking a deep breath, Minerva reached out with her front paws and attempted to pull herself up to the top edge. Her feet scrabbled for purchase against the wood. She managed to grab onto a carved ridge in the molding with her toes and reached her head into the small gap.

From there, it was easy. Once her head, arms, and torso were through, she could stretch herself out and shimmy the rest of her body up and into the crawl space. She wasn't sure what to expect, but she dearly hoped that she'd find some other pathway back to the store. Even if it meant traveling through the walls. She was sure her sharp teeth could gnaw through plaster, though she didn't want to test that theory. She didn't suspect aged plaster was nearly as palatable as aged cheddar.

As the lights came up in the space behind the crown molding

Minerva blinked and struggled to focus on the incredible sight before her. She was expecting to find herself in a rough and unfinished crevice, at best. She was certainly not expecting to see a wall-papered hallway with elaborate tiny paintings and sconces that stretched out before her like a dollhouse owner's dream.

Landing with a soft flump on the patterned carpet she marveled at her new surroundings. How could this be? She'd been certain she knew every nook and cranny of the Mudpuddle.

So how was it possible that she'd missed this tiny network of hallways and rooms, hiding in plain sight?

TWELVE

A RESTLESS NIGHT

The Butterfly Effect reveals a hidden truth: that the gentle beat of fragile wings can ripple across the fabric of existence itself. It suggests that the very smallest of actions can set into motion a series of events that reshape destiny.

In scientific terms, this phenomenon refers to the sensitivity of complex systems to initial conditions. It suggests that a butterfly's wing-flap might, in time, stir the winds into a tempest halfway around the globe. Yet, in the realm of magic, it exposes something more profound. There is a connection between all living things and the elements, a web of causality that may be manipulated.

We must embrace the duality of the Butterfly Effect. It reminds us that every creature, no matter how small, wields some power. Every action, however seemingly insignificant, has the potential to shape the course of our world.

–EXCERPT FROM THE MUDPUDDLE MANUAL OF NATURAL MAGIC

Maida hadn't meant to stay up all night reading. But after hours of scrubbing sinks, mopping floors, reshelving books and re-hanging her clothes, she hadn't been able to fall asleep. Even with new locks on the doors and a soothing bergamot and eucalyptus candle burning, her mind raced, buzzing relentlessly.

She was still awake reading a novel about a psychic detective when the phone rang once at three a.m. A few minutes later, it rang twice. Maida didn't wait for the third call. This was Zani's signal. She phoned her friend back right away and immediately launched into her own news, sharing all the details of the break-in. For once, she had something interesting to relate! And if the break-in had left her feeling anxious, she was sure Zani would be her rock. Her nomadic friend was fearless. Nothing shook her.

Maida fully expected Zani to respond with some wild story about exchanging phone numbers with a fellow hostage during a bank robbery. She didn't expect Zani to fuss and cluck at her like a mother hen.

"I think you should go back to Boston for a bit. Maybe stay at your dad's place? I'm worried about you. You shouldn't be alone there." Zani worried. "Is there anyone I can call?"

Her friend's reaction to the break-in surprised Maida.

"Are you going soft on me, Zani?"

"I don't know." Zani paused, and the line crackled, reminding Maida of how very far away her best friend was. "I just have a feeling about this. It's weird that they took nothing. It's like what they really wanted to get at was you."

She'd been so taken aback that she'd completely forgotten to tell Zani about the locket.

After that conversation, it was no surprise she hadn't been able to fall asleep. She kept being startled by thumps and bangs coming from other apartments. Each time, she imagined it was someone about to bang her door down.

Zani meant well, but her words only reminded Maida how alone she was. This was the biggest design flaw in her "simple life" plan. She really had nobody here in California. Not even a pet.

She knew she ought to try harder to make friends. But the more she thought about having to make small talk with strangers, the less she felt like making the effort.

Maida finished reading the last chapter of her novel shortly after sunrise. But she tossed and turned for two more hours before it was time to get up and get ready for her meeting with Will and the solicitor. Now she couldn't stop thinking about the mysterious inheritance Will had mentioned. Why the sudden urgency?

Questions tumbled and collided like rocks inside her head, polishing themselves smooth without answers.

When it was finally time to get out of bed and make herself presentable, Maida dragged herself to the bathroom and splashed some cold water on her face. She tried to wish the dark circles under her eyes away. Then she pinched her cheeks, trying to coax a bit of color into them. She couldn't stop yawning. When she stretched her arms over her head and yawned for the fifth time, her ears filled with the rushing sound of her own blood being forced to move. The coffee at The Bunny Hole had better be strong, she thought.

Even though she was tired and apprehensive about the meeting, it would be so nice to see a familiar face. She hoped the paperwork would be simple, so she and Will could send the solicitor back to wherever solicitors went when they weren't being contentious, and use the opportunity to catch up properly.

Thank goodness she didn't need to get fancy for Will. He accepted her just as she was. Maida twisted her mess of hair into a sloppy bun and didn't even bother changing out of her favorite pajamas. She simply threw on a cozy Shaker knit cardigan over the nightgown and pulled on some leggings underneath. Then she slipped her feet into some fuzzy, slipper-like boots. One of the nicest things about living by the beach in Southern California was that this was a perfectly normal outfit in which to leave home.

There was just enough time to water the plants before she left.

The fresh, cold ocean air slapped her awake as she stepped outside. She could smell sea spray and wood smoke, plus a hint of the burnt plastic odor that still lingered in the air. Maida poked a pinky finger into the soil of each plant, checking for dryness before she sprinkled them with water from a small metal watering can.

When she got to the end of the line, she spied the newcomer. Stapelia grandiflora. Someone had dropped it beside the pile of pot shards in the middle of the night. The ragged new arrival looked skittish. It hadn't so much grown, so much as flinched sideways out of its too-small pot.

"Don't worry. I've saved sadder specimens than the likes of you," Maida said, examining the cactus-like plant. It would be a fun one to sketch, laden as it was with odd black blooms that resembled paper lanterns.

She'd have to be quick about it. As soon as the blooms burst open, the hairy, dinner plate size flowers would stink like the bottom of a festering dumpster. It wasn't the poor plant's fault. All the same, she'd have to keep this one downwind of everyone's front door once it bloomed.

Addy's door swung open just as Maida was considering where to place it.

"Hey, Maida! You know what you should try with those plants?"

"Hmmm?" Maida answered distractedly, making space for the new plant between a jade and some milkweed.

Addy cleared her throat impatiently.

"I'm sorry," Maida sighed, "I was distracted. What were you saying, Addy?"

"Well." Addy glanced quickly back inside her apartment, then closed the door quietly behind her. "I was just about to give you a suggestion to help triage your patients here." She waved her clear plastic mug of green juice at the mess by Maida's door.

Maida gazed up at the pretty young woman. She was young. So young. Like many of Maida's neighbors, Addy had come to California with dreams of being an actress. And why not? She was beautiful, but more importantly, she was a chameleon. She cycled through aesthetics with uncanny ease and speed. Her features had a certain indeterminate ethnicity. She was a girl that could go blonder and portray a Viking shield maiden, or dye her hair darker and pass herself as an Indian princess. With the right accent training, Addy could be almost anyone.

But today she was just Addy, fresh faced, bohemian and barefoot, standing by her front door.

"What you should try," Addy pressed on authoritatively, bored with waiting for Maida to take the bait, "is some Nocturnaturals plant food! It's brand new and sold out everywhere, but I bet I can ask Cormac about getting some."

"About that...I probably shouldn't have given you his number. I'm not sure you should call him," Maida warned.

"Why not? Did you change your mind?" Addy's eyes narrowed defiantly, and she folded her arms across her chest. When she stuck out her lower lip, Maida half expected her to shout, "No take backs!"

"No. I wasn't interested yesterday and I'm still not interested today," Maida reassured her. "I don't think he was actually interested in me, anyway." She still couldn't quite put her finger on it but she still felt certain the come-on had been a ruse.

"You really shouldn't cut yourself down like that. I mean, you're older, but there's nothing obviously wrong with you. I'm sure if you made an effort you could find someone. I mean, maybe not someone like Cormac Vorador, but there has to be somebody." Addy frowned and picked at the peeling moon-shaped "Be Beautiful" Nocturnaturals patch on her upper arm. It reminded Maida of the other thing she needed to mention.

"That's the other thing. I meant to warn you. Someone broke into my place yesterday afternoon. They made a real mess." Maida pointed out the broken pot shards.

"That's a bummer, but what does any of that have to do with Cormac?" Addy examined her fingernails.

"Nothing. I just thought I'd mention it because there's been a rash of break-ins around here. People are claiming that the break-ins have a connection to Nocturnaturals products. You should probably be careful if you're selling that stuff. And I think you should also be careful with that guy."

"Thanks for the tip." Addy cocked a brow. "Your concern is super sweet, but your timing is totally off." Addy lowered her voice. "Cormac spent the night at my place."

Suddenly those thumps in the night took on a whole different meaning. She felt herself blushing.

"Sorry if we kept you up." Addy smiled a little too smugly.

But was she, really? Her slow, confident blink had the effect of a cocked and aimed gun as she waited, daring Maida to comment. Was Maida supposed to congratulate or admonish her on her conquest? She wasn't in the mood to play Russian roulette, so instead, she said nothing.

This sort of conversation was exactly why she preferred to keep to herself.

"I'm all done here." Maida stood up and brushed the dirt off her hands. "Nice dress. Got an audition today?" She was already planning her escape.

"I do!" Addy preened. "Cormac insisted I try out for his infomercial."

"Why don't you take one of these stones for luck?" Maida plucked an opalescent moonstone from the planter by the stairs and thrust it at Addy.

"Awww, you're so sweet, but I don't need that," Addy said, immediately tossing the stone back into another pot. "I don't believe in those kinds of charms. I think we all have to make our own luck."

"Okay...I guess you're good then. Best of luck!"

With this, Maida slipped past her chatty neighbor and took off down the stairs.

THIRTEEN

THE BUNNY HOLE

While certain naturalists may dismiss the notion of time travel or mystical portals as fanciful, the recent inexplicable emergence of formerly extinct species, such as the coelacanth, the takahē, and the Chacoan peccary, suggest otherwise. Lazarus species routinely emerge from the misty fog of the past, flaunting bold evidence of the hidden dimensions of reality.

Ordinary naturalists attribute the enigmatic return of these species to their ability to thrive surreptitiously in hidden or remote places. We can't fault them for their inability to intuit the wondrous and mystical fabric of reality like magical naturalists do.

-EXCERPT FROM THE MUDPUDDLE MANUAL OF NATURAL MAGIC

It was a short walk to The Bunny Hole from Maida's apartment. The donut shop was located just a block from the Pacific Coast Highway. You couldn't miss the giant, white-frosted, rotating donut mounted on top of the single-story building.

Ruby, Diamond, Agate...She strode briskly past the jewel-named streets of South Laguna. Maida was still thinking about the odd exchange with Addy and she wasn't watching where she was going.

This was how she almost ran into a tall dark-haired man waiting for the crosswalk light to change at the corner. He was waiting to cross the highway, headed in the other direction and stepped aside to avoid her.

"Sorry!" she breathed.

"You should slow down," he replied, pressing the button under the traffic signal twice in rapid succession, before looking down at her. His warm eyes widened with surprise and what seemed like recognition as he took her in. Did he know her? Or was he looking at someone else? She glanced over her shoulder, but there wasn't anyone behind her.

Maida felt her skin prickle as she leaned forward to press the button for the crosswalk in the direction she was heading. When she looked up again, he was still staring at her. He looked straight into her eyes, raising his brows and holding her gaze pointedly, as if he were waiting for her to say something, or answer a question. But what was she supposed to say? He hadn't asked her a question, had he?

She allowed her gaze to brush over him before looking away again. He was all polished angles and long limbs, swathed in a well cut and tailored tan trench coat. This man didn't look like he was from around here. Or even like he was from now. Who wore a trench coat to the beach? With posture like that?

She had the irritating feeling now that this man was someone she ought to recognize. It bothered her she couldn't recall from where? His high cheekbones, glossy chestnut brown hair and curious russet-colored eyes were so uniquely different, and yet so familiar. Was he someone famous? She tried not to stare as he brushed an unruly lock back from his forehead.

This happened a lot in Southern California. Film crews seemed to pop up around every corner. There were movie stars at the supermarket. But that didn't explain why he seemed to recognize *her*. She didn't have long to ponder it. A second later the light changed. His walk signal lit up, and he took off across the street.

Watching him walk away made her feel weirdly melancholic. She couldn't bring herself to look away. She just stood there watching him till he disappeared behind a row of parked trucks. She stood there in a bit of a sleep deprived stupor, until someone else walked by with coffee, which smelled wonderful. Then she finally snapped out of it and remembered where she was going.

From the street in front of the strip mall parking lot, Maida could see Will sitting inside The Bunny Hole. He was sitting in a corner booth by the front window, taking advantage of the light as he snapped photos of colorful donuts stacked in a pretty pink box. There were two paper cups of coffee on the table, one of which she hoped was hers.

Will pocketed the camera the instant he spied Maida and rushed out the door. Then he waved his arms over his head like he was some kind of wild rogue air traffic controller, guiding Maida in. A pair of power walkers slowed down to a slow stroll in order to get a better look at whatever was going on. One of them scowled at Will when he continued to wave his arms like a crazy person, even as they picked their way around him. That didn't faze Will. He was blissfully uninhibited. Same as always. And, she suspected, he was doing this to get a rise out of her.

Maida wondered, for the millionth time, how someone this colorful had ended up working for someone as beige as her father.

"Glad to see you're okay!" Will gave her a quick once over like he was checking for damage.

"Why wouldn't I be?" Maida made an exasperated face at him. First Zani, then Will. Did everyone think she was a child?

"Alien abduction, possessed dolls, bands of roving televangelists...You never know." Will pulled Maida into the shade of the donut shop's awning.

"What are you even talking about?" Maida shook her head. Will simply stood there and grinned back at her.

His mischievous smile had an immediate and predictable effect on her. When Will smiled at her, two things happened—one to her and the other to him. Her spirits lifted and his eyes got all skrinkle-y, disappearing into his face. The effect was so comically disconcerting that she always laughed at the sight of it, regardless of whether she wanted to.

Will didn't mind one bit. He knew how disarming this effect was and used it to his own advantage. He stepped forward and enveloped her in a big, hearty hug.

"Will? You're squishing me," Maida groaned.

"I'm just so happy to see you. You look good, Mayday. Radiant as always." Will released her and looked her over.

Maida knew Will was a smooth talker. She suspected he was just being flattering. They were both getting older, after all. Time was taking a toll.

But taking a second look at her father's right-hand man now that he'd finally released her from his bear hug, she couldn't help but wonder if he'd been granted some sort of special daylight savings pass on aging.

At forty-three, Will should have been trotting into silver fox territory, yet he still looked as youthful as he had in his twenties. His wavy red hair was just as thick and lustrous as ever, and his deep emerald colored eyes still sparkled with their signature green glint. Nothing about him seemed to be fading with time.

"Radiant, huh?" Maida said, reaching out to touch his face. His unwrinkled skin was so smooth. It felt bouncy. How?

"Why don't you ever seem to age?" Maida asked. "You'd tell me if you had work done, right? I don't think it's fair that I'm going to start getting all the character lines while you age backwards on me."

"Stop it." Will shook his head and swatted her hand away. But then he caught her hand in one of his and pulled it towards his face to examine the tattoo on her wrist. She had forgotten to cover the small act of rebellion from her college years. It had been so long since she'd gotten the word *abracadabra* inscribed that she often forgot it was there. The design was simple, the word inked in simple calligraphy with the image of an artist's pen nib inked into the final flourish—as if it were still being written.

"Why haven't I seen this before?" Will accused.

"It's nothing," Maida insisted, attempting to pull her hand away. But Will hadn't finished examining the tattoo. He even fished a pair of spectacles out from his brocade jacket pocket in order to get a better look.

Maida felt relieved by the sight of his small, thick iridescent glasses. So she wasn't the only one aging after all.

"Who designed this?" Will looked up for a moment.

"I did," Maida answered. "I've had it for ages. You don't need to mention this to my father, do you?"

She tried to pull her arm away again, but Will held it there. "Stay still, I'm admiring your work," he murmured as he studied it. "What were you thinking when you drew it?"

Maida gave him a wary look. The idea had just come to her in college, after auditing one of Zani's lectures on magical words. In it she had learned that the phrase Abracadabra came from the ancient Hebrew words for *I speak as I create* or, some thought, *I create what I speak.* Abracadabra was one of the oldest known magical words. Maida liked the notion of creating magic with one's words. Books were made of words too, and books were definitely magical for her. Most of all, she loved the idea of using one's imagination to create something brand new, something that had never existed before.

Despite her father and her strict upbringing, she'd wanted to believe there was something more. The tattoo was a representation of her own desire to do that—a reminder that she had the power to create and live the life she chose. Giving herself permission to believe in the possibility of magic and inscribing the hopeful word on her flesh had felt like breathing life into clay.

Maida didn't tell any of this to Will, of course. She shouldn't have to explain herself and there was a very good chance that even if he kept her "magical" tattoo a secret from her father, he'd never let her live it down.

"It's just a silly tattoo, Will. What can I say? I was young. I was having a moment."

Finally, after what Maida thought was a ridiculous amount of time to be fussing over an ordinary tattoo, Will let go of her arm.

"Okay." Will nodded sagely and repeated the word, almost as if speaking to himself. "Okay. You don't have to tell me right now. But I think we both know it's more than that."

Maida studied him, waiting for the teasing banter to resume. But it didn't happen. His expression remained serious.

"Come on, Mayday, let's go in before the coffee gets cold." Will reached out to hold the door for her.

The donut shop smelled of sugar, coffee, and decadence. Chocolate, Maple, Almond Cream. It was going to be a tough call. Perhaps the eclair? When they sat down at the booth, she reached for the box of treats, but Will swatted her hand away and tsk'd.

"You can't eat till everyone's here, Maida, you know the rules."

"Seriously?" Maida pouted. She'd almost forgotten about the solicitor.

Will nodded and pushed the paper coffee cup towards her. Maida took a sip. Of course, Will had remembered exactly how she took it. He was a stellar PA.

"So, where is the solicitor?" she asked, peering around the small space. The morning rush had subsided and most of the Formica booths were empty. There were just a couple of people lingering over a last cup of coffee, and one woman in line.

"Arthur went around the corner in search of a '*proper macchiato*.'" Will rolled his eyes as he imitated the solicitor.

"So what do you know about this inheritance, Will?" Maida took advantage of their alone time to ask the questions that had been plaguing her all morning. "What's with the urgency? Did my father tell you anything about this property?"

She fiddled with the silver locket while she spoke. She was already used to the way it hummed in her palm. It felt so comfortable there. When she released the locket, to take another sip of coffee, Will went absolutely goggle-eyed.

"Bless the sea fairies! What kind of mischief is *that*?" Breathless, he pointed at the locket. "Where did you get it?"

"This thing?" Maida glanced down. "I don't know. It just washed up on the beach yesterday, right at my feet. I have to admit, it was very..." she caught herself smiling before saying the word "magical."

"I'll bet it was." Will whipped out his spectacles again. "Allow me?" He leaned forward across the booth and cradled the locket in the flat palm of his hand, lifting and lowering it as if checking his weight. Then he traced the letter L with his index finger.

"This is beyond extraordinary, Mayday! Do you know what this is?" Will's cheeks were bright pink. He was talking fast, clearly excited.

"No?" She shook her head. "Should I?"

"I believe it's a gearheart locket. There's few of them left. Have you had a look inside it yet?" Will snatched at the locket, trying to push the lever on the side without even asking.

"Hey! Cut it out." Instinctively, Maida pulled away and closed her hand protectively around the locket. As much as she normally enjoyed Will's quirkiness, this felt like he was crossing a line. "I thought we were meeting here to discuss my inheritance." Maida frowned.

"Yes, yes, of course we are, and Arthur will get to that as soon as he secures his bougie brew. But this," Will pointed at the necklace, "this changes everything!"

And then, in a shocking breach of good manners, Will helped himself to a pink frosted donut with rainbow colored sprinkles.

FOURTEEN

A CHANGE OF PLANS

Blending in with Ordinary humans requires mastering their social cues, even when your otherworldly instincts may be triggered.

To prevent unplanned shifts, keep your emotions in check. Sudden noises or scents may excite your animalistic proclivities, but controlled breathing can help you stay calm. If needed, excuse yourself briefly to regain composure.

Avoid rigid or overly alert postures, as humans prefer a more relaxed stance. Prolonged eye contact and certain smiles can be misinterpreted, so maintaining a neutral expression is wise.

Subtle nods and calm gestures will allow you to engage smoothly while staying in control. A true gentleman adopts Ordinary behaviors without drawing attention.

-EXCERPT FROM THE METAMORPHIC MAN: A GENTLEMAN SHAPESHIFTER'S GUIDE TO CULTURED CONDUCT

Arthur's second port with Will had gone much smoother. This time, Arthur was ready when Will plunged them both into oblivion. After two quick steps, they emerged into a Wonderland themed party room, crammed into the back of a Laguna Beach donut shop. Red paper-covered tables decorated with confetti stood at the ready for a child's birthday party.

Reflected in the colorfully framed funhouse mirrors that lined the walls, Will looked like a giant, and Arthur appeared short and rotund.

Will inhaled, long and deep. "Smell that, Arthur? This is no ordinary donut shop. It was started by a pair of rabbit shifters but they've got a crew of world-class culinary elves doing the baking for them." Will pulled two wax paper wrapped bricks from his jacket pockets. "Ceylon cinnamon and cocoa from Ecuador." He winked. "Free use of the portal when you call ahead and bring the elves fresh ingredients."

"Do you always have to make arrangements to port?" Arthur asked. He was curious about how it worked. Twice they had come through mirrors, but when Will had thrown open the door to the van, the portal seemed to appear from nowhere. And Arthur was pretty sure there wasn't a mirror in his pantry.

"No." Will pocketed the powders again. "Anything can be a portal, so long as it's not warded. It's just safer to stay on the path. Porting is more predictable when you can call ahead to make sure the coast is clear. Best not to leave some things to chance."

This was probably the most practical thing that Will had ever said to Arthur, and he found it oddly endearing.

"Can I get you some coffee?" Will offered as they walked towards the front of the sunny, immaculate shop. "We're a bit early."

The glass cases held a collection of cleverly shaped and decorated baked goods, frosted in brilliant tones. Amongst the rainbow-colored donuts, Arthur spied crescent moon croissants and kouign-amann pastries adorned with spun sugar and gold leaf crowns.

As hungry as this made him, he wanted to stretch his legs and take a moment to think about his conversation with the Director before he spoke with Maida.

"If it's all the same to you," Arthur glanced out the door and down the street as he made his excuse, "I think I'll go find myself a proper macchiato."

"Okay, see you soon." Will waved distractedly and turned back towards the baker to place his order.

Walking down the street, Arthur recalled why he disliked Southern California. He ran hot. Even in the wintertime, it was too warm for him. He unbuttoned his trench coat as he walked alongside the busy coastal highway.

The Director had given him much to think about, but she had said nothing to convince Arthur that he ought to alter his plans. He believed that the simplest solutions were almost always the best. Therefore, he would begin by asking Maida to assign power of attorney over to him. He'd handled dozens of difficult clients. Arthur wasn't about to let a truculent house tell him how to do his job. He was still determined to get back to Boston in time for dinner. Without the Ordinary woman in tow.

He paused at a crosswalk. This quaint coastal stretch of the highway was packed with small shops, boutiques, and galleries. He spied the inevitable gourmet coffee shop a couple of blocks down on the ocean side of the road. He wasn't actually fussy about his brew. That had just been his excuse to go for a walk. But now that he smelled the roasty aromas wafting his way, he was glad he'd come.

Arthur was just getting ready to press the button to change the signal when the woman almost crashed into him. She seemed to be in a hurry, heading north towards the donut shop, lost in a dream, not paying attention to where she was going.

Thirty years later, and there was still no mistaking her. Those big curious eyes. That crazy hair? He would have recognized Maida Westabrook anywhere.

In general, Arthur tried to avoid eye contact with Ordinary women. He'd been stalked by besotted court reporters on more than one occasion. Animal magnetism was a real thing, and it wasn't only the noble beasts that benefitted. Even weasels and snake shifters had the power to attract undue attention. It made Ordinaries easy prey for unsavory shifters. He wanted no part of that.

One interesting thing Arthur had observed: however fascinated an Ordinary might become with a shifter, they couldn't maintain direct eye contact for more than a moment or two. The instant they saw the magical glints of gold in a shifter's eyes, their primal senses of self-preservation kicked in.

That didn't seem to be the case with Ms. Westabrook though.

Maida was staring right back at him, staring for a full ten seconds which was an all-time record for an Ordinary. He was so surprised, he almost forgot to breathe.

Was Director Berman right? Did she recognize him, too?

His foolish heart skipped a beat at the idea of this. But then she looked away, which was probably for the best.

She leaned forward to press the button for the crosswalk in the other direction, then stared down at her feet while waiting for it to change. He caught her scent on the breeze as she stood beside him. She smelled fresh, like meadow plants. Bee balm and mountain mint, with a hint of honeysuckle.

Fauns and leprechauns!

His head was swimming. She smelled so good that it was making him twitch and salivate. If he'd ever found such a delectably fragrant patch of earth in his stag form, he would have flung himself down and gleefully rolled about on it.

Arthur felt his skin tingle. He stood up straighter. Her proximity was shaking his molecules into a pre-shift state. He used the trick of counting and cataloging the bones in his human skeleton, working his way from the ground up as he waited for the moment to pass. He'd have to banish himself back to Ireland forever if he unintentionally shifted in front of her again. The prospect of it was mortifying. He would not succumb. But he felt the phantom of his antlers aching with the effort of it.

By the time his breathing calmed, he was already up to his patella. When the light changed, he practically bolted across the road.

Reaching the ocean side of the highway, Arthur turned west towards the Pacific Ocean. He cut down a side street, walking briskly towards a weather-beaten sign posted beside a steep staircase. It was only two stories down to the sand. Once on the beach, he kicked off his shoes and rolled his pant legs up to his knees. Then he walked straight into the water. He let the painfully icy surf smack his feet and ankles, washing away his ill-advised urge to make that woman laugh again like she had as a child.

Ten minutes later, and ten minutes late for their meeting, Arthur lingered outside the shop for one last moment, spying on Will and Maida through the window. Their interactions were easy, familiar.

He watched Will take a large bite from a lavish pink donut, grinning with impish delight. The fae PA was having far too much fun, given the serious nature of the situation. But it was Maida who held his attention more. Her pale hair looked almost opalescent, and he wished he could hear her laughing through the glass. Will and Maida were clearly comfortable with one another, joking like they were siblings. There wasn't anything more between them. Even though he felt sure of this, Arthur still felt an unexpected stab of possessive jealousy when Will playfully smashed his donut against Maida's face.

Arthur checked the contents of his briefcase one last time. The documents were still in order. Once she signed them, it would be done. He and Will would be on their way. He'd probably never have occasion to see her again.

Will waved to greet Arthur as he pushed through the door, but Maida was busy perusing a paper menu. She didn't look up until he was standing right in front of her.

When she did, she smiled warmly. "Hey, I know you!" she said. Her face was so open and unguarded it made the ache start all over again.

"Do you?" The words tumbled out of him, feeling sticky, sandy and stuck together as he wondered again if she had instantly known him, the way he'd known her.

"Sure—from the crosswalk." Her smile grew brighter. "*You're* the solicitor?"

"Yes." A curt nod was the best he could manage, as he felt that sensation of plummeting in his chest again. He hated to admit to himself that Director Berman's words had gotten his hopes up. *For what?*

Of course, Maida didn't remember their childhood encounter. Why should she remember it? She had been five years old. And her memory had been muddled. Their childhood encounter had rearranged his entire life, but for her, it had been just another ordinary Tuesday.

It meant nothing.

"Nice to meet you, Mr. Hart." Maida stuck out a hand. "I'm Maida."

"You can call me Arthur." He busied himself fiddling with his briefcase, pretending not to notice her gesture. He couldn't trust himself to touch her at the moment. Not now that he'd finally cleared the scent of her from his nose. It was best not to take chances. His nostrils quivered.

"Sit down, Arthur!" Will jumped up, gesturing for Arthur to take a seat on the bench opposite Maida, in the booth. Arthur slid in and moved towards the window, placing himself as far from her as he could.

"Hopefully, I won't take up too much of your time this morning Ms. Westabrook. If you could just sign the papers I've drafted, I'll be authorized to act as your agent and handle the sale or reassignment of the house for you." He removed the stack of papers from his briefcase and placed them on the table.

"What if she doesn't want to give up her house?" Will nudged Maida to slide further into the booth and took the seat next to her. She was now sitting directly across from Arthur, their knees knocking.

It took a few extra seconds for Will's words to penetrate the static filling Arthur's head.

"Wait. What do you mean?" Arthur stared icily at Will.

Will drummed his fingers against his jaw and gazed skyward, as if he were genuinely pondering the issue. "Well, I was just thinking that Maida should probably examine the property herself, before signing her rights away. As a solicitor, wouldn't that be the most prudent course of action to advise your client?"

If Will hadn't been his ticket back to Boston, Arthur would have reached across the table and wrung his neck.

FIFTEEN

DISAPPEARING INK

Patience is a practice that must be mastered in both human and animal forms. When your instincts urge you to act swiftly, it is often the perfect moment to embrace stillness and restraint. True strength lies not in haste, but in the art of waiting.

To maintain your dignity, try focusing on the small, deliberate motions that ground you in the present—whether it's adjusting a cufflink or tracing the rim of a glass. These subtle gestures provide an outlet for your instincts without betraying your impatience. Patience is not only a mark of refinement but also of control, allowing you to navigate both human society and the natural world with elegance and grace.

-EXCERPT FROM THE METAMORPHIC MAN: A GENTLEMAN SHAPESHIFTER'S GUIDE TO CULTURED CONDUCT

"Here, at least have a donut before making her sign anything." Will shook the donut box at Arthur. "It would be a crime for you to come all this way and not indulge a little."

Arthur hesitated, salivating over a bear claw. Will shook the box a second time.

"Come on, live a little."

Arthur capitulated, helping himself to a flaky, buttery, cinnamon-laced bear claw. The exterior of the pastry was covered with paper thin slivers of shaved nuts, resembling fur. The tip of each phalange of the bear's paw ended with a whole pointed almond evoking the claw. He could smell the rich marzipan and rum raisin filling. It was a work of art. Almost too beautiful to eat.

Arthur set the pastry down on a napkin. "The entire reason I'm here today is to save Ms. Westabrook the trouble and fuss of having to travel back to Boston to handle this matter."

"I do think I'd like to know a little more about the property, though," Maida interjected. "And about you too, Arthur. I knew you looked familiar at the crosswalk." She pulled a pencil from her pocket and began to doodle absent-mindedly on the back of the paper menu.

"You did?" Arthur raised a brow, casually, as if his heart hadn't resumed its frantic tap dance. He could feel her knees laced between his and it was making the hair beneath his pants leg grow. He didn't dare move. Friction would only make matters worse.

Desperate for a distraction, he tapped the pile of documents on the white Formica table to square the stack.

"Yes." Maida nodded. "I knew I knew you from somewhere. It must be because I knew your father. Although..." She looked up to study him again, taking stock of his face as though she were about to draw him. She tilted her head one way, then the other, and narrowed her eyes. "You don't seem anything like old Reggie."

"We weren't close," Arthur said. "I went away to school in Ireland, and was mostly raised by my family there."

"I was going to say, I can definitely hear a little Irish influence in your voice." Maida looked back down at her drawing.

She was turning bright pink. Did this mean she *liked* his

accent? He could have warmed his hands in the radiance of her blush. He glanced down at the donut and back up to the curve of her ear. It was a toss-up which one he wanted to nibble on more.

He closed his eyes for a moment and blew out a quick breath. "Back to these papers...I'd be happy to explain my thinking."

"Arthur?" Maida continued to sketch as she posed another question. "Why haven't I ever heard anything about this house until now?'

"The Lathrop family is notoriously private," Arthur acknowledged. "And there's not many of them left. I'm only aware of your mother's younger sister and the elderly aunt who has been taking care of the property in question."

"I have aunts?" A hurt expression crossed over Maida's eyes.

"Yes." Arthur nodded. "That's correct. Although one of them is missing at the moment, which is why I'm here."

"I don't understand."

Arthur suspected that Maida's confusion had little to do with him or the house. She was wondering why neither of her aunts had ever contacted her. That wasn't a matter he could address.

"Inheritance law can be very tricky. The bookstore was bequeathed to you, but until recently it's been held in trust. Are you following me?" Arthur looked into Maida's eyes again and was surprised when she stared back again, unblinking. It was as if she was searching for something. This time, he looked away first. "As I was saying, the property is matrilineally entailed."

"I think I understand that, but then why didn't my mother's sister inherit the bookstore once my mother passed away?" Maida questioned.

"In this type of 'fee tail female' entailment, the inheritance is passed down to the oldest daughter in each generation. Your mother's sister could not inherit because she wasn't eligible. Only you are, as the current oldest daughter of the oldest daughter of the Lathrop line."

Maida clutched at the locket that was hanging from a sinuous silver chain around her neck. Arthur could make out the letter L and wondered if the necklace might have belonged to her mother. Her brow was furrowed.

"What does the house look like?" Maida asked. She picked up her pencil with her free hand and started to idly sketch again. "Is it a cottage or a colonial style home? How many bedrooms? And what kind of neighborhood is it in?"

Arthur lowered his head to look at her. He chose his words of discouragement carefully, for maximum impact. "It's very, very old. The place requires constant upkeep. Aside from the expense, it would be a massive commitment. You'd have to give up your life here and move back to Boston."

He felt a tiny bead of sweat accumulating on his brow. *What would he do if she wouldn't sign?*

"It's a gorgeous old Queen Anne-style mansion," Will piped up. "With a wraparound porch and a turret. The whole first floor is a bookstore. There's also a delightful little coffee shop. I think you would love it! Can't you picture it?" He reached out to touch her locket and Maida swatted his hand away.

"Cut it out, Will." She frowned at him. Then she turned back to Arthur. "This place sounds quite charming. You don't have a picture you could show me, do you?"

"I'm afraid not," Arthur said. He could see Maida was sketching a house now, with a turret and a porch, not unlike the Mudpuddle's, probably as a result of Will's prattling on.

"Perhaps you can tell me more about the area where it's located? What's the address?"

"It doesn't have a street address. It's in a very exclusive area." Arthur pinched the bridge of his nose.

"Really? What neighborhood would that be?" Maida asked, raising an eyebrow as she added an eyebrow window into the roofline.

"Primrose Court," Arthur and Will both spoke at once. Maida stopped sketching, and held her pen in midair, looking at them quizzically.

"Am I supposed to know where that is?" she asked.

"It's a neighborhood in Boston," Arthur explained.

"No it's not. I grew up in Boston and I've never heard of it," Maida spoke skeptically.

She spun the menu around and started sketching something new in the blank spot.

"It's...tiny?" Arthur said. He hadn't meant it to sound like a question.

"Nope." Maida dug in her heels. "You haven't convinced me. There's got to be something else you're not telling me. I hate to say it, but I think this might be some kind of scam." Her pencil flew over the paper in a blur that left a wake of scribbled leaves, branches, and Arthur couldn't quite see what else.

"I assure you, this isn't a scam, Maida. I should have mentioned that I have personally been to the Mudpuddle, and met your aunts." He felt his grip on the situation starting to slip.

"The *Mudpuddle*?" Her brows drew together. "What's that?"

"I'm sorry," Arthur apologized, "the Mudpuddle *is* the house. It's also the name of the bookstore in the house. I'm not doing an adequate job of explaining."

"You're doing a *terrible* job," Will agreed.

"Wait. Have you been there too, Will?" Maida asked.

"Every year, as a kid. We'd go there on field trips." Will got a dreamy look on his face.

"What about my father?" Maida asked.

Will shook his head vehemently. "No way, Mayday. Primrose Court is an exclusively magical community. You have your witches, your shifters...there's even a few full fae living there. You kind of have to see it to believe it. Or maybe that's believe it to see it for most people." He twisted a paper straw wrapper into a tight, slender rope as he spoke.

Arthur's kick under the table was swift and targeted.

Will winced, swallowed, and continued on. He was displaying the same dogged determination he'd had when slogging past oblivion in the space between the portals. "You really need to come with me to see the place in person, Mayday."

Mayday? What kind of nickname was that? Arthur's next kick missed, probably because Will knew it was coming.

"Come on, Arthur, hear me out. I really think she deserves to know..." Will dropped the contorted bit of paper and wrung his hands instead.

"Is this your idea of a joke, Will? Or is it some kind of game? Can one of you please enlighten me?" Maida was getting agitated now, glancing back and forth between them.

Arthur bristled. He desperately wanted to enlighten her. In every possible way. But not enough to risk breaking her. It was cruel, not being able to tell her the truth about her own family.

"Magic is real, Maida!" Will blurted out. "Your whole family is magical. And so are we!"

Shut up. Shut up. Shut up!

Arthur rested his head in his hands and breathed slowly.

"You do realize how crazy you sound, Will?" Arthur fought to keep his voice calm and rational. "Enough with your joking. Nobody finds it funny."

"That's because I'm not joking! I told you, Arthur, I don't believe in gaslighting." Will's tone turned plaintive. "Maida deserves to know the truth. Why can't you see that she belongs in Primrose Court?"

"Okay, hang on a moment, Will. That's more than enough." Maida held up a hand to stop him from saying anything further. She shuddered a little. This was something Arthur had seen Ordinaries do before, when shaking off something magical that they weren't able to process. Sometimes it was accompanied by goosebumps and a cold sweat. And then they usually fainted. At least she was sitting down.

"I just wanted to get some information before I signed. I'm good now," Maida said. "Where are those papers?"

She seemed to be fine, and he didn't want to waste any more time. Arthur fanned the contract out in front of her and placed his fountain pen on top of the pile.

"No! I can't let her sign!" Will snatched the pen away.

"What has gotten into you today, Will? Maybe you should take some time off?" Maida admonished him. She wrested the pen back, and turned her attention back toward Arthur.

He paused for only the briefest of moments before pointing to the signature line on the last page. "Sign here."

"You know what?" Will pouted and jumped to his feet. "Have it your way, you two. One of these days, you'll learn to take me seriously, though." He narrowed his eyes. "I'm choosing not to take it personally. I'm going to order some more donuts." With this, Will stormed off towards the end of the line in front of the counter.

"Is he always this unhinged?" Arthur asked quietly.

Maida studied Will for a moment, a look of tenderness crossing her face. "I don't know. Will is special. He's very sensitive. And he has a vivid imagination. Possibly even wilder than my own. He'd say anything to get me to move back to Boston. I think he means well." She flipped through the pages of the contract, taking a moment to review the document before signing.

"Thank you for trusting me to handle this for you," Arthur said.

While she skimmed, Arthur examined the menu she'd been scribbling on. Besides the house that resembled the Mudpuddle, there was a willow tree. He recognized it immediately.

Arthur spun the page around to get a closer look.

Hanging from the tree was a child's rope swing. She had drawn it exactly as Arthur remembered it. There was even a cloud of butterflies gathered around the tree. Although the drawing was done in gray pencil, he didn't have to ask what color they'd be in reality.

"Can I have this?" he asked.

With a flourish, Maida signed her name on the last page and shoved the stack back at him. "Sure." she shrugged. "Keep it. Though I can't imagine what you'd want it for."

"Maybe I'm just one of those weirdos who likes to collect takeout menus." Arthur smiled wryly. He flipped the last page of the document to the front, in order to make sure her signature was clear and legible and to let the ink dry.

Maida slid sideways towards the outside of the booth. They knocked knees one last time. "I should probably get back home. My place was broken into yesterday and I've still got some cleaning up to do."

"What? Your place was broken into!" Will was back beside the table with abnormal speed. "Why didn't you say something sooner?" The panicked look on his face was a pretty accurate reflection of the alarm bells going off in Arthur's head.

"I don't know. I guess I didn't want you to freak out." Maida shrugged. "I handled it. I changed the locks. There's been a lot of break-ins lately."

"Did they take anything?" Arthur asked, hoping to hear they'd taken cash, electronics, or jewelry. These were the things Ordinary thieves tended to take. It would disturb him more if they had grabbed nothing.

"No, fortunately they took nothing," Maida said. She yawned and covered her mouth with a hand. "I have to admit I stayed up too late reading last night, so I'm also pretty tired. I'm just going to hit the restroom before I go."

"You know what? I've got to use the restroom as well!" Will said, putting an arm around Maida's shoulder and steering her toward the back. "Wait here, Arthur?"

"Okay." Arthur nodded. They had no reason to stick around Laguna any longer but he was suddenly loath to leave. He thought he should at least walk her home, make sure the break-in was as trivial as she seemed to think. If not...It was his turn to shudder. At least in Primrose Court there were wards to keep people safe.

Arthur glanced back down at the drawing, running his finger over the swing. He was doing the right thing, wasn't he? No matter what Director Berman had said about Maida's resiliency, it was safer to resolve the situation without dragging an innocent Ordinary into the thick of a magical community in crisis. He pocketed the drawing and stared out the window, watching all the Ordinary people out doing Ordinary things on an Ordinary day.

Director Berman had asked Arthur about what might have happened if Buffalo had given up his daughter all those years ago. It was the wrong question, Arthur thought. The question that plagued him more was what if Buffalo hadn't *had* to make that choice? He and Maida might have grown up side by side, two magical beings living on the same estate.

What then?

On the surface of the table, something caught Arthur's attention. An unexpected movement that stirred up microscopic dust and made the air shimmer. He stared down in disbelief at what was happening to Maida's signature.

Almost as if it were emerging from a cocoon, a butterfly emerged from the bottom of the page. First one wing slowly poked up forming from the letter *M*, then the other unfurled from the *W*. Next came the body, antennae and finally legs, rising and filling in from all the letters in between. By the time the butterfly was whole, the signature line was completely blank.

The blue beauty flapped its wings, waving away the wrinkles before attempting to fly. It left a trail of tiny blue dots as it walked off the page.

"Order Up for Arthur Hart!" a slight, elvish man in a paper baker's hat called out. "Arthur Hart?"

"I'm sorry, did you mean Will Porter?" asked Arthur, still staring at the butterfly.

"No, Will's gone, dude." The elvish baker screwed his face up at Arthur. "He and that blond girl went through the portal five minutes ago. But if you're Arthur, he told me to give you the donuts, and he left a commercial flight voucher for you."

SIXTEEN

BELIEVING IS SEEING

For centuries, travelers have told tales of spectral cities rising from the desert sands. Mirages, those beguiling optical illusions, can make distant objects appear and disappear in the most bewitching ways.

Is it merely a case of environmental sleight-of-hand? Or does the frequency of such anomalies around a common environmental convergence suggest an even greater truth?

The magical community makes the argument that mirages cannot manifest without the presence of magic. Conversely, the Ordinary community routinely attributes the sudden appearance of magic to mirage.

—EXCERPT FROM THE MUDPUDDLE MANUAL OF NATURAL MAGIC

When Maida came out of the restroom, she almost collided with Will. He was standing by the cluttered community bulletin board in the hallway, tidying up the flyers. His tantrum had passed, but his face was still uncharacteristically serious.

"Can we chat for a minute before you go?" Will asked.

"I'm not moving back to Boston, Will. I'm happy here. I have a life in Laguna."

"Do you? Really? When was the last time you went out on a date? Or had dinner with friends?" Will turned the knob on a door marked "private" and peeked inside. "Give me five minutes of your time."

Will being dramatic was par for the course. Will, being unhinged, to use Arthur Hart's description, was not. She knew she had to hear him out. Something wasn't right.

Maida glanced back out toward the seating area. The solicitor was sitting in the booth, looking out the window. There was still something so achingly familiar about him she couldn't quite name. A feeling? A character? An archetype? Something that stuck—like the smell of petrichor. The word for it was on the tip of her tongue. But she couldn't trick herself into recalling. She had a ridiculous urge to return to the table and sit back down beside him.

Such a shame that Arthur Hart lived in Boston. She'd probably never lay eyes on him again, and she didn't want to forget his face. His face was just so pleasing to look at. Especially when he smiled. She guessed he didn't do that nearly enough. He had too few laugh lines for a man his age. She'd observed a lot about the solicitor in the short time they'd spent together.

For example, she'd observed that one of his teeth was crooked, but the rest were straight. He had four gold flecks in one eye, seven in the other. The left side of his face was slimmer, and the hair on the right side of his head curled more. He was delightfully asymmetrical. She'd do a sketch from memory as soon as she got home.

"Maida, please?" Will repeated the question a bit more firmly. He acknowledged where she was looking because he added, "Don't worry about Arthur. He's not going anywhere without me."

"Fine," Maida capitulated. "Five minutes." She allowed Will to pull her into what appeared to be an empty children's party room. A hand-painted quote on the wall read *"We're All Mad Here."*

"Have I ever lied to you?" Will asked the moment the door was shut.

"No. You've always been an open book. I just don't think we're on the same page today." Maida studied herself in one of the room's many rippled mirrors. It made her look disconcertingly small.

"You're not on the same page as me because you've been reading the abridged version. You need to know the complete story." Will ran a hand through his hair, and gave it a frustrated tug.

"Whatever it is, you can tell me, Will. I know you work for my father, but we're friends, right?" She'd never seen him this agitated before, and it worried her.

Will put his hands on her shoulders and gazed into her eyes. She had never seen him look so intense. Did he mean to kiss her? Oh, no...She felt her eyelid twitch. Will was like a brother to her. She didn't care for him like that. Instinctively, she leaned away as his head lowered toward hers, and kept going.

If he meant to kiss her, he'd missed by a mile. She breathed a sigh of relief. But she wasn't out of the woods. Will was still holding her by the shoulders and staring down at her chest.

"The house is hiding inside your locket, Mayday, isn't it?"

"What do you mean?" Maida clutched the locket, confused. "That's ridiculous."

"Is it? Show me what's inside, then." Will stood up straight again, but dipped his chin down to meet her eyes. Then he glanced back down at the pendant in her hand.

Too flustered to object, Maida pressed the locket's lever. Nothing happened. She pressed it again. Still nothing. When she pressed it more insistently for a third time, the locket buzzed and zapped her.

"Ouch!" The current stung her hand, and she released the locket. It dropped and bounced against her breastbone. "Sorry. I think it's stuck. It won't open," she apologized.

"That's okay. I guess it doesn't feel safe with me yet. But I'm right, aren't I?" Will gave her shoulders a quick squeeze. "The Mudpuddle is in there?"

"Don't be silly, Will."

"Do I look like I'm joking?" He removed his arms from her shoulders and folded them across his chest. "Is there, or is there not a house in that locket?"

"Yes, there is a house," Maida agreed begrudgingly. "But it's not an actual house. It's a fantasy—like something out of a fairy tale."

"It's an actual house. It just isn't an *Ordinary* house," Will said. "I saw you drawing the Mudpuddle's eyebrow windows. Tell me, did the house in that locket wink at you?"

Goosebumps skittered over her skin in waves. How could Will possibly know the house in the locket had winked at her?

"What is going on here, Will?" Maida stared into the glass-green depths of Will's eyes. "I'm sorry I didn't show you my tattoo sooner but this seems a bit elaborate for a prank, don't you think?"

"If this was a prank, I'd have to have prescience because you found that locket before you came here."

He was right. There was no way he could have arranged for the locket to wash up at her feet like it had. The beach had been empty. If she'd come a second sooner or a moment later than she had, she wouldn't have found it. Her mind raced with the possibilities and kept coming back to a place of chaos and confusion.

"You have to come back to Boston with me, Mayday. Please. I'm thinking you're the only one who can bring the Mudpuddle back to Primrose Court."

"You said the house I inherited was in Primrose Court," Maida said. "How can I bring something back, if it's already there?"

"That's the whole issue, actually. It *was* there, until a couple of days ago, when it vanished," Will whispered, as if revealing a controversial secret.

"It vanished," Maida repeated. She took a step back, shaking her head vehemently. "That's impossible, Will. Houses don't just up and vanish. I'm sure I would have heard something on the news if something like that happened. There would be an international task force to study the phenomenon."

"Absolutely, if a house disappeared from an Ordinary neighborhood. But, as I told you, Primrose Court is a magical community. It's hardly the strangest thing to have happened there by non-magical standards."

Maida rolled her eyes.

"Okay then. So what was your plan to get it back? Were you going to send out a psychic search party? Try to track it with supernatural scent hounds?" Maida attempted to play along for a moment, but her sarcasm was thinly veiled.

Will didn't seem to notice it.

"Something like that." He grimaced. "Arthur seemed to think he could summon the house to return once he had the proper authority to do so." Will waved a hand to dismiss this thought. "It's a moot point now that your magic has manifested, and the house has made its way to you! Isn't it marvelous?" He bent forward so that he could address the locket directly. "What a clever little house! What a good, smart, beautiful house!" he cooed.

Maida could have sworn she felt the locket purr in response.

"Maybe you should just take this locket from me." She felt as crazy as the motto on the wall as she suggested this to Will. "You can give it to Arthur, and he can bring the 'house,'" she used air quotes here, "back to wherever it belongs."

She reached behind her neck to undo the clasp, but it wouldn't open. Fortunately, the chain was quite long. She reached to pull the locket off over her head.

This time, the voltage was even higher. Maida staggered backwards as the chain shocked her, tripping and nearly falling onto a table.

"Bloody briars!" she exclaimed.

"See? It has to be you. It's already formed an attachment." Will held a hand to his heart and stared at Maida with a look of wonder. "Do you have any idea how extraordinary this is? How lucky *you* are?"

She felt anything but lucky. She was tired and confused. All she wanted to do was go back to bed and pull the covers over her head. She could just pretend this entire crazy conversation had never happened.

Maida took a deep breath. "I do think I really need to go home now."

"Yes!" Will whooped. His face skrinkled up with sheer joy. "So you'll come back to Boston with me? I knew it! I knew you were magical. I've felt it all along! We have so much to talk about. I can't believe you've had to go through charmarche all on your own like this. When did you first start experiencing your magicality?" Impossible words and phrases kept coming out of him. She couldn't keep up.

"No. I'm not coming back to Boston with you." Maida shoved him away. "I'm going back to my apartment."

Will's smile dissolved as his face fell into the most sorrowful expression. He shook his head apologetically. "I'm so sorry, Mayday. I can't let you go back there. It's not safe for you here anymore."

"I told you it's fine. I changed the locks. They didn't take anything." She backed towards the door.

"That's because whoever it was, they didn't find what they wanted, Mayday. They wanted *you*." Will took her hand. Another chill traveled down Maida's spine as she remembered her friend Zani saying the same thing.

"Listen, Will, if it makes you feel better, I'll look up some flights as soon as I get home. I'll see if I can come for the weekend."

"No." Will shook his head again. His voice had a solemn iron-clad resolve she hadn't heard from him before. "You need to come with me. Right now."

"Come with you where, Will? Are you planning to throw me over your shoulder and drive me straight to the airport?" Maida attempted to call his bluff.

"I actually have something much quicker in mind." With no warning, Will swooped. He bent forward, reached an arm around her hips, and threw her over his shoulder. Will was not a particularly large man. Maida suspected he weighed less than her. Yet somehow, he'd hoisted her like she was no heavier than a sack of feathers.

"Put me down!" Dangling upside down, Maida kicked her legs and beat her fists on Will's back. It didn't seem to faze him. She kicked so hard, one of her boots nearly flew off. Will grabbed it and shoved it back on. "This isn't funny, Will!" she protested.

"I know. I'm sorry!" Will yelled.

Maida was considering whether to claw Will with her fingernails or punch him in the kidney when she was blindsided by a white light so bright, it was like the roof had just been ripped off. The room filled with rushing wind. Tissue paper confetti rose up off the tables and swirled around them like they were at the center of a tiny tornado.

"Remember when I said that magic is real?" Will shouted. "This is the part where I show, instead of tell you."

Maida opened her mouth to scream as Will took a giant step towards and through the wall. How was that possible? A moment ago, there had been a warped mirror there, but now there was nothing but nothingness. The sound of her scream came out wrong. It sounded muffled and far away. So did Will's voice when he called out to her a moment later. It sounded like he was shouting to her from the house next door, in the middle of a tornado.

"You should close your eyes. You might pass out if you don't. But don't worry, Mayday. I've got you. I won't let you fall."

SEVENTEEN

AN ENLIGHTENED HOMECOMING

Under the canopy of stars, across oceans and continents, there is an invisible network imbued with ancient earth magic. Ley lines make up the hidden map that traverses the earth, connecting people and places to time and the tides.

Only a few magical creatures possess the ability to navigate between the lines. Their gifts allow them to travel vast distances with speed and unerring precision. It might not surprise you to learn that their skills are always strongest when they are journeying home.

-EXCERPT FROM THE MUDPUDDLE MANUAL OF NATURAL MAGIC

Maida dozed in her seat. She was comfortably reclined and swaddled in a fleece blanket with her seatbelt on. Outside the tinted windows of the luxury passenger van, the world sped by. Her lids fluttered open and promptly shut again.

She saw the outlines of two men sitting in similar seats in front of her. But Maida's mouth was too dry to call out to them, and her brain felt too scrambled to form coherent words.

"She's waking up," one of the men said. She rubbed her eyes, willing them to focus.

The men swiveled their seats to face her. From the look on their faces, they were worried.

She recognized Will Porter first. He was wearing the same colorful jacket as the last time she'd seen him, at The Bunny Hole. When had that been? Or had she just dreamed it?

She hadn't seen Dr. Dvita in a very long time. He had been her pediatrician. She'd been sick so often as a child, he'd moved into their house.

This has to be a dream.

Maida turned her head to gaze out at the countryside streaming by. All the reds and greens and yellows of the autumn trees melted into one long variegated band, like a colorful marbled ribbon. She imagined the landscape would taste like a caramel apple if she could stick out her tongue and lick it.

"I told her to close her eyes," Will said. "She put up quite a fight." His voice echoed too loud inside her head. Maida placed her hands over her ears and closed her eyes again, wishing she could wake up from this strange dream. She had plants to re-pot.

A moment later, they turned off the highway. The woodland colors faded to the spongy blues and grays of sea and sky. Maida glimpsed familiar signs by the side of the road. Places she knew from her childhood. She closed her eyes again.

"Porting can be a shock to the system, even when someone is completely prepared for it," Dr. Dvita said. "Let's give her more time to recover."

What was Dr. Dvita doing in her dream? Not that she minded. She'd been fond of the short, pudgy man. He always dressed in white, which suited his egg-like roundness. She'd dubbed him Dr. Dumpty. He had such a reassuring presence.

The doctor looked exactly as she recalled him, from his white lab coat, to the smoky-lensed glasses resting just below the bridge of his nose. She smiled groggily at him.

"There you are! Good afternoon, Miss Maida. Welcome

home," the doctor said. He leaned forward to check her pulse and handed her a chilled bottle of water.

"Will Porter was just catching me up on everything that has transpired in Primrose Court and California over the past few days. I should have liked to have tried the donuts at that shop in Laguna."

Maida bolted upright. She remembered. She wasn't dreaming after all.

Her eyes filled with cold fire as she glared at Will. "What the Hecate, Will? What were you thinking? You *kidnapped* me!"

He winced.

"I know. I'm sorry. We needed to get you somewhere safer. Whoever broke into your apartment won't give up that easily. They must know about your connection to the Mudpuddle." Will glanced at the locket. "Your father's house has wards."

"And by wards, do you actually mean private security guards and surveillance equipment?"

Maida felt for the locket on her chest. Sure enough, it was still nestled there, pressing its warmth into her like a pet. She could almost feel the house's heartbeat as she stroked it.

Will must have drugged her. She was still hallucinating. There was no other explanation.

"I'm sorry I have to ask this, but how much of our conversation from The Bunny Hole do you remember? Do you feel okay?" Will reached into a large paper takeout bag and pulled out a fistful of French fries. He shoved seven of them into his mouth and turned to the doctor for some reassurance.

"Short term amnesia is a common side effect of porting," the doctor confirmed, cheerfully. "Perfectly harmless. Not to worry!"

Maida considered the question. Her head still felt fuzzy. "I recall you saying something about showing versus telling. Then I must have blacked out," she guessed. "What time is it? How long have we been in Boston? And why is the doctor here?"

Will, on his second fistful of fries, held up his pocket watch while he finished chewing. "We left The Bunny Hole almost fifteen minutes ago. I had my driver pick the doctor up just in case you suffered any ill effects from porting."

"That's impossible! It can't have only been fifteen minutes." Maida checked her watch, which was not synced with local time, but it agreed with Will's assertion.

"That's what I meant by *showing* you!" Will said. "I'm a porter. I can open portals between places and carry others through with me. It's my magical talent, if you will."

"Will's gift is exceptionally rare," Dr. Dvita confirmed. "There can't be more than a dozen other fae porters like him."

"Fae? As in *fairy*?" Her mouth was hanging open. She glanced back at the doctor.

Dr. Dvita nodded indulgently.

Will fished a sandwich out of the bag next. He devoured it in less than three bites. "Excuse me for being such a glutton. Porting uses up an incredible amount of energy. I need to eat a ton to regain my strength." He stifled a burp. "I really wish I had those donuts right now."

"You're fae..." Maida couldn't help but notice Will's ears. She'd always thought they were a little pointy. But that could be a coincidence. Was she stereotyping?

"Only half fae." Will polished off the rest of his French fries. "Who knows what else. I'm a proper magical mutt."

"Don't worry, dear." The doctor smiled reassuringly. "I know it all seems absurd right now, but it's early days. You've only just been granted enlightenment. In another day or two, magic will seem perfectly natural. The magical mind's ability to expand and embrace the true nature of the world is nothing short of a miracle."

Maida gulped some water and attempted to assimilate all this new information. The oddest thing about it was that it wasn't all that difficult. On some level, she had always known magic was real, hadn't she? She just hadn't known to what extent. She'd felt obliged to question it. Questioning magic was a given. It's what you do.

Will eyed her with suspicion. "Why aren't you freaking out more?"

Maida shrugged. "What would be the point?"

"Hang on a minute..." Will pulled out his camera and handed it to the doctor. "Take a picture of us? I want to record the moment. Arthur was so wrong. He was sure you'd be bound for Bedlam in a wheelbarrow if we told you the truth."

"Where *is* Arthur?" Maida stared at Will accusingly. "Is he still at the donut shop? You didn't just leave him sitting there alone, did you?"

"I bought some donuts to tide him over and left a flight voucher for him," Will said, somewhat defensively. "He'll be back by tomorrow morning. I got him booked on a red-eye."

"Why would you make him take a red-eye?" Maida looked horrified.

"It was the best I could do on such short notice! I pay out of pocket for the flight vouchers, I'll have you know." Will pouted.

"You couldn't have brought him back here at the same time?" Maida hated the thought of the solicitor just sitting there, all alone, waiting for them. How long had he waited before realizing they were gone?

"I'm not strong enough to carry two passengers at once." Will foraged in the console beside his seat for a bag of jelly beans and a candy bar. "Especially when one of them is a massive stag shifter the likes of Arthur Hart. What if he accidentally shifted en route?"

Stag shifter? Had Will just said those words. What did that even mean?

"Speaking of shifters...Can we talk about the elephant in the room?" Will wrinkled his nose as he picked the black jelly beans out of the bag.

"What?" The doctor looked worriedly at Maida. "You don't mean to say that she is an elephant shifter? Why didn't you say sooner! Perhaps we should pull over?"

"I didn't mean elephant like *that*." Will rolled his eyes. "The elephant in the room is that Maida's *not* an elephant shifter, or any kind of shifter so far as I can tell. But I don't think she's a witch either. Yet she clearly has come into her magic. Look at that aura of hers! I'm just not so sure exactly what her magic is."

"Does it matter?" Dr. Dvita asked.

"I should think so." Will raised an eyebrow. "How will she figure out what she can do, if she doesn't even know what she is?"

"How long did it take you to figure out you were a porter, Will?" Dr. Dvita asked.

Will pursed his lips. "Years," he finally admitted.

"She'll do just fine." Dr. Dvita patted the back of Maida's hand. "I've always suspected that if and when your magic manifested, it would be something really special. Just like you."

"I'm not sure what you're talking about." Maida felt her cheeks growing warm. "I can't open portals or morph into an animal form. There's nothing particularly magical about me."

But even as she said it, she remembered the way she'd been reading minds, and how lucky she always got at thrift stores and tag sales. Whatever she was looking for, just seemed to turn up.

Good luck locating a four slice used toaster hardly seemed to be on the same par as porting.

"Try to think," the doctor said. "Has anything unusual happened lately? Perhaps since you found that locket? Sometimes an object like that can be the catalyst." He gestured to the necklace.

"Maybe..." Maida said, thinking about the frog in her bag now too. Had she been wrong to assume that was a coincidence?

Dr. Dvita curled back into his chair, tucking his head between his shoulders. She noticed the curious way he retracted his limbs and tucked himself in when he wasn't speaking to anyone. Suddenly, she had a hunch.

"What kind of shifter are you, Dr. Dvita?" she questioned.

The doctor chortled. "What do you know? You're catching on quickly!"

"Maida, it's considered rude to ask someone like that," Will muttered under his breath.

"I don't mind, I don't mind at all." Dr. Dvita's beady black eyes twinkled. "But I do think it would be better to show you than tell you."

"Really?" Maida gulped. When she pictured a human turning into an animal, she imagined werewolves. In books and movies the metamorphosis was a painful process that involved flesh tearing and bones breaking. She had no interest in witnessing that. She was far too squeamish.

"It's really no big deal." The doctor removed his glasses and gave them a quick polish. "Just say the word. I'm happy to demonstrate."

Maida glanced over at Will, who shrugged, nonchalantly.

"Okay then." She nodded, gravely. She took a deep breath and folded her arms in front of herself, bracing for the demonstration.

"Relax, Mayday," Will said, passing her a handful of jelly beans. "It's not scary. It's kind of cool, actually. Just watch."

She wasn't even sure of the exact moment that it began. Much to her relief, the doctor's transformation did not involve any agonizing undulations. There wasn't a single shout of pain. Time just seemed indefinite for an instant, the way it always does in the last few moments of a sunset when the sun sits on the horizon.

One moment, Dr. Dvita, the man, was sitting across from her in the van. The next moment, the air around him began to crackle and pixelate. With a barely audible poof, he dissolved into a million tiny pieces. Molecules. Atoms. Possibly smaller. For an instant, all his energy simply hung there, suspended in the air. It shone in the flashes of dappled sunshine that strobed through the windows of the moving van.

"How is it possible that I can still see his smile?" Maida exclaimed.

"It's because he's shifting in slow motion. He's showing off for you. Not many shifters have as much control as the old doc." Will stuffed a candy bar in his mouth.

Without warning, the doctor's particles began to move in chaotic clouds. He came apart and flew back together again. His essence dipped and bobbed overhead, buzzing like a swarm of bees. With another poof, they vanished.

"Where did he go?" Maida asked, breathlessly.

"He's right there." Will pointed at the large tortoise that was now taking up the doctor's seat. The thick-shelled creature sat snuggled in the doctor's coat. Most comically, he had the doctor's smoke colored glasses balanced on the end of his beak.

Maida blinked at him, and he blinked back at her.

She looked from the tortoise to Will and back at the tortoise. She repeated this process a half dozen times before the doctor effortlessly shifted back into his human form.

"Thank you for showing me that, Dr. Dvita," she said.

Now she truly believed. Magic *was* real. Whatever lingering doubts that might have still been ailing her, the doctor had cured.

EIGHTEEN

CHARMARCHE

Within the chrysalis, an extraordinary alchemy unfolds. The caterpillar, encapsulated within, undergoes a remarkable metamorphosis. It liquefies its body into a primordial soup, from which it meticulously reconstructs itself into a winged wonder.

The very word "chrysalis" hails from the Greek "khrysallis," meaning "golden pupa of the butterfly," drawing a golden thread from ancient lore to the enchanting pupa it envelops.

-EXCERPT FROM THE MUDPUDDLE MANUAL OF NATURAL MAGIC

"Welcome home," Will said as the van pulled through the gated entry and onto the private drive that led to the Westabrook estate in Marblehead.

Maida had the distinct feeling that she was being welcomed into more than a house. She was being welcomed into a community. Everything looked the same as it always had. But it also looked so different. She glimpsed the groundskeeper's cottage through the woods. Will had mentioned something about Arthur Hart being a stag shifter. Did that mean his father had been a shifter, too?

Granny Luna. Reggie Hart. Will Porter. Who amongst her father's staff *hadn't* been magical? She couldn't believe how obvious it all was now. How had she missed it? And more importantly, why had the people closest to her hidden their true identity from her?

"My father has an awful lot of explaining to do," Maida mumbled to herself.

She heard the familiar crunch of gravel under the tires as the van pulled into the circular drive in front of the house.

"Your father's already on his way home. He'll be here first thing tomorrow morning. He wants to speak to you in person, Mayday. Go easy on him?"

Will's concern for her father chafed. Shouldn't it be the other way around? Her father and his staff had been lying to her for her entire life. She wasn't sure who to trust anymore. She bit the inside of her cheek.

"Well, I hope this means I won't need to hide my tarot cards anymore," she noted.

"Your well-being has always been your father's number one concern," the doctor insisted. "Try to bear that in mind and at least hear him out?"

"I have a lot of questions," Maida said.

"Naturally." The doctor nodded. "And you shall have answers. I'm sure you're overwhelmed right now. Dinner and a good night's sleep are what you need most. Doctor's orders!"

She suspected the doctor was right, but it was strange, being spoken to like she was still a child. Sleep would not come easy, no matter how tired she was. She had too much on her mind.

Finally, the van came to a halt in front of her childhood home.

Magic or not, Westabrook Manor was breathtaking. Its fluted columns, adorned with intricate carvings of ancient lore, rose from the foundation to the roof. Lush green vines scrambled up the arbor and into the eaves, whispering secrets into the breeze. Behind the lavender stained glass windows, lacy white curtains offered privacy, imbuing the home with a feeling of mystery.

The house had always felt magical to Maida.

Immediately, the massive oak front door swung open. A stone-faced, hoary, old man in butler's livery marched out to hold open the van's door for them. His movements appeared stiff and mechanical, yet he moved with surprising efficiency. How was Yves even still alive? He'd been ancient when Maida was a child. Why hadn't she thought to question things like this before?

"Hello, Yves." Maida accepted the butler's dry, papery hand, and leaned forward to kiss his desiccated cheek. Though crumpled and wrinkled, the folds of his face steamed themselves out at the sight of her, smoothing into something resembling good cheer.

"Will Porter! I have a bone to pick with you. Why wasn't I consulted about this mission?" a familiar, raspy voice rang out. Granny Luna was standing on the threshold of the house, arms akimbo.

She shook a finger at Will as he climbed out of the van. "And you!" Granny Luna glared at the doctor. "You didn't insist that he stop to pick me up? It'll be eons before I offer to wax your shell again!"

True to her rather eccentric form, Granny was wearing a black silk haute-couture gown under a hot pink fur stole. A pair of oversized designer sunglasses rested atop her head like a tiara. Although Granny Luna was barely five feet tall, her rhinestone studded platform trainers added almost four inches to her height. Her attitude contributed at least six more.

Maida hadn't realized how much she missed Granny Luna till she saw her.

"You couldn't have found a better way to do this? How dare you go kidnapping and enlightening her without me?"

"I would have been happy to have you along. But we didn't have time to stop and ogle the surfers or go shopping, Granny."

"Nonsense!" Granny Luna waved her hand dismissively at

Will and stepped out onto the porch, holding her arms out to embrace Maida. "Let me get a look at you, my lamb." She squeezed Maida so tight that she lifted her. Maida felt her feet leave the ground for an instant, and her heart felt airborne as well.

"My word! You look rough," Granny Luna said, releasing her. "Let's get you upstairs and washed up and changed for dinner, shall we?" She linked arms with Maida and spun her towards the stairs.

Maida glanced down at her rumpled clothing and smoothed her nightshirt. "I'm afraid this is it, Granny. I haven't brought any luggage."

"Don't be silly, dear. We'll just send Will to the store for something. Tell him your size. He can sort it out."

Will narrowed his eyes at Granny Luna.

"What store would that be, Granny?"

"Well..." She paused for a moment. "I was thinking of a particular shop in Paris. I'll give you a list. There's a few things I need as well."

"The shops are closed in Paris right now, Granny."

"Minor inconvenience. I'm sure you'll find a way in." She winked.

"That's theft you're advocating," Will argued.

"Can't you just leave a few bills on the counter?"

"No!" Will folded his arms and dug in his heels. "I'm tired, Granny. I've already ported twice today. I need to eat some more."

"Fine." Granny rolled her eyes at Will. "I'll just send Yves to the mall."

Maida's childhood room was exactly as she'd left it. The canopied bed was made up with fresh linens, and the exotic garden mural on the wall was still in full bloom.

"I wish I could have been the one to enlighten you," Granny Luna lamented. "I have been looking forward to this day for years.

The day you become a magical woman! Charmarche can be a very confusing time."

Maida sat on the edge of her bed. It was the second time she'd heard the term. "What exactly is charmarche?"

"It's the onset of magicality." Granny Luna touched her cheek, tenderly. "I never lost faith, child. I knew it would happen for you. Now don't be frightened. All the feelings you're feeling are perfectly natural."

"Granny, I'm thirty-five years old!" Maida laughed. "Hardly a child."

"Yes, but I've had this speech prepared for a long time." Granny Luna frowned. "It's usually a done deal by twelve or thirteen."

"It is?" Maida asked.

"Yes but there's no shame in being a late bloomer, my dear. It's only too late if you're dead!" Granny Luna went to the closet and pulled out a sack that was almost as big as she was. She dragged it towards the bed.

"Can I help you with that?" Maida asked.

"No, no. I can do it," Granny insisted. "Us fae wenches are a lot stronger than we look!" Her eyes glittered green and she heaved the bundle over her head and tossed the contents out onto the bed. With a shake and a snap, Granny Luna spread out the largest, busiest, most unapologetically outrageous crocheted blanket that Maida had ever seen.

"I started working on this for you when you were just a wee thing. Thought I'd either give it to you for your charmarche, or your eightieth birthday. Whichever came first?"

Maida was speechless. Lurid fuchsia, puce, and orange squares clashed with mustard, purple, and brown ones. Garish lime-green crocheted vines and leaves embellished the chaos, snaking from square to square, winding their way around ferociously fanged neon colored blooms. It was an absolute masterpiece of mismatchery.

"Shoots and buds, I'm not ashamed to admit I'm proud of this one! I've got my whole flutter in." Granny Luna beamed. "I know you're not my kin, Maida, but you've always been like family to me."

"Oh, Granny Luna! I love it so much," Maida said.

She wasn't lying. In fact, it was possible she loved it all the more for being so monstrous. Maida felt the soft wool and was instantly comforted. She could feel the love.

"It's been far too long, my dear. We have a great deal to catch up on, don't we? But before another moment passes, I'll just come out and ask you. What did you think of our Arthur?" Granny Luna leaned against the bed, smiling cannily.

"Arthur? The solicitor?" Maida felt herself flushing. "I mean, I don't know. He was pushy. But I guess that comes with the territory, given that he's—"

"Such a fine, strapping young buck! I mean, the *antlers* on him!"

Maida had been about to say, "a solicitor" but as Granny Luna finished her sentence so audaciously for her, she found her mouth kept moving with no sound coming out. She bit down on her lips to stop them flapping and slowly shook her head at the old woman, trying to regain her composure.

"What, child? We're all magical adults here!" Granny Luna looked quite pleased with herself. "And I've always been fond of the boy."

She perched on the edge of Maida's bed and swung one sparkly sneaker as she continued her questioning.

The antlers on him. Maida's mind was moving in a million different directions now as she pictured a half human, half beast version of the solicitor. She'd have to dig up her art supplies in the morning. She still wanted to sketch Arthur Hart before the memory faded.

Granny Luna interrupted her thoughts. "Tell me everything about California. I've heard stories about how long some of those surfers can stay up on their long boards! Did you meet any local Mer-folk?"

"Not that I know of?" Maida said. She wondered if there was some sort of tell.

"That's probably for the best. Mermen are diabolically good looking, but you can't trust them. They're cold blooded." Granny Luna nodded knowingly at Maida and she found herself nodding along to avoid being disagreeable. But what she really wanted was to curl up under the afghan and go to sleep. A profound wave of exhaustion broke over her, and she decided it wouldn't be so tough to fall asleep after all. In fact, she could do without dinner.

Granny Luna had other ideas.

"It's just so good to be so open with you. Finally! After all these years. Forgive me for getting carried away. I suppose I should have started by asking you if you were seeing anyone in California?"

"I mean, I date. Occasionally." Maida yawned.

"I'd wager none of those Ordinary boys were particularly magical in the sack though, were they?" Granny Luna snickered behind her.

"Granny!" Maida suppressed a snort as she kicked off her shoes. She crawled into the bed and pulled the blankets around herself. "I assure you I'm not sleeping with anyone! The truth is..." Maida closed her eyes so Granny wouldn't have to see the tears threatening to spill out of them. "I don't really have any friends in California. I've been trying so hard to build a life for myself there. But I don't fit in. It turns out that having a simple life isn't that simple after all. It's actually quite hard. And lonely, too." Maida heaved a sigh of relief. It felt so good to confess the truth. Like dropping a heavy burden.

Suddenly, she recalled something and rolled over onto her belly. She patted the bed and felt between the pillows.

"Looking for someone?" Granny Luna asked, plucking Mr. Pants off the apex of the headboard where he was resting like a regal ornament. Maida couldn't recall how she got the stuffed deer toy. She'd had it since before she could remember.

"I know! You've been so lonely, Mr. Pants. It really feels like we've been waiting forever for Maida to come back. She just had to sort a few things out first." Granny pretended to chat with and comfort the toy. "Well, she's here now, isn't she? Those aren't her people. She belongs back here." Granny held the deer to her ear and pretended to listen to him. She held a hand to her mouth in an expression of mock surprise. "Oh really? What's that you say? You think she should move to Primrose Court? And take me with her? I mean, if that's what you think is best..."

"Cut it out, Granny," Maida said sternly. "Give Mr. Pants back to me. He doesn't like being touched by other people."

"I'm sure." Granny nodded, dropping the toy back on the pillow. "He's fiercely loyal, that one. A girl could do worse for herself."

NINETEEN

MISCHIEF OF MICE

True nobility is revealed in one's unwavering poise, regardless of the circumstance. To lose composure is to expose a crack in the armor of one's heritage, a failing unworthy of those chosen to carry forward our sacred legacy. A pure-blooded witch or wizard must always uphold decorum—keep your wand steady and your potions well-stocked, for readiness breeds restraint.

Even in moments of great provocation, it is far more powerful to maintain grace than to descend into vulgar displays of emotion. A measured response speaks to the strength of character and superior breeding that define the pure-blooded line.

-EXCERPT FROM THE ARCANE ELITE: UPHOLDING THE SANCTITY OF WITCH BLOODLINES

Minerva had always enjoyed an excellent sense of direction, but now that she was navigating within the walls, she was all turned around. It was as if she'd lost her inner compass.

"You're such a good house," Minerva said. "Can I trust you'll show me the way to the clock?"

The lights flashed twice in response and Minerva continued to follow them through the maze of corridors within the walls.

Great care had gone into creating these spaces for someone. Minerva marveled at the fine workmanship and clever details. Lilliputian brass and crystal sconces were mounted on the wall beside each of the closed doors, and each door had a brass plaque engraved with a number, like an apartment or a fancy, old world hotel room.

Minerva had always loved miniatures. But no dollhouse she'd ever seen could hold a candle to this minuscule enclave. Everything was perfectly sized for a mouse. How had the house kept this a secret for so long? She never would have guessed this tiny world existed right under her nose. These carefully crafted spaces were not just for show. Someone had obviously lived here. But she did not know who, or when.

Judging by the way the dust piled like snowdrifts in some areas, it must have been a very long time ago. Cobwebs formed lacy curtains in every corner. Minerva sneezed seven times in quick succession. A good omen. She must be on the right path.

When she turned the corner, the hallway grew wider. The celestial lights guided her into a shrunken yet luxurious ballroom, with stunning parquet floors and ornate crystal chandeliers. Even with all the dust, Minerva caught the ghost of a sparkle glinting from the fine, faceted venetian glass. This room was like something from a palace. No detail had been spared.

The trail of lights led her up a Persian carpet lined staircase to the second level. Minerva paused to look down at the view from the balcony, imagining the room packed full with a mischief of mice. What a scene that must have been! She could image all the mouse does and bucks, dressed in their best finery and dancing a quadrille.

There was no time to dawdle, though. The lights raced on down another hallway without her.

"Slow down!" Minerva huffed. "I'm coming!" The lights reversed, coming back to meet her, but there was no question that they were getting impatient with her. They sped her along at a jog. She dared not linger anywhere to have a look around, lest she get stranded in the dark again.

Oh, what torture it was, not to be able to pause and have a poke around the library! She could see there were rows and rows of shelves lined with books. But her mouse vision was too poor to read any of the titles without getting closer. As she passed, she pocketed a small handwritten volume left out on one of the tables. It would be so nice to have something to read later on. Perhaps it would ease her loneliness.

Beyond the library, there was a family gallery. Minerva recognized several of the portraits hanging there as she trotted past. They were exact replicas of the full-sized ones hanging in the stairwell of the Mudpuddle. At the center of the gallery was a portrait of a sweet-faced, silvery gray mouse, wearing a shiny silver locket engraved with the letter "L". Minerva thought she looked familiar.

A moment later, as she whizzed by a large silver urn and caught her own reflection, she was startled to learn why. The portrait looked almost exactly like Minerva now did. All that was missing was the locket.

She was getting winded, but she kept going—up two more floors and down another hall. When she reached the end, she stood in front of a steep, simple wooden staircase that appeared to go nowhere. A dead end.

But she could hear the clock tick-tock ticking away on the other side of the wall, much louder than before. She knew she must be close.

Resolutely, Minerva climbed up the staircase. Much to her relief, when she reached the top and peeked over the crown molding, she discovered she was directly above Papa Lathrop's clock.

She almost jumped for joy at the sight of it. How spry and limber she felt in mouse form with four legs to climb and a tail to steady her! Minerva took a moment to acknowledge these blessings as she scampered down onto the top of the clock.

From there she easily hopped down the clock's cleverly stepped sides, onto the mantel itself. How many times had Minerva looked at that clock, never once noticing the carved details that made it so convenient to climb down now? One more thing to be grateful for. That and the fact that the numbers on the clock face were large enough for her to read, even with her terrible eyesight. Finally, she knew how much time had passed.

Two days! It had been two full days since she'd woken up in her bed, full of hope for the future. Two days since that putrid mage had destroyed that hope forever. Oh, how Minerva hated that her last encounter with Zephyr had been so contentious. She never would have dropped him on the street like that, had she known she'd never see him alive again!

She and Zephyr had weathered their share of missed connections and false starts over the years. But they had finally been in a place where their relationship could work. He'd said he still wanted that. She'd never stopped wanting it, either. Why hadn't she said as much?

A fresh wave of grief washed over her again, followed by the predictable ebb tide of loneliness.

They would have buried Zephyr by now, she knew. He'd be nothing but dust. And she hadn't even been able to attend his celebration of life. He was the last of his family line. He'd dedicated his life to the Society and had no descendants. So who would be there for him? Who would say the proper incantations for him and observe the month of mourning? She ought to be covering her mirrors, at the very least.

Minerva's stomach growled, reminding her she needed to eat again. Mouse metabolisms were so swift. She would have to collect more food. Minerva lay flat on her belly on the mantel, facing the coffee shop in the room next door. So close, and yet so very far away.

"I don't suppose you know the way from here to the coffee shop?" Minerva asked the house, hopefully.

At once, the lights began to gather and pool on the left side of the mantel behind another bit of familiar woodwork. She adored the oversized pine cone finials that topped off the barley twist carved columns on either side of the fireplace surround. She especially appreciated that they were the perfect size to display festive hats when she decorated for the holidays. But now they looked absolutely monolithic to her. They were more than twice her height. Imposing. She edged towards them.

The light was guiding her to the narrow crack behind the finials. It was a snug fit. Minerva had to flatten her back against the wall, suck in her tummy and wiggle sideways. It was a good thing she wasn't claustrophobic! Thankfully, as she got closer to the center point of the finial, she noticed she had a smidge more whisker room. Someone had carved out a shallow depression in the back of the wooden ornament, forming a niche. And at the center of this niche, was a perfectly round, mouse sized hole.

The lights flashed in a spiral around and into the hole, briefly forming an instructive arrow.

"You want me to go in there?" Staring into the darkness, Minerva was quite dubious.

Once again, the lights twinkled and gathered into the arrow symbol. This time, they flashed twice.

Minerva attempted to peer into the hole, but she couldn't see a thing. She could feel with her paws and sense with her whiskers that it sloped off at a steep angle. There were no stairs. The walls were slick, and she couldn't find anything to grab onto.

"I don't understand! How do you propose I navigate through there?" Minerva argued with the house's insistent flashing arrows. "It's pitch dark and slippery!"

"Bong! Bong! Bong! Bong!"

The clock's chime was shockingly loud at such close range. It startled Minerva, making her jump. With nothing to hold on to, she lost her footing and fell, head first, into the hole.

Suddenly she was tumbling, falling, slipping and sliding in circles through what could only be the interior of the barley twist column.

She slid so fast that her hat came off her head. It landed at the bottom, several seconds after she did, resuming its usual place, but with a much more jaunty angle.

Minerva's heart was pumping and her cheeks, had they been able to flush, would certainly have turned pink. She hadn't done anything as exhilarating as that for years! It was almost as thrilling as the first time she rode her broom.

She'd gone so fast, she must have shed sparks! She could see them floating in the fireplace now, winking warmly like fireflies.

Minerva stood and brushed herself off. "Next time," she addressed the house, "I think I'd prefer to try that on my bottom!"

TWENTY

THE MISSING MANUAL

Fossils are nature's way of sending messages from the distant past into the present.

Whether it's the imprint of an ancient leaf, the bones of a long-lost creature, or a spiraling shell bridging epochs, each fossil tells a story of life once lived.

Encased in timeless stone, these relics whisper secrets of survival, evolution, and transformation. Their quiet presence offers us glimpses into the very mystery of existence.

-EXCERPT FROM THE MUDPUDDLE MANUAL OF NATURAL MAGIC

Morning light filtered through the trees outside Maida's window, and the early birds were chittering away.

Waking up in her childhood bedroom felt both strange and familiar. Her sleep had been deep and dreamless, which was just as well. What was the point of dreaming when your waking hours were just as strange as any dream could ever be?

"Morning, Mr. Pants." Maida stretched.

She'd drifted off with her soft furry toy's head tucked beneath her chin, the same as when she was a little girl. His antlers cupped the sides of her face and nuzzled cozily behind her ears.

She was far too grown for the comfort of stuffed animals, but she had to admit the soft weight of the buckwheat filled animal against her chest was quite literally heartwarming. Her locket was nestled in the space between, and felt warm to the touch.

After a deliciously hot shower, Maida changed into some of the clothing that Yves had left in a shopping bag beside her door. She picked out a soft, flowing pair of black palazzo pants and an ivory hand knit cardigan with charming floral embroidered embellishments. The comfortable items he'd selected were almost exactly what she would have chosen for herself. There was even a selection of comfortable shoes for her to choose from. Maida slipped her feet into a tan pair of booties made from sueded fabric.

There was still half an hour before her father was due to arrive home and Maida knew exactly how she was going to use that time. She crossed to her desk to look for a sketchpad and paper. If she closed her eyes, she could still recall Arthur Hart's face perfectly. The memory was like a snapshot.

Maida pulled open the top drawer. Mints, a lip balm, a tiny tin full of crystals, a raven's feather, two pens, a hair tie, some hand sanitizer, and some loose change rattled around inside the paper lined drawer.

She tugged at one of the deeper side drawers, certain that she'd left a blank book or two in there, ages ago. The drawer opened a few inches and stuck. Reaching a hand in, she felt the tooled leather of a large, thick book. Someone had wedged the book into the small space.

That was odd. She couldn't recall leaving behind a book like that. But of course it had been years since she'd used this room, and someone else might have stashed it there. Maida slid her fingers under the book, shifting, repositioning and wiggling it in order to maneuver it out of the drawer.

Finally free, the book slipped right out of her hands and fell onto the floor with the rumbling thunk of a thunderclap. Warily, she bent to examine it. The title was spelled out with intricate gold foil letters.

The Mudpuddle Manual of Natural Magic.

Mudpuddle. There was that name again.

Iridescent embossed butterflies fluttered across the midnight blue leather cover and the paper edges were elegantly decorated with painted vines and flowers. Maida stared at the intriguing book for a moment. Then her curiosity kicked in, and she cracked it open.

The water marbled lining paper was just as exquisite as the cover and painted edges. She ran an appreciative finger over the beautiful patterns before turning the page.

Much to her delight, there was an inscription written in deep purple ink.

To our darling Larkspur on your thirteenth birthday,

We wish to officially, joyfully welcome you into the Primrose Court community.

As you may have already realized, the pursuit of knowledge in the field of Magical Naturalism is a lifelong endeavor.

It would be impossible for one book to hold all the answers, but you can trust this manual to help you ask the right questions. It is constantly being updated with the latest observations from Magical Naturalists worldwide, and more importantly, it is the perfect place to record your own observations.

We're so proud of you and how you've blossomed into such a promising young witch. We hope you will make your family proud.

All our love,
Mother and Father

Maida felt a lump forming in her throat upon reading these words. It was so bittersweet to read these loving words from the grandparents she had never met to the mother who died giving life to her. She sniffed the ink, which still held a hint of violets and lilac.

Maida flipped through the book. The paper was as fine as dragonfly wings, packed with text and illustrations. As her hands passed over the margins, hidden notes and information were revealed, developing before her eyes like a palimpsest. She leafed back towards the beginning in search of a table of contents. Instead, the book fell open to the title page, where there was a simple dedication and note from the publisher. The publisher's logo was a small butterfly, and below this, the words Mudpuddle Books, Primrose Court, MA.

The dedication read:

To all those magical beings who gather to draw strength from the abundant earth. Where some see mud, we recognize magic.

Maida searched for a date, but there was none. She closed the book and turned it back over again, realization dawning.

Mudpuddle Books? Was this the same Mudpuddle as the bookstore in Primrose Court? Her Mudpuddle? How strange that she was already thinking of it that way.

Of course! It had to be!

Maida tilted the book back and forth, admiring the way the butterflies appeared to be flapping their wings as she did so.

A firm knock outside her door interrupted her. "Hello? Am I interrupting anything?" She heard her father's voice in the hall. A second later, an impossibly large man stuck his head in the door.

Maida looked up from her book, so initially happy to see her father that for an instant that she almost forgot she was furious with him. Almost.

She studied his familiar form through a new lens. The lens of truth. A week ago she hadn't known *what* her father was, but she'd felt sure she knew *who* he was. Now the opposite was true. She knew what he was, but she no longer felt she knew the famously successful, large and proud man standing before her.

Buffalo Westabrook had no problems measuring up to his name.

Anyone would know at once why pundits and cartoonists represented him with the head of a buffalo. With his thick mane of rusty brown hair, he definitely looked far more like a bison than a Jerome. She had to give him credit for not attempting to hide his nature.

Like the animal he was linked to, Buffalo's human head was large and powerful. There was also something about how his massive head sat on his equally oversized shoulders. When Buffalo was sizing you up, you could not help but feel small. He had wide-set brown eyes and a broad nose that had a tendency to flare.

The otherworldly intensity of his unblinking gaze was a test for even the most steady souls. What had one of the news magazines said about him? *Never bluff a Buffalo.*

Even though her father was so formidable looking, it had never occurred to Maida to be afraid of him. Only of disappointing him. That much hadn't changed.

Reflexively she slid the book under her pillow, only to withdraw it again. She had nothing to hide from her father now.

He was the one who had all the explaining to do.

"I was just reading this field guide." Maida was unable to keep a hint of defiance from her voice. "It's called *The Mudpuddle Manual of Natural Magic*. Are you familiar with it?"

"Yes." Buffalo nodded. "It's a classic."

"That's all you have to say about it?" Maida arched a brow.

"I'm glad you found your mother's copy. It was a special edition. She took great care of it, too."

Buffalo sighed heavily and shook his head. "I couldn't afford a copy when I was a kid. Probably would have been lost, anyway. We moved around so much."

"You've seen this book before?" Maida asked.

"Of course. It was one of the few things your mother hung on to when she moved in with me." Buffalo's eyes were sad.

"Why didn't you ever show it to me?" Maida ran a hand across the cover. "Didn't you think I deserved to see it?"

"I wish I could have," Buffalo said, loosening his tie and unbuttoning the top button of his white shirt. "Look, Maida, I understand you're angry with me, and I suppose you have every right to be, but I'd like the chance to explain. I've been cooped up in planes and cars for what feels like days, and frankly, I'm feeling claustrophobic. Too many walls. Will you take a walk outside in the garden with me?"

"Okay." Maida set the book back down on her desk. She'd always loved her father's lush gardens. It was where she'd developed a love for plants, and where she'd always gone to sit and sketch. "I suppose I wouldn't mind having a look around the old garden."

She also knew that this would go far better outdoors. She had so much to say, and so many questions to ask, that she was afraid the house couldn't contain their conversation.

TWENTY-ONE

THE TRUTH AT LAST

Though trees appear to stand in solitude, they are eloquent communicators. Trees connect via a remarkable system known as the wood wide web. Fungi are the conduits for this coded conversation. They link the roots of different trees and allow them to share their secrets. This silent dialogue enables trees to support one another, broadcast warnings, and maintain the balance of the forest.

But where there is light, you must guard against darkness. Malevolent, sentient fungi can corrupt entire forests. Shadowveil Mycelium mimics the natural communication between trees and manipulates their messages. They sap their vitality and sow destruction.

-EXCERPT FROM THE MUDPUDDLE MANUAL OF NATURAL MAGIC

Buffalo Westabrook's garden covered five acres of sprawling grounds. The garden was divided into different areas and habitats. There was an aquatic area that boasted a large lily pad filled pond full of koi fish, several fountains, and a waterfall. The flower gardens and greenhouses were full of prized roses, orchids, and dinner-plate sized dahlias. These kept the vases inside the house full almost all year round. The fragrant lilacs, lily of the valley, and thickly ruffled peonies were Maida's favorites.

A grassy playing field, large enough for games of rugby and level enough to pitch palatial tents for corporate events, lay beside a sprawling hedge maze. Maida had always disliked the maze. Her father insisted that wandering inside the tall green prison was a meditative act, but the thought of getting lost there disturbed her.

Maida's favorite part of the garden was the fruit orchard and raised beds, where they used to grow the household's herbs and vegetables. This section of the property was ringed by paths that led back to the back door of the house. She had many happy memories of pedaling her bike in circles while Granny Luna and the chef gossiped and drank coffee.

When Maida grew tired of riding in circles, she would park herself on the swing under the old weeping willow tree. It was, by far, the largest tree in the garden.

Maida had loved to make believe her swing was a magical airship, carrying her away on adventures in exotic places. If only she'd known Will Porter back then! She walked with her father now, noting all the changes time had wrought. Some large, and some small.

"You aren't growing vegetables any more?" She was sad to see the manicured grass where there used to be wooden containers for lettuce, tomatoes, squash, and beans.

"Not enough people living here to eat them." Buffalo shook his head and stopped walking. He looked thoughtfully at his daughter. His eyes had an unguarded wistfulness that she'd only caught glimpses of in the past. "Your mother made me promise to keep a garden for you to tend. She wanted you to grow up around plants. She was a hedge witch. For a mental magic type, she wielded a lot of persuasive power over living things. She could get anything to grow. Including you. Against all odds."

Maida's eyes widened. She couldn't believe her normally recalcitrant father was talking about her mother. Openly. He almost seemed relieved to be speaking about her.

"My mother was a witch. Shouldn't you have told me a bit more about that?" Maida asked.

Was this about her mother's addiction?

What happened to my mother? What was wrong with me? Why did you lie?

She didn't have to give voice to all these questions. But surely, they were showing in her eyes. Her father had always read her like a book. His instincts were almost unnerving at times.

Buffalo sighed. "I'm not even sure where to start. But I suppose it should be with 'I'm sorry.'"

"You're sorry?" Maida parroted. She felt her anger building like a storm surge. "How about you start at the part where you kept me in the dark about basically everything? My whole life has been a lie. And if that's not enough, everyone else around me has always known the truth. You, Will, Dr. Dvita, Granny Luna...who else was in on this elaborate charade?"

Her heart was pounding harder now, and she picked up the pace. Buffalo easily remained beside her, a single one of his long strides equaling three of hers.

"Do you think this was what I wanted? Maida, please! I couldn't risk losing you too. After your mother died, you were all I had. And for a while there, we weren't even sure you would survive. I was at the end of my rope."

Maida turned to face her father. "Is that why you hired Dr. Dvita? To monitor me for signs of addiction, too?" Here she hesitated, voice wavering. "Or did you need his help to fix something even worse that was wrong with me?"

What could be worse, Maida wondered? What had her father been so afraid of? But in her heart, she knew what was worse. With two magical parents, it should have been a simple equation. But in her case, one plus one added up to zero. She'd been born an Ordinary. What a shocking disappointment she must have been.

"The issues with your mother weren't what you think. It's

likely she wouldn't have survived delivery, regardless." Buffalo kept pace with his daughter.

"So you're saying I killed her?" Maida said. It was nothing she had not thought a thousand times. But saying it out loud was like vomiting hot glass. She felt the prickle of tears threatening to gather in the corners of her eyes. She blinked them back. "What a waste, considering I came out so...defective." Maida spat out the word. "Is that why you couldn't stand any reminders of magic in your life? Too painful?"

Buffalo raced past Maida and stopped in front of her. He placed his hands on her cheeks.

"There was nothing wrong with you, my darling. Nothing. You were perfect."

"If I was perfect," Maida shook her head, shaking his hands away, "we wouldn't be having this conversation."

Buffalo flinched. "After you were born, we had to treat you with some powerful substances to clear the effects of your mother's addiction from your system. They worked. Thank the stars, they worked! But there was a cost. They had the side effect of suppressing and inhibiting the growth of your natural magic. There was no detectable magic left in you by the time your treatment was complete."

"I see." Maida wrapped her sweater tighter around herself. The morning air in New England was far chillier than California. But it was also her emotional state that was making her tremble.

"There are strict rules about Ordinary folk growing up in openly magical households, Maida. Not only is it forbidden by our kind, it's also dangerous for the Ordinaries. The risks are too great. In most cases like this, the child is placed with an Ordinary family, either in foster care or in an adoptive home. When you were only a few days old, I had to make choices for both of us."

Buffalo inhaled deeply and exhaled slowly. "I was selfish. I chose for myself. I chose you."

Maida continued walking, a little more slowly, as she considered this. Buffalo followed close beside her, matching her pace. She was grateful for the heat he radiated.

"What drugs did my mother take?" Maida looked over her shoulder. She was dying to know now. She'd always suspected, and now here, at last was her proof. "Painkillers? Speed?"

"No. Nothing like that. Your mother was addicted to magic." Buffalo's head was hanging as he answered. "And when you were first born, so were you. Specifically, synthetic magic." He said the words with obvious distaste. "It wasn't entirely her fault. I was to blame as well. I did nothing to stop her from using it. We both just wanted her to carry to term."

"What the heck is synthetic magic?" Maida drew back at the unfamiliar term. She'd heard of many crazy names for street drugs, but this wasn't one of them.

"Man made. Lab created. Artificial. Fake," Buffalo spat out synonyms. "Synthetic magic."

Maida cocked her head. "That's a thing?"

"It's nothing new. It's been around in many forms. Ancient alchemists were blatant about their quest to create it. Mages, necromancers, and dark wizards have dabbled with it since the dawn of time. There are still studies happening at well-known Ordinary institutions. They are harnessing the latest technological advances to speed up their exploration of ancient magic. Some of them have made alarming advances, actually. But to answer your original question, yes, it's still out there and it's extremely dangerous. It shows up in unexpected places."

"Like the Mudpuddle?" Maida ventured a guess. "Did the disappearance of the Mudpuddle have anything to do with synthetic magic?"

"We don't know for sure, but Arthur seems to suspect that's the case. Whatever happened there was serious. The house has never disappeared for days. We really need to get to the bottom of it." Buffalo kicked at a clump of grass, sending it flying across the yard and into some bushes.

"And you need my help to do that?" Maida asked, feeling the pendant buzz against her chest.

"Unfortunately, yes." Buffalo stared at the ground. "I hate the idea of putting you in danger. But it appears you're the only one who can bring the place back."

How ironic, Maida thought. Here she'd been kept away from magic her whole life, and now she was going to have to help get a bunch of the people who'd kept it from her out of a magical pickle.

She had many more questions.

"What happens to people who become addicted to synthetic magic?" Maida asked. She turned the corner, passed the frog pond and headed towards the willow.

"The long-term effects on Ordinary humans are subtle. Depression, brain fog, body aches, rashes, impotence, insomnia, migraine headaches, lethargy." Buffalo ticked off a laundry list of symptoms.

"Sounds like the cautionary tale in every drug commercial I've ever heard." Maida rolled her eyes.

"In rare cases, it can cause allergic reactions. Some cases of cancer have been found." Buffalo smiled wryly. He threaded his hands together and stretched. Maida heard his knuckles crack. "The effect on magical folk is more profound. We're still learning about it. We have a much lower tolerance for synthetic magic and a much higher tendency to become addicted. And once addicted, it's very hard to recover. Shifters become volatile, and then eventually catatonic. Witches simply go mad. We call the disease 'the languor.'"

"Is that what happened to my mother and me?" Maida asked.

"Your mother showed all the classic signs of the langour, although back then we didn't have a name for it. And you were born a very sick baby," Buffalo confirmed. "We couldn't know how much was because of the synthetic magic your mother was using while she was pregnant with you, and how much was because of other things."

"What other things?" Maida asked.

"Prematurity, the difficulty of the pregnancy, and mixed genetics. It's not only taboo for different magical types to mate because of outdated pure blood ideology. It can often also be a risk to both mother and child. Not that this deterred Larkspur. She was determined to fight discrimination with her whole self—body and soul, if need be."

"And you?" Maida asked. "How did you feel about that?"

Buffalo looked away from her now. "Let's just say I was already in love with another witch, and very aware that it would be an uphill battle for both of us to pursue a relationship. But I was willing to try. One night she came to me..."

They had come to a stop near the weeping willow and Maida was pleased to see her swing was still there. It looked like the rope had been replaced, but otherwise the same broad, simple board was hanging where she remembered it.

"I don't need to know the details, Dad..." Maida spied a small green frog by the side of the frog pond. When she bent to take a closer look he hopped away towards the tree.

"The witch that came to me? She wasn't who I thought. We'd all been drinking and Larkspur had thought it would be funny to employ a glamor, and show up in my room looking like her roommate. She suspected how I felt about Amrita."

"Oh no..." Maida's hand flew to her mouth. "That's terrible! How could you ever forgive her?"

"We were all so young. Kids do stupid things. Magical kids do especially stupid things."

Maida looked longingly at the swing. It was practically begging for her to sit down on it, and so she did.

"So she tricked you into getting her pregnant?" Maida asked.

Buffalo leaned back against the tree trunk, studying her, appearing to weigh his words before continuing.

"Not exactly. She tricked me, but it wasn't as nefarious as that. I don't think she actually intended to conceive a child." Her father shifted from foot to foot as he spoke, clearly less than comfortable with the details he was sharing. But he was also determined to spare none of them. "But once she did, there was no way that she wasn't going through with it. Even when the doctors told her how dangerous it would be, given my size and her congenital condition. It was a miracle that she became pregnant at all."

"What condition would that be?" Maida asked.

"She had an abnormally small uterus. Mouse sized." Buffalo grimaced. "'Incompatible with gestation' was what the doctors said."

"Oh," Maida said, gathering her thoughts. She felt awful asking the next question, but she felt she must. "Why didn't she just consider termination?"

"Fates no! She was convinced you were special. She wouldn't think of it. Even when her family threatened to cut her off if she went through with it. She was so determined. She turned to synthetic magic because it was the only way she could carry you to term. There was no talking her out of it. And by that point, she'd convinced me as well. You should know this, Maida. I may not have intended to bring you into the world, but once I knew you existed, I was willing to do anything to hold you in my arms and bring you home."

"Why did her family cut her off?" Maida rocked gently on the swing, needing the motion to take the edge off this conversation. She had one foot tucked under her bottom and nudged herself with the other, pushing against the bulky roots that bulged up from the ground in front of her.

"We've had brief periods in history where witches and shifters have gotten along and lived together in harmony. Usually when we've had to stick together to face a common enemy. Primrose Court was founded around the same time as the Salem witch trials. And many of the first shifters to settle there were blamed in one form or another for the outbreaks of plague in the old country. But even at the best of times, there's been a double standard. It's one thing for witches to mingle socially with shifters. It's another thing entirely to mix bloodlines," Buffalo explained.

"Why not? It's obviously possible." Maida tilted her head and gestured down at herself.

"Yes, obviously." Buffalo smiled at her, his pride shining in his eyes. "But the Lathrops are a prominent family. Very proper. It didn't help that your mother was very young and so was I. Plus, she dropped out of school. This was a true scandal. They wanted me to talk her out of it, even offered me money to go away. When I refused, they had me banished from Primrose Court."

"I see." Maida swallowed. "So I guess I'm pretty lucky to be here." She toyed with the locket, considering whether she even wanted to meet her two remaining aunts. Now that she'd heard this story, she wasn't so sure. "I guess I understand why my aunts never reached out to me now."

"Minerva Lathrop wasn't one to poke her nose in other people's affairs. She's always kept to herself, running that bookshop. She's been the caretaker for generations. Your mother's sister is another story. Lucretia was very jealous of Larkspur, but she looked up to her as well. She lost her sister, and then her parents not long after. It wasn't easy for her, and she's grown into a very rigid person. Lucretia blamed me when the synthetic magic made Larkspur go mad. And I don't blame her for that."

"But it wasn't your fault. It was her decision to take it."

Buffalo turned away from Maida and walked a few paces. She couldn't see his face. She could only see his shoulders moving up and down as he breathed. There was the slightest shudder as he exhaled.

"I could have stopped her."

"If you had, you wouldn't have had to give up your magic. Your life would have proceeded differently. I can understand if you have regrets." As she pumped her legs to swing higher, her momentum caused a slight breeze. She felt one of the long branches of the tree brush against her arm. She swatted it away.

"No! I was going to say it was what she wanted, but it was what I wanted too. I could have stopped her, but I didn't, and I wouldn't if I had to do it over again. I'm terribly sorry for what happened to your mother and to the Lathrops but I can't regret it. I won't ever regret it."

"Even though you thought I was Ordinary?" Maida called out while swinging out and away from him. She was gathering speed. Another branch whipped against her arm, and the swing went sideways for a second before righting itself.

"I was so relieved when you tested negative for magic!" Buffalo paced back and forth. "You have no idea! I was *thrilled.* I didn't want you to have anything to do with magic. After all that had transpired, I was willing to live out my own days without ever shifting again. I started a business in the human world and cut magic out of my life entirely. No looking back. It hasn't been all bad, has it?"

"Ow!" Maida tried to slow the swing. The higher she swung, the more tangled she was getting in the long branches. They whipped her as she flew past. "Speak for yourself. You wouldn't even let me make a wish on a wishbone! You put me in time out once for crossing my fingers!"

"I couldn't take any chances, Maida. I just wanted you to be safe and have a normal life."

Maida attempted to say something, but the words stuck in her mouth as a thick rope of tree tendrils rapidly twined up from between her legs, reaching around her shoulders and throat. At the top of the swing's arc, she had to let go of the swing's ropes to claw at the choking shoots. The swing swung out and away from her. Desperate to save herself, Maida wrapped her legs around the bundled branches, pulling them away from her neck and face. She gathered the branches in fistfuls, holding on for dear life as she gasped for air.

She felt herself rising, and fast, up, up, up into the tree.

"Maida?!" Buffalo's voice sounded distant, and growing even farther as the branches rocketed her skyward.

"Dad!" she sputtered.

She gulped lungfuls of air. The tree seemed less interested in choking her to death and more interested in her locket. The branches slithered around her torso like snakes, curling under her shirt and around her waist.

"Shadow of a serpent! I thought we were old friends!" Maida cursed, fighting the willow and kicking at its boughs, to no avail. The more she struggled, the worse things got. Like quicksand. She had to force herself to remain calm and stay still.

Now would be a good time for her newly minted magic to manifest, she thought. What was the point of having magic if you couldn't use it to stop a tree from acting like a vindictive snake?

No sooner than the thought crossed her mind, a half dozen snakes slipped from the tips of the tree's trailing branches where they touched the ground. She watched them as they slithered away. They only made it a few feet past the tree's shadow before changing back into willow branches. Maida shuddered. Had she somehow done that? She peered through the greenery forming a mesh around her.

Her father was gone. The place where he'd been standing moments earlier shimmered and shook like a mirage. There was a great cloud of dust being kicked up and then she heard thundering hooves as Buffalo, truly a buffalo now, charged at the tree.

The first blow shook the tree so hard it felt like an earthquake. There was a pause, but the tenacious branches quickly resumed their careful exploration of her collarbones, moving on to the locket's chain. They tugged at it, attempting to slide it off over her head. But the locket would not budge. It also fought back, sending out shocks which filled the air with the smell of singed wood. This only seemed to discourage the tendrils for a moment or two. Fresh green wood sprouted from the charred areas.

The second blow shook the tree even harder than the first. It caused some branches to break off. One of them hit Maida's head, and she saw a brilliant swarm of bright stars swimming around her face and head.

Suddenly, the tree lurched sideways and Maida felt as though she were seated in a slingshot. The branches that cocooned her whipped her around and spun her in a spiral, twisting and untwisting her as she dangled.

"Hold on!" a voice bellowed out and Maida saw Will and another man racing through the garden, toward the tree. She struggled to maintain consciousness. She imagined she saw Granny Luna in the tree beside her, slashing at the branches with the sharp edge of a crystal dagger.

Maida felt a searing pain across the back of her neck as the tree yanked the locket's chain even harder. Almost as if it meant to behead her with it.

"Oh no you don't, you slithering eel weeds! Not on my watch!" Granny Luna bit into the willow bark, baring razor-sharp fangs that cut clean through the branches.

The third blow to the tree felled it. Maida felt herself falling again and shut her eyes tight.

Just before she ought to have hit the ground, a pair of long, muscular arms caught her. They belonged to someone with an unequal amount of golden glints in each eye.

It was Arthur, and she remembered him this time—not just from California.

"I saw your antlers," she whispered. "We were right here."

TWENTY-TWO

A TREACHEROUS TREE

Offering a sincere apology is a mark of true character, no matter the form you take. A proper apology begins with accepting responsibility—no deflecting blame onto your animal instincts.

Keep your apology simple and direct. Acknowledge the harm done, express genuine remorse, and, where possible, offer to make amends. Avoid overexplaining or making excuses—whether in human or animal form, a gentleman's word should be as steady as his shift.

-EXCERPT FROM THE METAMORPHIC MAN: A GENTLEMAN SHAPESHIFTER'S GUIDE TO CULTURED CONDUCT

Arthur's return trip to Boston was an exercise in patience and human origami.

He was eager to resolve the situation with the Mudpuddle. He couldn't wait to see Maida again and he couldn't wait to throttle Will Porter for leaving him stranded. But all the slow motion hours in crawling traffic, and waiting in airports, had given Arthur much needed time to reflect. He'd been so stubbornly focused on the execution of his initial plan, and so distracted by meeting Maida again, that he hadn't listened to what Will was trying to tell him. Maida was not Ordinary, after all. Will had been right. Arthur was not too proud to admit when he was wrong.

As soon as he reached the airport, he ducked into a pay phone to check in with Rosie and let her know he wouldn't be home till morning. He wasn't thrilled about leaving his daughter alone overnight, but as she reminded him, she was almost seventeen—hardly a baby. She promised to bolt the door.

After that, he gave Director Berman a call. He was expecting her to admonish him for not heeding her warning about his plan. He suspected he was done—that this would be the end of his first and only mission for the Society. When would he have this sort of opportunity to work with them again? He should have felt relieved, but he felt a sinking, shrinking sensation that he recognized as disappointment. He was disappointed in himself, mostly. Fate had given him a second chance with Maida Westabrook and he had failed her again.

"I'm sorry, Director Berman. I could not complete the assignment you gave me. The fault was entirely my own. I should have handled things differently. It seemed like the simplest solution to me, but I was clearly wrong."

"So her magic has come back to her at last." Amrita Berman smiled through the phone lines. "I always suspected it would. Perhaps the locket was a catalyst."

"Perhaps the tests that were done when she was a child were mistaken," Arthur suggested boldly. He had seen it when they were children, hadn't he? Why hadn't anyone else?

"Perhaps," Amrita admitted. "But better to err on the side of caution than risk losing her altogether."

Arthur wasn't sure he agreed. All magic came at a cost, according to Ordinary lore. But what was the price of having it denied for so long?

He'd never witnessed magic like Maida's. By comparison, his

abilities were trivial. Drawing life, literally creating life from ink on paper, was a unique talent. It was manifestation magic. He'd heard that such things were possible. But not like this. Witches needed clay, earth, or something that was once living to conjure an existence. Dark rituals and forced, forbidden magic were usually associated with the practice. The idea that she had casually, innocently, and possibly accidentally manifested new life so easily was almost mind boggling.

"What now?" Arthur asked. "Does the Society still need my services?" Best to get it over with, he thought.

Director Berman had not hesitated to reply. "I warned you I had concerns about your plans." She paused and Arthur braced himself for what came next. "This just means you'll need to pivot. There's no need for power of attorney or reassigning her inheritance, unless she finds it burdensome, which hopefully won't happen. I still expect you to accompany Maida to Primrose Court and help guide her through this process."

"Legally speaking?" Arthur asked. This wasn't what he was expecting.

"Yes," Director Berman said. "But more than that if you can manage it. I want you to look out for her. Guide her. Protect her. This isn't a trivial ask, Arthur. Maida is the key to bringing back the Mudpuddle. The community in Primrose Court is already suffering in its absence. It may seem trivial to you, but large rifts start small."

"There's still no word on Minerva?" Arthur knew the rumor mill in Primrose Court. Every day that went by without answers, seeded new debates and theories.

"Nothing. And the town council has contacted me about Zephyr. I understand you went by the morgue to pay your respects?"

"I did," Arthur said. "I assume there's been no change in his... condition?"

"No change," she confirmed. "But we have a team analyzing

his shoes to see if we can determine anything else about the incident but—"

"Synthetic magic is difficult to trace," Arthur finished the thought.

"That it is." Amrita sighed. "So highly processed and volatile. Short-lived as well."

"It could be a red herring," Arthur suggested. "Perhaps it was used to throw us off the scent of the real culprit." Quite literally, he thought, recalling the stench.

"It's hard to imagine who that might be," Amrita said, "or what their motivation might have been. Zephyr and Minerva were so beloved. But I suppose everyone has enemies. Or perhaps it was a matter of being in the wrong place, at the wrong time."

"I would like to know what happened to Zephyr and Minerva," Arthur said, thinking specifically of Bardo Chan and worrying. "It would quell the rumors and in-fighting between the magical types."

"We have other methods of scrying if it comes to it, but we'll have to wait till some of the synthetic magic dissipates. I'm afraid I'll have to be present for those rituals myself," Amrita said. "If Zephyr's remains stick around for that long."

"Absolute truth?" Arthur asked. It was the gold standard in magical courtrooms, but only senior members of the Society could perform the secretive ritual.

"If it comes to it," Amrita confirmed. "For now, I'd like you to focus on keeping Maida safe, and helping her to bring back the Mudpuddle. Do you think you can do that, Arthur?"

"Why me?" It was the most basic question, but he felt the need to ask.

"It has to be you, Arthur. You and Maida have a special connection."

When Arthur reached Logan Airport, he was greeted by an Ordinary driver holding a card with his name on it. The driver led him to the car that was waiting for him. It was to deliver him directly to the Westabrook estate, he was told. But Arthur did not know what was waiting for him there. Would Maida be more or perhaps less inclined to accept her inheritance, now that she knew the truth about her family?

And if she accepted it, would the Mudpuddle simply reappear? Did the Lathrops have specific rituals or practices for securing the property? He steeled himself for the inevitable. They would need to ask Lucretia Lathrop for her help. He didn't want to give her too much time to think about it. Best to just show up at the apothecary.

And then what?

If Maida was successful, would she consider staying on in Primrose Court? He found it surprising how much the prospect of this lifted his spirits.

Arthur was getting ahead of himself. He felt drained from his hours on the plane, cramped into a middle seat. His limbs ached. His eyes drooped and his head bobbed, and soon he was asleep and dreaming of the willow tree again.

The car came to a halt on the gravel in front of Buffalo Westabrook's mansion, waking him with a start. It had been decades since he'd been back to the Westabrook estate.

Once Arthur's driver departed, he stood in the circular driveway for a moment or two, simply listening to the early morning birdsong. It was still such a familiar sound. Standing there, he was overwhelmed by the smells of fall leaves and freshly mown grass that summoned a flood of early childhood memories. Some of the memories were bad, but some were also good. He wondered who was living in the groundskeeper's cottage now. They were doing a fine job, but not as good as Reggie had. It was evident to Arthur that many of the trees had been pruned improperly.

Was it too early to ring the doorbell? Should he knock instead?

He was still considering his options when Will Porter raced out the front door in a breathless panic. "Hurry!" Will yanked on Arthur's arm. "It's Maida!"

The instant Will tagged him, he felt the slingshot sensation of time gathering speed. They sped toward the garden, running headlong down a path that Arthur remembered, towards the tree that still haunted his dreams.

The willow looked nothing like the graceful giant that he recalled. It had transformed into a malicious arboreal beast. It flailed and twisted from side to side. Its long, sinewy branches slashed into the earth and whistled as they whipped through the air.

"The willow has her!" Will pointed high in the tree. Alarmingly high. From what Arthur could see, Maida's legs were wrapped around a thick bundle of branches, but there was nothing else holding her there besides the network of tangled green tendrils crawling over her. She screamed.

Arthur's blood ran cold, as if he'd had an infusion of ice water injected into his veins. This time it smelled more like burnt rubber, and hot metal. It tasted like copper and stung his nose and throat.

This was certainly synthetic magic, and if there'd been any doubt before that Maida was the intended target, there was none now.

"Hold on, Mayday!" Will hollered.

Before they could reach the base of the tree, Arthur heard the thunder of hooves and the sharp crack of wood as Buffalo charged, ramming his horns into the trunk. The ground shook, and the boughs shivered. A tangle of snakes unraveled themselves from the lower branches, wriggling in every direction, their venomous fangs bared. Arthur nimbly hurdled over them, just as they were transforming back into sticks.

The tree was leaning sideways now. It swung Maida as if it meant to fling her. She was barely hanging on.

Will stared helplessly up into the branches. He had taken a small knife out and held it out in front of himself, slashing at the whiplike branches.

Buffalo was charging again. His horns punctured the tree's bloated trunk and emerged tarry, dripping with toxic, invasive magic.

"Look out!" Arthur warned. A quiver of cobras emerged from the freshly fallen branches, raising their heads as if they meant to strike. They reverted back to wood as Buffalo reduced them to a pulp beneath his hooves.

"I've got the tree. I need you to catch her."

Buffalo hadn't made a sound, yet when the older man met his eye, Arthur understood his intent. They both spoke an ancient language easily understood by their animal selves. Buffalo pawed the ground and made a gruff sound that was somewhere between a snuff and a snort. He looked at Arthur again and lowered his head.

"Don't let me down."

Buffalo took off running in the opposite direction of the tree, he would need the distance in order to build momentum for his next charge.

Arthur positioned himself under the tree's canopy, staying beneath Maida, as best he could. He softened his knees and held his arms outstretched and ready. He didn't dare take his eyes off her. He didn't blink, not even when he heard the cracking death blow of Buffalo's horns splitting the trunk of the willow in two.

Everything teetered for a dizzy second, before the rest of the tree slumped. The branches released their hold and then Maida was tumbling, free falling through the air like a rag doll.

Arthur dove forward, reliving the horrifying sense of helplessness he'd felt the last time he saw her there. She'd almost fallen out of this same tree then. But this time there was no one holding him back. He caught her easily in his outstretched arms and pulled her close.

"You're safe," he spoke into her hair, which was damp with sweat from her struggles. Her eyes blinked open and then opened wider still, pupils dilated with recognition.

"I remember you," Maida said. "I saw your antlers." Her eyes closed again, and she went limp against him. Buffalo was panting by the shattered trunk of the tree, and Will was racing toward them. Arthur pulled her closer still.

"I've got her. She's okay!" Arthur shouted. "You're okay," he repeated in a whisper, placing his forehead against hers.

TWENTY-THREE

GEARHEART LOCKETS

A good night's sleep is more than just a luxury—it's essential for maintaining balance. A well-rested gentleman is sharp, composed, and less prone to those regrettable outbursts that come with exhaustion.

Prioritize your rest by establishing a consistent routine. Ensure your sleeping space is both comfortable and secure, regardless of which form you may find yourself in come morning.

-EXCERPT FROM THE METAMORPHIC MAN: A GENTLEMAN SHAPESHIFTER'S GUIDE TO CULTURED CONDUCT

The moment Arthur laid Maida on the couch in the library, her eyes opened. She sat upright. Her hand flew to the back of her head where she had a goose egg, and she winced.

If that bump was the worst of it, she was lucky. He stepped back to observe her. Her body was covered with scratches, but miraculously she didn't appear to have been seriously injured.

"Let's just have a look, shall we?" Arthur recognized Dr. Dvita at once and was relieved to see him there.

The doctor was still in his slippers and wearing his white lab coat like a bathrobe over his pajamas. His stethoscope hung around his neck.

Will stood anxiously in the corner with his back turned, fists clenched. "Is it safe to turn around?" Will asked. "I don't want to pass out. I get a little weird around blood."

Maida patted her head and glanced down worriedly at her hands. "Am I bleeding?"

"No. It's okay, Maida. You're okay," the doctor soothed. "Try to stay still for a moment while I have a look at you? You fainted and I want to make sure you don't have a concussion."

"Was I out for long?" Maida asked.

"Just a few seconds," Dr. Dvita reassured her. He shone a light in both of her eyes. "I think it was a shock more than anything. And likely a lack of food. You've eaten very little since yesterday. I think once you catch your breath and have a little something to eat and drink, you'll be just fine. Now, where's my newspaper?"

Arthur breathed a sigh of relief.

The doctor packed his stethoscope into his satchel and pulled out a newspaper, which he tucked under his arm. The headline read *Mudpuddle Still Missing: Theories Abound.*

"Oh! It's safe to turn around, Will. There's no blood. Maida's going to be fine," the doctor called out as he settled into a rocking chair near the bookcases.

"Thank the stars!" Will spun around. He didn't seem to want to make eye contact with Arthur.

"How about I see what I can round up for breakfast?" Will suggested.

He didn't wait for an answer before rushing off towards the kitchen. He was in such a hurry, he almost collided with Granny Luna. She was holding two cups of coffee in one hand and an ice pack in the other. There was also a scraggly, shabby stuffed animal tucked under her arm.

"Here's some coffee for the two of you." Granny fussed. "And an ice pack for that bump on the back of your head, Maida. That should help the swelling."

She set the mugs on the coffee table and handed the ice pack to Maida. Then she turned to admire Arthur. "Such a fine shaper you are, Arthur Hart. Quite the hero, too!"

Granny Luna snapped the toy at him like she was snapping a tea towel. Then she tossed it to Maida. "I've brought you Mr. Pants for comfort as well."

Arthur did a double take at the toy. Mr. Pants? Where had he come from?

Maida caught the stuffed animal and set it on the couch beside her. She placed the ice pack against her head briefly, but quickly set it back down again so she could drink her coffee. Granny Luna frowned.

"You should be icing!" Granny scolded. "And you don't want to get a chill, do you?" She draped another one of her afghans over Maida's shoulders.

"I'm *fine*, Granny," Maida argued. "You don't need to fuss. It barely hurts." Then she helped herself to a large sip of the coffee, closing her eyes as she swallowed.

A moment later, Maida set her coffee down shakily. "I loved that old tree," she said. She leaned back and hugged the old toy to her chest, absent-mindedly flossing the fingers of her left hand with its velvet coated antlers. "I always thought of that tree as my friend. Why would it do something like that?"

"It wasn't the tree's fault, dear. 'Twas enchanted," Granny Luna said, leaning over the back of the sofa beside Maida. "Particularly nasty bit of magic, if you ask me. You might have been killed."

"I'm not so sure it wanted to kill me." Maida shook her head. "It definitely wanted to take my locket, though." She touched the locket with her free hand.

Arthur carried his mug to a club chair on the far side of the sofa. His coffee was black like he preferred it, and strong like he needed it. He settled into the plush, comfortable seat, allowing some of his tension to ease.

"You know," Granny perched on the arm of the doctor's chair, "whoever hexed that tree couldn't have been all that bright. Such a shame. The poor tree didn't stand a chance against Buffalo's horns. It was magnificent to see him in full form again, though, wasn't it?"

There was something savagely proud in the way Granny Luna's eyes flashed. Dr. Dvita lowered the paper and set aside his pipe to respond.

"I'll say! What a sight that was to see him shift after all that time, Beryl!" He addressed Granny by her first name. "Did you ever think you'd see the day?"

"No, Tarquin, I most certainly did not!" Granny replied to Dr. Dvita. She smoothed his lab coat affectionately.

Granny Luna turned back to Maida, eyes shining. "I wish you could have seen it, Maida! Your da shifted so quickly, so seamlessly, even after thirty-five years. It was simply spectacular!"

"Has it really been that long?" Maida asked. Her brow furrowed as she considered this.

"Your father hasn't allowed a lick of magic here since the day you were born. It was quite a challenge for my old bones, you know. Walking is not what fairy feet were made for." Granny Luna reached back and pulled a long, slender leaf from her carefully coiffed hair. "Fiddleferns! I thought I got them all."

"That really was you up in the tree?" Maida blew out a long sigh. She stared at Granny with a mix of horror and respect, as if she were truly seeing her for the first time. "Granny! You were savage. You *bit* right through the branches that were strangling me!"

"Well, of course I did. My dentist is always going on about the importance of flossing. It's just been a while since I did it with willow bark." She winked at Maida, who still appeared to be processing the somewhat feral nature of her fae guardian.

"Glad to see you've kept your teeth as sharp as your tongue,

Granny." Buffalo's colossal form momentarily blocked the light as he crossed through the doorway.

He'd shifted back into human form again, but the smells of grass and earth still clung to him. His hair was mussed, and his eyes glimmered with lingering golden sparks of fresh magic. Most noticeably, his posture had changed. It was subtle, yet unmistakable. Buffalo stood taller, prouder, and stronger.

Thirty-five years of suppressing one's true nature? It caused Arthur physical pain just thinking about it. Buffalo must have read Arthur's thoughts, because the older man's mouth tilted up on one side as he nodded in acknowledgement. Then Buffalo's attention was locked on his daughter. He rushed across the room to embrace his Maida, but at the last minute reconsidered, kissing the top of her head gently, instead. She looked so small next to his hulking form.

"I'm okay, Dad," Maida said.

"I can see that," Buffalo said. He settled on the edge of the coffee table in front of her. "Have you thanked Arthur Hart for catching you?"

"She doesn't have to thank me," Arthur objected. He scraped a hand through his hair and attempted to change the subject. "I'm glad I could help. Right place, right time, et cetera." He was babbling. He felt his cheeks redden.

"Wait. What are you doing here, Arthur?" Maida's cool eyes sought his own in a curious, but not unkind, way. "I thought I already signed the papers you needed."

"Yes, indeed, but the circumstances have changed now that you've been enlightened. There's no need for me to act as your proxy now that you're here. Speaking of which," he turned to address Buffalo, "I'd like for Maida to come to Primrose Court with me shortly, assuming she's up to it. I thought we might visit the apothecary and speak to Lucretia. She might have some ideas about how to secure Maida's inheritance."

"You're assuming Maida wants to go there and claim it." Buffalo looked sternly at Arthur and turned back to Maida. "You don't have to go anywhere you don't want to go, darling. You're more than welcome to stay here and rest."

Arthur returned his gaze to Maida. She was still studying him as if she were weighing a decision. "Lucretia is my mother's sister?"

"Yes." Arthur nodded.

Maida set the ice pack on the table. She sat up straighter, leaning towards her father, chin out and head held high. "I'm fine, Dad. I'm here now, and I want to go. I want to meet this aunt of mine." She smiled a weak smile at her father, then turned to look at Arthur.

"Okay." Arthur held her gaze for a moment, then glanced back at Buffalo. "The sooner we settle this, the better." He rubbed his hands together. "Whoever broke into Maida's apartment and enchanted the tree is still out there."

"What do you suppose they want?" Maida crossed her arms protectively in front of herself.

"They want her gearheart locket, obviously." Will Porter burst back into the room, laden with pink and white bakery bags that bore a now familiar logo.

Arthur felt his eyes bugging when he read the name. *The Bunny Hole.*

"Who's hungry?" Will asked cheerfully.

"Are you kidding me, Will? You made me take a ten hour red-eye home from Los Angeles, but you just popped back out to California to pick up donuts?"

"There's a limit to how many times I can port and how much cargo I can carry in one day!" Will dropped the bag at the center of the coffee table and held up his hands. "I'm a porter, Arthur, not a sherpa!" He handed Arthur a bear claw. "Here. I got this one for you."

"Thank you, Will." Arthur took the bear claw and met the other man's eyes. "I'm sorry I didn't listen to you sooner yesterday." He took a bite. "But you still shouldn't have left me stranded like that."

"I left you a *voucher!*" Will said.

"When was the last time you had to book a same day plane ticket using an expired voucher?" Arthur asked. Will shrugged sheepishly and Arthur decided to change the subject. "What do we know about this locket?"

"It's a gearheart locket," Will volunteered.

"And what exactly is a gearheart locket?" Arthur asked.

"They are a fine bit of metallurgical wizardry that involves the marriage of intricate clockworks and spell work. They are very efficient," Buffalo explained, standing and sipping his coffee as he slowly paced the perimeter of the room. "Only a handful of them were ever made, several hundred years ago. There's a lot of secrecy around them and their manufacture, which isn't surprising. Those weren't the safest of times for witches." He stopped in front of the fireplace, staring at the mantel clock, thoughtfully. "One theory is that they were the handiwork of Lionel Lathrop, Maida's fifth great grandfather."

"Interesting. What do they do?" Arthur asked. He had noticed the distinctive locket, but he hadn't examined it. He moved closer to Maida now, sitting on the edge of the coffee table in the spot her father had vacated.

"They don't do anything per se. It's more about what they are —pocket universes, designed to provide protection and a safe place to hide. Legend has it that there is no penetrating a gearheart locket. It will only work for its maker or its owner. I've never seen one firsthand. I always sort of thought they were magical Macguffins," Buffalo replied. "Clever of Will to recognize what it was."

Will preened at this praise, taking a formal bow. Observing this, Maida rolled her eyes. Such a quick gesture that nearly everyone else had missed it. But Arthur hadn't. He bit his cheek to avoid smiling. Why did she make him feel so light, even when they were discussing such heavy things?

"How did you know what it was, Will?" Maida forced her features into a more serious semblance and looked back at him.

"The porter I trained under was obsessed with them. He

desperately wanted to find one. Thought it would come in handy, given our profession."

"Are you sure he wasn't just trying to hide from you?" Maida teased. Arthur envied the easy way she and Will traded banter. They acted very much like siblings.

Maida was still clutching the old stuffed toy on her lap. Arthur stared at it, wondering who'd given it to her.

"May I see it?" Arthur asked.

Maida glanced down at the toy for a moment, almost as if she'd read his mind. She held it out to Arthur, and he took it. Their fingers brushed, and Arthur felt it in every follicle.

"I think he actually meant the locket, Maida, not that toy." Buffalo sat down on the couch opposite her.

"Oh, of course!" She blushed and her hand flew to her neck—holding the pendant away from her chest for examination. Arthur slid into the seat beside her. She tilted her chin back, baring her throat to him. He held out two fingers and touched the locket gently as she related the story of how the locket came to be in her possession. Much to his surprise, the locket vibrated beneath his fingers as he traced the letter L. Hastily, Arthur snatched his fingers away.

"It does that," Maida said. "I know it sounds crazy, but I think it hums when it's content."

"And when it's not happy?" Buffalo put on a pair of reading glasses and leaned across the coffee table to study the locket, but refrained from touching it. "How can you tell?"

"That's a little more obvious." Maida grimaced. "It shocked me when I tried to open it for Will. And it shocked the tree."

"Can I see it again?" Will flopped onto the sofa on Maida's other side. He reached out to touch the locket.

"Will, I don't think—" Maida objected, but she was too late. Will jumped back and shook his hand as if the locket had bitten him.

"Cursed Currents! I don't know what the Mudpuddle has against me," Will snapped. He stuck his sore finger in his mouth.

"What are you talking about, Will?" Arthur frowned.

"The Mudpuddle. It's in that locket." Will rolled his eyes dramatically at Arthur. "Obviously."

The room went silent as everyone stared at Will, and the locket.

"I just don't know why it's taken such a dislike to me. I've never been disrespectful while visiting, I always tip well in the cafe. Do you think the house might have a problem with fae?"

"Don't be a daft bunny!" Granny snapped at Will. "I hate to tell you, Will, but there's always going to be some folk for whom you're not their cup of tea. And in this case, folk includes enchanted houses trapped inside lockets."

"It's not trapped." Will pouted. "It's hiding."

"A house inside the locket," Arthur mused, leaning forward, daring to touch it again and look closer. Although there were no inscriptions or maker's marks on the back, from the way it nestled into the hollow of her throat, there was no mistaking that the locket, and whatever was inside, belonged to her and her alone. It had chosen her.

Maida drew her hand away, allowing Arthur to weigh the locket in his palm. It was heavier than it looked, and felt warm from her skin.

"It's quite remarkable," Arthur said. "Have you looked inside?"

His fingertips grazed her collarbone as he gently placed the locket back against her. He could see she had goosebumps. He prayed they were like his—the good kind.

"There is the image of a house in there. I'm not so sure it's the Mudpuddle, but Will seems certain that it is," Maida said. "Thanks for not demanding that I show it to you right now. I just have this weird feeling that it doesn't want me to open it here. Isn't that strange?"

Arthur nodded, recalling what Director Berman had said about the house having a mind of its own.

"I don't think it's strange at all. The Mudpuddle is behaving like a frightened child. It's going to stay hidden in that locket until it feels it's safe to come out again. At least now we know where it's hiding. That's progress!" Arthur said.

TWENTY-FOUR

THE COMFORT OF FRIENDS

The luminous language of bioluminescence is spoken by countless creatures and organisms and serves as a silent yet profound means of connection within the natural world.

Fireflies use it to woo potential mates. Deep-sea inhabitants signal to one another in the darkest depths, and countless other organisms summon it to convey messages, announce their presence, or evade predators.

What can we learn from these creatures? It is up to us to find our own ways to glow.

EXCERPT FROM THE MUDPUDDLE MANUAL OF NATURAL MAGIC

Maida excused herself to her room to freshen up before heading out to Primrose Court. She was stalling. Although she'd put a brave face on for her father and Arthur, she wasn't actually sure she was ready. Her legs were still shaking from her morning misadventure in the tree.

She needed more time to process that magic was real.

It was something she'd always wished for, hadn't she?

She'd spent so much time seeking it out, and sketching it. She'd stashed bits and pieces of it in drawers and on bookshelves. Under her pillow, in her pockets when she went on beach walks, and spilling from the pots on her balcony. For most of her life, Maida had been cataloging and collecting snippets of magic like it was evidence with which she would one day make her case.

And today was that day. She was surprised, but she was not shocked.

Perhaps she had known it all along. She'd been waiting for this moment of enlightenment. All she'd needed was permission to believe in what she already knew. But it still felt like a dream, this world of shifters, witches, and fae. Like she'd stepped sideways into an alternate universe—a world that was basically the same, but with portals in donut shops and pendants that contained pocket universes.

One moment it all made sense, and the next, it seemed preposterous.

She had the overwhelming urge to call Zani. Her friend would be worried about her, particularly if she'd tried to call last night. She needed to let Zani know that she was safely back in Boston. But beyond that, she was less sure about what she could share.

If anyone was going to listen with an open mind, it was Zanfira. But she didn't want to put her friend in danger. It was difficult to decide what to say when she hardly knew the rules. It was possible that Zani would think she was crazy if she told her the truth. But it was also possible that she already knew.

As if on cue, the phone on her nightstand rang once and went silent. Then it rang twice.

Maida didn't wait for it to ring a third time. Considering Zani's uncanny knack of calling or texting her, precisely whenever Maida needed her most, she played her hunch.

"How long have you known?" Maida asked.

She heard Zani's sigh. The line was silent, save for the crackle of long distance wires, as Zani considered her reply. Had she been ready with a flippant reply or made a joke, Maida would have known that Zani was Ordinary. But the time Zani was taking with the reply was a tell.

Finally, the response to Maida's question came through with another question.

"About magic, or yours specifically?"

There it was.

"You knew magic was real?" Maida accused.

"Of course. I'm a witch, Maida. I've been studying magic all my life. I don't do a very good job of hiding that." Zani had a point. Her favorite tee shirt was emblazoned with the slogan 'wandering witch' and she'd gone so far as to top her graduation cap with a witch's hat. Maida had chalked all that up to her friend being eccentric, like her.

"You knew about my family?" Maida asked.

Zani snorted. "I'm an archaeologist who specializes in folklore, legends, and cursed items. Your family's story has all the above." Maida could practically hear the eye roll in Zani's voice, and it irritated her that her friend didn't seem to be taking her big news seriously. "Are you going to stay there in Boston?"

"Wait. How did you know I came home?" Maida peeked out the window to where the others were waiting by the van.

"Will Porter popped by this morning. I guess it was last night, your time? He filled me in. I hope whoever broke into your place didn't follow you! I can't wait to see that gearheart locket. What a find!" Zani said.

"Will just popped in?" Maida was surprised.

"Well yes." Zani sounded flustered. "I messaged him when I couldn't reach you. I was so worried. He just wanted to reassure me you were okay, and he explained the whole situation to me. I'm glad he brought you home. I think that was the right thing to do."

Maida decided not to mention the mess with the tree just now. Or anything about Arthur. There wasn't enough time, and she wasn't ready to discuss the feelings Arthur had stirred.

"What are you doing right now?" Zani asked.

"I'm just about to leave for Primrose Court. I can't believe you're a witch, Zani. And magic is real!" Maida blurted.

"And yet we still can't fix climate change." Zani sighed.

"My father is working on it," Maida said. "Also he is a buffalo shifter. Were you aware?"

"I was," Zani confessed.

"My mother was a witch," Maida blurted.

"I know. Larkspur Lathrop was a legend!" Zani's excitement was palpable, but so were the stabbing pangs of betrayal that Maida was feeling. Zani had been her closest, and perhaps only true friend for the last seventeen years. But this hadn't been the friendship she'd thought it was.

"You knew..." Maida could not complete the sentence, so she started again. "Why didn't you tell me any of this?"

"Would you have believed me?" Zani's voice was sad and apologetic.

"Maybe?" Maida swallowed the lump in her throat. "I might have. But you never gave me the chance."

"Please forgive me, Maida?" Zani pleaded. "I need you to know that I never believed you were Ordinary, and even if you were, I didn't care. You were and still are my best friend. But there are rules about sharing, and trust me, there are sound reasons these rules exist."

"Such as?" Maida asked. She was weary of hearing about the rules for everyone. Her heart was still having trouble understanding the reasons for those rules.

"Ordinaries aren't meant to see beyond the veil," Zani explained, listing out the reasons. "They go crazy, fall prey to dark influences, waste their lives trying to prove or be something they're not meant to be. Knowing the truth about magic when you command none is not a comfort, Maida. It's a curse. More often than not, a death sentence."

"I still wish you would have considered making an exception," Maida grumbled.

"There's no way I was going to risk losing you like that." Much like Buffalo had been, Zani was resolute. "I'm sorry. Enlightening you wasn't an option. Not without a clear sign of your magical endowment."

"Some endowment," Maida said. "I'm not so sure what the point is when I don't have any idea what it is I am or what I'm supposed to do."

"That part will come," Zani assured her. "Give it time. You see people. Really see them. And you've always had the ability to make something from nothing. Your touch brings things to life. I can't think of anyone better to bring people together and bring back the Mudpuddle. Haven't you always dreamed of living in a bookshop?"

"Yes," Maida admitted. "But that's mostly because I wouldn't have to go out as much. I don't know that I have what it takes to bring people together. I'm a loner."

"I don't know, Maida. I think maybe you just haven't found your tribe yet."

Maida heard the honk of a horn and glanced out the window. Granny and Will were waving at her to come down. Arthur and her father were already seated in the van.

"I've got to go, Zani, but let's talk again real soon?" Maida said.

"Just you try and keep me away, Maida. I can't wait to see you when I'm back in the States. We have so much to talk about."

TWENTY-FIVE

PRIMROSE PASSAGE

Have you ever wondered who first whispered the enchantment to transform humble acorns into sprawling shade trees?

The answer lies with our friends, the squirrels. These capricious creatures are known for scattering their precious seeds in hidden alcoves across the land. From these nascent acorns, towering trees emerge. Was it forgetfulness or a grand design that led the squirrels to abandon their treasures to the earth's embrace?

The line between hapless hoarders and prudent planners remains blurred, a riddle yet to be unraveled. One thing is certain in every realm: a friendly rapport with your local scurry is a magical alliance worth cultivating.

–EXCERPT FROM THE MUDPUDDLE MANUAL OF NATURAL MAGIC

In the van, Buffalo Westabrook was engrossed in taking notes on a technical drawing of a windmill. He squinted as he peered through a pair of reading glasses that were almost comically small on him. Those were new. Maida hadn't seen her father wearing them before. There was something endearing about the way he kept pushing them up every time they slid down his nose. He made a note in the margins.

Maida was seeing her father in a whole new light. She felt her memories shifting, pieces rearranging themselves to form new pictures, like one of those sliding puzzles. Some pieces still didn't fit.

Buffalo looked up, caught her staring, and easily read her mind. "There are a lot of new options open to you, and the world might seem to be a very different place, Maida. But there are certain things that haven't changed one bit. Family is family. Our bonds create their own kind of magic and you know what? All the sappy Ordinary clichés are true. Love is the strongest magic there is. There's no point in driving yourself crazy with might-have-beens."

"I'm assuming you've already been down that road?" she guessed.

"Clever girl." Buffalo pushed his glasses up again.

"Just down the hill and then to the left." Dr. Dvita, who was seated towards the front of the van, pressed a button to instruct their driver via intercom.

They had entered a rougher, older neighborhood. The very type of place Granny Luna had cautioned Maida against, when she was young.

Dr. Dvita pressed the button again. "Perfect. Now turn in there. Just over by that dumpster."

A heavy bank of fog was rolling in from the coast, although the sky had been clear before they got to this part of town. By the time the van pulled over beside the gated driveway, the mist seemed to engulf them. It was pouring out from the alley beyond the gate.

Dr. Dvita produced a key card, which he passed forward to the driver.

With a wave of the card, the gates parted, allowing them entry into the narrow lane that seemed to lead to nowhere. The cobblestone street was bumpy and the tall brick buildings on either side loomed close on either side. If the van got stuck here, there would be no way to get out. Day turned to night as the fog blocked out the sun. The cabin of the van was dark as midnight.

Maida felt the hairs on the end of her arms stand up as a bat shaped shadow passed by the window.

"Are you sure this is safe?" Maida asked. None of the other passengers seemed perturbed. Granny was still crocheting. Her father was still reading his work papers with a flashlight, and the doctor was sitting watchfully by the front window, one claw-like finger poised above the intercom. Arthur was seated up front with the driver, so she couldn't see him. She wished she could, though. He had the most reassuring face.

She couldn't stop imagining his antlers.

Will pressed a button, lighting up the interior. "We're perfectly safe. It's just the wards. Think of it like the soundtrack in the lobby of a haunted house in a theme park."

"Why can't we skip the lobby and port in?" Maida looked quizzically at Will.

"I can't port in with an entire entourage, can I? And we're already here. It makes no sense to wear myself out going back and forth to move you all a mere half mile." Will's expression went from cheerful to beleaguered in an instant.

"But you could port into anywhere else that you wanted?" Maida asked, suddenly thinking of a dozen places she would love to go in an instant. "You went to Romania to see my friend Zani?"

"She pinged me on my T-watch after you didn't answer your phone last night. I think she was ready to send out a search party." Will held up his right wrist to display his watch. When Maida looked blank, he added, "Right. How would you know? It's a magical watch that helps members of our community stay connected."

"It's a terrible idea if you ask me." Granny Luna tutted. "Seems like these devices cause more problems than they solve. Nothing wrong with sending an owl or a raven. You young folks don't worry one whit about privacy. That'll come back to bite you!"

"We're still working out some kinks." Will rolled his eyes.

"So you just popped in to see her?" Maida reiterated. She raised a brow.

"Why not? I've always wanted to meet her. I love reading her articles about her conservation work." Will looked pleased with himself. "I offered my services to her, should she ever find herself in a spot of danger."

"I think as an occult antiquities conservationist, those kind of spots are her specialty," Maida said, thinking that Will might come to regret that offer. "How did you find her? Do you need an address? Or is it like tracing a phone call?"

"Not exactly. I have to feel my way. It helps if there's a connection to the person or place. I have to get the ley lines right to port in precisely. It takes a fair amount of practice. There are established portals that make it easier. Like your donut shop."

"The Bunny Hole is a portal?" Maida's eyes widened.

"It's kind of obvious from the name, don't you think?" Will lowered his chin and widened his eyes back at her.

"Just a bit further," Dr. Dvita announced. "And from there, we'll go on foot." He turned to Maida to explain. "Primrose Court is a self-contained pedestrian friendly zone. There are no automobiles allowed in the neighborhood. Just a few enchanted carriages."

A moment later, the narrow brick passage widened. Will slid the side door open as the van slowed down and came to a stop. Maida could see the front of a rusted old billboard that was turned on its side, propped against the wall in front of the van. It carried the flaking remnants of several old ads under layers of spray paint and tags. They appeared to be at a dead end.

"Come now, we're here." Dr. Dvita unbuckled his seat belt and hopped out. "It's been ages since I last visited. I can't wait to see what's changed."

Maida took the doctor's hand and stepped out. Granny stepped out behind her, and then Will. There wasn't much room to maneuver. They all turned sideways to thread their way to the front of the van. Maida could see Arthur waiting for them to pass in the front seat. Peering back in the van, she noticed her father still seated, his focus still intent as he continued to scratch out notes on his papers.

"Aren't you coming?" Maida asked.

"I'll wait here," Buffalo said. "I have a bit of work I need to finish. Arthur and Will know how to reach me if you need anything." Buffalo tapped his wrist. Maida noticed he was wearing a watch similar to Will's.

Then he turned his full focus back to the document he was reading.

As they inched past the front bumper, Maida looked dubiously at the narrow passage behind them. "How is the van going to turn around?" she asked the doctor.

"Don't worry about that." Dr. Dvita turned to wink at her. "Your father's driver is skilled. He's a cat shifter."

After they all passed, Arthur jumped out to join their party. Maida noticed he was wearing a similar watch to the one Will and her father wore, but he had it turned backwards and was speaking into it as he walked. His voice was a curious mixture of sternness and affection.

"I thought I told you to stay put until I got home," he said. He shut the van door behind him. "No, I don't think running out of Gemini's preferred brand of kibble qualifies as an emergency." He held up a finger, asking them to wait as he finished his conversation. "I'd have been happy to pick it up for you, if you had mentioned it. I'm headed into Primrose Court myself right now."

Arthur paused and ran a hand through his dark hair, disheveling it for a moment before most of it settled back into place neatly, almost as if it didn't know how to misbehave. Almost. That one wavy lock in the front refused to lie straight.

"Yes, Rosie, I'm aware it's a teacher development day and that you don't have classes." He sighed and turned away from them as he continued to chat more quietly. "No, now is not a good time for you to meet Maida. Get your cat food and head straight home. Just lock up and let me know once you get there." His voice softened. "Love you, Ro."

Arthur rotated the watch and turned back to their party of five. "I'm sorry, my daughter is actually on her way to Primrose as well. Her cat has a penchant for the magical kibble that they only sell at the shop here."

"I saw that beast at your place." Will shook his head at Arthur. "It looked ferocious. If it wants magical kibble, you'd best feed it magical kibble."

Arthur smirked at Will.

"That cat is fine with table scraps. I just think Rosie wants to check on the Mudpuddle. She and her friends spend a lot of time there, and they're very anxious about it."

"Shake a leg, you lot!" Granny admonished. "I have some shopping to do. I want to get to the market before the best crystals are gone. It's moonstone season." She darted ahead and ducked nimbly behind the billboard, Will trailing in her wake.

They emerged into a niche at the center of a lush green park. Weathered wooden benches flanked the path on either side of the bricked-in arch they'd just passed through. Thousands of carved signatures covered the seats. The effect was artistic. More like a tattoo than a tag.

As they made their way out of the park, Maida thought Primrose Court reminded her of many other older urban neighborhoods arranged around parks, but there were subtle differences. Although they were definitely still in Boston, and in an urban area, it was remarkably quiet here. The constant background sounds of cars, trucks, planes, people, and humming machines had fallen away. She heard birdsong and the sound of the breeze.

"Is this the right way?" she asked, staring at the path to the right of where she was standing. Her locket grew warm and buzzed even before the other members of her party could answer in the affirmative.

Peering through a screen of foliage, she caught sight of the expansive, sunlit street just outside the park's gate. As she grew closer, she could see a row of shopfronts, all on the ground floor of row houses. But this wasn't where she was headed. She was being pulled, as if by magnets or an invisible tether, towards a larger fenced-in lot on the corner. The property stood empty.

She needed to get closer.

In almost no time at all, they were all standing in front of the houseless lot surrounded by a wrought-iron fence. The front gate stood propped open.

Beautiful trees shaded the yard—maples beginning to flame and horse-chestnuts whose leaves had aged to burnished shades of brown. Maida breathed deeply. The fresh air smelled of fallen leaves, old roses, wood smoke, and coffee. It swirled in Maida's nostrils, evoking a feeling of nostalgia, though she wasn't even sure what she was feeling nostalgic for. Slowly, she spun in a circle, staring up at the canopy of leaves above. She was certain she could hear the old trees whispering to her. Were they welcoming her? Or was that just her imagination?

"My goodness me!" Dr. Dvita exclaimed as they stood in the dappled shade of the yard. "How large the lot looks without the house on it, and how narrow the street has grown! Even the trees aren't as tall as they should be."

The trees looked enormous to Maida. Elms, she thought. A rare sight because a blight destroyed most of the other trees in the city decades ago. A lovely hedge of rosemary planted along the perimeter of the property was another welcome sight. Until she noticed a singed section. She pointed at the small garden shed. The grass in front of it was black and charred. "What happened there?"

"I think that's the question everyone wants answered." Arthur sighed. "Do you want to go in?" His hand was resting on the gate, which Maida only saw now was 'decorated' with a "No trespassing" sign and purple police tape. The locket shuddered, which made her hesitate.

Dr. Dvita came to her rescue, patting her hand and redirecting her attention to the house across the street. He pointed proudly at the ivy covered mansion on the corner opposite.

"See that gray stone house there, Maida? That is where I grew up. We lived in the third story apartment. The old swing used to hang from that tree."

Maida pointed up to the eaves of the old home. "So that's the garret window where the squirrels used to come in for book club meetings?" she exclaimed. Her eyes brightened as she recognized the legendary structure. She remembered the ridiculous sounding tales about his childhood that the doctor used to tell her.

"The same!" Dr. Dvita shimmied as he laughed. "You forget nothing!"

"How could I forget a family of literate squirrels?" Maida felt her lips curling into a smile. She'd always assumed the doctor was telling her tall tales, of course. But just then, a big-toothed, bushy tailed rodent wearing a waistcoat dashed across the roofline and under the eaves.

Maida gasped. "The squirrels are real?"

"Of course. I'm quite creative, but I didn't make them up." Dr. Dvita blinked. He squinted at the house and frowned as his eyes pored over the property, taking in all the details. She could see him weighing and measuring the differences in his mind. "My family were boarders, mind you. We didn't own the house."

"That's quite enough reminiscing," Granny Luna scolded. "Let's leave these kids to their business, Tarquin. We'll be heading off to the market, now." Granny Luna linked her arm with the doctor's. "Shall we meet you back here in an hour or so?"

"Don't buy anything I wouldn't buy," Will called after them. "But do buy me some of the pickled lemons?"

When Granny and the doctor were out of earshot Will spoke again. "I do think Granny may have a shopping problem."

Arthur glanced at his watch. "The apothecary should be open any moment now. It's just down the street this way."

Out of habit Maida stopped at the curb, looking both ways for cars. But there were none.

"They don't allow cars here." Arthur put a hand on her arm and stepped into the street with her. "But you do have to look out for the K-bikes."

"K-bikes?" Maida asked.

"It's the modern version of a broomstick," Will supplied.

"Kinetic bikes. Environmentally friendly. They resemble Ordinary bikes, so they can be used almost anywhere without drawing too much attention. As long as the riders stay on the ground," Arthur explained.

As if on cue, a dark-haired, teenage girl in a scarlet sweater and a matching hand knit hat came flying at top speed around the corner. Her black hair was streaming out behind her and her cheeks were pink. She seemed to be in a hurry. Without even casting a glance back at them, she swung her leg over the bar and dismounted while the bike was still rolling. The bike came to a halt as soon as her feet hit the ground. She plucked a small purse out of the basket before ducking into one of the stores down the street. The sign on the sandwich board in front of the shop read Galaxy Pets.

Maida watched with interest as the bike parked itself in a rack in front of the shop.

Arthur dropped Maida's hand. His eyes narrowed, and he frowned, looking from Maida to the shop and back to her, as if he was torn about which way he wanted to go.

"Pretty girl," Maida commented.

"That was my daughter, Rosie," Arthur grumbled. "And she absolutely should have been watching where she was going. And wearing a helmet." He had a pained look on his face as he turned back to the shops. "Do you mind if we head over to the apothecary to see Lucretia now?" He eyed the two shops. "I think I probably should pop next door and speak with Rosie about her driving afterward."

TWENTY-SIX

A VISIT TO THE APOTHECARY

Deep within the heart of the forest, bullfrogs sing in perfect harmony as they serenade the moon. Fireflies blink in waves, creating mesmerizing shows. High above, migratory birds slip silently through the night sky on transcontinental journeys. Bees swarm, fish school, and ants march in perfectly timed performances.

No living being is immune to the earth's unseen natural forces. We wake and sleep, bleed and breed, live and die in a perennial dance with the moon, time, and the tides.

What is all this if not magic?

—EXCERPT FROM THE MUDPUDDLE MANUAL OF NATURAL MAGIC

The brass bells on the door to the apothecary chimed when Maida, Will, and Arthur entered. The shop was small, neat, and clean. Scrubbed pine floors met whitewashed wooden walls with wainscoting and simple shelving. The air was redolent with the aromas of camphor and clover, making the interior feel much like a doctor's office. The counter at the front was a deep peacock blue topped with a marble slab. Behind it were still more shelves. They extended to the ceiling, accessible by a rolling ladder.

Tall glass jars of herbs and powders, tiny glass vials containing tinctures, oils, and elixirs, and tins of ointments and balms filled these shelves to the brim. She wanted to open them up and sniff them all. A tester bottle with a pump lid sat on the marble counter. The hand drawn label identified it as honey and lavender hand cream. A note taped to the front read "Try Me."

"Can I help—" A middle-aged woman bustled out from the back then froze in her tracks. "It's you!" she said, staring wide-eyed at Maida, holding a hand to her mouth in a rather old-fashioned gesture. Maida wasn't sure if the woman was shocked or merely suppressing a burp.

"Good morning, Lucretia," Arthur said, coolly.

Lucretia tugged at her jacket and adjusted her skirt as she stepped towards them in brisk mincing steps. The tweedy woolen fabric of her suit looked very itchy to Maida. Her pointy high-heeled shoes also looked quite uncomfortable. Everything about her aunt looked pinched. Maida felt a stab of sympathy for her.

"I suppose you are here for the spare key. And I am duty bound to hand it over. Although I can't see what good it will do you when there's no house to use it on." Her gaze skittered across Will and Arthur before landing on Maida, sizing her up. Lucretia pressed her lips together tightly.

"I see you have her hair color and her eyes, but other than that, there's hardly any resemblance to my sister. If we had bumped into each other on the street, I wouldn't have noticed you at all. I don't sense any Lathrop magic in you whatsoever."

"Do you make your own products here?" Maida ignored the insult. She helped herself to some of the honey and lavender lotion. She traced the bee on the label with one finger, whispering the Latin name for a familiar species. "Xylocopa sonorina." The giant blue-black bees were one of her favorites.

"What's that?" Lucretia scowled.

"Nothing. I like your packaging," Maida answered.

Lucretia patted her honey colored hair. "Thank you. I make everything here and I draw the labels myself."

"I like to sketch too." Maida glanced up at her aunt. But if she was hoping for a positive reaction, or some kind of bonding over a shared trait, she was going to be waiting a long, long time.

Lucretia had turned her gaze to Arthur. She was looking at him with a certain repugnance, as if she were being forced to hold her nose. After a moment, she turned back to Maida.

"Don't get your hopes up, Maida. Even if the house reappears, it doesn't mean it will let you in. It might not take kindly to a half blood like you. If you ask me, the community might be better off without that place. I know Minerva had a soft spot for the bookstore, but it never should have been open to the public like that. Especially considering the value of the sensitive items stored in the family Archives. With all the animalistic riff-raff tromping through that place, it was only a matter of time till something untoward like this happened. Poor Minerva—" Lucretia reached into her pocket and withdrew a lacey handkerchief.

Arthur's jaw set into a hard line as he folded his arms against his chest. He exhaled slowly before speaking coolly, in a voice that was utterly devoid of emotion. "There's no reason to speak that way about your non-witch neighbors. In fact, it's quite unbecoming. Do you even hear yourself, Lucretia?"

"I do," the woman met his icy gaze with equal amounts of chill, "I'm not casting aspersions on *all* of your kind, Arthur. There are still a few good eggs out there. I'm just noting that it's probably for the best if we don't forget ourselves and get too intimately involved with one another." The shop bells tinkled again as someone dropped off a package, but Lucretia was too distracted to notice. She swatted at something flying near her face. "No good can come of indiscriminate couplings." She sneered at Maida. "Why my sister ever chose to mate with one of those creatures...He didn't even want—"

Lucretia didn't get to complete the sentence. With a shower of bells, the shop door burst open. In strode Buffalo. Taking long, purposeful strides, he marched straight up to the counter. His expression was hard, brows drawn and determined.

"I will never, ever, regret bringing my beautiful daughter into this world."

"You fancy yourself as quite the hero, don't you?" Lucretia's face was bright red now. Her feet were planted firmly in place, but the tremor in her hand betrayed the brave face she was trying to present. She couldn't look Buffalo straight in the eye. Instead, she cast about for a less formidable opponent, her dark beady eyes settling on Will with a look of disgust. "Let me guess. Next you'll be wanting me to congratulate you for rescuing this fae abomination?"

Maida eyed Lucretia, and then her father, cautiously. Buffalo's eyes were hooded, and Maida knew he was holding something of himself back. Will was staring at the wall, perhaps considering whether he should port out. She wouldn't blame him if he did. He shouldn't have to take that kind of abuse.

When Will glanced sideways at Maida's father, she was surprised to see a flood of tenderness warming Buffalo's eyes. She watched as he nodded subtly at Will, as if to say, "I've got you." Will's nod in return seemed to say, "I'm not going anywhere." The two men had come to some sort of mutual understanding. Will turned back to face Lucretia.

An awkward silence ensued.

Finally, Arthur cleared his throat and spoke in clipped tones. "Let's get this over with, Lucretia. We're here for a specific purpose. Do you have any ideas about how we might bring the Mudpuddle back? Any special incantations or rituals you can share?"

Lucretia pursed her lips tighter, and straightened to her full height, seeming to reach a decision.

"No. I've fulfilled my duty. I will not waste any more time here," she said. She spun on her pointy heel. "Good luck and good day!" she said in a voice dripping with sarcasm. Then she flung the velvet pouch over her shoulder and made a beeline for the back room.

The velvet missile flew towards Maida, landing in her hand as if drawn there by a magnet.

"Ummm..." Will was wide-eyed, pointing at Lucretia, who had suddenly stopped in her tracks. She stood frozen a few steps from the door to the back. An enormous purple black bee had affixed itself to the top of her head. It was buzzing up a storm.

"Get it off!" she hissed. "I'm allergic to bees."

Arthur reached for the lotion bottle on the counter, picking it up and examining it curiously. "Was it my imagination or was there a bee on this label just a few moments ago?"

"Hold still. I've got it." Will vaulted over the counter. He stood behind Lucretia and held out his index finger. The bee immediately crawled onto it.

"It's just a carpenter bee," he said. "They rarely sting. Although, this one does seem to have an enormous stinger. Perhaps it's a rare poisonous variety?" He held the bee up to show off its shiny barb.

Maida could see the sweat beading on Lucretia's forehead. "Take it away!" she whimpered.

Calmly, Will walked back around the counter, crossed to the front door and released it outdoors.

"How did you do that?" Lucretia whispered.

"Bees love abominations." Will smiled a tight-lipped smile. "Drawn to us like honey."

"I wasn't talking about that," Lucretia hissed. "I was talking about the purple bee. It was printed on there," she pointed at the lotion, "and then it was attacking me." Lucretia narrowed her eyes at Maida.

"You're not quite what you seem, are you, Miss Maida Westabrook? What kind of spell was that? Were you trying to kill me with my own products? And what about Minerva? Did you do something to her, too?"

"What? No! I..." Maida stammered and backed up. Surely she

hadn't conjured the bee, had she? Much as she'd taken an instant dislike to her aunt, she didn't want to kill her.

"Something similar happened at The Bunny Hole." Arthur set the lotion back on the counter. There was a large blank spot at the center of the label where the bee had been. Arthur looked from Maida to the other men.

"I, I don't know what to say. I don't seem to have any control of it. Stuff like this has just been happening ever since I found the locket." Maida's hand went back to her throat.

Lucretia's eyes bugged in shock at the sight of the silver pendant in Maida's hand. She gazed imperiously at Arthur and pointed an accusatory finger at Maida. Maida flinched. She half expected a bolt of lightning to burst out of her aunt's extended digit.

"She stole Grandmere Lathrop's locket!" Lucretia accused. "That locket has been missing for hundreds of years!"

"I found it on the beach!" Maida huffed, indignantly. "I've never been to Primrose Court before. To be quite honest, if the rest of your family is anything like you, I can see why my mother left here."

"Give it to me!" Lucretia rushed out from behind the corner to lunge at Maida.

"I will not!" Maida held up her hands, prepared to defend herself and the locket, but she needn't have bothered. The moment Lucretia's fingers reached for it, the locket retaliated, shooting a plume of silvery threads that floated in the air like jellyfish tentacles. They swayed and wrapped themselves around her aunt's fingers. Lucretia yelped and yanked her arm away. She cradled it as she whimpered at the offense.

"Now she is attacking me! Arrest her, Mr. Hart!" Lucretia sniveled.

"Even if I had the authority to make an arrest, I'd hardly arrest my own client," Arthur said.

"She's a liar and a murderer! She's been hiding her gifts. And you've been a party to this! Was that your plan all along?" Lucretia's voice was shrill now as she turned back to Buffalo. She pulled out a slim birch wand and held it aloft, pointed at Buffalo.

"Put down your wand, Lucretia," Arthur intoned. He didn't seem particularly worried about the threat. Maida wondered if he was being a bit cavalier. Lucretia's wand swayed like a switch. The tip was glowing an ominous shade of green.

"I think the Society would be interested in hearing more about what these creatures are up to, Mr. Hart. You are in over your head."

"Actually." Arthur pulled a notice from his pocket. The scroll floated over to Lucretia and unfurled itself in front of her. A large silvery seal glowed at the center. "I'm here on official Society business. I don't think the Director would look kindly on your interference."

"Your accusations are quite inflammatory, Lucretia. I'd hold my tongue if I were you." Buffalo squared his shoulders, glaring at the woman.

A wrinkle appeared in Lucretia's brow, but she slid the wand back into her breast pocket. Her eyes welled with frustrated tears.

"If you did anything to Minerva...so help me! You've no right to hold her as a prisoner like that. You'd better let her out of there!" Lucretia demanded.

"Surely you don't think Minerva's inside that locket?" Buffalo looked at Lucretia skeptically.

"Lucretia," Arthur questioned, "why do you think Minerva is trapped in Maida's locket?"

"Papa Lathrop made those lockets to protect our family from harm. They were a sort of insurance policy. The spells were in place—waiting to be activated at the first sign of danger. My aunt simply disappeared without a trace. She didn't even leave a note, which is very unlike her. And I don't think I should need to mention it again, but Maida had everything to gain from Minerva's disappearance. I bet if we opened it up right now, we'd see Minerva's photo. Wouldn't we, Maida?" Lucretia smugly ticked off the evidence on her fingers like an amateur investigator who's cracked the tough case that her more qualified colleagues had fumbled. "Bet you didn't count on the house disappearing too, though, did you?"

"Minerva's photo is not in the locket," Maida said quietly. "I assure you. Do you want me to show you?"

"Maida, are you sure you should do that?" her father asked. "Didn't the locket shock you before when you tried to show it to Will?"

"It did," Maida said. "But I don't think it will now."

Cautiously, she slid her hand along the side of the locket and found the clasp. This time, when she pressed the latch, the locket sprang right open with no resistance whatsoever.

"See for yourself," Maida said, holding out the locket. "There's not a person in here. Just a house."

Lucretia squinted her eyes and screwed up her face. "Is this supposed to be a joke? There's not a house there."

Maida tilted the locket back up towards herself and looked down. Lucretia was right. The place where the house had been was blank. In its place was a mirror. She was staring at her own face.

Suddenly, the door flew open again and a young woman burst in. Maida recognized Arthur's daughter, Rosie. The girl dropped her packages by the door.

"It's back, Dad! It just appeared out of nowhere!" Rosie shouted breathlessly. "Thank the goddesses! And you! You did it! You brought the Mudpuddle back!"

Then she ran to her father and flung her arms gratefully around him.

TWENTY-SEVEN

GRANDMERE'S JOURNAL

A word of caution to all pure-blooded witches and wizards: Once committed to parchment, secrets are no longer truly your own. To record private thoughts, spells, or family lore is to invite prying eyes—intentional or otherwise—into the sanctity of your mind and lineage. Such writings should be confined strictly to one's family grimoire, and even then, must be protected by layers of charms, hexes, and enchantments, ensuring only the worthy may access it.

Particularly perilous is the growing trend of keeping an Ordinary journal, a frivolous indulgence of lesser beings. While these lesser folk may have little to lose, a pure-blooded witch's every word carries weight. Should such writings fall into the wrong hands, even the most innocent reflections could be twisted into weapons against you.

-EXCERPT FROM THE ARCANE ELITE: UPHOLDING THE SANCTITY OF WITCH BLOODLINES

Minerva managed to swipe some biscuit bits from the coffee shop, but the cheese fridge had bested her. It was almost torture, seeing the Gruyere through the glass and being unable to reach it. The door was just too heavy. She even tried to summon her broom again, in the hopes that it could act as a lever. But she only heard the distant clatter of the enchanted object falling over. Try as she might, she could not get her faithful ride to do her bidding.

Still, this was progress. She'd gotten the thing to move.

At first when she returned to the fireplace she wondered how she was going to get back up the precipitous slide. But upon inspection, Minerva discovered that the opposite column contained a spiral staircase beneath its twisted barley carved design.

"You might have led me to this one and saved me the bumps and bruises," she grumbled at the house. It seemed to chuckle back at her, lights twinkling.

After she climbed her way back up, she stopped for a nibble, settling herself on the mantel beside Papa Lathrop's clock. She pulled out the small journal that she'd swiped in passing from the library. The once violet ink was faded to a claret color, too old to even leave a trace scent. The writing was in French, a fine loopy script that was still perfectly legible. Fortunately for Minerva, French was one of the nine languages she was well studied in.

She'd suspected whose journal it was, and these suspicions were confirmed upon reading the very first entry. Grandmere.

My name is Flora Lathrop and I am 24 years old, in human years. I am writing this entry from the deck of my ship. The year is 1685 and my husband and I have set sail for the colonies. I know not what lies ahead, all I know is that it is not safe for our kind to remain in France any longer. From the Affair of the Poisons to the Dancing Plagues, our kind are in constant fear of discovery. If discovered there would be no question as to our fate. We are in the gravest danger.

For my beloved and I the risk is even greater, as neither of us can rely on the shelter and protection of our native communities any longer.

Lionel and I first met at the court in Versailles. In such a place, infested with intrigue and charged with the magic of many charlatans, it was necessary for those with real magic to avoid too much scrutiny. We both stuck to the shadows, hiding our true selves.

Happenstance placed us both in the palace library on the fated day we met. Has it really been three years hence? It didn't take long for us to form an allegiance. We immediately recognized each other for what we were.

For whatever reasons, thank the stars, neither of us have carried the burden of past prejudices forward into our hearts and minds. It was simply wonderful to find a friend in this potentially hostile territory.

How many times has our alliance served us? I do not think either of us would be alive to tell our tale had we not met. My magic gives me unique access to Les Ordinaires, including those at the highest levels of court. Lionel's gifts have also come in handy. His talent for magical contrivances is unparalleled, allowing him to rise in the ranks of courtly craftsmen quickly.

To be sure, he could have taken almost any young witch in Paris as a wife. In fact, his family thrust many options upon him. But it was too late. We were already in love. The heart, once decided, pays no attention to the outdated rules of society. And so, neither have we. We do not feel, nor accept, that such rules should apply to us.

Yet there was no way that his family, or mine if they were still alive, would have accepted such a forbidden union. We had no choice but to—

Here the writing trailed off, as though the author had been

interrupted mid thought. Minerva took a bite of her biscuit and considered the entry. Papa Lathrop was a legendary figure in her family lore, but his first wife, Flora, was less well known. Quiet and bookish, she had started the library within the Mudpuddle that had grown into the bookstore and Archives that still existed today. But beyond this, Minerva knew very little about her third great grandmother.

Minerva turned the minuscule book over in her paws and flipped through the pages. There were small sketches scattered throughout. Flowers, landscapes and more than one sketch of Papa Lathrop. The next entry had him standing at the rails of the ship.

Lionel is much more himself since we have arrived. The sickness we'd hoped was only due to the passage has proven as much. He continues to gain strength daily. With the money we accumulated at court, we have been able to purchase a sizable plot of land, hidden inside the small British village of Charlestown. Leo hopes to build a house there, and we both agree that a library will be its central feature. The house will be large, and Lionel promises me that there will be space for both of our families to seek refuge there, should the need arise. In time we hope they will come to accept our union.

But I fear his family would never knowingly wish to dwell where my kind lives and the opposite is also quite true.

Her 'kind'? Minerva wasn't sure what Flora could have meant by that. Perhaps they were from rival wizarding families?

Minerva flipped towards the middle of the journal. Flora appeared to have abandoned writing for several years, as the entries grew farther apart, and increasingly more mundane in nature. Her ancestor wrote about shopping trips and the scarcity of certain goods.

She drew dozens of illustrations of flowers, small delicate bouquets tied with bows. Some of the entries were tearstained. Minerva didn't have to wonder what had happened those years.

She could easily guess. A row of tiny gravestones in the family cemetery documented Flora's sad story, in a different way.

Were these the flowers that she'd laid on the graves of her still-born children? She traced a finger over the inscription beneath one bouquet. Posey. There was a stone with that name in the plot. She felt quite certain the years would correspond.

Finally in 1690 the entries began to take form again. Flora wrote about the troubles in Salem and her fears for herself, Lionel and their children.

We did not come all this way to continue on in so much danger," Flora had penned in her signature plum colored ink. "But Lionel thinks he has a solution. He has purchased more land, and invited other magical folk to take refuge. Primrose Court, for that is what we have decided to call it, will always be a haven for magic and those who would otherwise be persecuted for their inheritance of the trait.

There was a drawing of a basket of yarn at the end of the entry. It looked surprisingly like the one Minerva had fallen asleep in, back in the Mudroom. And coincidentally, there was a tiny mouse sleeping in the basket in the drawing as well.

Minerva yawned and stretched. Now that her belly was full, she was already tired again. She closed the diary and gathered up her bundle of biscuit bits and pieces. She stared sadly at the cafe, thinking it could really use a good dusting. She missed the smell of baking and, handy as it was, she might have traded her tail for a good cup of tea.

But there was nothing she could do about any of that right now. She needed to bide her time, continue to do research, and rest. Rest was not a thing that came naturally to Minerva. Sleeping past daybreak, and taking a nap were two things that were literally unheard of in her world. Yet here she was, plotting her path back to one of the mouse sized apartments. Surely there were beds in them —and it was barely noon.

Suddenly the clock chimed and Minerva jumped. The book

fell out of her hands, opening to another page with a drawing of a mouse in it.

The entry read:

Auntie Estelle on the day she came to visit us in Primrose. We have opened the home to my family at last. Lionel has contrived a way to bring the court to them, within the walls of the Mudpuddle. At long last we shall be one happy family again. If only his family were a bit more open minded about our union. Perhaps when Mirabelle is a bit older. They cannot help but find her charming. She is so like her father. In fact her likeness to me has lessened with each passing month. Perhaps this is for the best. She is an easy baby. In many ways she is like my second child.

The first of course, being this magical house.

Minerva slammed the book shut.

"Mother of all moonbeam madness!" Minerva cried out. "Was my great, great, great grandmother a mouse shifter?"

The lights flickered all around her, as if in answer to the question. Then the mantel shook somewhat violently. Minerva heard the distinct clatter of books falling from the shelves and hitting the carpet in the reading rooms next door. Was she experiencing an earthquake? She clung to the pine cone finial she'd been leaning against, hopeful she'd be able to ride whatever it was out.

The thought of Zephyr flew through her mind once more.

Oh, Zephyr! What would he have thought of her now? As broad minded as he was, she still worried that he wouldn't have wanted her if he'd known the truth about the Lathrops. Nobody would have.

Ever since Mirabelle and her younger half-brothers grew this community into what it is today, it has been an unspoken agreement that in times of trouble, it was acceptable for magical folk to band together and act as allies, and even possibly fraternize. But it should never go beyond that.

Mating between species was a dangerous and terrible idea.

She thought of the row of tiny gravestones again. There was a larger stone beside them, decorated with a wreath of flowers. Flora had only lived to the age of thirty-five.

Minerva squeezed her eyes shut tight as the house shook again, swaying from side to side like a ship backing into its berth.

Then, with one last jolt and a short shudder, the shaking of the house ceased. All was eerily still. Everything felt solid again.

Minerva opened one eye to peek at the damage.

Much to her surprise, daylight was pouring through the windows. She could hear the birds chirping outside.

"Well, well, well!" she squeaked. Her mouse voice was starting to sound more familiar to her own ears. "You decided it was time to go home. What a good girl! But whatever changed your mind?"

She patted and stroked the pine cone finial as if she was coddling a pet.

The house did not reply, and the flickering lights in the walls were no longer visible either. For a moment Minerva was sad. The house hadn't been such terrible company for the past few days.

"Nevermind, I'm sure you'll tell me when you can." Minerva sighed. "In the meantime, I have a lot of work to do, don't I?"

She was still tired. Perhaps even more so when she considered her predicament. Even though the house was back where it belonged, how would she ever be able to communicate what had happened? Who would listen to a mouse?

Partly from relief, partly from a food coma, and partly as the result of all her exertions, the exhaustion was overwhelming her now. She needed to lie down for a bit. The important thing was, her home was home.

When she woke, she would make a new plan.

TWENTY-EIGHT

SETTLING IN

Straddling the realm between science and magic, we find the phenomenon colloquially called "The calm before the storm." It is more than a meteorological event.

The calm before the storm is a breath held in anticipation.

If you listen to the silence, you will hear whispers, wingbeats, and the quiet stirrings of creatures who are better suited to sense these shifts.

–EXCERPT FROM THE MUDPUDDLE MANUAL OF NATURAL MAGIC

Maida stood in the Mudpuddle, taking stock of her handiwork. She appreciated the design of the shop, but was also determined to put her own stamp on the house she had inherited.

The heart of the bookshop was a large open area that had been fashioned by combining the home's original parlor and drawing rooms. Floor-to-ceiling wooden bookcases lined the entire room. Wooden ladders attached to brass rails allowed access to the highest shelves. Deep drawers beneath the shelves held additional copies of books, assorted supplies, and seasonal display items.

The area was divided into three distinct zones. These were a sort of command-central station for the bookstore, a small cafe, and a reading nook, tucked in the turret off to one side.

A sturdy, horseshoe-shaped wooden countertop formed an island on the side closest to the entrance foyer. Maida guessed this was the area where her great aunt Minerva had stationed herself to greet customers, answer questions, and ring up sales. A large ancient cash register with shiny brass keys held pride of place atop the countertop. The contraption sprang to life as Maida touched it. Humming, clacking, and whirring, the keys depressed themselves rapidly and rhythmically, producing a tune. Suddenly, the cash drawer flew open. There was a note inside, printed on receipt paper. Maida unfolded and read it.

Welcome Maida. You're going to do just fine.

She smiled and tucked the paper into her apron pocket.

The other half of the large space housed the cafe. Maida couldn't wait to see the bakery case full of staples like blueberry muffins and croissants. Tall glass canisters full of roast coffee beans flanked the brass espresso and cappuccino machines. A marble-topped coffee bar awaited frothy drinks. There was even a small cheese refrigerator, with a collection of gourmet cheeses behind the counter. And there were a generous number of seats. A collection of mismatched, upholstered armchairs and quilt covered wing chairs cozied up to small painted tables. She was delighted to see the tabletops were decorated with assorted game boards. She could see why Rosie and her friends enjoyed getting together here for game night.

There was more seating and a larger circular table in the round reading nook, which she guessed was a coveted spot to gather. The large windows offered a great view of the front yard and the street beyond.

Everything about the Mudpuddle was cozy, comfortable and well loved, but still in perfect working order. She could not fault Minerva for her upkeep of the place. Nothing appeared to be broken or run-down. It was nearly perfect. Just the sort of place Maida could picture spending an afternoon curled up with one of her favorite novels and a steaming cup of cocoa.

Maida didn't want to change much about the Mudpuddle. But there were some small changes that she couldn't resist implementing.

For example, she'd rearranged the books displayed in the main area when she discovered that the shelves closest to the register were packed with highly technical and obscure-sounding tomes. She suspected that the average customer was not looking for *Chloromancy: The Arcane Mechanics of Photosynthetic Power*. Nor was *The Ley line Nexus: Mapping and Manipulating Earth's Energetic Vascular System* topping any charts—though she did set the second title aside to show Will. Instead, she thought she would prioritize some impulse items and feel-good titles. She hoped those in search of headier stuff would have the patience to search the stacks. It was her wish that customers would stick around long enough to explore the other rooms full of books. And of course everyone was welcome to enjoy the free lending library on the wraparound porch.

Maida could get lost exploring the eight smaller rooms towards the back of the house. These rooms contained books on just about every subject under the sun. There was a room dedicated to fiction, folklore, and fairy tales. Another held books with recipes, spells, and instructions for crafting magical feasts. Then there were the rooms full of books on botany, animal husbandry, travel, and all kinds of crafts and a formal reading room dedicated to magical naturalism and the history of magical folk. Even the bathroom walls were papered with the pages of books, enchanted to reflect the reader's preferences, according to Arthur's daughter Rosie. One could not choose their bathroom reading, the house simply delivered it to them.

"It takes some time for the house to get to know you, but you'll find the selections get better each time you visit the privy," Rosie promised. She'd also warned Maida that many people liked to keep their bathroom reading private, so it was impolite to ask anyone about it.

Maida picked out a selection of tarot decks, crystal divination books, and palmistry guides and placed them on the two shelves nearest to the register. On a whim, she cleared a third shelf, which she filled with her own favorite romantic and fantasy novels.

One other small change Maida instituted was to set up a wrapping station, inspired by one of her favorite book shops in California. She loved how they wrapped the books in colorful tissue paper and cellophane, added confetti, and tied it with ribbons. It made every purchase feel like a special gift.

This was precisely how Maida wanted the patrons at the Mudpuddle to feel when they shopped in her bookshop.

Maida put the books she'd pulled on a cart to return them to their shelves. In the reading room, she ran a finger against the spines of the beautiful leather-bound gilt embossed titles. Surely there was a book in this collection that would help her understand and master her own gifts.

So far, her attempts to recreate the type of incidents that had happened at the apothecary and the donut shop had yielded no results. She'd felt silly doodling butterflies in her sketchbook and willing them to flutter from the page. She'd felt even more foolish when nothing happened. One time, she'd tried clutching the locket in one hand as she drew with the other. Again, nothing. Maida still couldn't figure out what to think or do in order to make the magic happen. She searched and searched through the stacks but none of the books in the shop seemed to have the answers.

Feeling frustrated as she was, she wasn't particularly in the mood to chat with Zani, but she ran back to the heart of the bookshop to answer the heavy old phone as soon as she heard it ring once, then twice.

"I don't understand it," she complained. "I may actually be Ordinary after all."

"I think you're trying too hard," Zani said. "You're sabotaging yourself. You have to just let the magic flow."

"Easy for you to say," Maida complained. "You were probably born with a magical machete in your hand and the inborn ability to vanquish demons with a subtle twitch of your nose."

"If only." Zani laughed. "It took me years to master my demon vanquishing twitch. It comes in handy at Ordinary bars occasionally."

"The thing is, you had somebody to train you and guide you and teach you about your magic," Maida said. "I don't know how I'm supposed to do this alone."

"I had help for sure," Zani acknowledged. "But try to imagine a coven full of opinionated witches each with a different plan and agenda for me arguing over the right way to do everything. I couldn't even get dressed in the morning without six of my aunties telling me my outfit was wrong."

"Is that why you attended an Ordinary school for college?" Maida asked.

"Oh yeah. The aunties were not thrilled with that decision. But I needed to spend some time on my own and get away from all of those voices before they took up permanent residency in my head. I isolated myself from the magical world to prioritize my own true passions."

"That must have been hard for you," Maida commiserated. She'd always envied Zani's freedom—nobody tying her down or telling her what to do. She could see now that she'd been very mistaken.

"It was actually a lot easier than living at home. I had a fantastic roommate."

"I miss those days sometimes."

"Has the solicitor moved in with you yet?" Zani was not doing a very good job of disguising her curiosity about Arthur Hart. "I've heard he's quite handsome?"

"He's just doing his job. There are still some issues with the paperwork because of my aunt being missing. Plus, my father doesn't want me to live here alone," Maida explained. "He thinks it's not safe."

"Well, I agree with that," Zani said. "I imagine it would be nice to have some company. When is he coming?"

"Arthur and his daughter Rosie are actually moving in today," Maida said. "I'm so grateful for their help."

"How old is his daughter? Sixteen? Lucky kid!" Zani exclaimed. "I don't think you understand how special the Mudpuddle is. I would have given anything to live there at her age. What an adventure for her!"

Maida pictured Zani sitting in her hotel room at some quaint inn perched on the edge of a cliff in the most remote village, located in the middle of nowhere. She'd only been half-joking about the machete. At the very least, Zani was probably sleeping with a dagger under her pillow and a can of mace in her pocket.

"So tell me more about this mysterious mission," Maida asked. "And don't leave out the details you'd normally gloss over. I want the whole story, now."

"Well, currently I'm working on recovering Catherine de' Medici's bloodstone amulet. I've been tracking the vampires who stole it for weeks. I'm super close now. I'll probably be infiltrating their nest next week, actually. Don't freak out if you don't hear from me for a few days. Mmph...that's an exquisite piece of chocolate." Zani paused for a moment, taking a bite of something. She then washed it down with what Maida imagined was hot tea with a shot of spicy brandy—Zani's signature evening drink. "By the way, I found some really gorgeous local pottery here. Do you want me to pick up some mugs for the bookshop?"

"That would be lovely," Maida said. "But more importantly, vampires?! For real? Are you sure there isn't anyone else who could infiltrate the vampire nest and collect the amulet for you?"

"I'm afraid not." Zani sighed. "That's why I'm paid so well to do what I do. Don't fret Maida. I've been at this for years."

"Perhaps I was better off not knowing..." Maida twirled the long phone cord around her wrist, stretching and unstretching the coils as she considered this. "What do people want these things for? Is there much of a resale market for stolen magical objects?"

She imagined there would be, but it was hard to picture who was doing the buying and selling.

"Of course!" Zani said. "I mostly work with museums sanctioned by the Society, but there are collectors all over the world who will pay top dollar for mystical artifacts. It's always been a weird market. But lately it's gotten weirder. Items are getting harder and harder to come by. I can't figure it out."

The light shifted and a ray of sunshine streamed through the stained-glass windows, painting a rainbow of colors across the floor. Maida stood and leaned forward to check the clock on the mantel in the foyer. It was nearly ten a.m. and Arthur and Rosie would arrive soon.

"I've got to go in a minute," Zani said. "I'm having cocktails with a local madame who wants to introduce me to her 'influential gentleman friends.'" Maida could hear the air quotes in Zani's voice. "And by that I mean I think she's planning to put me on the menu."

"No! Zani!" Maida gasped. She had always suspected her friend's job was far more dangerous than she let on but having her suspicions confirmed in such lurid detail was still shocking.

"Don't worry, I've been dealing with opportunists like her since I was a toddler. I just have to show her she'd be better off serving the vampires to me than vice versa. Easy-peasy."

"Please stay in touch?" Maida begged. "I'm totally confident in your skills, but I will still worry about you. Much more so now that I know what you're really up to."

"You know, that's kind of sweet," Zani admitted. "It's nice to have somebody who worries about you. And likewise. I have complete faith in you. But keep me posted. Especially about Arthur Hart."

Through the window, Maida could make out the father and

daughter pair walking towards the Mudpuddle. Arthur was dragging two suitcases behind him and Rosie was carrying something in a large case.

"Love you, Zani, talk to you soon. Be safe!" Maida said before hanging up the call. Then she went out to the porch to greet her company.

TWENTY-NINE

A FRESH START

Whether you are attending a dinner party in human form or staying at a friend's home during a particularly transformative full moon, arriving with a thoughtful gift shows your appreciation for the host's efforts and generosity.

A gift need not be extravagant, but it should reflect the tastes of your host and the spirit of the occasion. In some cases, a small token—perhaps a rare herb for an herbalist or a handcrafted trinket—can speak volumes. The gesture itself fosters goodwill, strengthens bonds, and, most importantly, reflects the refined manners of a true gentleman, who understands that a well-chosen gift is the hallmark of gracious living in any form.

–EXCERPT FROM THE METAMORPHIC MAN: A GENTLEMAN SHAPESHIFTER'S GUIDE TO CULTURED CONDUCT

"I can't believe I'm going to get to live in the Mudpuddle!" Rosie squealed. She was walking beside Arthur, rolling a colorful, sticker-covered suitcase with one hand, and carrying an oversized cat carrier in the other arm. Sitting regally inside the carrier was a large ball of white fluff. One eye was bright yellow and the other blue. Gemini observed Primrose Passage calmly and dispassionately through the clear window, like a princess being carried home in her litter.

Weren't cats supposed to hate being confined and carted about, Arthur wondered?

"How soon do you think I can transfer to the school here? Wait till I tell my friends! I'm going to join some clubs. How am I ever going to choose? I'd love to learn more about mythological beasts and be part of the folklore squad," Rosie chattered on. "But I love the idea of developing new and interesting potions and I'm pretty good at baking." She frowned, considering the difficult choices ahead.

Although it felt like more time had passed, it was only three days since the house had reappeared. The plan for Arthur and Rosie to stay with Maida at the Mudpuddle for a few months had come together quickly. Admittedly, Arthur had some trepidations about any of them attempting to live there. What if the bookshop disappeared again?

Amrita had minimized these concerns. "It's extremely unlikely to happen again now that Maida is assuming guardianship of the property. The house went to great lengths to find her, and obviously felt safe enough to reappear," she'd argued.

He maneuvered his suitcase around a pothole and turned back towards his daughter, considering her for a moment and wondering, yet again, if she'd experienced a full shift yet. For years now, there had been glimmers, but nothing decisive. He had no idea whether she would favor his side or her mother's. She wouldn't talk about it with him, but he wished she would.

"You know this is only temporary, Ro. I'm just helping Ms. Westabrook get settled. It might only be a few weeks. A few months at best. Just as long as there's still an ongoing investigation at the Mudpuddle, and there are still legal issues. Are you really sure it's wise to switch schools for such a short time?"

He already knew the answer that Rosie would give, so when he turned his head, the same look of utter disdain from both his daughter and her cat greeted him. It was as if they were both summoning all their patience not to snap at him.

"You know it's always been my dream since I was little to live in Primrose Court. All my friends are here. For once, I could just be normal and be myself. Don't you want that for me?" Rosie's eyes narrowed. "Perhaps," she swallowed, and lifted her chin, "she'll let us stay longer. I can help with the investigation. I'll make myself useful."

It was the slight wobble to her chin that did Arthur in. He knew how much this move meant to her, perhaps more than anyone. He'd longed to live in the magical community for his entire childhood, even after he'd been sent halfway around the world. Perhaps it had been a mistake to hire Pearl to babysit Rosie when his daughter had been so young and impressionable. All of her first friends, and many of her memories, had been made here.

Bardo Chan still lived here.

"We'll see," he said. "You know I want what's best for you."

"Well, it's certainly safer in Primrose." Rosie pointed out as she picked her way through the passage. Arthur was amused to see she was barely looking where she was going, muscle memory guiding her past jutting curbs, and uneven stones. He could navigate that passage with his eyes closed as well.

Rosie had a point. She was a tough kid, streetwise and capable of protecting herself. She'd had to be. Arthur and Rosie hadn't ever lived in the best neighborhoods. He'd wanted to be close to clients, and his clients lived in rough areas. The crime rate in Primrose was negligible compared to downtown Boston.

Living in the Mudpuddle was also a dream come true for him. Who wouldn't want to dwell in the magical home that was so central to the entire community? Maybe she would feel more comfortable surrounded by peers. Comfortable enough to commit to a full public shift.

If Arthur was being completely honest with himself, as happy as he was for his daughter, he wasn't only excited by the prospect of living in Primrose Court's most famous domicile. He was also thinking about Maida. A strange mix of curiosity and protectiveness tugged at his core. He hated the thought of her living in the Mudpuddle all alone. Maida wasn't helpless, but she was in extremely unfamiliar territory. She was going to need an ally, or at the very least, an advocate. As her solicitor, he could provide a buffer between her and those that might give her a hard time. He could help her explore her burgeoning powers.

He could catch her in his arms, should she fall?

That was as far as he let his mind wander. He wasn't prepared to address the more primal feelings he was experiencing beneath his calm facade. Thank goodness he was adept at hiding his feelings. But beneath his skin, his blood was moving faster than it had in years. He was on high alert and had a heightened sense of his surroundings, unlike his usual experience when walking as a human. It was like someone had stirred the soup of his soul with a stick and all the sediment was swirling.

"It has to be you, Arthur. You and Maida have a special connection."

He couldn't forget Amrita's words. They fluttered through his mind, along with the memory of the ephemeral blue butterfly that came from Maida's signature.

Whatever the spell was, he was driven by it. Unable to resist. He didn't just desire to protect her; he ached to be by her side. Primrose Court was pulling him back as if by some sort of force. It made him impatient, inclined to rush, as if every second he delayed, a pot might boil over and snuff out the flame. He couldn't get there quick enough, and wished he had a porter.

"Slow down," Rosie complained. "Some of us aren't giants."

"I'm sorry. I just want to get there already." Arthur slowed his pace, giving Rosie a moment to catch up.

"Let me take your bag for you, Ro." He reached for the handle to the colorful suitcase that she was struggling with. Gemini blinked approvingly at him as he took it, and Rosie shifted the pet carrier to her dominant hand.

At last, Arthur stepped out into the sunshine filled park at the center of the magical community. He waited while Rosie set the cat carrier down on the bench and bent to tie the lace on her shoe that had come undone.

"Let me get it." Arthur kneeled to tie her shoelaces, making a double knot like he had a thousand times when she was a little girl. On the bench beside him, Gemini basked in the sunlight bathing her carrier and purred. "I think she approves of this place." He smiled as he straightened, glancing back down at the cat.

His heart nearly skipped a beat when he spied something next to Gemini's carrier. He ran a finger over the familiar, clumsily carved signature. *Arthur S. Hart.* He couldn't believe the letters were still here. He'd scratched them on the bench as a child when he'd been coming to school here. But they'd faded as soon as he moved away. These benches held space for the tagging of current residents only. An odd sort of local privilege.

"I guess I don't see the harm in your transferring schools." Arthur exhaled slowly. "As long as you understand, it might only be for a few months."

"Of course." Rosie nodded excitedly. "And I can help with the shop. I mean it. I'd really love to do some baking. I have a few ideas for things that might be a hit." She considered something. "You know, Bardo says they have excellent culinary arts classes at the Academy. If you can even get into that conservatory. That one's super competitive. It's mostly witches. And I'm no witch but my dragon fruit, poppy seed muffins are practically addictive."

"Did Bardo say that too?" Arthur's brows drew together.

"Maybe addictive wasn't the right word." Rosie rolled her eyes and picked up the cat's carrier. "But yes, Bardo also thinks my muffins are delicious. He certainly tried enough of them while I was perfecting the recipe. Ah Ma Pearl was the one who first suggested the crystalized ginger in the streusel, remember? I don't know why you're always picking on Bardo. What do you have against him?" Her tone had taken on a sharp snap, and her pace was a great deal faster. Now he was the one stepping more quickly to catch up.

Even Bardo's own grandmother thought he was trouble.

It was a good thing, Arthur thought, that he wasn't currently using a T-watch to communicate with his daughter. This wasn't the time or place to pick a fight.

"Your muffins are very yummy, indeed. The ginger was the perfect touch," he said amiably.

He carried the suitcases up the short stone flight of stairs and stopped again at the bubbling fountain. Pausing for a moment, he reached into his breast pocket and pulled out two coins. He handed one of them to Rosie, before proceeding to toss a coin over his left shoulder with a bit of a flourish. It wasn't like him to indulge in common superstitions, but he thought he might make an exception today.

Rosie clasped her chest dramatically with her free hand. "Oh my gods, Daddy! Did you just make a *wish*?"

Arthur couldn't recall the last time Rosie had called him Daddy. Just Dad. Or Arthur. Lately she'd taken to testing his patience by addressing him with his given name.

"I'd love to be able to afford something here, so you could go to school with your friends and see them more," Arthur admitted. "But maybe not that Bardo Chan."

Rosie's expression darkened again. "You're as bad as some of the stuck-up witches. He's not who you think he is. He's had a tough home life, and he's misunderstood. I would think you of all folk would be more sympathetic!" She took off down the path ahead of Arthur before he could respond. So much for calling him Daddy again. The ray of sun had disappeared back behind the clouds.

Arthur didn't wholly disagree with Rosie. It wasn't Bardo's fault his parents had been criminals who abandoned him to be raised by an elderly grandmother. Part of what drove him to ask Pearl to watch Rosie was that he'd recognized how great their need was. He'd wanted to help, and he'd tried. He'd done as much as he could. But it was different when the kids were small.

As a public defender, Arthur had seen a thousand Bardo Chans get carried away by the undertow of crime, succumbing to dark magic. It was tricky. He wanted to help, but he also didn't want his daughter getting sucked in.

"I swear you're going as fast as you go on that blasted K-bike," Arthur complained. Normally, it would be no effort to keep up with his daughter, but she really was racing. Plus he was carrying two heavily laden suitcases tucked under his arms now, rather than hassling with the ways the wheels kept catching in the cobblestones.

"Speaking of which, when can I have my bike back?" Rosie asked.

"Next week," Arthur said. "And you'll need to promise me you won't forget your helmet again."

Rosie made a sort of "hmmmph!" sound that Arthur thought didn't sound all that promising.

"Almost there, Gemmy!" Rosie was talking to her cat. "See those shops through the trees? It's at the end of that block. That big house on the corner with the porch that looks like the helm of a pirate ship?" She stuck a finger into the cage to touch her cat's nose. "We're going to have so much fun and make so many new friends there! Even if it's only temporary and Dad's being such a doom druid about it."

Arthur heard the wistful tone in Rosie's voice and cringed. He could empathize with how she felt. Always an outsider. There weren't any other kids with magical heritage in the Ordinary high school she was attending. She had friends, but none that she'd stay in touch with once she graduated. All of her true friends were here in Primrose. He considered the fact, yet again, that in just two short years, his daughter would likely be gone from his daily life. His influence on her was waning daily. The least he could do was make the most of the time they had left together.

"I'll put out the word and seriously start looking for a place here, Ro," Arthur said. "It will probably be smaller than our apartment." That part was going to be a problem for him more than her. He was already using their dining room table as his office. But if he could find anything in Primrose Court, he would make it work, at least for the next couple of years.

"I thought you said it's hard to get a place in Primrose?" Rosie eyed him with suspicion. Now that he was finally giving in, her eyes were guarded. That was on him. He'd only just told her not to get her hopes up, hadn't he?

Arthur set one of the cases down on the sidewalk as they exited the park. He ran a hand through his hair. "Things tend to turn up and get snatched up quickly, but it's easier if you're already living here," he assured her. "I'm sure we can figure something out if it's that important to you."

"Sure." Rosie shrugged, chin wobbling again. "We'll see."

Her feigned nonchalance hurt his heart. How many times had he done the same? Pretending he didn't care at all about the things that mattered the most. The apple didn't fall far from the tree. It doubled his resolve to make this happen for Rosie.

A few moments later they paused at the corner outside the gate to the Mudpuddle.

"We're home, Gemmy!" Rosie exclaimed, holding up the cat carrier for Gemini to get a better view. "Home for now, anyway." She glanced back at Arthur cautiously, amending her statement. "Isn't she beautiful?"

Gemini responded with an enthusiastic meow.

"But...Something's different," Rosie stared at the house. "The plants are all different. There's so many flowers. Everything looks more colorful. Did somebody paint?"

It was quite the transformation. The house had simply slipped into a new color scheme, like it was putting on a dress.

"The house painted itself," Arthur said. "And I think Maida has a way with plants." He thought he'd never seen the Mudpuddle look more welcoming, however a moment later when the new proprietress stepped out onto the porch, he completely revised that thought.

Maida was luminous in the morning sunshine. Her silver white hair glowed like a halo. She tucked a strand behind her ear and smiled at him, raising her hand in a shy half wave. She was wearing a simple gray knit dress and an old-fashioned apron like an artist's smock. It had large pockets in the front, and Arthur could make out a book, possibly her sketchbook, in one of them. On anyone else, this ensemble might look frumpy. But Maida somehow made it her own. There was something that was both endearing and wickedly challenging about that many buttons and ties. Like a thoughtfully wrapped present.

Maida looked down at him from the top of the stairs, snaring his eyes with her own. He wondered if she'd read his mind as she wrapped the strings of her apron back around to her front, and tied them securely at her waist. She didn't seem angry. A small smile played about her lips.

Rosie set the cat carrier down on the top step and ran to throw her arms around Maida, nearly bowling her over in one of her signature, Rosie-style hugs. Arthur so rarely got to experience those hugs these days. The last time he'd had the honor was when the Mudpuddle reappeared. He couldn't recall the time before.

"Thank you so much for letting us stay here, Maida. Thank you, thank you, thank you! I don't know how we can ever make this up to you. Whatever you need help with, I'm willing to work. I'll bake cookies, wash the floors, shelve books, whatever you need!"

"My goodness." Maida seemed a little overwhelmed by Rosie, which was not surprising. "That's quite a greeting. But I think you've got it wrong. You and your dad are doing me a favor, not the other way round."

"It's a privilege to stay here with you while you get settled." Arthur set down the suitcases on the front porch. It was the truth. Staying at the Mudpuddle was every magical child's fantasy, and he was sure more than a few adults as well. Staying there with Maida only made it more so.

"Please, stay as long as you like." Maida relaxed a bit and patted Rosie's back now. "This place is enormous."

"Thanks for letting me bring Gemmy too!" Rosie said, remembering the cat now. She lifted the carrier for Maida to see the cat. Gemini stared out at Maida with sphinx-like calm.

"What a beauty!" Maida exclaimed.

When Maida bent forward to greet her, the normally impassive cat blinked lovingly at her.

"She won't be any bother," Rosie promised. "She's very clean and I look after her."

"Yes, well, I keep thinking I'm seeing a mouse in there." Maida gestured back towards the house. "Maybe Gemini can scare it away?" She glanced up at Arthur, who had now reached the top step. He set down his luggage and as he reached for the banister, his hand grazed hers. She met his eye again. There was still something burning there, some white spark of curiosity in the gray. He wasn't imagining it, was he?

He reached into the pocket of his overcoat and pulled out a bottle of champagne with a blue bow. It was a rare vintage, dating back to the year they'd first met as children. It had been a bit extravagant, given his meager salary. He didn't know if she would notice, but he'd hoped she would.

"You know, I think I'm going to like it here, Arthur." Maida moved her hand closer to his and smiled shyly.

"Who wouldn't?" Rosie enthused.

It was then that Arthur understood that Rosie wasn't the only one in danger of getting their hopes up.

THIRTY

MISTER PLANTS

Sentimentality is an oft-overlooked aspect of shifter nature, and there's no shame in it. A true gentleman knows he need not always be stoic. Embracing vulnerability is a source of strength, fostering deeper empathy with others.

By acknowledging and sharing your feelings, you not only connect more deeply but also invite others to do the same, forging bonds that transcend both species and form.

-EXCERPT FROM THE METAMORPHIC MAN: A GENTLEMAN SHAPESHIFTER'S GUIDE TO CULTURED CONDUCT

Later that evening, Arthur and Maida sat on the broad wooden rocking chairs on the front porch, drinking steaming mugs of cocoa and nibbling at the cookies that Rosie had baked before taking off to see some of her local friends.

"She wasn't kidding!" Maida exclaimed, dunking a spicy snickerdoodle into her mug. "Rosie really is an accomplished baker. I can't believe she just whipped these up."

"She's so happy just to be here. You have no idea." Arthur

smiled. "Staying here for her—for really any magical kid—is like having the run of an entire theme park."

"My father rented out a theme park for me on one of my birthdays," Maida admitted. "It was kind of overrated. Especially with my father making a point of explaining exactly how every illusion and magical effect was achieved."

Her face was sad for an instant, and Arthur recalled the strict rules he had been forced to memorize before accompanying his father to work. And the consequences for letting that facade slip. Still, Maida had never been sent away. She'd been pampered and cosseted, kept safe from all trauma. He couldn't say the same for himself.

Arthur's teen years abroad had been rough. His education at the overpriced boarding school for shifters had been anything but easy. He had physical scars and mental ones. In shifter schools, everything was a battle for dominance. Plus, you still had to get the grades to attend university. His poor relations in Ireland never took a shine to him and resented the idea of having to buy extra holiday gifts. So Arthur spent his weekends and holidays alone, studying for exams and mastering his gifts. It was why he'd excelled in his academic career. But there was a cost. He'd been so isolated. He'd chosen differently for Rosie.

Arthur didn't want to think about that now. He rocked slowly and then turned back towards Maida, who was wrapped up in a hideous floral afghan. She held her hands to either side of the mug she was holding, as if to warm them. The night was chilly, but not so much to Arthur. He didn't get cold as easily as most folk.

"There's something I've been dying to ask you about," he admitted. "Tell me about that stuffed animal you had back at your father's house? The stag?"

"Mr. Pants?" Maida blushed. "I don't know why Granny's always making a thing about him. Apparently, I was obsessed with the toy as a kid. Refused to go anywhere without it. Everyone was terrified about the prospect of it getting lost. My father even tried to have a backup made but I spied that counterfeit right away and wasn't having any of it. Nothing but the real Mr. Pants for me!"

"Absolutely." Arthur couldn't help but release a corner of the smile he was holding back. "Anything else would be a travesty. But how did it come to be yours?"

"Actually?" Maida's brow creased, and she gazed skyward, as if extracting a missing memory from the stars. "I think it was your father who gave him to me!"

"Is that so?" Arthur raised an eyebrow.

"Yes." Maida shrugged. "I'm sorry. I can't recall the occasion. I was only four or five. I didn't know your dad well, but for some reason I really, really loved that toy. He was my favorite for years. I even brought him to college with me. Don't tease me. Every kid has one of those special toys, don't they?"

"The lucky ones do." Arthur swallowed. He had been somewhat lucky till he'd been sent away. "I did, at least for a time."

Maida studied him. "I'm having a hard time picturing you as a child, Arthur Hart. Even as a boy, when I think back on it, you seemed more like a man to me."

Arthur sighed.

"Well, I assure you, I was a boy, and a fairly sentimental one at that. I was very attached to my stuffie as well. His name was Mister *Plants*."

Arthur had actually named the toy after his own father. Back when Reggie was still a hero in his eyes.

"Mr. Plants?" Maida made a quizzical face. "That's so funny. It's so close..."

"Yes. Well, I suppose the fact that you were only four or five exonerates you," Arthur interrupted her. "I'm sure you had no idea that you were accepting stolen goods."

"Pardon?" Maida stopped rocking and sat up straight. She set down her mug on the side table. The afghan slipped off her shoulder. Arthur tugged it gently back up.

"Don't worry. I'm not going to ask for him back. I'm just glad to know he found a new home with you. I was afraid my father threw him away after I left for boarding school."

"Mr. Pants is Mister Plants?" Maida gathered the afghan back around her shoulders. She shook her head as if trying to make sense of it.

"It's okay that you changed his name." Arthur nodded. "You had primary custody at the time."

"I'm not so sure I did change it, at least not intentionally. I couldn't say my l's." Maida retrieved her mug, took a sip and set it back down. "So your father gave me *your* toy? Why?"

Arthur had been wondering the same thing. He'd suspected as much the moment he saw the toy, but he still couldn't fathom why or how Maida had come to be in possession of his childhood bed partner.

"We may never know." Arthur sighed. "But I guess in a weird way, it makes us related. I mean, we've both slept with the same guy."

Maida swatted him playfully. "Very funny."

He was only half joking, though. He felt so close to Maida, and the connection felt so natural, despite being so difficult to explain.

"I'd like to be more than your solicitor, Maida. I'd like to be your friend," he said.

Off in one of the trees, an owl screeched. Maida startled, knocking the table and spilling some of the cocoa left in her mug.

"It's okay." Arthur reached out a hand to steady her. He could feel her pulse throbbing beneath his fingertips. "You're okay."

"I'm sorry." Maida took a deep, steadying breath. "It's all so unfamiliar. This whole place. I feel like...I don't know what's safe. I don't know who or what's real anymore."

"I'm real." Arthur gave her shoulder a squeeze. "And I'm here to keep you safe. As your solicitor and as your friend. You can ask me anything."

"Thank you," she murmured, staring into the dark night beyond.

He reached out and placed a finger gently under her chin,

drawing her face back toward his. "Look at me, Maida. I'm an open book. I will not lie to you about anything."

He might, however, omit the truth about how delicious her slightly parted lips looked to him right now. It would be so easy to lean forward and kiss her in the moonlight. He could well imagine the taste of cinnamon and chocolate lingering in their mingled breath and the smell of fall leaves and distant fires.

Now it was his turn to pull away. He folded his arms across his chest and leaned back in his chair.

"Are we really safe here?" Maida asked quietly. "After what happened to my great aunt and to that wizard, Zephyr?"

"I think we are probably safer here than anywhere else," Arthur said. "But," he conceded, "I won't lie to you and say there's no danger. We don't know exactly what happened here. And that is also part of why I'm here. The Society isn't finished with their investigation."

"I have a million more questions about that," Maida admitted. "Have you met the director, Amrita Berman?"

"I have." Arthur smiled. "She's a formidable witch."

"And my godmother, apparently. She was my mother's college roommate."

"So I've been told." Arthur nodded. "She's very excited to meet you. She's coming here next week to perform a ritual to help the town council of elders decide what to do with Zephyr's remains. Honestly, I don't think she needed to be the one to come for that. She could have sent someone else. I think she wanted to see you. I'm sure you'll have many questions for her as well."

Maida considered this for a moment, and nodded. She pulled the blanket closer around herself.

"So what's the story with Zephyr? Has nobody claimed his remains? Why can't he be buried?" She cocked her head considering this. "Or cremated? I'm not sure what's customary with magical folk."

"Of course not," Arthur rocked slowly, "why would you be?" He scooted his chair closer to hers and explained the situation.

"Witch and wizard bodies usually transform to dust as their souls are released. It can happen in an instant, or sometimes it might take up to a day. But it never takes this long."

"Poor Zephyr," Maida shook her head. "Do you think his soul is in limbo?"

"Nobody knows." Arthur shrugged. "It's never happened."

"And what about Minerva?" Maida asked. "Do you think she's—"

Maida didn't get to finish the thought because at that moment Will Porter threw open the front door. He had a box of items from Maida's apartment under one arm. In his other hand, he held a scraggly succulent that was covered with enormous furry black blooms. He was holding it as far away from himself as possible.

"I grabbed the things you wanted, Mayday!" he announced. "And Addy insisted I take this weird plant of yours too. But whew...does it ever stink! Hot garbage!" He set the box and the plant down next to her and flopped into one of the empty chairs. "That neighbor of yours sure is a talker. Asked me a million questions about you. Oh, and she sent a card." Will pointed to an envelope stuck in the pot. "You should probably write back to her with your dad's address. She asked where to forward your mail."

Maida reached for the note, and Arthur shot out a hand to stop her.

"I don't think you should open that," he warned. He wasn't sure why, but he had a bad feeling.

Maida swiped the envelope away. "Addy is annoying, but she's harmless. I think it's sweet that she asked about me."

Arthur frowned. Something about that plant unsettled him.

Maida opened the envelope and drew out the card, which was decorated with flowers and a sad-looking cartoon kitten.

"I think I ought to take that plant downwind a bit," Arthur said.

"I think I should take it a lot further than that. Is there anyone you hate whose house I could drop it off at? Preferably on another continent?" Will waved a hand.

"Don't you dare!" Maida objected. She lifted the pot protectively. "It isn't the stapelia's fault it smells so awful. It's just growing pains. She'll be back to normal in a couple of weeks." She placed the pot by the front steps, talking quietly to the plant "Don't worry, we'll find a nice spot for you tomorrow."

"Hey, what did Addy's note say?" Will asked as Maida as she collected their mugs to bring them inside.

"Nothing much," Maida answered. "Just that she broke up with the guy she's been seeing and that she missed me."

THIRTY-ONE

GEMINI AND SCORPIO

Germination is a pivotal moment in a seed's journey to becoming a plant, an alchemical process where nature's precise ingredients come together. Water softens the seed, allowing a sprout to emerge, while light gently warms the earth, urging the sprout upward.

But beyond these elements, magic is the constant force. It bridges environmental gaps, sustains life in impossible conditions, and sparks growth in the most unlikely places. For those who can see, magic is omnipresent, even in the most inhospitable cracks and corners, quietly fueling life's emergence.

-EXCERPT FROM THE MUDPUDDLE MANUAL OF NATURAL MAGIC

Maida stood behind the counter trying, and likely failing, to commit the names of today's customers to memory. She doodled a puffer fish, making a note in her sketchbook to commemorate the most recent shopper.

Hildegarde Fish: enjoys books about landscaping and gardening.

She could still see the adorable middle-aged woman as she toddled her way back to the street. Ms. Fish used a plump hip to bump open the gate, since she was flipping through the pages of an oversized coffee table book as she strolled. Maida couldn't blame her for being mesmerized by the glossy images of exotic courtyards. She just hoped the woman wouldn't trip and fall.

After a busy day, she welcomed the afternoon lull. She was finally alone. Mostly, alone. Mr. Pants sat on the counter, beside the cash till, as impassive as a British Beefeater. It was silly that a stuffed animal should bring so much comfort, but he did. He'd always been her emotional support stag. Mr. Pants was soothing in a familiar way. Having him there as the shop's mascot eased some of the awkwardness of having a man, who should feel more like a stranger, living with her.

That Arthur felt so familiar to her was one of the most disconcerting things about him. She knew his smell, and the crease in his brow that appeared when he was worrying about Rosie. She knew he loved honey in his tea but routinely denied himself this small pleasure. And she knew when he was watching her. Not just watching, but affected by her. She could sense the shift in his molecules. The reaction was like fire, wild and alchemical. She felt something shifting too, even though her physical form was not made to show it.

Her cheeks flamed as her thoughts traveled down this warm passage. Glancing back at her companion on the counter, she shook her head. She was lonely, but needed to stick to the type of friendship that existed on solid ground. Not the type that dissolved into fantastical silken dreams. Her new world was fantastical enough.

And yet, this world was also familiar. As if she'd always been here. The house was still shifting slightly to accommodate her. She noticed small changes daily. Wall colors changed, and carpets appeared. These changes were subtle, like someone brushing their hair, or sliding over a bit to make room on a bench. They'd be easy to miss if you weren't paying attention. She felt as if the house had embraced her—gathering her up and providing a soft landing.

Since moving into the Mudpuddle, she had never been too hot or too cold. Whatever she was looking for seemed to appear exactly where she expected it to be. The house even smelled hospitable, sending her whiffs of coffee, books, and freshly baked cinnamon rolls. Most inexplicably, when she cracked her window at night, she could still hear her beloved Pacific Ocean waves lulling her to sleep at night. When the breeze brushed against her forehead, as gentle as a mother's touch, she drifted off, knowing she was where she was meant to be.

Even at the finest hotels, and in her own snug apartment, Maida had never felt this welcome. With all her books and favorite things from her apartment in place, the Mudpuddle felt like home.

The past week had flown by, sped along by a seemingly endless stream of introductions. New people, new places, new ideas. She, Arthur, and Rosie had a daily routine. They ate breakfast together, and then Rosie went to school while Arthur worked on his cases in the reading room. On some afternoons, like today, he had to go back to the office in Boston for a few hours, but Maida was never alone for very long. She glanced at the clock. Rosie would be home in less than an hour.

Gemini wound around Maida's feet, then took off running. Maida worried it was the mouse she kept spying out of the corner of her eye. As jarring as it was to see a mouse, she didn't wish the creature any harm, so she followed Gemini down the hall.

When she saw that whatever the cat was batting about between its paws was something silvery and papery, she relaxed.

Was it a candy wrapper, perhaps? It skittered down the hallway towards the mudroom. At least it was keeping her entertained.

Maida paused to pick up a small zodiac-inspired, catnip filled toy and stashed it in her pocket, lest someone trip on it. She'd tidy up later, after Rosie got home. She didn't want to leave the cash register unmanned. She hoped that Rosie might also come with her to deliver the basket of books she'd discovered in the mudroom. From what the doctor had told her, the squirrels might get testy if they didn't get their book club selection in a timely fashion.

By now, Maida had explored most of the property. The only exceptions were the apartment that Rosie and Arthur occupied and the Arcane Archives in the cellar. She didn't even know how she might get into the Archives. The only way into the vault was through a large metal door, decorated with a massive skull shaped ornament at the center. Maida supposed the death's head was also the doorknob, but it didn't matter, since she didn't have the key. That was something else they needed to sort out.

Arthur didn't think it was safe for Maida to go down there alone, and Zani seemed to agree. Her advice seemed hypocritical however, given that it was coming from a woman who was currently infiltrating a nest of vampires.

As it usually happened, the moment Maida thought of her friend, the telephone on the shop's countertop rang.

The sound startled the small gray mouse who'd been hiding in the crevice behind the apparatus. With a squeak and a frantic scamper the mouse sped across the counter, skidding in place on a toppled stack of promotional bookmarks momentarily before disappearing into a tiny crack in the wall.

Maida was extremely relieved that Gemini was occupied elsewhere.

The phone trilled again, somehow managing to sound even more insistent this time.

"Hello?" Maida lifted the receiver.

"Collect call from Zanfira Marinescu, do you accept the charges?" the voice on the other end was distant and echoing. She sounded far enough away for a stiff breeze to break the connection.

"Yes! Yes of course!" Maida spoke quickly and a little too loudly, thinking of the vampires. "Zani? Are you there? Are you okay?"

"Of course I'm okay. This is hardly my first vampire nest, Maida. Let me tell you, these Carpathian leeches are notoriously slow moving and yet they're so cocky, they don't even bother to ward their colonies. I swear they all have a touch of age related dementia, along with serious iron deficiencies. Those misogynistic soul suckers never see me coming."

Maida shuddered, not wanting to picture the evil entities her friend was dealing with. She definitely preferred her magic to be cozier and more delicious. Maida rubbed her thumb absent-mindedly against the rough burlap toy in her pocket, counting the knotted stitches along the edges with her index finger.

"So," Zani continued, "I got the bloodstone back, plus I've recovered some other really cool artifacts I can't wait to bring to the Archives. I can't really talk on the phone about what they are. But let's just say I've invested in a lead-lined case to keep them in. I know that Minerva Lathrop would have loved to get her hands on these. Any new clues as to her whereabouts, by the way?"

"No," Maida said. "It's baffling. Nothing new. The director is coming here later this week to help with the investigation and to decide what to do about Zephyr and the Archives."

"I'm jealous you're getting to meet the legendary Director Berman."

"Well, she is my godmother," Maida said, the word "godmother" still sounding unnatural to her as she spoke it. "I don't know why it's taken so long." Maida wasn't sure but she strongly suspected the reasons had more to do with her father than her.

"Tell me more about Arthur," Zani said.

"He's good. Very helpful," Maida said.

"Hmmmm. Good? Helpful?" Zani's tone was as canny as a raised brow. "Care to be more specific?"

"Not really." Maida squirmed and fiddled with the toy in her pocket, feeling the rough surface grow smoother and harder as her thumb rubbed and circled against it.

"Perhaps this is a conversation for next week, when I get there in person?" Zani laughed. "I know a good story when it's being suppressed." Maida heard a few clicks and some more static on the line. "Anyway, I'm coming in a week from Wed—"

When the line went dead, Maida laid the receiver on the counter. She was reluctant to hang up and acknowledge the call was over. It was always great to talk to Zani, but even more so now that there were no secrets between them. Only when the phone complained about being left off the hook did she replace the receiver to silence the beeping.

Something was poking her leg. She reached into her pocket to withdraw the cat toy. But instead of pulling out a burlap pouch stuffed with catnip, she discovered she was holding a live scorpion by its tail. Its shell was green and speckled with shiny iridescent dots. Its claws and legs flailed as it lifted its head to look at her.

"Oh, my gods!" Maida flung the scorpion away from herself.

Before the venomous creature could land anywhere, Gemini reappeared. She flew through the air, leaping at the flying scorpion and catching it in her mouth.

"No, Gemini!" Maida shrieked as the cat crashed to the floor beside her water bowl, spilling the contents.

The scorpion was no longer in the cat's mouth, but she was crouched down, holding something between her paws. What had she done? Had she done that, actually turned an inanimate object into a living one? Maida lunged forward and Gemini hissed.

"Leave it, Gem!" she implored. Gemini stared back at her, obstinately refusing to move.

"Please, Gemini." Maida was near tears. She squatted down, trying to use a pencil to get the deadly creature away from Rosie's beloved cat.

Finally, with a bored look, the cat stood up and walked to the water dish for a drink. Maida was prepared to see a mangled arthropod. But the only thing that had been sitting beneath Gemini's paw was the burlap toy. It stared up at her with empty eyes, embroidered with x's.

Gemini came back towards her purring loudly, and nudged the toy back towards her, as if to ask her to throw it again.

She was afraid to touch it. Or anything. Between this and the incident with the bee, she was beginning to wonder if she might be a danger to others.

"That's so cute! Is Gemmy playing fetch with you?" Rosie burst through the door and flung her backpack to the floor. Her cheeks were pink, and she sounded breathless, as if she'd run the entire way home from school. "What did I miss? Anyone interesting come in today? It's so hard wanting to be in two places at once, Maida! Can we take the books over to the squirrels later? You didn't go without me, did you? I hope not. Those squirrels can get nasty with Ordinaries. Not that you're uh...Ordinary...Sorry." Rosie bit her lip and twirled the end of one of her dark curls between two fingers.

For the first time since her enlightenment, Maida wished she was.

"Tell me everything that happened today. I want to know exactly who came in, what they bought—leave nothing out!" Rosie demanded.

The teenager's enthusiasm was a welcome distraction.

"How about we have a snack first." Maida gestured at the bakery case. "I'll tell you about my day, and I want to hear about yours as well. After that, if it's still slow, we can close up for a break and go deliver the books to the squirrels."

"Bardo says it's not unusual for some shifters to try out different shapes before settling. We have more agency than our parents have led us to believe. Some things are inborn, but we still can choose," Rosie was saying.

The basket of books for the squirrels was swinging from Rosie's arm as they made their way across the lawn to the house next door. Per Granny's advice, Maida was carrying a second basket, filled with bundles of nuts and wedges of cheese.

"You never want to cross a squirrel," Granny had warned. "They're terribly vengeful and gossips to boot. Luckily, the doctor put in a word for you."

"Lots of shifters like to test out different shapes," Rosie asserted. "It's totally natural. It's not a big deal."

"Mmm hmmm."

Maida loved hearing about the magical community from Rosie's perspective. She couldn't help feeling jealous of the way Arthur's daughter, Rosie, was raised with one foot in the magical community and the other in the Ordinary world.

But today she was distracted. She couldn't stop thinking about the scorpion. Perhaps she had just imagined it coming to life in her pocket—a trick of the light, or her imagination running away from her. If only she could ask Gemini the cat if she'd seen it too.

"I can't really talk about this stuff with my dad..." Rosie sighed, snapping Maida back to attention.

She studied Rosie. The young girl was so tough, and resilient. She was very pretty, with her glossy dark curls, pale skin, and fiery eyes. Maida could see Arthur's influence in her eye color. Genetics were a wondrous thing that way. But she had no idea how magical genes were expressed. Not for Rosie, and certainly not for herself.

"Why can't you talk to your dad?"

Despite Rosie's tough exterior, she still had a certain youthful vulnerability that it was impossible for Maida to miss. Rosie let out a dismissive snort and rolled her eyes, but Maida sensed this was bravado. Something was bothering the girl.

"You might not have noticed, but my dad is really uptight. He's very much into following the rules. That's probably why he became a solicitor. I think he spends too much time with the Ordinaries. Who knows when the last time he even shifted was?" Rosie scoffed. "He might have forgotten how."

Maida bristled, thinking of her own father suppressing that side of himself for decades.

"I don't think he'd ever forget something so essential," she said, knowing it was the truth. She hesitated before asking the next question. "What about your mother? Can you speak to her?"

Rosie laughed a little bitterly, and stopped in her tracks to examine Maida, a challenge in her eyes. "Very funny!"

"I'm sorry if I've overstepped," Maida apologized immediately. "My mother passed when I was a baby, so I should have considered—"

"She's not dead," Rosie interjected. "My mom's very much alive. She's just the exact opposite of my dad. Completely wild. She went full-time caribou and left for the wilderness when I was only three years old. Apparently, raising a child was too boring for her. Good luck finding her."

"Oh." Maida was at a loss for words. "I'm so sorry, Rosie. That—"

"—sucks," Rosie completed the sentence.

"Yes. Yes it does," Maida concurred.

"Anyway...I just thought since we're both learning and going through stuff, maybe we could be friends? Just promise me you'll keep this conversation strictly between us girls," Rosie said. "And you can ask me anything as well." Rosie winked. "But we might want to save the rest of this conversation for later."

They'd arrived in front of the squirrel's house, and Rosie raised her brows, jerking her head towards the front door. She held a finger in front of her lips.

"Right." Maida nodded. Their neighbors were bright-eyed, bushy-tailed and big-eared.

No sooner had they placed the baskets on the doorstep, when three oversized squirrels danced out to gather them. The male wore a velvet waistcoat, while the females were outfitted in elaborately embroidered frocks made of pastel colored silks. They looked nothing like any squirrels Maida had ever observed before, and she might have been shocked by their unusual appearance and period costume, if not for Dr. Dvita's excellent descriptions of these particular literary squirrels in the stories he'd told her throughout her childhood.

She curtsied and introduced herself. "Pleased to meet you. I'm Maida Lathrop. I understand you were expecting the books for your monthly book club meeting to arrive last week? Please accept my apologies for the delay."

"We've brought you some snacks, too." Rosie pointed at the smaller basket where the treats were bundled up in colorful squares of calico print fabric.

"Am I to believe that the Mudpuddle is here to stay put, then?" the male squirrel, who was the largest of the three, asked. He had the air of someone whose patience was being tested, as if he'd dialed a number for help, then waited far too long to speak with an agent. Without lowering his narrow snout, he glanced down at the larger basket and nudged aside the cloth covering the books. He examined the contents suspiciously. "Or are we going to make other arrangements for our club in the future?"

The plumper of the two females sniffed the air and reached out tentatively towards the treat basket, but the large male squirrel slapped her hand away. He adjusted his monocle and stared snootily at Maida. The effect was disconcerting as it made one of his eyes appear to be three times the size of the other. This plus the overbite and twitching whiskers made it very difficult to take him seriously, which she knew she must.

She could hear Rosie's sharp intake of breath but didn't dare glance over at her. It was hard enough, maintaining her composure.

"The house is mine, and I intend to stay put," she asserted, meeting the squirrel leader's eye, "so we must assume the Mudpuddle isn't going anywhere."

The squirrel nodded and removed the book, examining its cover and spine more appreciatively.

"We were hoping as much," he conceded. "But we didn't want to jump to any conclusions."

"We value your patronage." Maida nodded. "I hope you all enjoy this month's selection." It was an interesting choice. She recognized the bestselling murder mystery title, but was a bit baffled by why a true crime novel would appeal to a community of magical squirrels.

"Of course we will." The male fluffed up his tail and stood straighter. "Nothing but the *best* books for us."

"Everyone's reading it!" the smallest of the three, a female in a yellow silk dress and matching bonnet, squealed. Before the larger squirrel could stop her, she reached into the basket and snatched out a book for herself. She immediately fanned out the pages and held it up against her face to sniff it, before holding it in front of her dress. "I do think the blue cover complements my dress perfectly, don't you? I just can't wait to be seen with it!"

She paused upon seeing the recriminating eyeball in the monocle that was now directed at her. Batting her lashes, she revised her statement. "What I mean is...I can't wait to be seen reading it!"

"Wonderful, perhaps you'll lead the group discussion and grace us with your insight, my dear?" the male squirrel called her bluff.

"I errr...uh...wouldn't want to assume..." The female in the yellow dress placed the book back down and wrung her hand.

The moment stretched on awkwardly until Rosie cleared her throat. "We'd best be getting back, Maida, I have some homework I need to do."

"Right." Maida curtsied again. "So lovely to meet you all. Please let me know of any special requests, and I will order and deliver your next selection in a timely fashion."

"Of course, lovely to meet you ladies as well. Good day! Off you go then!" The officious male spoke for the group. Maida turned to go, following Rosie back towards the Mudpuddle.

"Do give our regards to Minerva if you see her around!" Behind her, the plumper female squeaked. "I hope she's feeling more herself soon."

Maida froze, confused. "Wait. What do you mean 'give your regards' to Minerva? Do you know what happened to my aunt?" She spun back around to face the odd ensemble.

But it was too late. The porch was bare. They were already gone.

THIRTY-TWO

FORGOTTEN SPELLS

The shaping of a pure-blooded witch or wizard begins in early childhood, making it essential for arcane education to start as soon as possible. A disciplined young mind is fertile soil, ready to absorb the most potent magic. Foundational spells, passed down through generations, should be instilled from the moment a child can speak.

Memorizing these core spells safeguards our legacy. A young witch or wizard, armed with these essentials, is prepared for any challenge. Let no child be left untrained, for in their mastery lies the future of our kind.

-EXCERPT FROM THE ARCANE ELITE: UPHOLDING THE SANCTITY OF WITCH BLOODLINES

Minerva was forgetting things. She couldn't recall the name of the herb in the tincture that Lucretia concocted to ease her arthritic hands. Each time she tried to recite the summoning spell to call her broom, it came out a little differently.

She needed to recall that broom spell if she was to get hold of that candy wrapper. Once she had it, she was going to deliver it to Arthur Hart. She'd overheard him telling Maida that he was working with the Director. She'd always liked the boy—so much more than his surly father. Arthur seemed quite capable.

She'd have done it days ago, if only it wasn't for that blasted cat stalking the halls. The cat, when it wasn't trying to make a meal of her, seemed quite fond of batting the balled-up bit of silvery plastic around.

Which was why she needed the broom.

She'd spent countless hours remembering and reciting for nothing. Every attempt was a failure. Minerva was exhausted. She must be emphasizing the wrong syllables, or perhaps she'd reversed the word order? One time she'd got the broom to topple over. Maida investigated the sound and stood the broom back up against the wall.

Wand or no, it was ridiculous that she couldn't even perform a simple child's spell.

And yet she wasn't as fussed as she normally would have been. The more time she spent as a mouse, the less bothered she was about the sort of things that normally would have had her apron strings in a tangle.

When her grandniece rearranged the furniture in Minerva's bedroom, it hardly bothered her at all. When Maida brought all the romance and cozy mysteries to the front of the shop, relegating the more technical tomes to the back rooms, Minerva had merely shrugged her tiny shoulders. Much to her surprise in the following days, she saw sales were picking up. People were willing to take the time to browse the stacks for a specific book they'd come in to buy. And meanwhile, they were tempted to buy additional books that they had to pass by on their way in and out.

She realized she should have done something like this long ago.

The speed with which Maida had picked up the shop's accounting and organizational systems impressed Minerva. The girl was a natural. If Minerva had suspected this was possible, that Larkspur's daughter could tend to the bookshop properly, she would have sought her niece out much sooner. She'd worked so hard, all by herself, for so long. And she hadn't needed to!

She could have taken it easy, gone out with friends. Surely she would have made some if she hadn't put all her energy into running the bookshop. She could have indulged in reading books, too, rather than just selling them.

None of that mattered anymore.

She had nothing left to look forward to. Nobody to scold for having crumbs in their beard. The shop could and would go on without her. Quite swimmingly. With Zephyr gone and the care and keeping of the Mudpuddle seen to, Minerva was no longer needed. She was an extraneous mouse. She might as well just stay disappeared and sleep all day. Minerva rather enjoyed sleeping in, she had discovered.

But the sound of that blasted crinkly wrapper plagued her. Every time she heard the cat swiping it about, she remembered the mage. He'd come close to breaking into the Archives, but he hadn't been successful. Minerva felt certain he'd be back. The least she could do was warn Maida and Arthur.

Afterwards, she could take a nice long nap.

She waited until Maida and Rosie went out on an errand, and Gemini the cat was sprawled out snoring on a sunny windowsill in the mudroom, before making another attempt at summoning her broom. Stealthily, she crept along the hidden ledge, getting as close as possible to the corner where the broom rested. She could see Gemini's whiskers twitching and the golden claws of her paw gleaming as she batted at something in her dreams.

Bristle, handle, wind, and air,
Come to me with haste and care.
Broom of magic heed my plea,
This ancient charm now wake for me!

Minerva chanted the spell, as best she could recall it, taking care to pronounce each syllable. This time, it seemed to work. For a giddy moment, hope filled her heart. The simple wooden broom levitated off the ground and hovered for a moment. The bristles ruffled and the air around the broom vibrated with magic. Minerva crouched. This was the furthest she'd come. Now she only had to get her broom level and bring it closer. She took a deep breath, readying herself to leap onto the handle.

Thistle, candle, wind, and air,
Fly to me if you dare.
Broom of magic heed my plea,
This ancient spell now weaves for me!

The broom tipped into a horizontal position. *Slowly, slowly...* Minerva exhaled the chant again, this time in a whisper, struggling to enunciate as much as her mouse voice would allow it. The air in the mudroom was crackling with electricity now. Some of the hair on Gemini's back was standing on end. The oversized cat rolled over onto its back, basking in a sunbeam.

Just a little closer...

The broom quivered, and Minerva tried harder to focus on casting the spell, ignoring the sleeping monster below.

Gemini stretched and opened one large blue eye. The eye focused on Minerva. It stared up at her brazenly, knowingly, *hungrily,* she thought. Well, good luck with that. There was no way for Gemini to reach her up near the ceiling.

Then, as the cat shifted, baring more of her belly, Minerva heard the familiar crackle. Gemini was laying on top of the wrapper.

Toadstools and fungus!

There was no way she'd be able to retrieve it from beneath the cat.

With a clash and a clatter, the broom crashed back down onto the floor. The cat hissed, but did not budge. Minerva felt hot tears coming to her eyes.

"You ignominious, idiotic feline," she ranted. "Why won't you just let me get that wrapper so I can give it to Arthur?"

Gemini blinked at her impassively and licked her paws.

"Don't you know everyone could be in danger? Including you and Rosie?" She shook her fist at the cat.

At this, the cat froze, still glaring back up at her. Minerva could swear she understood, although she herself had always found cats to be terrible listeners. Just one of the many reasons none of the Lathrops had ever bothered with a feline familiar, she thought. Cats were too narcissistic to be relied upon.

Gemini licked her chops and stared up at her. Her predatory gaze made Minerva feel tiny and vulnerable. Suddenly, Minerva intuited another, much better reason why the Lathrops might have eschewed cats.

She felt goosebumps rising.

"I'm on to you, you flea-bitten failure of a familiar! You'll have me to answer to if that awful mage gets back in here."

The cat blinked twice at her then closed her eyes and curled back up with the wrapper.

"Fine," Minerva grumbled. "I'll just have to find another way."

It would have to wait for another day, though. Minerva was sleepy now but she didn't feel like going back to the mouse apartments. She retraced her steps back to the foyer and curled up behind one of the pine cone finials on the fireplace mantel. If Gemini could sleep on a windowsill, then why couldn't she sleep on the mantel?

The smell of woodsmoke, mixed with the warmth of the lit fireplace carried her quickly off to dreamland.

"Wake up, Minnie!"

The face in front of her consisted entirely of sparks. Zephyr's breath smelled of cedar, and charred oak.

She blinked at the vision. This had to be a dream.

"Wake up!" he demanded more insistently. "I need you to go to the Archives and get something for me. You need to remember who you are."

Minerva rubbed her eyes. "Zippy? Is that you?"

"We're running out of time, Minnie, you need to go *soon.*"

She folded her arms across her chest. Sleeping or awake, there was little sense in arguing with an apparition, and yet she felt compelled. "How do you propose I do that? Can't you see I am now a mouse? That same mage who cursed you transformed me into this."

Minerva gestured at herself.

The apparition of Zephyr shook his head vehemently, sending sparks scattering so far and wide it worried her that the books might catch fire. "No, Minnie. The wizard didn't do this to you. He was using synthetic magic, remember? If he had hit you with a transformative curse, it would be wearing off by now. But if anything, it seems to have grown stronger."

Minerva cocked her head, considering this.

"You need to fetch the hand mirror I checked into the Archives after my first mission with the Society. Do you recall it, Minnie?"

Of course she remembered it, and the charming tale he told her about it. She'd still been a girl, full of hopes and dreams then. He'd dared her to look into it, but she hadn't taken the bait. Not once in over eighty years. The mirror remained locked in a glass display case at the center of the Archives. The very same case where she kept the items she was fondest of.

It was a memento of another time.

"What is it you want with that mirror?" Minerva asked the apparition. She knew it was just a dream and that it wasn't really Zephyr, but now that she was chatting with him she dearly wished it wasn't her mind playing tricks. She didn't want the dream to end. Continuing the conversation was her desire.

"You need to look into it," Zephyr said. "And then you need to come and find me."

"What do you mean, come and find you?" Minerva asked. "On the other side? What is it like there, Zippy?"

"I wouldn't know," Zephyr said. "All I know is I miss your biscuits and—"

Cling! Clang! Clingle, Tingle, Ding!

The bells on the shop door startled and woke Minerva. Maida and Rosie were back from delivering the books to the squirrels.

"Does it smell smokier than usual here?" Maida sniffed the air.

"Must have been something in the wood in the fireplace." Rosie wrinkled her nose. "There's a lot of ash on the floor. Let me fetch a broom.

"Thanks! There's one in the corner of the mudroom," Maida volunteered.

Minerva pinched herself, hard. She was definitely awake now. She could have sworn she'd just been speaking with Zephyr. But it must have been a dream.

THIRTY-THREE

DINNER PLANS

Every shifter, whether carnivore or vegetarian, should have a signature dish or two perfected for those moments when company unexpectedly arrives. Be it a hearty stew, a beautifully garnished pizza, or a simple yet elegant dessert, having a reliable go-to recipe allows you to impress guests effortlessly.

A well-prepared meal not only showcases your culinary skills but also demonstrates your readiness and hospitality, ensuring your guests feel both welcome and well-fed, regardless of the occasion—or their form.

-EXCERPT FROM THE METAMORPHIC MAN: A GENTLEMAN SHAPESHIFTER'S GUIDE TO CULTURED CONDUCT

Arthur piled a second helping of pasta onto Maida's plate, while she poured him a second glass of wine. The evening was going very well. Rosie was eating at a friend's house, and everyone else seemed to be otherwise engaged. For the first time in the week since he'd moved in, it was just him and Maida, alone, having dinner together. A single candle illuminated the table, holding them close in a warm, safe cocoon of light. They were dining in the turret reading nook. Like a blanket fort or a treehouse aerie, it was the kind of atmosphere that fostered intimacy, and the swapping of secrets. Everything and everyone else fell away into the night that surrounded them, and even the most trivial things suddenly seemed of great importance.

"Favorite flavor of ice cream?" he asked casually.

"Hazelnut," she answered. "Don't tell me you know how to make ice cream as well?" Maida twirled a long strand of fettuccine Alfredo around her fork and took an appreciative bite. "This is ridiculously delicious, Arthur. If being a solicitor ever gets old, you could always consider becoming a chef."

He enjoyed watching her eat. She did nothing to hide her glee, which made him ache to please her more. He could make a career of that.

"Sadly, I fear I'd be a terrible chef." Arthur smiled wryly. "I can't stand cooking for people I don't like. Plus, to be a chef, you have to be creative. It requires the ability to come up with something new. I'm more suited to sticking to a recipe. I'd be happy to find one for hazelnut ice cream and make it for you. Even though," and here his mouth twitched into a lopsided smile as he raised his brows in a challenge, "Marionberry is clearly the best flavor."

"Hardly!" She laughed.

Arthur liked making her laugh, too. Possibly even more than watching her eat. He only wished they had met sooner, or under different circumstances. Or maybe even not at all until they were both adults.

He wished he'd had the chance to woo her and take her out to dinner. If they'd both been Ordinary and never met as children, maybe he might have bumped into her accidentally, in Los Angeles or Boston. Surely the Fates would have made it so?

How foolish he was to speculate like this. But how could he think of anything else when she was sitting so close? Close enough to kiss, if he was willing to risk it.

The possibility hung in the air between them, like a rain laden cloud that was ready to burst. He would have to wait for it to pass. He knew better than to complicate matters. It was just a wish, and a wish it would have to remain.

He couldn't risk this.

"What are you thinking about?" Maida placed two fingers on his forehead and slid them gently across his brow as if she were ironing out a wrinkle. "You look so serious." Arthur jumped back at her touch and regretted it instantly. Wasn't this what he so desperately wanted? To touch her and be touched by her? So why was he recoiling so at the slightest gesture of intimacy?

Come on, Arthur, keep your antlers in check.

Maida was going to move on from here, or maybe he was. He'd have to move out at some point. And then Rosie was going to leave and then he was going to be alone again. This was his fate. The sooner and more completely he accepted this, the happier he would be.

"I was thinking about you," Arthur answered honestly, if not completely.

"Well then, I wish you wouldn't make a face like that." Maida sighed. "I don't want to be the one responsible for giving you wrinkles."

"I have a teenage daughter, Maida. You'll have to get in line." Arthur relaxed a little. He placed his hand over hers and gave it a squeeze. "I can't help being concerned for the people I care about." Then he changed the subject to the matter he'd meant to discuss with Maida this evening, ever since she'd told him what transpired earlier that day. "Tell me again about the scorpion? Are you sure it became real?"

Now it was Maida's turn to frown. She withdrew her hand and smoothed out her napkin. "I am as sure as one can be about that sort of thing. It's all so new to me."

"So one moment it was a cloth toy in your pocket, and the next?"

"The next moment it was alive and twisting around in my

hand." Maida looked down at her palms. "But it didn't stay that way. I threw it and the cat was there and she saw it and she pounced. But then at some point it transformed back into a toy. I can't say when. I'm just glad she didn't get hurt." Maida gestured towards the cat and shuddered at the memory. "I'm so sorry, Arthur. I still don't even know for sure if it was me? Did I make that happen?"

"I'm not sure," Arthur said. "I think it's likely, though. I've never met a manifester before." Then, noting her distress, he softened his tone. "The most skilled witches can affect physical transformations, but bringing inanimate things to life is a very rare gift."

"You call that a gift? Your daughter's cat could have been killed!" She was wringing her hands now, and berating herself. He recognized all the signs. "I don't know how I did it," Maida confessed. "I'm afraid to touch anything at this point. I don't want to hurt anyone. Or anything."

Arthur laid his hands over hers, noting how small her hands seemed in his. They were trembling.

"The onset of magic is always a little unsettling, Maida. But there are many people here to help and guide you. I'll tell you something that I've observed over the years. The practitioner's intentions power most magic. Energy flows where attention goes. If you don't have clear and definite negative intentions, it's unlikely that you'll achieve negative outcomes. That's why I'm not afraid of you, and I don't think you need to be afraid either." He gave her hands a squeeze.

Her expression softened a bit and when she slumped back in her seat, Arthur could still see the fear in her eyes, but it stopped well short of panic. Beneath that fear was pride and determination.

He pulled his hand away, busying himself with straightening the napkin on his lap.

"I'm sure Amrita will have better advice for you when she comes," Arthur said. "She's an interesting character. I think you'll like her. Have you thought more about what you want to ask her?"

"I have so many questions. Mostly about my mother. I'd like to know what she was like." Maida raised her wine glass to her lips. She paused. "And I'm interested in learning more about the Archives. If I'm to manage this whole place, I'm going to need to learn about the things that are locked down there, and how to keep those secrets safe."

At the mention of the Archives, Arthur felt a frisson of fear. The Archives contained many wondrous items. But there were also cursed items locked in the vault below the house. Evil objects powered by dark magic, cruel intentions, and hate fueled chaos.

"Being the caretaker of the Mudpuddle is one thing, taking responsibility for the Archives is another. One step at a time," Arthur said, mirroring her and lifting his glass to his lips. But the plaintive yowl of the cat at his feet had him setting the glass right back down again. "What is it, Gemini?"

The cat yowled again, and rubbed against his leg. When he reached down to pet her, she even purred. "*Now* you suddenly warm up to me?" Arthur asked. "Did Rosie forget to feed you or something?"

"Maybe she's hoping to score some of your fettuccini?" Maida said.

"Maybe?" Arthur froze as Gemini abruptly leapt onto his lap and placed her paws on the table. She leaned her head over his plate, sniffing the remains of the sauce. The cat's sudden interest in him flummoxed him. "Is that it, Gemmy?" he scratched behind her ears. "Do you find my Alfredo sauce irresistible?"

Gemini gave her head a little shake and coughed as if to extract a hairball. The coughing rapidly escalated to a gag. The ice cubes in their drinks clinked together. Gemini was shaking the whole table.

"Oh! Umm..." Maida leaned back.

Arthur froze, undecided whether to fling the cat away or hold still. But the point was moot, as a balled-up, silvery candy bar wrapper came flying out of the cat's mouth. It landed on the plate. Maida gasped.

The wrapper was stuck to the remaining sauce on the plate. Gemini rotated her head back to face Arthur and meowed again, as if to make a point. Then, with no warning, she took off again.

"What the..." Arthur's voice trailed off as he leaned forward to examine the wrapper. It appeared somehow dry, and nearly whole. He was grateful that the remnants of the cat's last meal did not accompany it. He prodded it with his fork and a butter knife, pinning the corners down to confirm his suspicions.

"What is it?" Maida asked. "Some kind of wrapper? I thought I saw her playing with a bit of trash earlier. I wasn't sure if it was another toy."

"Stars curse it, Rosie!" Anger surged through him upon recognition of the nefarious Nocturnaturals logo on the candy bar that his daughter's cat was playing with. "Nocturnaturals," he spat out. "These things are outlawed in Primrose Court."

Maida leaned forward for a better look. "Really? They're so popular in California. Everyone is either buying them or selling them, or selling them to afford buying them. Do you really think it's that bad?"

"Yes it's that bad!" Arthur threw his napkin onto the table. "These products have ruined lives. They are highly addictive, and destructive. There's an active epidemic amongst magical folk that can be directly traced to the use of Nocturnaturals edibles, patches, and oils."

"An *epidemic*?" Maida raised a skeptical brow. "This stuff isn't even classified as a drug. It's just wishful thinking in a pretty package." She waved her hand.

"I wish you were right." Arthur pushed back his seat and stood up. He couldn't sit any longer. He paced as he explained further.

"That may be the case for Ordinaries, but Nocturnaturals contain synthetic magic. And the fact that it's a mass produced, mass market item...It's everywhere. I don't know how you combat that?"

Maida stood and examined the wrapper. Her face had grown pale. She reached for her wine glass and crossed the room to where Arthur was standing. Her next words were tentative, and quiet. "You wouldn't know this, Arthur, but my mother didn't simply die in childbirth. She'd been sick for a long time. Synthetic magic is what actually killed her. It nearly killed me too."

She placed a hand on his shoulder. "I did not know that Nocturnaturals were so dangerous. I just thought it was crazy how people were going nuts over a bunch of silly patches and candy bars. I guess I should be grateful I never jumped on the bandwagon."

Arthur shook his head and paced back to the table. "This shouldn't be here. There's a ban in place. Whoever brought this to our community needs to be held accountable." His mind was racing in circles. It kept coming back to one person.

"I'm still not sure I understand how it works?" Maida said. "Maybe you can explain it better to me? What happens? Does it make magical folk feel high when they consume that stuff?"

"Initially. There's an intense feeling of euphoria, followed by a surge of power. Synthetic magic amplifies users' innate abilities and grants them temporary extra skills. It's hard to predict what those will be. Like a surprise gift!" Arthur could hear the sarcasm in his voice, and took a deep breath. His emotions were getting the best of him.

"It's addictive because the cravings set in immediately, but it also becomes less effective with repeated use. Over time, it obliterates users' natural talents, while giving them a false sense of power. It messes with their heads, impairs their judgment. Younger folks are particularly susceptible."

"That's horrible." Maida set her wine glass down on the counter. "What can we do about this?"

Arthur stared at his hands, both balled up in fists. He stared up at the ceiling, then back down at his feet on the floor. Then he exhaled and said it. He couldn't hold his fears back any longer.

"I'm afraid that a friend of Rosie's, Bardo Chan, has been using it. It's one reason I didn't want Rosie spending time with him. Now

I'm worried I might have been too late." Arthur raked a hand through his hair.

Which friend had Rosie said she was hanging out with tonight? What were they doing?

The temptation to use his T-watch to track her and bring her home immediately was strong, but he didn't want to risk sharing this with the entire community.

How had that wrapper ended in Rosie's cat's belly?

"You don't really think that wrapper is Rosie's?" Maida asked, horrified.

"It's the only logical explanation, isn't it?" Arthur said, shoving his hands into his pockets and balling them into fist.

"No." Maida stood slowly. "I'm sure there are other explanations. I don't think you should jump to conclusions. The Mudpuddle is a public place, lots of people are in and out of here."

"True," Arthur conceded. "But given the fines for possession, I cannot imagine anyone being so careless with the wrapper, especially in such a public place. And Rosie has been so secretive lately. My gods. How could I have let this happen?"

He had to fight the ripple of magic that swept over him with the powerful emotions he was feeling. The sting of an imminent shift felt like pinpricks in his pores and the walls were too close. He wished to be outdoors in a large field. Somewhere he could run and stomp and bray at the moon till exhaustion obliterated the guilt he was feeling. Right under his nose. He'd allowed his own daughter to fall prey to a petty synthetic magic pusher, right under his own nose.

"Arthur, please calm down. You don't have all the facts." Maida laid a clean, manicured hand on his shoulder. He stared at her. It looked too perfect up against his increasingly hairy arm. He could hold back the full shift, but not all the effects.

She stared down at the thick hairs sprouting beneath her fingers. He had to look away as he jerked his arm away from her hand. He couldn't bear to see the disgust he suspected must be on her face right now.

"You don't know what you're talking about, Maida. Rosie is my daughter, and this is my business!"

Maida winced. "Arthur, please. I spent a lot of time in my teens butting heads with my father. Give her a chance to explain."

"This isn't the kind of situation where you get second chances, Maida. I'm not sure you understand."

And with this statement, he stepped out into the starless night.

THIRTY-FOUR

PEARL CHAN'S COMPENDIUM OF DRAGONS

The role of biological catalysts in DNA replication is a testament to the enduring magic that binds all living things. The double helix of DNA unfurls like a cherished scroll.

DNA polymerases, the magicians of genetic code, meticulously inscribe the new strand, while helicases, the custodians of time, unravel the secrets of the past. The outcome is a mystical replication of life's ancient script.

We must not underestimate their significance, for in their seemingly ordinary forms, they wield the power to etch the signature of life itself.

-EXCERPT FROM THE MUDPUDDLE MANUAL OF NATURAL MAGIC

The following weekend, Will and Granny paid a visit to the bookshop. During a lull between customers, they gathered round a table in the cafe.

"I think the place is busier now than ever," Will said. "You must be doing something right."

"People are just curious," Maida insisted.

"That's malarkey!" Granny cooed. "You've breathed new life into this place and you ought to take credit for it. Any wizard would! The place suits you."

"Thank you, Granny." Maida sorted through a stack of beautiful handmade bookmarks she found in a drawer. "It's been hard work, but I'm enjoying it."

"You know," Granny feigned a casual disinterest as she stirred her tea, "I could be a big help around here. I've got impeccable taste and am very knowledgeable about all the folk living here in Primrose Court. Just say the word."

"By this, she means she's got the best gossip. Not that it's a bad thing." Will Porter rolled his eyes. "Might actually be good for business." He stole a snickerdoodle from Granny's plate.

"Oh. My. Fairies! This is so good! What on earth do you think Rosie's putting in these cookies?"

At the mention of her name, Rosie, who was working behind the counter in the cafe, froze. A worried look shot across her face and she scanned the cafe nervously, speaking quickly and defensively. "Nothing! There's *nothing* magical in them at all. I promise! It's just ordinary cinnamon and sugar with a pinch of cayenne!"

"Rosie is an extremely talented baker," Maida intervened. "She's a natural."

Rosie shot her a quick look of gratitude that was almost heartbreaking before returning her attention to a mythology book on the counter. Maida knew she was cramming for finals. That wasn't the reason the normally bubbly girl seemed so skittish, though.

Ever since the night that Gemini coughed up the candy wrapper, Rosie had been quiet and withdrawn. She'd barely left the house, other than to attend classes. "I may as well work more shifts," she'd said that morning, "since I'm grounded till I'm eighty."

Maida had heard nothing else from Arthur. In fact, she'd barely seen him all week, except in passing. He dedicated his time to meeting with the town council, working from his apartment, and traveling to meet clients on the Ordinary side of Boston.

"Where's Arthur?" Will asked, looking around. "I was hoping to catch up with him while I was here. I could use some advice about where to get a pint in Ireland."

"Well, I could help you with that!" Granny punched Will in the arm. "You don't need to go bothering the solicitor for that information."

"I was hoping he'd join me." Will shrugged. "Remember what happened the last time I took you to a pub, Granny?" Will looked down his nose at the spritely woman. "We don't want a repeat of that, do we?"

"How was I to know he was a selkie?" Granny held her hands up in self-defense. "He was dazzlingly handsome."

"I think that's the point," Will teased.

"Sorry, Will, I don't know where he is. I haven't seen much of him today, or yesterday for that matter," Maida apologized.

"Well, if Will won't have me, maybe you will?" Granny turned back to Maida. "You know I'm just flapping my wings over at your father's place. He's hardly ever there. It's just me and that old gargoyle, Yves. You'd be doing me a favor."

"I could definitely use some more help around here, particularly in the cafe." Maida considered the offer. She really needed help. "Rosie is doing an excellent job, but we get a big rush in here every morning and midafternoon when school lets out. Do you think you might be interested in working in the cafe? I'm not sure how much the business could pay you, but I could probably make up the difference."

"Nonsense!" Granny clucked, jumping up immediately and pulling the spare barista apron off the peg. "You don't have to pay me. I don't need money. Just let me stay here and help you out. I'm grateful for the chance to be useful again."

"Be careful," Will warned. "If you turn your back on her she might bedazzle the books."

Granny wrapped the apron strings around herself three times and tied it off in a bow. Even with the top bloused up, the garment was far too big on her and trailed to the floor. "I'm going to have to get something more appropriate made. Maybe in purple? We should have shop colors, no?"

"Sure." Rosie, who was drawing up a family tree of all the Greek gods, barely looked up to answer. Granny examined her drawing.

"Not bad," she said. "But I think Hephaestus needs more facial hair."

"Sure..." Rosie chewed the end of her pencil. She was so engrossed in her project that she did not notice the hulking figure standing by the door, waving to get her attention.

"Rosie, dear, I think there's someone here to see you," Granny said in a stage whisper that was loud enough for everyone to hear. She nudged Rosie. "Maybe you should go see what he wants."

Maida watched as Rosie looked up towards the door, wide-eyed. Suddenly, it seemed like everyone in the Mudpuddle was staring at the large, surly looking boy standing between them and the exit.

Will let out a low whistle. He leaned in to whisper in Maida's ear. "He's got some horns, coming back in here after everyone said he was responsible for Zephyr and Minerva's deaths."

"Sorry to bug you at work, Rosie." The boy's eyes seemed wild, darting here, there and everywhere. "I was hoping to borrow that book we discussed? The one my Ah Ma gave you? I need to get some of her recipes for a friend?"

"I'm working, Bardo." Rosie tapped her pencil on her drawing.

"That's okay, you can give me the book and I'll make copies and bring it back."

"I'm not giving you the book. What if something happens to it?" Rosie snapped. "That book is irreplaceable."

"Don't you think I know that?" Bardo glowered. "She was *my* Ah Ma. I just want to get what's mine."

"She gave the book to me, though," Rosie retorted. "Anyway, I don't have it on me right now. Come back next week."

"Next week's too long!" Bardo whined. His eyes were imploring. "Please, Rosie, I don't want to fight with you. Can't you just help me out?"

"Fine." She closed her textbook. "Come back tomorrow. But this is it, Bardo." She shook a finger at him. "Last time I'm helping you out."

"See you tomorrow then, Rosie!" Bardo slapped a hand on the door frame before departing. "Don't forget the book!"

That night, it was just Maida and Rosie. Arthur was working late and Granny had gone home to fetch a bag of her things. Rosie reheated some homemade chili while Maida locked up and set one of the tables in the cafe for a simple meal.

"I'm just going to close the drapes," Rosie said. "Give us some privacy. I hate feeling like I'm sitting in a fishbowl."

Maida shrugged. The shop windows didn't bother her. They were set back enough from the street and evenings were quiet, so the shop windows didn't bother her. But if it made Rosie more comfortable, she supposed there was no harm. She'd gone through an intensely private phase as a teenager, too. Maida propped her feet up on an ottoman and leaned back in her seat. She was tired after a long day of helping customers find the perfect titles.

"Please don't tell my father that Bardo stopped by the shop today?" Rosie begged Maida. She set her backpack on the floor beside the table and settled into the seat opposite Maida.

"I can't lie for you, Rosie," Maida said.

"It wouldn't be a lie. Maybe just don't mention it? Nothing happened. He just wanted to borrow this book." Rosie reached into her backpack and withdrew an unusual-looking tome. Metallic pink, fuchsia, and scarlet scales covered the exterior of the book. The page edges were gold. A blue metal clasp, inlaid with a glass dragon's eye, kept it locked shut.

Rosie stroked the cover reverently. "Ah Ma Pearl left it to me."

There was no title on the cover or the spine.

"What's the book about?" Maida asked.

Rosie looked around suspiciously, as if she thought there might be spies present. "If I tell you, you can't tell anyone."

"Rosie, you can tell me anything. I won't judge you. But I'm not sure that I'm the person you should be sharing secrets with. Wouldn't it be better to speak to your father?"

"I can't. He wouldn't listen. And he wouldn't understand," Rosie said. "Can I have your word to keep my secrets?" Rosie asked.

"I've already said I won't lie for you," Maida repeated.

Rosie folded her arms across her chest. "You don't have to lie for me. Give it another hour or two and the rumor mill will have Bardo proposing to me in the middle of the store. My dad is going to hear about his visit, whether or not you tell him. And I am going to tell him about what's in the book...eventually. I'm just not ready yet. I don't have anyone else to talk to, Maida. Please?"

Rosie's imploring eyes were her undoing.

"Fine," she said. "But please don't ask me to cover up for you and your boyfriend again."

At this, Rosie snorted. "Me and Bardo? Hardly! We've known each other since we were little kids. His grandmother watched me when I was little so my dad could work. Ah Ma Pearl said she knew what I was the moment she saw me, because she was like me. She's been gone a little over a year now." Rosie dabbed at her eyes.

Gemini jumped up onto Rosie's lap, purring like a motor. When the cat blinked her eyes at Maida, she couldn't help reaching out to scratch her head as well.

"What about the wrapper?" Maida asked, recalling the regurgitated matter that had sent Arthur into such a tailspin. "Was it yours or not?"

Rosie stared agape at Maida. "Do you think I'm an idiot? Do you know what that stuff does to people?"

"I've heard," Maida said. "Though I've never seen it firsthand. Have you?"

Rosie's features went a little too blank at the question. It was a practiced poker face, leading Maida to believe Rosie had something to hide.

"Was the wrapper Bardo's then?" she asked.

"No! I mean...." Rosie scrambled to find the right words. "I don't think so. I don't think the wrapper was his. He's not stupid enough to leave a trail like that."

Maida sat down at one of the bistro tables and sighed. "So your dad was right to be concerned, then."

"Bardo would never do anything to hurt me, Maida."

"I'd like to believe you, Rosie, but addiction can make people do uncharacteristic things." Maida chose her words carefully.

"Poor Bardo," Rosie said. "He was always the scrawniest little kid, always getting picked on. It took some time for him to grow into his form. His first few shifts were terrifying for him."

"I can only imagine," Maida said.

"Just between you and me, he's not the brightest beast in the bunch." Rosie sighed. "He's always trying to get the other guys to respect him. He makes bad choices."

"Was experimenting with Nocturnaturals part of that?" Maida asked. She was struggling to keep her voice calm and judgment free. But what she wanted to tell Rosie was probably the same exact thing her father had yelled.

Stay away from that boy!

"It's okay now. Everything's fine. He swears he's stopped," Rosie assured her.

"So if it's not your wrapper, and it's not Bardo's, then whose was it?"

"No clue. And that's not what I wanted to talk to you about." Rosie frowned and tapped her book.

"This book explains what I am," Rosie tapped a finger on the cover, "and it explains why it's a little awkward for me to talk to my father."

"What do you mean?" Maida asked. "Aren't you a shifter like your parents?"

"I am a shifter," Rosie said. "But I am *nothing* like my parents. Some of us are just born a little different from our parents."

Maida could hardly argue with this, so she simply nodded and gestured for Rosie to go on.

"Look at you." Rosie pointed at Maida. "You're half witch, half shifter, right? You probably never should have been born."

Maida winced at this, and Rosie recanted. "I don't mean it like that. What I mean is, statistically speaking, it was highly unlikely. And yet here we both are. I don't think we need to think of it like we're freaks. I think we should embrace the fact that we're extra special." Rosie spoke like she was parroting a script, but there was growing confidence in her voice as well, as if upon hearing herself speak the words out loud, she was delighted to discover she actually believed them.

With a flourish, she flipped open the book. Maida leaned forward to read the title page. The writing on the title page was childish, and somewhat faded. It read *Pearl Chan's Complete Compendium of Domestic Dragons.*

"What is this?" Maida leaned forward to touch the thin parchment paper of the book. She flipped a page and was amused to see a family portrait that included a red mama dragon, a viridian green papa dragon and a small pink baby dragon. All three dragons were smiling. At the bottom of the page, someone had scrawled the name Pearl.

"This is Pearl Chan's Dragon Grimoire."

"Her grimoire?" Maida paused, confused. As far as she knew, only witches kept grimoires. "Is this a work of fiction? Was she hoping to publish this?"

"No." Rosie shook her head, a bit frustrated. She flipped further into the book, where the drawings became increasingly more elaborate and detailed. "I don't think you understand. This is her *life's work.*"

Maida pulled the book closer, admiring the almost photorealistic quality of the pen and ink drawings. The images seemed to shimmer.

"These are exquisite, but of course dragons are mythical beasts. They aren't real, are they? I mean, Bardo is a yak shifter and my father is a Buffalo and your parents are—"

"Red deer and caribou, I know!" Rosie finished impatiently. "But recessive genes, mutations, spontaneous magic..." She was growing flushed now, two bright scarlet patches glowed on each of her cheeks.

"Of course." Maida nodded, still studying the fantastical drawings. "But dragons, Rosie? Seriously? Are you pulling a prank on me?"

"Ughhhh." Rosie groaned. "Promise me you won't freak out?"

A wave of heat was followed by a resounding *fffwomp* sound that reminded Maida of the sound of a gas stove being lit. The pages of the book ruffled in the hot breeze and Maida leapt to her feet, instinctively. She almost collided with the massive dragon crouched in the center of the cafe. It was slowly flapping its oversized wings, careful not to knock over the furniture.

Maida's first instinct was to scream, but she was careful to stifle her urge because the last thing she wanted to do was overreact. There was no question that the creature before her was none other than Rosie.

But this version of Rosie was so much larger, so much more mythological, and so much more dangerous. The scarlet circles on her cheek still glowed and shimmered with an iridescent sheen. Her nostrils were flared and her eyes were a mirror of the flames she surely contained. A small tendril of smoke wafted out from between her front fangs.

Maida felt a trail of sweat rolling down her spine. This was only partially due to the sudden rise in temperature. It was impossible not to feel nervous standing beneath a living, breathing, modern day dragon.

If there are fairies and talking squirrels, why shouldn't there be dragons as well?

Maida grasped a chair for balance and chided herself for questioning what Rosie had been trying to tell her.

In dragon form or human, it was still Rosie, she reminded herself.

Just Rosie.

She looked up so she could take in the whole of her.

Now that Maida had the chance to look at her, really see her in all her natural glory, she could appreciate the beauty Rosie was. Every scale was polished to perfection and glowing, streaked with a palette to rival the most exotic flower petals. The colors of her scales ranged from pale green to gold to magenta. They changed like prisms, reflecting the light differently from every angle.

"My gods you're gorgeous!" Maida praised. She reached out a hand but stopped just short of touching Rosie's left wing, a miracle of sinew and finely veined skin as delicate as lacework.

"May I?" she asked.

Rosie held out her wing, allowing Maida to run her hand along the silky surface. She wrapped her hand around Rosie's sharp talon as if to shake hands. "I am most honored to make your acquaintance, Rosie. You are my first dragon, and if I say so myself, you are smokin' hot."

In the next instant, she was holding Rosie's human hand, and the girl was grinning ear to ear, a human once more. "I can't believe you said that. That was the worst joke ever!"

After they both stopped laughing, Rosie flipped back through the book until she found a drawing of a dragon very similar to herself. "I think I'm most like her. I've got the same colors."

"Are there many of you?" Maida asked, glancing from the drawing and back to the girl.

"No. Most folk will never see a dragon in their entire lifetime," she said. "It's a rare occurrence. Pearl's family was an exception. Both of her parents were dragons. But Pearl's son, and his sons, were yak shifters—same as her own grandparents had been. She was very bitter about that." Rosie had a pained expression on her face.

"But she was kind to you?" Maida asked.

"So kind. She's always spoiled me—making me gifts and telling me stories. I felt bad taking the book. Bardo should have had it."

"It was Pearl's book to give as she chose, and I think she chose well," Maida said. "What would Bardo have done with the book?"

"Sold it, probably, to buy a new K-bike." Rosie sighed. "Dragon grimoires are exceptionally rare. I think we should probably keep it in the Archives." She stroked Gemini absent-mindedly as she spoke. "As far as I know, dragons are the only shifters to keep grimoires, and familiars."

"So Gemmy is your familiar?" Maida raised a brow.

"You didn't think she was a regular house cat, did you?" The corner of Rosie's mouth twitched into a smile that was so much like her father's.

"We should clean up from dinner," Maida suggested, "unless you have some special dragon magic for sanitizing dishes with fire?"

Rosie's eyes flashed.

"Too soon?" Maida bit her lip. "I'm sorry, I won't tease you if it's offensive."

"No," Rosie giggled, "I'm not that thin skinned. *Literally*. It's just so strange to be teased. Nobody else knows, except for Bardo."

"He figured it out?" Maida was surprised.

"Yeah, he acted like it was no big deal, but I think he felt..." Rosie paused to hunt for the word she wanted to use.

"Jealous?" Maida asked.

"Maybe. But not that. More like 'bad'. He never wanted to be a dragon. He's perfectly happy being a yak. He just wished that had been enough for his grandma." Rosie sighed and stood to clear the table. She stacked the plates and turned toward the kitchen.

"You're a good friend, Rosie." Maida hugged the girl. "I hope Bardo appreciates that."

THIRTY-FIVE

FAIRY CLEANING LADY

A pure-blooded witch's home must embody the same precision and care demanded in all aspects of her life. Cleanliness is not merely a matter of hygiene, but a reflection of discipline and respect for one's heritage.

Best practices include the diligent use of self-sweeping brooms, dust-repelling charms, and potions to banish clutter. Every room should be immaculate, with magical artifacts displayed tastefully, untouched by dust or disorder. A well-kept home is a testament to the character and clarity of mind of its owner, ensuring her surroundings mirror the excellence of her lineage.

-EXCERPT FROM THE ARCANE ELITE: UPHOLDING THE SANCTITY OF WITCH BLOODLINES

Minerva had done her best. She might have failed to retrieve the wrapper, but it had still found its way to Arthur. She deserved to rest.

Being a mouse was nice, in some ways. She had no guilt about her new, lazy ways. She could sleep in till nine, have a snack and nap till noon. So what if the mouse apartments were a mess again? There was nobody to keep up appearances for. The dust gathered in giant drifts that rivaled the snow now gathering on the shop's windowsills. So what? Nobody minded.

This was a much nicer way to think about it.

The fact that she could probably disappear forever and nobody would *care* was a much more bitter pill to swallow.

Who had even missed her? Not one soul had thought to pay their respects since the Mudpuddle had returned. Not even Lucretia. She would have expected her niece to at least stop by and offer to arrange a celebration of life. Organize a search party. Do something.

The customers didn't seem to miss her. They were just as happy to buy their books from Maida. Even the squirrels seemed to like Maida's snacks just as much as they had enjoyed hers.

Over in the cafe, Rosie's snickerdoodles were almost as popular as her lemon biscuits. But Rosie's cookies were *Ordinary*—baked with no real magic unless you counted the final blast of dragon fire that gave them a gooey caramelized crust. It was practically preposterous how delicious they were. Minerva had to give credit where credit was due.

This entire experience was humbling.

Primrose Court didn't need her anymore. With or without her, the Mudpuddle was still standing; the shop was still prospering, the coffee shop patrons were klatching and as far as she could tell, the contents of the Archives were still contained—thank the fates for that.

How long had she been living like this? A few days? A couple of weeks? A month?

Judging by the amount of snow falling outside the shop's windows, it had to be closer to a month, she thought. An entire month since that mage had blasted her with his wretched fake magic and she was still a mouse. Shouldn't the spell be worn off already?

What if she stayed stuck like this forever?

The bed was comfortable and warm, at least. Especially when piled high with the quilts she'd scavenged from the other empty apartments. Beneath the covers, Minerva chased her tail. She completed three circuits during which she made a fresh donut shaped depression in the tiny mouse feather bed. She sniffed and snuffled as she hunkered down, ready to descend back into dreamland, where she hoped she might encounter Zephyr again.

Seeing him so regularly in her dreams helped with the loneliness. She just wished he would stop going on about that magic mirror. How on earth did he expect her to get down to the Archives?

Perhaps today would be different. Perhaps today she would dream about sharing a nice wedge of cheddar or a creamy hunk of brie with Zippy. That was a dream she would not mind having again and again.

"I know you're in there Minerva Lathrop! There's no point in hiding. You're not fooling me!"

Minerva's eyes shot up. Were her ears deceiving her? Was that someone speaking to her? How?

"Come on now. Get out of bed. You've done a terrible job of keeping this place up. The least you can do is get up and have a spot of tea with me."

Minerva's curiosity was piqued when she heard the clink of china. Just enough to ask a question, though. Not enough to come out.

"Who is that?" she squeaked. "Who's there?"

"It's me, you old fool!" The quilts were ripped off the bed rather unceremoniously, leaving Minerva exposed to the cool morning air. She shivered and blinked, willing her eyes to focus on the owner of the voice that sounded so familiar.

"Is that you, Beryl?" Minerva squinted. She thought she recognized the fairy Beryl Luna. Fairies could shrink and grow at will, but this did not explain what Beryl was doing standing in the mouse apartments.

"Fair as the forest it is I!" the well-aged fairy hooted. "And I can't believe you've been holding out on me all these years, you old witch. How long have you been sitting on this micro estate?"

"You can understand me?" Minerva asked.

"Why not?" Granny shrugged.

"Because I'm a MOUSE." Minerva frowned. "Hadn't you noticed?"

"Well you've always been a bit mousy," Granny teased. "So I *hardly* noticed."

Minerva didn't hesitate. She snapped her tail at Beryl.

"Now, now, you wouldn't want to spill the tea, would you?" Granny chided. "It's not very neighborly of you to lash out at me when I've come to pay you a visit and done you such a big favor. Come and have your tea."

"Favor? What favor? Why couldn't you just let me sleep!" Minerva grumbled.

"I've cleaned your whole apartment and what's more, I've made you fresh tea and cakes!" Granny sounded affronted now. "And, I've brought you fresh clothes. Those rags you have on are filthy!"

Minerva blinked again, willing the sunspots away and her cloudy vision to clear. But even before she could see, she could smell the tea. When Granny held the cup beneath her nose she inhaled.

"Sweet elixir of life!" Minerva moaned.

"I told you, I've done your dishes and ironed your sheets as well. Have you never had a proper fairy housekeeper then?"

"Well...no," Minerva confessed. "We didn't go in for such luxuries in my family."

"More's the pity, you could have done with a bit of pampering." Granny sniffed and patted the doll-sized ball gowns hanging on the rolling rack beside the bed.

"Where did you even find those?" Minerva blinked.

"Toy store," Granny admitted. "But I had them altered."

"How are you here? Why are you here?" Minerva asked. She

was thinking she was dreaming again. She took a scone from the plate Granny was proffering and took a bite. It was scrumptious, buttery and soft and flavored with juicy bits of raspberry. She had to admit that short of a dream involving Zephyr and cheese, this was the best dream she'd had in ages. Her eyes began to slide half shut as she dozed into her pleasure.

"Wake up!" Granny pinched her. "This is not a dream! I'm here to bail you out. Bring you back. Rescue you."

"Ouch!" Minerva cried out. Now when she looked around, she could see that the apartment had been cleaned. Every surface glistened and glowed as if it had been given a fresh coat of paint and a polish.

"You did all this for me?" Minerva marveled.

"I did." Granny dropped down into the chair beside the bed and helped herself to a scone. "'Twas nothing for a fairy."

"But why?"

"Because we older folk need to stick together."

"I can't go back like this." Minerva looked down at her ragged clothes and furry appendages. "Who would take me seriously? They barely took notice of me when I was a witch. I'm no longer needed out there. Leave me be. Let me live my mouse life." She waved a dismissive hand towards the wall.

"Is that what you call what you're doing now?" Granny Luna arched her brow and tapped a bedazzled sneaker. "Sleeping the days away, creeping about and stealing food. And here I thought you were just trying to avoid being charged with murder."

"I didn't do anything to Zephyr!" Minerva squeaked defensively.

"I believe you, and I'm sure the others will." Granny dusted some crumbs off her skirt. "We'll just get you cleaned up and you can speak to a constable."

"And what then? Maida and Arthur make me their pet?" Minerva protested. "No thanks. That's no life. Living with a cat and a dragon probably isn't the greatest thing for my health." Minerva sipped her tea.

"A dragon?" Beryl's eyes grew wide. "What are you talking about, Minnie? Have you been nibbling on some toadstools?"

"No, Beryl. I saw Rosie shift with my own eyes," Minerva bragged. "Bad as my eyes are, that was one shift I couldn't mistake. But you musn't tell anyone."

Minerva hated to admit it, but she rather enjoyed having the scoop. For once she wasn't the last one on the street to hear the good gossip.

She'd missed out on female friendships for so long. Certainly her family would never have allowed her to socialize with a fairy. But Beryl was a lot of fun. And Minerva had nothing to lose. So long as the fairy kept her secrets.

"Promise you won't tell anyone about me, Beryl? You're welcome to visit me here whenever you like. You can even take up residence in one of the apartments. Have some friends over. Throw a party in the ballroom. Just don't tell anyone that I'm still here."

Granny Luna's eyes grew wide at the mention of the ballroom. "That would be so much fun. But not without you, Minerva! More tea?"

Minerva nodded and allowed her to pour a second cup of the strawberry scented tea.

"There are plenty of folk who miss you. I miss you. I do wish you'd reconsider and let me tell the others you're okay," Granny Luna tried again.

"I'm not okay. I'm a mouse who can't do magic anymore," Minerva lamented. "You can shrink and grow, and come and go as you like. But I'm stuck like this."

"We could still play tricks on the customers in the bookshop," Granny suggested.

"No," Minerva argued. "Even if I wanted to do that, it wouldn't be the same for me. I don't want anybody to see me like this. How do you think it feels to actually become a mouse after being called mousy for most of my life?"

"May the Morrigan take your detractors away!" Beryl cursed. "I'm sorry I said you smell. You're really not all that bad, you know.

I actually think you're kind of cute. I, for one, don't care one whit whether you're a mouse or a witch. In fact, I think I might prefer you this way. Will you at least think about it?"

"Fine." Minerva nodded. Now that her belly was full, her lids were growing heavy again. "I promise I will think about it."

"That's all I'm asking," Beryl said.

"How did you figure out I was here?" Minerva asked, struggling to stay awake long enough to hear the answer.

"Sure as the winds, Rosie's cat showed me."

Zephyr came to Minerva almost immediately, somewhere in the space between dreams and waking. He was more insistent than ever.

"My mirror, Minnie! You need to get it. Go and get it right now."

"Get your own mirror, Zippy," Minerva mumbled, snuggling into her donut shaped hole. "I don't care how you look, anyway. Don't you know that already, you old fool? I loved you even when you had crumbs in your beard."

"No, Minnie. You have to get the mirror." There were tears in his eyes now. "Please. It's important. It's not just for me, Minnie. It's for you!"

And then he was gone. The dream was gone. And she was awake.

Minerva sat up in the darkened apartment, dazed, confused and foggy, feeling more alone than she ever had.

There was only one thing to be done. She was going to have to find a way into the Archives, already. She was sick of always dreaming the same dream.

THIRTY-SIX

UN-FAIRY GODMOTHER

In the natural world, it's not uncommon to find birds fostering orphaned chicks or mammals like dolphins and primates adopting unrelated young. Time and again, nature shows us that deep connections can, and often do, extend beyond blood ties.

Non-biological mothers form bonds just as profound and meaningful with their adopted offspring, offering the same protection, nourishment, and love as any biological parent. These relationships remind us that the magic of nurturing isn't confined to lineage—it flows from the universal instinct to care for and protect life in all its forms.

-EXCERPT FROM THE MUDPUDDLE MANUAL OF NATURAL MAGIC

Maida and Arthur paced the sheltered atrium of the town hall in silence, walking separately and avoiding eye contact each time they met in the middle.

Will would arrive any moment with Amrita Berman. Zephyr's

remains had remained unchanged. The town's residents were demanding answers. More than a few had gathered outside the town hall, hoping to get a glimpse of the Director.

But Zephyr was not the only reason Amrita was en route. She was coming to meet Maida.

Maida was inexplicably nervous about this.

"Are you okay?" Arthur asked on their fifth rotation around the enclosed space.

Maida nodded and continued to walk in circles.

She didn't want to talk about it, and she also didn't want to talk about the way Arthur had stormed out the other night. She especially didn't want to talk about Rosie being a dragon shifter. That was Rosie's secret to share.

Round and round she went.

Finally, the Director arrived.

Maida's first impression of Amrita Berman was that she was as perfectly polished as river rock, and just as free from artifice. She knew they'd met before, but she had a hard time believing this, because she didn't remember her. The Director seemed like the type of woman who was unforgettable.

Amrita traded a look with Arthur, and he nodded and turned towards the door. He hesitated before leaving them, turning to address Maida.

"Will and I will be right inside."

When she looked into his warm eyes, the empathy she saw there overwhelmed her. His gaze was like honey, and it soothed her raw nerves. She felt the urge to run over and embrace him.

"Thank you, Arthur," the Director said. Arthur turned to address her.

"The council is still gathering. We'll head over to view Zephyr as soon as you two are ready."

And then he left her alone in the atrium with her godmother.

Amrita rushed right up to her, smiling proudly.

"Oh my. Let me look at you!" Amrita exclaimed, reaching out

to touch Maida's hair. She placed a hand under Maida's chin. "You have your mother's eyes. But I can see some of your father in you as well. His cheekbones..." She tilted her head and narrowed her eyes. "And his stubborn streak." Amrita smiled. "Let's sit, shall we?"

Amrita pointed to a concrete bench at the center of the atrium and grasped Maida's hand. The midday sun cast harsh shadows through the trees, giving everything cold, sharp edges. In contrast, Amrita's hands were warm, her presence comforting. They sat facing each other and Amrita continued.

"Not that your mother wasn't stubborn. She was just less idealistic. More oppositional. You and your father are more prone to dig your heels in when you feel a sense of conviction, no?" Amrita clarified.

"I can't argue with that." Maida smiled a small half smile.

Despite her reserve, she felt instantly at ease with Amrita Berman. Studying the older woman, she spoke plainly. "I have so many questions about my mother. Aside from my father and my aunt, who I've just met, I don't really know anyone who actually knew her."

"And neither one of them will talk ill of the dead, I take it?" Amrita raised her eyebrows.

"They're not really willing to talk, period." Maida shrugged. "For the longest time, I thought there must have been something terribly wrong with her. And possibly me."

"Oh dear. There's nothing wrong with you." Amrita sighed. "But I will not lie to you about your mother. She was a difficult person. Easy to love, and possibly easier to hate. It's hard to come clean when your feelings about a person are complicated and just about everyone who knew your mother had complicated feelings about her."

"Including you?" Maida asked.

"Especially me. She was my best friend. And she betrayed me, most cruelly." Amrita pressed her lips together and looked up at the sky, as if seeking answers she knew would never come.

"But you forgave her?" Maida asked.

"Not entirely," Amrita admitted. "You can forgive the person, but not the act." She smoothed her skirt and folded her hands on her lap. "In the end, I felt sorry for her. I don't think she got what she deserved. She paid for her mistakes with her life."

Amrita leaned forward to pull a faded photo from her bag. In it, the two young women were sitting on the edge of a bunk bed in a dorm room, not unlike the one she'd shared with Zani. They were both wearing school uniforms with bulky sweaters. Their arms were wrapped around each other and they were laughing. Maida recognized Amrita, immediately. Her mother looked like any other pretty, young, blond college co-ed. She handed the photo to Maida.

"That's yours. Keep it."

"Thank you." Maida took the photo.

"I'm sorry. I should have started by asking what you already knew," Amrita apologized. "Rather than lobbing all my random thoughts at you. I've just waited such a long time to meet you. It's a little like meeting a celebrity you've stalked for years."

This made Maida smile. "I think that's how my friend Zani feels about you, actually." She held up the photo and studied it some more. "So what I know...I know you and my mother were roommates. And I know that she was unhappy about your relationship with my father."

"Then you know quite a bit, actually." Amrita nodded. "Your mother was raised in a strict household. Mingling with other types of folk was not tolerated. To be fair, that was most households, at the time. My parents were unusually liberal. But even they had their limits. I didn't tell them I was seeing a shifter. I didn't think there was any reason to tell them."

"So my mother didn't approve of your relationship with my dad?"

"Your mother was jealous. My attention was less focused on our friendship. Meanwhile, she was desperate to rebel against her strict upbringing. We stole her thunder. Buffalo and I broke all the rules. We weren't doing it for attention. We genuinely cared about each other. But attention was what we got. Good and bad." Amrita closed her eyes for a moment, remembering. "Your mother was used to being the center of attention. She thrived on it. But suddenly she found herself alone, standing in the shadows. So she took a bit of my hair from my hairbrush and used it to work a glamor."

"My father thought she was *you*," Maida whispered.

"That was his claim. Your mother had a different story, of course. It's not for me to say what actually happened behind closed doors, except to say a child was conceived."

"Me." Maida laid a hand on her own chest, and Amrita covered it with her own.

"Yes, you blessed woman." She clasped her hands to her own chest. "I will never fail to give thanks that so much beauty and kindness could come from such a deception. No matter how devious of an act your mother's glamor spell was, her ill intentions didn't take root in your soul. Her entire pregnancy defied the odds. You shouldn't even be here. And yet here you are. You came into this world with your own unique endowments, a manifester and a miracle."

Maida dragged the toe of her shoe through the pebbled soil. "That all sounds so wonderful. But truthfully, I have always felt like more of a disappointment—like I was too ordinary, even before I knew the real meaning of the word."

"Please don't be too hard on your father, Maida. He tried to do right by you. Particularly after seeing what synthetic magic did to your mother. It's obvious why he wanted to raise you in a different world. I think he was relieved when they pronounced you Ordinary. Even though there were those that had their doubts, he considered your Ordinaryness a blessing. He loves you so much. All he ever wanted to do was to keep you safe."

"What about *you*?" Maida asked Amrita. "Where do you fit in?"

"Magic is my whole world." Amrita smiled enigmatically.

"There's not a lot of room for much else when you're the Director of the Society."

"No relationships?" Maida arched a brow.

"No time." Amrita shook her head. "And no inclination, to be honest."

"So you have no children of your own."

"I think of you like a daughter," Amrita admitted. "Even though you're not mine. I've always been there in the background, checking in on you, watching over you. I like to think of myself as your fairy godmother. Although, Goddess help me if Granny Luna were to hear me use that term. She'd shove a stone in my ear."

Maida smiled at the thought of this. "I can picture that."

"I know you have probably felt alone," Amrita continued, "but you had a lot of folk watching over you, including me. I always suspected you had a bit of Papa Lathrop in you. I saw some glimmers of manifestation magic in you from the time you were four years old. Just nothing profound enough to put you through the enlightenment."

"Papa Lathrop was a manifester?" Maida asked, touching her locket gently.

"He was." Amrita nodded. "And a talented inventor as well. I see you still have the gearheart locket."

"I do." Maida held the locket in her hand. She was hoping to learn more about it, and more about Papa Lathrop. "What does it mean to be a manifester?"

"It means what it sounds like. You have the ability to speak things into existence." Amrita reached for her hand again, turning it over to expose the tattoo on Maida's wrist. "It's this. Except in your case, I think you may draw things into existence as well."

The conversation was cut short by the sound of approaching footsteps and the creak of a door.

"I'm sorry to interrupt," Arthur apologized, "but they're ready for us at the morgue. The council is anxious for the Director to help them make a decision about what they should do with Zephyr."

"Right," said Amrita, rising gracefully. "We'll chat more about this later. I've got to get back to Los Angeles tonight, but I would love to spend some more time in Primrose Court next week. It wouldn't hurt for you and I to have a look around the Archives together, would it?" She pointed to Maida's chest where the locket still hung from its chain. "If the house trusts you with that locket, I don't think you'll even need a key."

THIRTY-SEVEN

ABSOLUTE TRUTH

For most shifters, honesty comes naturally, as our true nature often shines through, even when we shift forms. However, there are some who find the temptation to conceal the truth as easy as changing their appearance. While maintaining honesty is the mark of a true gentleman, it's important to remember that not every truth needs to be told in full.

Oversharing can lead to unnecessary complications, especially when discussing matters related to shifting with those who might not understand. The art lies in finding the balance—being truthful without revealing too much.

-EXCERPT FROM THE METAMORPHIC MAN: A GENTLEMAN SHAPESHIFTER'S GUIDE TO CULTURED CONDUCT

"Well he certainly doesn't smell dead!" Will was the first to enter the chamber where Zephyr's lifeless body was laid out. He leaned over the body, sniffing the air again cautiously. "No rot, no decay. Nothing," Will said.

"Maybe you should show a little more respect, Will..." Maida chided.

Amrita strode slowly around Zephyr's lifeless form. She crouched down to examine him from different angles.

"Most unusual!" Amrita frowned. "Has there been any change at all to his corporeal vessel since he was brought in?"

"Not that I'm aware of," Arthur answered. Zephyr's body looked exactly the same as the first time he'd paid a visit to the morgue. There were no signs of deterioration and none of the unpleasant smells that inevitably accompanied decomposition. Other than the slightest trace of synthetic magic that still lingered in the surrounding air, the only aromas that Arthur could attribute to the wizard were a hint of spruce scented beard oil and cherry tobacco. "It's rather strange, isn't it?"

"How do you know he's dead?" Maida spoke from her corner by the door, keeping herself to the farthest point in the room.

"No pulse, no respiration, no reflexes, and a clear case of rigor mortis." Will demonstrated by attempting to lift a stiffened arm. He pushed back the old wizard's sleeve, revealing a tightly clutched fist.

"What's in his hand?" Maida asked, watching as Amrita bent to investigate.

"We're not sure," Arthur said. "We can't get his hand open. There's been a few theories though. Some folks think it's a talisman of some sort. Others think it might be Minerva's wand."

"That's quite an incriminating idea!" Will observed.

"It's forbidden to handle another witch or wizard's wand," Amrita explained to Maida "Except in rare cases of self-defense and preservation, such as when one is in the process of disarming a foe."

"I imagine if you can't touch another witch or wizard's wand, you shouldn't be buried with it either?" Maida guessed.

"Correct." Amrita nodded. "This presents us with quite a challenge."

"I find it hard to believe that Minerva did this to Zephyr," Will scoffed. "Mousy little Minerva?"

"Well let's see what we can divine from the ashes before we bother to speculate, shall we?"

Amrita pulled out a small purple leather bag from her framed valise. From it she withdrew a kit containing two small vials and a sharp silver implement. She clipped the kit to her belt and withdrew the chisel shaped tool.

Amrita leaned forward to probe the burnt object in Zephyr's hand once more. Carefully, she poked it with the blunt end of the silver tool. Holding the empty vial directly beneath the burnt bit of wood; she used the chisel to scrape the smallest bit of soot into a vial. "Hold this for me?" She held out the vial to Maida. "Try not to breathe on it."

Maida stepped forward, tentatively, to accept the vial from Amrita. The older witch sheathed the tool and pulled out the second vial, which held a cloudy silver liquid. It reminded Arthur of mercury. "It's never too early to begin your formal education, Maida. I'm shocked that nobody's thought to perform a spell-seeking test on this item already." She gestured at the object and then looked pointedly at Arthur. His face grew hot at the unspoken accusation.

"Of course we thought of that. Immediately! But I'm not a wizard and nobody in Primrose Court has the authority to perform such intrusive spells. We filed the paperwork weeks ago," he grumbled. "Does no one in your organization answer calls?"

"Not nearly quickly enough." Amrita grimaced. "Good thing I'm here now then, isn't it?" Her eyes gleamed as she used her teeth to loosen the cap on the smaller vial. Will gasped and took a step back.

"Don't worry, Porter. I will not spill a single drop of this," Amrita reassured him. She turned back to Maida and Arthur to explain. "It takes over a thousand years to brew a single drop of absolute truth. One misplaced drop has the power to destroy an entire civilization."

"How did you know what that stuff is?" Arthur questioned Will.

"I've seen it before. It gathers in puddles around the edges of oblivion. It's the number one reason most porters eventually go mad. First rule of porting, keep your boots dry!" Will's eyes stayed trained on the vial.

"Precisely why we don't sanction the use of it for most applications, or allow many witches permission to handle it. Imagine if it got into the wrong hands." Amrita's hands were steady as she finished unscrewing the vial. "Are you ready to perform your first ritual? As a blood relative of Minerva, it's much more likely for this to work if you take part."

Maida nodded solemnly. She was still clutching the vial with the ashes. Seeing that her hands weren't shaking either, Arthur felt impressed.

"Will the spell tell us what happened to Zephyr and Minerva?" Maida asked.

"Possibly." Amrita tapped the vial, causing the truth inside to swirl and coat the glass. "If that is indeed Minerva's wand, we'll learn the absolute truth about its recent spell history. That's about all we can risk using it for. We'll have to use our wits to figure out the rest. The truth is ultimately a matter that requires some interpretation, right, Arthur?" She held his gaze for a moment, her eyes filled with respect.

Amrita now turned towards Will, whose face was pale. Her features softened. "Even as trained practitioners of the mysterious arts, sometimes the best we can do is trust each other, keep going and keep our boots dry."

Finally, she turned back to Maida.

"Hold still," Amrita warned. "And whatever is revealed, Will and Arthur, I'll need you to keep your eyes open. You are both serving as witnesses."

Amrita removed the lid from the vial and the room filled with a bright white light, not unlike the light of Will's portals. The light spread everywhere, revealing Zephyr's body clearly and removing all shadows. The vial was an even brighter pinhole now, a single point through which one viewed an eclipse.

"Drop the ashes in, Maida," Amrita commanded.

Maida stepped forward and turned her vial over, allowing the contents to fall directly into the brilliant white spot. And then the room went pitch dark.

Arthur wasn't sure what to expect. Once or twice in his career, he'd heard testimony from expert witnesses that involved these sorts of absolute truth rituals. But he had certainly never participated in one.

"Eyes open!" Amrita commanded. "Look sharp, everyone. The truth is being revealed."

The room was still dark, but not completely. Tiny bits and pieces of light were swarming together, gathering to form shapes and crawling up the walls to create moving pictures. The images became more and more realistic as he watched, developing like moving photographs.

"I can see Minerva!" Will exclaimed. "She's standing in the Mudpuddle. She is scowling! And she's using her wand on someone. He's tumbling out the door. I can just see him..."

"My Gods, It's Zephyr." Arthur groaned.

"So you can see it too?" Amrita sighed. "That's three of us. We can confirm that Minerva's wand was used against Zephyr, quite recently. Yes? What else do you see?"

"I see something...silver," Maida volunteered. She pointed at a thread of light that extended from Zephyr's hand towards the ceiling.

"Yes, I see it too," Arthur agreed. It looked like a bolt of distant lightning, highlighted against the night sky.

"What is that?" Maida asked.

They all watched as the thread fracture and come together again, spinning itself into a silver ball that grew larger and larger. It hung for a moment, like a poorly sketched moon in the blackest of skies, and then it flew directly at them. Arthur flinched, ducking instinctively. Maida lunged sideways. She gripped the marble slab. Floating directly above the wizard was an image of Zephyr. He was lying on the ground, one hand outstretched. He waved it in the air, trying to catch something.

"There's someone else over there, too." Maida pointed toward the corner, where Arthur could barely make out the fleeting image of a cloaked figure running away.

"Thorny hawthorn splinters! Is that a broom?" Will groaned and closed his eyes as the flying object barreled by him, sailing straight through Arthur's chest.

"It's not real, Will!" Arthur reminded him.

"Eyes open!" Amrita called out again. "There are no second chances. We only get one shot at the truth."

"I'm seeing quite a few squirrels," Will commented. "Anybody else? They're just sitting in the trees watching like they've got nothing better to do."

"Arthur, look!" Maida called out, pointing at a small silvery, papery object blowing in the broom's wake. There was no mistaking it.

"The wrapper!" he exclaimed.

And just like that, the entire vision ended.

"That was awesome!" Will shouted.

"Don't get any ideas." Amrita cast him a warning look.

Will held his hands up in surrender. "Respectfully, I'm quite aware that I can't handle the truth. I was just grateful to be a passenger on this adventure."

Amrita patted him on the shoulder. "You are a great porter, Will. You deserve people in your life who will carry you as well."

"So now what?" Arthur asked. His heart was beating almost as hard as when he ported for the first time.

"Now we take a moment to record what we saw, compare notes, and share our findings with the constable. Then we put our heads together to deliberate and come to a quorum about what to do with Zephyr's body. He deserves to be laid to rest." Amrita used her free hand to smooth a lock of Zephyr's hair off his forehead. "I don't think there's anything else he can tell us now."

"Are you sure about that, Amrita?" Arthur leaned in closer for a better look. He couldn't believe what he was seeing. Two small droplets of liquid were pooled in the corners of the old wizard's glassy, unseeing blue eyes.

THIRTY-EIGHT

THE PERILS OF EMPATHY

When a crow dies, its companions gather in a solemn, ritual-like manner, cawing and circling above the fallen member. These gatherings, often called "crow funerals," seem to transcend instinct, as the birds pause to share a collective moment of mourning.

This practice is believed to help the community assess the cause of death while expressing a shared sense of loss. It is a striking example of empathy in the natural world, reflecting the crows' deep intelligence and strong social bonds. These rituals reveal a profound connection among the flock, where even death is met with understanding and respect.

-EXCERPT FROM THE MUDPUDDLE MANUAL OF NATURAL MAGIC

Maida kicked at the dead leaves on the sidewalk as she and Arthur made their way back to the Mudpuddle. It was a clear, crisp day with bright sunshine that had made short work of the dusting of snow in Primrose Court. But it was still quite cold. The air had the snap of incoming frost, and wood smoke wafted from the chimneys. Maida rubbed her hands together and blew on them.

"Here." Arthur removed his right glove and passed it to her. "Put this on." Then he took her bare hand in his and tucked both their hands into his coat pocket. "That's better, no?"

"Yes," Maida said. He could feel her fingers flex against his pocket. This was reckless. But life was brief. If anything, the visit to the morgue reinforced that. He gave Maida's hand a quick squeeze.

"Warmth in winter is a perk of having creature blood. At least for some of us. I can't speak for the doctor," Arthur said. "Witches get cold easily. There's a cottage industry built on that fact. I once had a client who worked in a witch's cloak atelier. He was accused of stealing woolen cloaks for his family. I had the case thrown out because there was no reason marmot shifters would covet witch cloaks."

"Those poor marmots!" Maida wiggled her fingers against his again and he had to concentrate to keep his feet moving forward. Was it static electricity? Magic? His imagination? Holding her hand felt dangerous and wonderful at the same time.

"Do you think Zephyr's tears were real?" Maida asked.

"The chamber was already quite humid and absolute truth can really mess with the atmosphere. It might have been condensation," Arthur said. "Amrita didn't think we should place too much stock in it."

Maida balled her hand into a fist, then spread her fingers back out and interlaced them with his. Tiny sparkles fizzed against his palm and crackled between his digits. Even in minute doses, he liked the feel of her flesh pressed up against his, so very, very much.

"This is dangerous. But I also like it too much to stop," Maida murmured.

"Is that what you were just thinking?" Arthur asked. "Or can you do mental magic now too."

"I'm not *trying* to read your mind. It's just what I imagined you were thinking." Maida gave his hand a reassuring squeeze. "Or maybe I'm projecting this on you because it's what I'm thinking. It's all very confusing, Arthur." She kept her eyes straight ahead and her pace steady as they walked.

"Does it even matter if we were both thinking it?" Arthur asked.

Maida slowed to gaze into the apothecary as they passed. Arthur could see Lucretia bustling around behind the counter, fetching products for a cloaked customer. She seemed to be making quite a fuss.

"I feel bad about the bee," Maida said. "When I looked at the label, I was thinking that it looked a lot more like a carpenter bee than a honeybee. Carpenter bees get a bad rap. Especially the giant ones we have in California. They're fantastic pollinators and they almost never sting—only if seriously provoked. Plus, they're so exquisite. Have you ever seen one? I was thinking about how misunderstood they are. I don't think my manifesting that bee served any real purpose. Lucretia was genuinely terrified and so was the bee."

"Will got to be the hero. Lucretia's been a lot kinder to him since that day. She even made him some special 'OPF face cream' to use while porting."

"OPF?" Maida was puzzled.

"Oblivion protection factor?" Arthur surmised. "I suspect you've been blessed with an extra helping of empathy, Maida."

"Blessed or cursed?" Maida mumbled.

"Both, most likely. Empathy can be a heavy burden, to be sure."

"What's the point of empathy if one is powerless to change things?" Maida asked.

"But that's the point—you aren't powerless. You can create change in impossible ways. It's a fantastic power and one that's going to require a fair amount of practice to master, I imagine." Arthur took a deep breath. "But what an amazing opportunity you have to repair the world, Maida. You can see into hearts and change dreams into reality. It's not just bees and butterflies. It's hopes and dreams and..."

"Love?" Maida stopped at the gate to the Mudpuddle and turned towards Arthur.

"That too." He swallowed.

"Do you think Zephyr's at peace?" Maida asked. Her brow was wrinkled. "I'm worried about him. What if it wasn't just condensation? What if he's pining for Minerva?"

"I don't want to talk about Zephyr anymore," Arthur spoke softly, pulling her closer as they climbed the porch steps. "I want to apologize about the way I left things the other evening."

"You were upset...The wrapper..." Maida nodded.

"I don't want to talk about the wrapper right now either," Arthur said. He slid his free hand beneath her curls, reveling in the short shiver this caused, and how she moved still closer to his warmth.

"What do you want to talk about, then?" Maida asked, her lips so close he could taste her breath.

"I don't actually want to talk at all," Arthur admitted. "I want to kiss you." He moved close enough for his lips to graze hers as he spoke the words against her mouth. "I've wanted to kiss you for a very long time." He pulled her into an alcove on the porch where they were blocked by a bay window and were no longer visible from the street. "I'm not sure I can resist any more."

For a moment, they just stared into each other's eyes.

He ripped off his other glove with his teeth and threw it to the ground. Traditions, history, all of it be damned. Her face felt delightfully cool against his overheated hands.

She tangled her hands in his hair, ran them down his back, and nuzzled her head in the crook of his neck.

"Arthur? I'd really like to see all of you." Maida's lips buzzed against his Adam's apple. She leaned back and looked up into his eyes.

Arthur bit his lip. It was already taking superhuman effort to stay completely in his human form. This level of desire was spurring his animalistic qualities to express themselves.

"I wouldn't want to frighten you," he said. It was all too easy to imagine a look of horror on her face. Or worse, revulsion. He closed his eyes tight, willing the image away.

"Look at me. I'm not frightened." Maida placed her hands on his cheeks. Her eyes were wide, dilated pools, beckoning him in. He could drown in those eyes.

He touched his forehead against hers. "Soon," he breathed. "Just not now."

"I think you're beautiful," Maida spoke. "I always have. Even when I thought I dreamed you."

Arthur pressed his lips against hers. Maida didn't pull away. Her hands formed fists around the cloth of his coat and she pulled him closer, kissing him back with equal enthusiasm. He heard the roar of the ocean where there was none and saw stars that had nothing to do with space. It was a bit like stepping into oblivion.

Engaged with each other as they were, it was all too easy to ignore the sounds of tapping on glass, and the polite thwunk thwunk thwunk of a gently used door knocker.

It was only when the knocking refashioned itself into a more insistent pounding on the bookshop door that reality registered, breaking the airlock they'd generated between them. Maida gasped and Arthur drew in a long breath as they struggled to regain their wits.

"Hello? Maida? Anyone? Is anybody here? I've come to collect that bonsai book!"

Hildegarde Fish rattled the front door of the shop. She had worked herself into quite a state. "Surely someone must be here? I was told my book would be in today. I must say, Minerva never shut the shop during regular operating hours."

"Where's Rosie?" Maida mouthed. She smoothed her rumpled clothing.

"I don't know!" Arthur mouthed back as he straightened and buttoned his overcoat.

The hairs stood up on the back of his neck. Rosie was rebellious, but not irresponsible. She wouldn't leave the bookshop unattended.

"And where's Granny?" Maida whispered and frowned.

They both strode briskly towards the entrance, startling poor Hildegarde as they came around the corner of the porch.

"Oh! Were the two of you there all along?" she exclaimed, clutching her chest. Her lips formed a perfect o as she stared dumbfounded at them. "Quite rude not to let me in. You're lucky I didn't hex you both. You gave me such a fright."

"We've just come from a council meeting," Arthur interjected. "What seems to be the problem?"

"You tell me!" Hildegarde folded her arms across her chest and pointed at a handwritten sign tacked up in the door.

Gone to help a friend with something. Back shortly.
- R

The note was written in Rosie's hand.

"Gone to help a friend?" Arthur could feel his eyes bugging out. His daughter was grounded. He could feel a hot wave of outrage settling in. *What was she doing?* Unless she was carrying home a bag of books for a differently abled customer, his daughter was in a lot of trouble. "Back shortly? Define shortly!"

"My sentiments exactly!" Hildegarde tapped her umbrella for emphasis. "I was here two and a half hours ago. I was willing to be patient then. I did a bit of shopping and took a walk in the park. But enough is enough. I'd like my book already, as promised." She eyed Maida accusatorially.

"Of course, Ms. Fish," Maida said soothingly as she undid the lock. "Why don't you come in now and I will fetch it for you? I'd be happy to offer you some tea and cakes as well. On the house, of course." Maida held open the door. "Why don't you go get comfy and I'll be right with you. I'll bring a selection of teas and cookies so you can decide what you're most in the mood for."

"Well that's more like it, dear. I could do with a spot of tea," Hildegarde cooed. "And some of those snickerdoodles, if you don't mind, with a bit of apricot jam?"

"Coming right up!" Maida called cheerily after her. She glanced back at Arthur, worried. "It was probably something innocent. Are you going to be okay?"

"No. I will not be okay." Arthur paced back and forth on the porch, jabbing a finger against his T-watch. "Come on, Rosie. If you don't answer me in the next ten seconds, so help me gods, I'm going to drag you back to Boston. You'll never set foot in Primrose Court again."

"I'm sure she's fine," Maida said. "Rosie's a smart girl and she can take care of herself. At least give her a chance to explain before you freak out."

"What do you know?" Arthur glowered at Maida. "She's a child."

"She's young, and she's headstrong, but I don't think she's reckless. Or helpless." Maida tilted her head and placed a hand on her hip. "I think you're being a little unfair. You might try talking to her. Share some of your own feelings with her? Maybe then she wouldn't feel like she can't open up."

"Try talking to her?" Arthur was gobsmacked. "Don't you think I've tried? She barely says two words to me these days. She won't even show herself to me. I've never seen her in a full shift. I don't know if she takes after me, or her mother..."

Arthur's stomach was roiling.

"Or maybe neither of you." Maida shrugged.

"What do you mean by that?" Arthur narrowed his eyes. "What do you know that you're not telling me?"

"Talk to your daughter, Arthur. Not to me." Maida glanced in the shop, checking to make sure her customer was still getting settled. "I will say that one thing you both definitely have in common is that you are ridiculous about opening up to people who care about you."

"You don't understand what it's like to be a father," Arthur rumbled.

"And you don't understand what it's like to be a daughter," Maida countered. She took a tentative step into the shop. "I need to go help Hildegarde, Arthur. We can't afford to lose customers."

"I just want her to be safe." Arthur followed Maida into the shop, waiting behind the counter, while she sorted through the boxes of special orders. He checked the watch again. Nothing but gossip, conspiracy theories, and questionable wart remedies. Precisely why he hated these newfound conveniences. A network, indeed. More like a public clothesline for the airing of personal laundry.

I bet she's run off with that Bardo boy.

It's too bad about that Hart girl. When will these kids learn not to mess with synthetics?

She's a good kid. Probably just hanging out with a girlfriend and lost track of time.

Probably dead in a ditch, like poor Zephyr.

Have you considered putting your teen on a strict vegan diet?

Every thought he could have, would have, had already had, was flashing across the watch screen faster than he could articulate his hopes and fears.

"It's not like her not to pick up. She always picks up, Maida." He jabbed at the useless watch again.

"Oh dear," Maida exclaimed. She was standing beside the register, holding a second piece of paper in her hand. This one was folded into thirds and had Maida's name on it. It was also written in Rosie's handwriting.

"Give it to me," Arthur demanded. His voice had gone cold and hard now. He had hoped Maida might be a positive role model, perhaps help Rosie open up a bit to him. As difficult as Maida's relationship with her father was, he knew she'd always remained close to Buffalo. The last person he would have expected to come between him and his daughter was Maida.

"I can't do that." Maida shook her head and slipped the note under a book on the counter. "She specifically asked me not to."

"Hecate's owls you can't!"

"I think you should trust her on this." Maida's chin jutted out.

"I don't think you know what you're talking about." Arthur's teeth were clenched as he spoke. "If she's with Bardo, she probably isn't safe. Have you seen the size of that boy in full yak shift?"

"Pffft." Granny Luna appeared, as if out of nowhere, and blew a raspberry at Arthur. "She could take him."

"Granny!" Maida exclaimed. "How long have you been here? Where were you?"

"I went to visit a friend and then I popped off to the reading room for a quick nap, which I was enjoying until I heard all this shouting. What are you all on about? Rosie's only gone off to meet with her fellow about some rare book he wanted to borrow. Hardly worth all this fuss. She'll be back by half noon."

"It's after three, Granny."

"Is it? Oh dear..." Granny frowned. "I should go check in with Minerva."

"Minerva?" Arthur snapped to attention. "She has some explaining to do. Is she back?"

"No!" Granny stammered. "No, no, no—pay no mind to this sleep soaked sprite! 'Twas only a nickname I gave to that pesky little house mouse we keep seeing here and there. Been cleaning up after her all day. No wonder I needed a nap!"

"You named a mouse after my great aunt?" Maida asked skeptically.

"Why not? Do you have any better names?" Granny Luna flashed an innocent smile and promptly changed the subject. "Anyway, where do you two suppose Rosie's got off to? I suppose she could be halfway to Canada by now." Granny shrugged, distracted by something she was reading on her watch.

"What do you mean by that?" Arthur asked.

He didn't have to wait long for an answer. His wrist had begun to buzz as well, flooded with incoming messages about Bardo Chan and his daughter running away together. The list of places they had been spotted was long, and someone even snapped a picture of the "lovebirds" leaving town, hauling luggage and backpacks.

"This makes no sense." Maida scrutinized the image and glanced back at the note. She bit her lip worriedly.

"Granny, go and help Ms. Fish. Arthur and I need to call Will. I think Rosie might actually be in a spot of trouble."

"Nonsense. She has nothing to fear. A powerful dragon shifter like her?" Granny clucked. "I would think that's one big perk of being her father, no? You don't have to worry that your little girlie can't take care of herself. She could probably take care of all of us in one fell swoop!"

"Granny!" Maida snapped. Her eyes were wide, pleading with the fairy.

"Dragon? What in the howling hollows are you going on about now?" Arthur was losing patience with the fairy, who was beginning to show signs of dementia.

He looked from Granny to Maida. Maida looked away. She wouldn't meet his eye.

"I'm just saying..." Granny refused to let it go. "It's nothing to be ashamed of. In fact, I'd think you must be quite proud. It's like Maida said. The girl is fierce! The scales on her, Arthur. And the claws! I can imagine an entire couture line being based on the glorious sheen of her toenails alone." Granny smiled wide enough to expose her tiny pointed fangs.

"Is this a joke, Granny?" Arthur asked. "Are you suggesting that my daughter, my Rosie, is a *dragon* shifter?"

He'd always wondered, of course, what his daughter might become. Worried a bit too, if he was being honest. He'd never longed for her to embody a gnu, or worse, a goat. But there was no shame in shifting into an adjacent species. Plenty of kids did that. Particularly when they were the product of a mixed shifter marriage.

But a *dragon*? Of all the reasons he could think of for Rosie to keep her shifting attempts private, the thought that she might be a dragon had never crossed his mind. Why would it. It was simply too far-fetched.

He wasn't even sure he believed in the old lore. When did the last official sighting of a live dragon occur? Not in his lifetime.

Quickly, before Maida could stop him, he snatched Rosie's second note from the counter.

Bardo needs me to be a dragon for him. He's finally doing the right thing. Sorry to leave the shop. It shouldn't take long. Granny's around here somewhere. Try not to worry. And don't tell my dad.

Arthur read and reread the words, trying to make sense of them.

He could feel his reality shifting, and it made the world feel slightly off kilter. He shivered at the cold creeping realization that he'd crossed a threshold and there would be no turning back. Nothing would ever be the same. He swiveled to face Maida.

"My daughter is a dragon shifter?" He could hardly believe the words as he spoke them along. "She's a dragon, and *you knew*?"

She didn't answer.

"You knew, and you didn't tell me?" He couldn't keep the feeling of betrayal out of his voice or his heart.

"I wanted to, but it wasn't my place, Arthur." Maida shook her head. "I begged her to tell you."

"And you knew about her and that Chan kid?" His realization of her betrayal caused his words to erupt out of him like hot acid, burning him first before damaging her.

"It's not what you think." Maida defended his daughter.

"How would you know what I thought? Unless you're performing your mental magic on me now, too? Is that what's been going on between us?" Arthur scowled.

Maida flinched.

"I trusted you." Arthur spat out the phrase, knowing he had himself to blame as much as her. He'd known better than to give into the temptation for companionship, for comfort, for something more.

"I haven't lied to you, Arthur. My intentions were good."

He couldn't look at her. He didn't want to see her face, or face the witchcraft in her eyes.

"I want to believe you. But so help me if anything happens to my daughter..."

Arthur dropped the note and stormed out the door. Wherever Rosie and Bardo were, he was going to find them.

THIRTY-NINE

LOST AND FOUND

Tales of mythical creatures like the Loch Ness Monster, the Leviathan, and dragons persist precisely because we know nature holds countless secrets.

Just as species once thought extinct reappear, the idea that legendary beings exist in remote, hidden realms is not beyond possibility.

Ancient stories and sightings may be whispers of creatures that dwell beyond the edges of our understanding, waiting to be rediscovered.

In nature's vast and mysterious tapestry, there is always room.

—EXCERPT FROM THE MUDPUDDLE MANUAL OF NATURAL MAGIC

"Storm's fury." Maida cursed softly under her breath as the door slammed behind Arthur. She, too, was worried. Arthur was right. Rosie had been gone too long.

Maida hastily wrapped Hildegarde's book in orange-colored tissue and tossed a handful of tissue paper hearts into the bag, before tying it with a turquoise silk ribbon. Wrapping the package did nothing to calm her nerves.

She was upset with Arthur for storming off, but she was even more upset with herself. She'd let her guard down and allowed herself to get swept up in other people's business. Coming between Arthur and his daughter was the last thing she'd intended.

Gemini twined between her legs, looking up at her anxiously.

"I know," Maida sympathized.

Gemini butted her head against Maida and she scratched the cat behind the ears. "I'm sure she's just fine." Maida wanted to believe the words she was saying.

While Granny made a fuss, delivering tea and snacks to Hildegarde, Maida straightened the checkout counter. She searched for any clues where Rosie might have gone. But other than the note, a half-finished cookie, a chewed up pencil and a half completed crossword puzzle, there was nothing.

Gemini seemed impatient as well. She couldn't seem to settle on any one spot to sit. Her tail flicked back and forth like a whip, and she kept glancing at the door.

Finally, Granny came back to the counter to join her. She was holding a pair of quilted oven mitts shaped like trout.

"I have some good news!" Granny boasted. "That went swimmingly. I don't think Hildegarde Fish will be giving us a hard time anymore. She even gave *me* a gift. I'm very good with the disgruntled customers."

Maida leaned forward to observe Hildegarde. She was curled up in a corduroy armchair, happily sipping her tea and sampling items from the three tiered tower of treats that Granny had delivered to the side table beside her. A stack of books sat beside the tower, awaiting her perusal.

"I also have some bad news," Granny continued. "These oven mitts are awful. Apparently, every spell Hildegarde casts turns into fish. We're stuck with her for a bit. She's not going anywhere anytime soon."

Granny used her sleeve to polish a bit of dust off the counter and rearranged the velvet pouches of runes that were on display in a large brass bowl.

"What *exactly* did Rosie say to you when she left?" Maida asked. Rosie wouldn't have simply up and left with no explanation.

"She said she was going out for a few minutes to meet up with that Chan boy. He came back to borrow that dragon book he wanted yesterday."

"Did she bring it to him?" Maida asked.

"Well, how am I to know?" Granny shrugged. "She had her backpack on. But I don't make a habit of going through other people's things."

Maida raised her brows. "You most certainly make a habit of going through other people's things. I think that's my headband you're wearing right now." Maida pointed at the simple elastic band that Granny had embellished with a large crystal brooch.

"Well, you don't count. You're not other people. You're *my* people." Granny waved a hand and gave a little shrug, as if this was the most obvious point in the world. "Doesn't it look nicer this way?" She ran her fingers over the sparkly flower. "I fixed it up!"

"I didn't need you to bedazzle my headband. I needed you to watch the bookshop and look out for Rosie!" Maida snapped, regretting it instantly.

Granny winced.

"I'm sorry, Granny," she amended. "I don't mean to give you the impression that I don't appreciate all the things you do for me."

"Once a nan, always a nan. I'm afraid you're stuck with me." Moving so fast that her image almost blurred, Granny Luna flitted back to the cafe and ducked behind the cafe counter.

"We just need to set better boundaries," Maida added. "You don't have to assist with my wardrobe."

"So you only want help with the tedious bits, then?" Granny stooped to retrieve an oversized feather duster. The colorful cleaning tool was at least as tall as she was and almost as wide. "It's you who's doing me a favor. Such a pleasure to flex my wings again and do things properly. 'Tis a burden keeping secrets."

Maida leaned across the counter and scrutinized Granny. "I don't see any wings?"

"Well, of course not, Maida. I don't go about in public with my wings showing!" Granny scoffed. "I'm a lady."

"Are there any other secrets you might be keeping from me?"

"House fairies are *full* of secrets, Maida dear. It's part of our charm! That and our impeccable sense of style." As Granny waved the duster over the countertop, empty plates, and containers stacked themselves by size, largest to smallest. Then they floated off toward the kitchen. Stray crumbs assembled into neat piles that marched off like deployed troops, heading towards the trash.

Even the unsold goods in the bakery case scrambled to sort themselves out. They scrambled over one another, piling into picturesque towers as if styled by a photographer.

"There now, that's much better." Granny smiled and put down the duster.

"Did you read Rosie's book, Granny?" Maida asked. "Tell the truth."

"Haven't had the chance yet." Granny wrinkled her nose. "She hardly lets it out of her sight."

"Then how did you know it was a dragon grimoire?" Maida folded her arms across her chest.

"Because she and Bardo were talking about it." Granny rolled her eyes at Maida. "Obviously."

"So you listened to their conversation?"

"Of course I did. Why wouldn't I? If folks don't want to be eavesdropped upon, they'd best be clearing the house of fairies. We can't help having such acute hearing."

"Just tell me everything they said? It's important," she implored.

"Fine, child." Granny relented. "But maybe you can help me wind the clock in the foyer first?" She jerked her head towards the fireplace in the front room, where the antique clock held pride of place.

"Does it need winding?" Maida frowned. The clock always kept perfect time, and she hadn't wound it once since arriving.

"It couldn't hurt." Granny cast a meaningful glance back at Hildegarde, who was now leaning back in the recliner, snoring gently. An empty cup of tea sat beside a half finished scone. "We wouldn't want to disturb our patron while she's resting."

"Granny! What did you give her?" Maida's eyes narrowed with suspicion.

"Just a little lavender and chamomile tea, dear. With a touch of lemongrass, some cornflower, and a few grains of valerian. Same as I gave you when you were a little girl and couldn't sleep."

"You drugged me too?" Maida clapped a hand over her mouth.

"Hardly! It's a fine herbal tisane," Granny whispered defensively. "Do you know how many times Lucretia's tried to pry that recipe out of me? That brew's been in my family for ages. Hildegarde will be just fine. Better than fine. She'll be out till morning, then she'll wake up refreshed and right as springtime rain." Granny's eyes were a pale glacial blue beneath her finely arched brows. She reached in her tote bag and pulled out a half finished afghan. It continued to finish crocheting itself as she draped it across Hildegarde's lap.

"It can't hurt to make her comfy." Granny shrugged. Then, with a final flick of her feather duster, she dimmed the lights and turned up the soft classical music playing on the shop's speakers. "There now. I think it's safe for us to chat some more."

Maida followed the fairy to the foyer and picked up where she left off.

"Bardo Chan was in quite a state. But then when isn't he? I can see why poor Pearl was always so disappointed in him."

"That's not relevant right now, is it, Granny?" Maida was inclined to agree that Bardo was bad news. But listening to the ticking of the clock on the mantel, she felt acutely aware of time passing. "I think the sooner we can help Arthur find his daughter, the better."

"They could be anywhere." Granny wrung her hands. "Would

that I'd dropped a tracking stone in her bag like I used to do with you."

"Tracking stone?" Maida rubbed her forehead.

Granny waved a dismissive hand, declining to comment, and continued. "Bardo kept repeating that he was 'just gonna do it, already' and that he was 'getting out, once and for all,' whatever that means. But he needed to borrow the book his Ah Ma gave to her."

Although Maida was new to the magical community, she knew that the sharing of family grimoires was not something done lightly, if at all. She thought of what Rosie had said about the book and the secrets it contained.

"She agreed to this?" Maida asked.

"She argued with him, but Bardo insisted it was his legacy as well. And he sounded desperate."

"What did Rosie say?"

"She said wherever the book went, she went, so she was coming with him."

"And he agreed to that?"

"He didn't fight very hard. Told her to meet him at the passage, said he'd already packed everything up."

"And by everything, what do you think he meant?" Maida asked.

Granny hesitated, wringing her hands. When she looked up, the conflict was evident on Granny's face.

"Nocturnaturals stuff. He wasn't selling the stuff here in Primrose Court, though. He was repping them in Boston," Granny said, confirming what Rosie had told her.

"You knew about this? Why wouldn't you have told anyone?" Maida bit her cheek.

"It's not a fairy's place to meddle." Granny frowned. Standing on her tippy toes, she repositioned a trio of candles and turned a stack of books to lean against the carved finial at the corner of the mantel.

"But you're telling me now," Maida pointed out. "Why?"

"Because you're family. And Rosie and Arthur are starting to feel like family too." Granny's eyes darted back up to the mantel. She ran a finger along its edge, checking for dust, and finding none, she brushed her hands together and smiled a small satisfied smile. "I've been a part of your family since before you were born, dear. But it's been quite a while since I've felt needed."

According to the clock on the mantel it had been almost five hours since Rosie left the shop. Maida leaned against the wall for support, wishing the house would help her.

"I can't just sit here waiting for the phone to ring. We should at least make calls. Maybe organize a search party? I can't concentrate. Let's close up the shop," Maida said. She locked the cash register. Any bookish emergencies would just have to wait until Rosie was found.

"I'll go pack up the cafe, then." Granny was already halfway to the coffee bar by the time she finished speaking.

"Wait! What about Hildegarde?" Maida could hear the steady gentle snores filtering in from the next room.

"Just leave her in place. She'll be grand," Granny called. Hildegarde, snorted, snuffled and snuggled with her book.

Maida was busy stacking books on the cart for reshelving, so she didn't notice one last customer walking up the path. The bells startled her.

"Well hello there, I hope I'm not interrupting anything?"

The silken voice coming from the entry foyer was familiar, but she was too distracted to recall why.

"It's fine," Maida called over her shoulder. "We were just about to close but maybe I can help if there's something in particular you were looking for?"

"The opposite, actually," the man answered. "I thought it might be you who was looking for a lost book. I found this crazy book in the park. Looks really old." He set a paper bag on the mantel.

Maida stepped into the foyer. She recognized the chiseled features set in a perfectly symmetrical face, at once.

"Cormac? What are you doing here?"

"Small world, isn't it?" He smiled rakishly at her.

"Are you stalking me?" She glanced around for Granny, but the elderly fairy was suddenly nowhere to be found.

"This place suits you. I believe you've found your element, Maida Lathrop. You're practically glowing." His eyes trailed over her appreciatively. He was flirting shamelessly.

"Answer my question," Maida said.

Cormac shook his head and sighed. "Why can't you ever accept a compliment?"

"So you came here to see me then?" Maida asked.

"No," Cormac admitted. "As delighted as I am to see you again so serendipitously, I had my own reasons for visiting Primrose Court." He toyed with the candles on the mantel. "Why did you tell me you *weren't* related to Lucretia Lathrop? I've been visiting her apothecary shop for years. It's been such a strong influence on our branding. I was just discussing some additions to the Nocturnaturals spring catalog with her."

"But your products are outlawed here!" Maida protested.

"Technically correct." Cormac nodded. His face was a mask of reasoned agreement. "But I'm not. My grandmother was a witch. I've always had a pinch of the sight, even though I was raised as an Ordinary. You know what that's like. No wonder we were so drawn to each other. I knew there was something special about you the moment I saw you sitting in that coffee shop." Cormac picked a candle up from the mantel. "Or maybe it was that candle you lit? I've always been a sucker for a well-crafted love spell." Cormac leaned closer and lowered his voice. "I was disappointed when it was Addy that phoned me."

"That wasn't the impression I had the next morning." Maida smiled tightly.

"Come now. Don't be jealous. She threw herself at me." Cormac shrugged. "I didn't want to hurt her feelings."

Maida couldn't deny his sex appeal. His tousled hair was silken and luxurious. His cologne smelled expensive. Dangerous and intoxicating. It was almost as mesmerizing as his strange backlit eyes. Even his skin shone, where it wasn't dusted with a five o'clock shadow. He had just enough stubble to highlight his maleness without turning a kiss into a tango with sandpaper. He was beautiful, if cold. Like polar ice.

Arthur's kiss flashed through her mind again, hot and sweet, and enough of a distraction to reduce Cormac's sex appeal to a sodden puddle.

"Why on earth would you recruit a shifter to sell Nocturnaturals?" Maida folded her arms across her chest.

"Who are you referring to?" Cormac looked up from the candles, tilting his head.

"Bardo Chan?" Maida said the boy's name.

Cormac's face fell. At once his features were serious, and concerned.

"Yes I know about Bardo. I feel so terrible about that kid." He leaned against the mantel and folded his arms across his chest as he searched for his words. "The simple answer is we didn't know he was a shifter when he joined the team." Cormac stared more deeply into her eyes. "I know. I know it's not an excuse. We're working on ways to screen our sales reps better. It's just tricky, you know? We're an Ordinary company, with Ordinary employees. Our target market is Ordinary people. And suffice to say we've terminated our contract with Bardo."

"Your products put a lot of magical folk at risk. Don't you care about that?" Maida stood up straighter.

"Of course. Safeguarding the magical community is also a top priority for me. It's one of the reasons I visit so frequently." Cormac leaned toward her and reached out to brush a stray lock of hair from her face. "Did you know Bardo?"

"Not personally," Maida admitted, stepping back. She eyed the bag on the mantel. "What's in the bag?"

"Ah yes! The whole reason I came in." Cormac mocked smacking his forehead. "I was so delighted to see you here, I almost forgot. Crazy story. This book was just lying on the ground in the park!" Cormac affected a look of concern, and took another step towards her. "I imagine someone's going to be very upset when they realize they've lost it."

"Thanks for bringing it in. Hopefully, we'll be able to get it back to its owner," Maida said. She stood on her tiptoes, trying to see what was in the bag.

"Oh right, let me show it to you." Cormac reached between them to pull the book out of the bag. He was close enough that she could feel his breath, which was surprisingly cool. It smelled of nothing.

He lifted Rosie's book out of the bag and handed it to her.

Maida's heart was racing. Before she was worried. Now she was scared. Rosie would never have been so careless as to drop her book in the park. Not unless something was terribly wrong.

"It doesn't take an expert to recognize a rare and valuable book. Something like that ought to be locked up safe in the Archives, don't you think?" Cormac peered over her shoulder. "Aren't you going to invite me in?"

Where was Granny?

"Sorry, now's not such a great time," Maida apologized. "I was just in the middle of something."

Cormac looked crestfallen. "But I've come such a long way. I believe there's a book that used to belong to my family, down in the vault. Minerva promised she'd find it for me when I was next in town. If you're taking that book down, maybe we can have a look around for mine at the same time?"

"Actually, young man, we were just closing up. We have some stocktaking to do." Granny Luna reappeared. Maida was relieved to see her. "Perhaps you could stop by tomorrow?" Granny suggested sweetly. "We open at ten."

"Alright then." Cormac sighed. "My flight back to New Orleans doesn't leave till tomorrow afternoon. I'm staying above the apothecary if you change your mind."

"See you tomorrow, then." Granny opened the door, flipping the sign on the front to "Closed".

Cormac lingered a moment.

"Addy's been really worried about you, by the way. She'll be glad to know you got that plant she sent with your friend. I saw it out on the porch. I'll have to let her know that I saw you, too. I'll tell her it was in Boston, of course. Can't mention Primrose to the Ordinaries, can we?" He tapped the side of his nose.

Finally, he was gone.

FORTY

THE INSUFFERABLE WAIT OF POSSIBILITIES

Even under stress, a gentleman must always present himself well—including the matter of scent. Whether in human form or otherwise, a sudden whiff of panic is never becoming.

Start with the essentials: proper grooming and a touch of cologne to mask any untimely odors. Should stress bring out your more natural musk, a quick excuse for fresh air or a discreet splash of water will do wonders. And for emergencies, a sprig of mint or lavender in your pocket can keep things refreshingly civilized.

-EXCERPT FROM THE METAMORPHIC MAN: A GENTLEMAN SHAPESHIFTER'S GUIDE TO CULTURED CONDUCT

Arthur checked all the usual places for Rosie. First, he went to Bardo Chan's house. The lights were all out, and the door was locked. Peering through the windows he was dismayed to find the living room, that Pearl had always kept spotless, was now an indoor junkyard. Food containers, empty boxes, papers, and piles of clothing were everywhere. But there was no sign of his daughter.

When he arrived at his apartment in Boston, he half expected to see Rosie concocting something in the kitchen. He could picture her sitting at their dining room table, eating a slice of pizza with extra hot sauce. He would have welcomed the mess.

Arthur visited the apothecary, the pet store, and stopped by several of her friend's houses too. No sign of her on either the magical or Ordinary side.

He wracked his brain for additional places to search and came up empty.

At least Rosie hadn't taken her bike. It was still parked in the corner of the living room. Since moving to Primrose Court, she hadn't bothered with it. That was one less thing to worry about.

Arthur shook this broken thought from his head. What was he thinking? Rosie was a *dragon* shifter. With or without a bike, she had the gift of flight. No wonder she's been so fearless on it. Had she flown before? He imagined her soaring undetected through the night skies of Boston and the pit of his stomach dropped, like he was the one in a free fall. Would her magic keep her cloaked?

Finally, at a loss for other places to look, he returned to Primrose Court. He sat on a park bench, watching the clouds above and searching frantically for a shadow, or any other sign. But there was nothing but the rustle of bare branches and the sound of the wind that whistled past them.

Unable to sit for very long, Arthur patrolled the park's perimeter. His senses were on high alert. A night hawk's scream. A snapped branch. Twice he shifted unintentionally when startled. The night was too quiet, otherwise. It reminded him of the eye of a hurricane.

Walking in circles, his thoughts swirled like storm clouds. Arthur reflected on the past, berating himself for not noticing Rosie's differences sooner. Her smooth hairless skin and her proclivity for spice. What kind of father doesn't notice these sorts of things?

He'd been wrong, cruel even, to be so angry with Maida. Arthur was ashamed of his reaction. It was unfair, and it wasn't even indicative of how he really felt. If anything, he was grateful Rosie felt some sort of kinship with Maida.

He even found himself re-examining his thoughts about the Chan family. All those years that Pearl was Rosie's babysitter, he'd known that Rosie was a light in the old woman's life. He knew she looked forward to seeing his daughter as much as Rosie had looked forward to seeing her. Their relationship was special. But he'd never understood, never dreamed of the reasons why.

On his fourth lap around the park, Arthur spied Will rushing out from the passage. The porter looked exhausted. He was holding a hoagie sandwich in one hand and a bottle of pop in the other.

"I came as soon as I could," Will called out to Arthur. "I've just spoken to Maida."

"What about the Director? Does Amrita know?" He didn't know how much Maida had told Will about Rosie's unusual gifts. He didn't even know if she'd told Will anything.

"About Rosie running off with Bardo?" Will frowned. "Of course, Maida called both of us when we got to LA. That's why I'm here."

Maida clearly hadn't told Will about Rosie being a dragon shifter. If she had, Will would be driving him mad, peppering him with questions right now.

"What did Amrita think?"

"About Rosie or Bardo?" Will took a big bite from the sandwich.

"Both."

"That it's worrisome they've disappeared, but the Society can't get involved over every pair of teenagers that run off together." Will looked apologetic. "I tried to get her to come back with me but she's staying with Buffalo tonight. I think they're planning to fly back here tomorrow."

Arthur didn't expect Amrita to drop everything for a runaway teenager, but of course Rosie was no Ordinary teenager. Then again, what could Amrita do, that they weren't already doing?

"I'm not sure there's much they can do to help," Arthur said. "Rosie and Bardo could be anywhere."

"Just give me a few moments to refuel and process, and I think I'll be ready to port again." Will polished off the sandwich. "We should probably head back to the Mudpuddle, though. Granny and Maida are making calls. They're pretty worried about you too."

Arthur wasn't sure he deserved it. "I stormed out of there earlier," he admitted. "I was so crazed with worry." He still was, but his fear was no longer seeking a target.

"That's understandable," Will acknowledged. "You know, you're the only one who expects you to be perfect, Arthur. Think about where you'd like me to take you. We'll find her. I promise."

"There's something else you should know." Arthur stopped walking. He'd made up his mind. He could trust Will, and if the porter was going to help, he needed to know the whole truth. "It's about Rosie."

It was well past suppertime when the small group assembled in the reading nook of the Mudpuddle. Granny made sandwiches for Arthur and Will, who was always hungry for more after porting.

Maida sat down next to Arthur and gave his hand a squeeze.

Such a small gesture, yet it made his knees weak. Her forgiveness was so easy, and so freely given. This was not something he'd ever experienced before, nor was it something he ever wanted to abuse.

"What's next?" Will asked. "Can you think of anywhere else she might be?" He wiped his mouth and folded his napkin. "Just say the word."

"I wish I knew where else to look," Arthur admitted. His worry was becoming a palpable sensation now. His head ached with the weight of it and his heart ached with the overwhelming feeling of failure. It stuck in his throat, threatening to choke him. He was sick with that feeling.

Everyone was looking expectantly at him, waiting for their assignment, but his mind was blank.

"I really don't know what to do," Arthur admitted. "I don't even know what to think. I think..." he considered it for a moment. The words felt strange in his mouth. "I think I need your help."

"Of course." Granny Luna nodded and patted his shoulder. "That's what family is for. I'll put on a kettle of tea."

When the telephone on the countertop rang, Maida and Arthur both stood.

"I'll get it," Maida spoke firmly. The phone rang a second time, then a third, seeming louder and more insistent with each ring. "It might just be normal bookshop business," she said over her shoulder.

Then again, Arthur thought it might not. It could be good news. Or it could be the most awful.

In the long seconds between the third and the fourth ring, time seemed to freeze. He was acutely aware of still living in a world full of possibilities. He was also acutely aware of how many possibilities could vanish in the time it took to take a breath.

"It's for you." Maida's face was solemn as she held out the shiny black receiver. "Boston PD."

Arthur closed his eyes, slowly exhaling all the air from his lungs. He took a deep breath before placing the receiver to his ear. He held the phone gingerly, as if that could influence the outcome of the call, and walked as far as the coiled tether allowed. Then he turned to face the corner of the room, so nobody would see his face.

"I'm afraid I have bad news." The voice on the other end was curt and to the point. Arthur braced himself, fearing the worst. "It's not about your daughter," the officer quickly clarified. "It's about a friend of hers? She says his name is Bardo Chan. We've just recovered his body from the river. Your daughter is waiting for you here at the station."

FORTY-ONE

THE MAGIC OF CATS

Cats, long favored as familiars by witches, offer a certain elegance and independence that aligns with the pure-blooded lifestyle. Their keen intuition and ability to sense magical energies make them valuable companions for detecting unseen threats or disturbances.

However, their aloof nature can sometimes prove a disadvantage, as they may be less obedient or reliable in certain situations. Moreover, their tendency to attract Ordinary attention may compromise discretion, an essential trait for any well-bred witch. Careful consideration should be given as to whether a cat's temperament truly complements the household's needs.

-EXCERPT FROM THE ARCANE ELITE: UPHOLDING THE SANCTITY OF WITCH BLOODLINES

Minerva made her way back to the foyer and ducked into the dusty space between the walls. While not ideal for navigating the house, it did bring her closer to the Archives. As far as she could tell, there were no mouse passages that could deliver her down to where she needed to go. She would have to make her way down the long hallway to the cellar door.

She would have to elude Gemini.

How absurd, after a lifetime of facing so many wicked and whimsical beasts, to find herself quaking over a common house cat.

Creeping a few feet further, Minerva peeked through the ornate iron grate. As far as she could tell, the coast was clear. No shadows shifted to reveal the furry beast. She pressed her ear to the grate as well, listening for the sly footfall of her new nemesis.

Once she slipped out through the grate, there would be no turning back. She would have to make it all the way down the hallway to the reinforced iron door. There was no room for error. She'd have to be quick.

Once inside the vault she planned to rappel down the side of the staircase, directly to the cellar floor. She wondered if the house might help her. It had been so quiet of late. Minerva feared it had moved on, now that she was no longer its mistress.

She'd stuffed her apron pockets full of all sorts of useful things; a jar of sticky jam, a thick length of rainbow colored rope, and an assortment of snacks. She would need to keep nibbling to keep her energy up.

She felt the rope one more time, running her fingers over the cabled bundle and checking the slip knot. The rope was braided from scraps of yarn pulled from the unraveled edge of one of the half-finished mittens in the mudroom. The fine merino wool was well up to the task of holding her weight when she rappelled. She also intended to use the rope as a lasso, using it to pull herself up to undo the latch on the center of the Archives door.

She was probably half mad to be attempting something so dangerous. But she couldn't keep having the same repetitive dreams about Zephyr and his mirror night after night. Minerva rotated her neck and did a quick set of stretches in the little crawlspace, limbering up and giving herself a pep talk.

Once she made it up to the large skull shaped knob that

worked the latch, she would be home free. Two pokes in the left eyeball, one in the right, pick the nose and wiggle the eyeteeth.

She didn't even need her wand to unlock it. She had the perfect tool for picking the persnickety lock.

Minerva jumped at the sound of footsteps. She felt the rush of cold air through the grate as the front door was opened and shut again. There were voices in the bookshop. Maida, Arthur, Granny Luna and someone else—was that Will Porter?

They were speaking in the sort of low, hushed tones one tended to use at funerals, or after getting particularly bad news. Her stomach dropped, fearing the worst for Rosie. She hesitated, listening, pressing her soft cheek against the grate. She could barely make out their shadows moving in the distance. They seemed miles away.

"Then it's settled," Granny was saying. "Will and Arthur will go meet with the police and fetch Rosie. I'll go back to Boston and wake the doctor and bring him back here, in case we need him for anything. It's looking like it might be a long night."

"And I'll stay put, wait for you all here," Maida finished.

"You shouldn't be alone!" Arthur objected.

"I'll be fine," Maida argued. "It's just for a little bit. I never really feel completely alone here, you know. The house has a certain presence. And I've got Hildegarde," she gestured to the sleeping witch.

"At least when she's sleeping she can't turn anything into a fish," Will said.

"Poor Hildegarde." Granny tutted. "It must be frustrating to have all your spells come out so scaly." She turned to Maida. "You'll be just fine, love. I'll be back in two twinkles of a shooting star."

"Beryl!!!" Minerva shouted as loud as she could. If only she could get Granny Luna to listen to her and warn the others about that mage who'd stopped by earlier. But it was too late. The fairy had already flitted out the front door.

"I can't thank you enough for all your help. You were there for

Rosie when she felt like she couldn't turn to me." Arthur was staring into Maida's eyes now. Minerva couldn't see this exactly, but she could make out their silhouettes in the hallway. They were standing close, and he had one hand placed beneath her chin. Then the shifter leaned forward to plant a quick kiss on her lips!

Minerva's hand flew to her chest, an old habit. But as she held it there, she realized it was not the scandalousness of that kiss that she was feeling. It was joy. She was happy for her great niece. Whatever happened next, she knew Maida wouldn't have to spend the next eighty years alone, as she had.

"We should go now," Will said to Arthur. "I'm ready if you are."

Minerva watched as the porter use his hand to quickly draw a circle on the wall near the end of the hallway. There was a flash of bright light and a sucking sound as the world inside the circle fell away. She had to squint, to avoid being blinded by the bright light streaming in through the grate. Lacy shadows sped across the walls behind her, making her feel dizzy. The vacuum effect threatened to suck the air from her lungs.

She took a deep breath and wrapped her paws around the grate, rattling it as hard as she could.

"No! Don't you all leave! The Mudpuddle isn't safe!" Minerva squealed in vain. "Don't go! Don't leave us here alone!"

The portal closed with a pop. The hallway seemed darker, gloomier in the aftermath.

"No!" Minerva felt the tears rolling down her cheeks again.

"We'll be just fine, won't we?" Maida was saying. For a moment Minerva thought she was talking to her. Was that possible? She gave the grate a cautious shove and slipped out through the space she'd made in the bottom corner.

"It's just you and me, Hildegarde," Maida was saying now.

Minerva heard snoring coming from the back of the cafe. It reminded her of Zephyr, but this was a soft snore, nothing like the old wizard's rasp. Peeking around the corner, she recognized the bumbling witch's sensible shoes. But that's not all she recognized.

Seated in Hildegarde's lap, curled up in an unfinished afghan, she saw a large cat shaped blob of white fur. The plume of Gemini's tail dangled down towards the floor, sweeping back and forth like a metronome, stirring up dust.

"Grizzled gremlins!" Minerva sucked her breath in through her teeth and flattened herself against the wall. She didn't think the beast had seen her, at least.

Quietly, she crept along the baseboards, moving more slowly than she would have liked. But she didn't want to dart too fast. The cat's eyesight was far keener than her own. Everyone knew that the worst thing to do when confronted by a ferocious feline was to turn your back and run away.

She passed the hall closet and the door to the mudroom. From here, she could no longer see the main lobby of the bookstore and cafe. But she could hear Maida talking to Gemini.

"I'm so sorry, Gemmy. Nobody's fed you tonight, have they? Where does Rosie keep your food?"

Minerva glanced back at the closet, where she knew Gemini's smelly kibble was kept. She could still duck into the mudroom if needed, but it would mean abandoning her mission. The cellar door was so close now.

"Come on, Gem," Maida called. Minerva heard footsteps and picked up the pace. Her skirts swirled around her petite feet as she silently sidled along.

Another two yards, and she'd be there.

"Come on, Hildegarde's lap will still be there after you've eaten." Maida paused in the doorway to the hall, calling to the cat.

And then Minerva heard the most dreadful sound. A muffled deadly thunk as four paws touched down on the wood floor. She could feel the floorboards vibrating, even though she was yards away. Instinctively, her right hand curled around the end of her tail. Her left hand reached into her pocket and pulled out the closed jar of jam. The glass jar would make a perfect missile to lob at the cat if need be.

Now she was moving more quickly, hopping and skipping sideways along the baseboards as fast as she could scurry. She didn't dare look up. She kept her eyes fixed on the floor, pausing only briefly to check her progress. Finally, she was close enough to cast her rope. But she would need to move to the center of the hallway to get the right angle. She needed the lasso to catch on the knob. Minerva withdrew the colorful cord from her pocket. She wrapped the loose end around her waist and recited a charm for luck.

The low growl that came from the other end of the hallway sounded like a cross between a lion and a hellhound. Minerva didn't want to look. She knew she *shouldn't* look. Meeting a predator's gaze was almost as bad as turning your back and running. Which was precisely what she felt like doing at the moment.

"What is it, Gemini? Do you see something there?" Maida asked. "I don't see anything. It's so dark. Should I turn on the light?"

Minerva's great niece fumbled on the wall, feeling for light switches where Minerva knew well there were none.

The cat growled again.

"Hang on," Maida said. She tucked the book she was carrying under her other arm and felt her way along the wall on the other side of the hall. Now she was getting closer to the switch outside the mudroom.

She heard a wet, smacking sound. Presumably the cat, licking its chops. It made her very bones shiver.

Minerva found she could no longer resist. She tilted her chin up and risked a glance over her shoulder. Two glowing orbs—one a celestial blue and the other a cosmic starlit gold, reflected at her. Long silvery whiskers fanned out in plumes to either side of the crouching feline, twitching like antennae.

She was only going to get one shot with the lasso and she would not screw it up.

Everything happened so quickly, and yet somehow in slow motion as well.

With her left hand she lobbed the jam jar, aiming squarely at the cat's head and putting as much shoulder into it as her slight frame could manage. She was going for maximum impact.

She missed by a mile. She heard the plink of glass hitting the ground and the disappointing susurrus of the minuscule jar rolling away. Gemini lunged forward to catch the jar in her giant paws, batting and pouncing on it like one of her toys.

"What have you got there now?" Maida stepped forward, straining to see.

There was no time to waste. She had to do it while the cat was distracted. Unfortunately, there was no way she would be successful unless she turned her back. Without allowing herself to second guess the decision, Minerva swung the small lasso above her head. She was determined to loop the cord around the doorknob on her first and likely only attempt.

"There's the switch," Maida said, fumbling with the levers along the wall. Nothing happened. "That's strange," she mused. "I wonder if the power is out."

"I'll be right back, Gem. I'm going to go see if there's any candles in the mudroom," Maida said.

One...Two...Three...

Minerva kept one eye open, and squinted the other one half shut, like a marksman, trying to create a sightline. But as she was half blind, with only one eye open, she had barely a quarter's worth of the sight she needed. At the last moment, she closed both eyes tight and let go, saying a prayer, chanting a spell, making a wish.

Suddenly, she was airborne, swinging from the taut rope that she was now clinging to with all four paws and her tail. The adrenaline surge hit even harder and sweeter than Rosie's snickerdoodles. She'd done it! She'd lassoed the doorknob. It was a miracle! Such an adventure, at her age! What a story this would make. Zephyr would be so proud, if only she could tell him. She pulled herself up the rope, claws over tail.

But the next instant, the loop slid down off the smooth metal skull and she was all tangled up and falling towards the cold stone floor. Too fast. Too hard. She braced herself for the impact, eyes squinched shut.

When the impact came, it was not the blow she expected. Instead, she crashed against something soft, warm and...wet? Something that stank of fish breath.

Gemini landed gracefully in front of the door. She stood up on her rear paws, placing the front two against the door, just below the doorknob. Her sharp white teeth held Minerva caged in her mouth. One of them grazed Minerva's right leg, another was pressed up against her ribs. A few millimeters in any direction and she'd be done for. She didn't dare move her body, but she did turn her head to protest.

"Put me down!" she demanded. "Do you know who I am? You must know that I'm trying to help here. Not just myself. I'm trying to help Maida and Arthur, and *Rosie*," she squeaked.

At the sound of Rosie's name, Gemini's pupils widened and contracted.

"That's right." Minerva risked wriggling her right arm and tail free. "Also, I'm just a scrawny little mouse. Why would you want to eat me when you've got such delicious kibble waiting for you upstairs?"

Gemini tilted her head up towards the doorknob and loosened her jaws enough for Minerva to sit upright.

"Please," Minerva decided to try a different tack, "I promise to share all my snacks with you. I know how to get the refrigerator open. Do cats like cheese?"

Abruptly, the cat nudged her forward, bringing her nose to nose with the door to the Archives.

"Wait? Are you trying to help me get into the Archives?" Minerva asked. It was a good thing she was already sitting down. How had she gotten it so wrong? This lovely beast didn't want to eat her. It wanted to be her friend!

Gemini began to purr so loudly and deliciously that suddenly Minerva didn't mind her terrible breath. The good vibrations tickled her toes and her nerves. The louder the cat purred, the less her bones ached. More than this, she felt a sense of hope returning. How was it she'd never appreciated the magic of cats before?

When she reached for her own tail, she felt a renewed sense of purpose.

"Let's do this, Gemini." Minerva poked the eyeballs, stuck her tail up the skull's nose and reached out with both hands to wiggle the death head's eyeteeth. She heard the click of the lock, and was grateful for Gemini's grace as the door swung open.

The great furry beast carried her all the way down the stairs and deposited her gently on the oriental rug by the landing.

"Thank you, Gemini. I think what I'm looking for is actually in the vertical files at the back," Minerva said.

The cat settled down in a sphinx-like pose, watching the door. She gave Minerva two slow blinks from her mismatched eyes and nodded.

One thing was for sure, Minerva decided. If she ever found a way out of this mess, she was going to have to reconsider her attitude towards cats.

FORTY-TWO

LIGHTS OUT

The phrase "just the tip of the iceberg" reminds us that much lies hidden beneath the surface.

Though science and effort can sometimes reveal these mysteries, the journey stirs emotions—fear, curiosity, wonder.

As disciples of Magical Naturalism, we embrace these unknowns, understanding that not every iceberg can be fully measured. Instead, we explore with open minds, always marveling at the magic and mystery that awaits discovery.

–EXCERPT FROM THE MUDPUDDLE MANUAL OF NATURAL MAGIC

Maida couldn't stand simply sitting there, waiting for news. She paced from the cafe to the checkout counter, pointlessly rearranged a few items on the shelves, then put them back. She stared at the silent phone, the bell above the door, Rosie's grimoire on the counter. The shop was too quiet.

In the foyer, the clock on the mantel chimed out the midnight hour.

She carried Rosie's grimoire to the bistro table across from

Hildegarde, who was still clutching the book she'd been reading when she dozed off. Rosie's cat was snoozing on Hildegarde's lap. Maida set down the grimoire, then gently slipped the book out of Hildegarde's hands. She sat down to peruse it.

Spells for Magical Pondscaping, Terrariums and Aquariums was full of the types of gardens she thought only existed in Las Vegas hotel lobbies. Fantastical floating bubbles filled with colorful tropical fish filled one page. Sequin lined ponds full of ferocious flowers plucked straight from one of Granny's afghans. There was even a whimsical aquarium that resembled a neon-lit man cave, where a group of five octopuses were engaged in a game of high stakes poker.

Magic unlocked so many possibilities for creativity. It made things she had never considered before possible. If only she could figure out how to harness her own magic without harming anyone. She wished that someone would have provided her with a guide. Like Rosie's grimoire.

Maida studied the book on the table. She would have liked to look at some of the images again, but she didn't want to pry, and anyway, the book was locked. She turned it over in her hands, and ran her fingertips along the scales until, quite accidentally, her pinky found a button to release the latch.

She hadn't even considered pressing it, when the book started heating up. In a matter of seconds the cover went from room temperature to the red hot searing temp of a branding iron. She barely had the wherewithal to drop the book before the scales left a permanent scar.

The instant it landed on the table, the book cooled off. The noise woke the cat, and Gemini sat up and scratched her ear. She gazed from the book, back to Maida, with half-closed eyes full of approbation.

"I would never read Rosie's book. It's not what you're thinking!" Maida whisper-talked at Gemini. She could not believe she was defending herself to a feline.

The cat stretched lazily before shooting back a judgmental

"sure it isn't" expression. Her whiskers tweaked haughtily as she sniffed at the crumbs on Hildegarde's plate.

"I'm so sorry, Gemmy. Nobody's fed you tonight, have they? Where does Rosie keep your food?"

Maida stood and tucked the Dragon Grimoire under her arm. Perhaps Cormac was right. A book that could burst into flames didn't belong in a bookshop full of paperback novels and spell books. She really ought to take it down to the Archives for safekeeping. And what could it hurt, Maida decided, if she were to poke around to see if there were any books about manifesting while she was down there?

All of this, she noted, was completely dependent on the Archives opening for her. She had no doubts about Amrita, but it almost seemed too simple to believe she could simply walk downstairs and check out the Arcane Archives as easily as if she was heading down to the basement to toss in a load of laundry.

She wouldn't stay long or do anything crazy. She was just going to feed the cat, drop off the book and have a quick glance at the bookshelves. If the Archives were arranged like the shop, she shouldn't have too much trouble finding things.

"Come on, Gem," Maida called the cat. But Gemini wasn't interested. She curled back up again on their sleeping patron.

"Come on, Hildegarde's lap will still be there after you've eaten," Maida coaxed, heading towards the darkened hallway.

Finally, begrudgingly, Gemini jumped down, though Maida wasn't entirely sure whether she was following out of hunger, or if she was simply determined not to let Rosie's book out of her sight.

The minute they reached the hallway, the cat started acting strangely again. She crouched and prowled and pounced. What was it? A marble? A penny? She could faintly hear something rolling down the hall. At least it wasn't another wrapper. She hoped it wasn't that poor mouse.

Maida felt for the light switch on the wall. She was still learning where things were, and she was half hoping one would simply materialize now. It had been days since the house had done any small favors like this. She hoped she hadn't worn out her welcome. Feeling foolish, she slid her hand along the wainscoting, just past the mudroom on the opposite wall. There they were.

Quickly, she flipped all four switches. But nothing happened. Looking back, she could see the front of the house was dark now as well. The power was out. Maida was used to this, having grown up in an older home. She recalled having seen a stack of beeswax candles and a box of matches in the mudroom.

"I'll be right back, Gem. I'm going to go see if there're any candles in the mudroom." Maida crossed her fingers that the mouse, or whatever the cat was hunting, would manage to get away in the meantime.

FORTY-THREE

DRAGON FLIGHT

For the shapeshifter, dealing with Ordinary bureaucracies can be a tedious, if not downright exasperating, task. Forms, queues, and endless paperwork may test your patience, but maintaining composure is crucial if you wish to avoid drawing unwanted attention.

Try to approach all matters of paperwork with an air of calm efficiency. Avoid letting frustration show—gritted teeth or tapping fingers are sure to raise suspicions. When in doubt, ask polite questions and double-check the fine print before signing anything.

-EXCERPT FROM THE METAMORPHIC MAN: A GENTLEMAN SHAPESHIFTER'S GUIDE TO CULTURED CONDUCT

"I tried to stop him. He wouldn't listen," a tearful Rosie told the Ordinary officer. "He was mixed up with some pretty bad people, drugs...Ever since his grandmother passed away he's been alone."

Technically, this was all true. But it was only half the story, and

Arthur was growing impatient. Rosie wouldn't look at him. She kept glancing at the door.

"Where's Maida?" she asked, suddenly.

"Back at the bookshop," Arthur answered. "Will Porter's waiting downstairs. He's got Buffalo's van, he'll drive us home."

Arthur would have liked to open a hole in the wall of the interview room and sweep his daughter into it, and emerge into the Mudpuddle on the other side. Rosie's eyes were hollow. Rather than their usual fire, they reflected the fluorescent lights above. She'd been chewing her fingernails. Her polish was chipped. Her hair hung limply. She leaned forward and folded her head into her arms, burying her face in the crook of her elbow.

"Can we please go home now?" she asked in a monotone.

Arthur glared at the officer, who'd already gone over the story twice. "My daughter has been through a traumatic event. It's after midnight. Would you mind if I took her home now?"

Another officer, this one a woman, came into the room. She seemed more sympathetic. She handed Rosie a box of tissues and patted her on the shoulder. "I'm so sorry, hon. There's nothing you could have done." Rosie took a tissue and blew her nose. Arthur watched in shock as a bit of ash floated up to the ceiling, thankfully extinguishing itself en route.

"Is someone smoking in the building again?" the female officer wrinkled her nose. "Or is that just you that smells like cigarettes, Officer Brown?" She set a piece of paper in front of the other officer.

As he read it, he frowned. "Does this Bardo kid not have any other kin who might come forward for his body?"

Rosie stood up too quickly, pushing her chair back so hard it fell. "I'm leaving," she said. "Now."

The female officer glared at the man. "Sensitivity training?" she mouthed.

"Fine, fine, you're free to go," Officer Brown said, waving a hand without looking away from the stack of paperwork in front of him. "Call us if you think of anything, or anyone else we should talk to. What a mess. Another unclaimed body. Just what we needed."

Arthur pressed his card into the officer's hand. "I'll take care of the funeral arrangements. The Chan family were friends of ours. Have the coroner call me."

Then he placed his arm around his daughter and held her close, silently steering her out of this Ordinary hell.

The van was parked illegally in front of the police station, but at this hour nobody seemed to notice or care. Will was holding the door open for them. Impulsively, he threw his arms around Rosie. "Don't mind me," he said as he released her. "I'll just tell the driver to drive us around the block a few times. I can sit up front if you like. You two can talk. I'm just so glad you're okay." Will used the cuff of his jacket to buff away a tear from the corner of his eye.

"There's no time for that!" Rosie glanced back and forth, as if checking whether the coast was clear, before jumping to the van. "That man's still out there. Tell the driver to head back towards the passage."

"Slow down." Arthur climbed in behind her and Will slid the door shut. "Tell us what happened with Bardo. And don't leave anything out this time."

Rosie wrapped her arms around herself and rocked in the seat. "You know, then? About me?"

Arthur nodded curtly. Rosie groaned. Will looked away.

"I can go if you two need a moment," Will offered.

"No. Stay," Rosie said. She squeezed his hand and raised her chin. "I have nothing to hide. I'm not ashamed of being a dragon."

"Well of course you're not!" Will said incredulously. He held out his hand to slap hers and quickly took a seat on the other side. "Why would anyone be?!"

"When we were little, Bardo used to mock me when I said I

wanted my shift to settle as something mythical, like a dragon. He called me names like lizard legs. I knew he was just jealous, though. Ah Ma Pearl paid more attention to me than him, and he was her own flesh and blood. I felt sorry for him."

"That was very mature of you, Rosie." Will nodded. "Few kids can sympathize with their bullies."

"Bardo could be nice, too. He always shared his snacks with me and he used to pick flowers for me." Rosie closed her eyes tight and rubbed her temples as she recalled this.

"I didn't even suspect what I was 'til a couple of years ago," Rosie admitted. "I just thought I was a late shifter, an ugly girl with unusually dry skin and red eyes. To be honest, I was afraid I'd turn out to be a goat." She sniffled as she laughed. "At least I'm not a goat."

"There's nothing wrong with goats," Arthur said.

"Right." Rosie nodded. "So, none of this actually matters. I know I'm not making sense. But I just want you to know that it's not entirely Bardo's fault that he is...was..." she paused and swallowed. "It's not entirely Bardo's fault that he was such a cloud headed clod."

Tears streamed down her face again as she said this, and Arthur slid closer, holding his daughter in his arms.

"Oh, Daddy..." she cried, the floodgates releasing as she remained there, shaking and sobbing.

He waited as long as he possibly could, which probably wasn't long at all, before asking.

"What happened, Rosie?"

"You know how Bardo was selling Nocturnaturals?" Rosie whispered.

"No!" Will gasped, holding a hand over his mouth.

Arthur pulled away, leaning back to look at his daughter. He felt like he hardly knew her, and this realization hurt.

"Not to magicals!" she corrected. "And not illegally, technically! It wasn't like he was dealing street drugs. It was all legit. He was a...what do you call it when Ordinaries sign up to sell things from home?"

"He was a sales rep," Will furnished the term.

He was a mark.

Arthur kept the thought to himself.

"That!" Rosie pointed a finger at Will. "He was a sales rep. His territory was Boston, and only Boston. He didn't sell to anyone in Primrose Court. And he was making decent money. He was doing it for Ah Ma, he said. To pay her medical bills." Rosie frowned. "Except..."

"Except what?" Will asked before Arthur could.

"Except he had to bring all his samples home with him, and some of the tougher shifters he's friends with thought it might be fun to try the stuff."

"He gave Nocturnaturals to other kids in Primrose Court?" Arthur's blood was approaching a full boil again.

"No. They *stole* it from him. And when he got angry with them, they called him a coward. This was around the same time Ah Ma got real, real sick. And then she told Bardo that she was giving her grimoire to me, even though it was a valuable family heirloom. She said that I deserved it more." Rosie's eyes were shining. Her voice cracked. "She told him she still loved him, even though he was such a...yak." She took a deep breath before going on. "We both knew what she really meant. She meant he was a disappointment. That's when Bardo started experimenting with a few of the products himself. I think he felt like he had nothing to lose."

"Oh no..." Will rested his head in his hands. "That's so sad."

Rosie turned her face up to Arthur's. He could see the ocean of tears that threatened to drown her fire. It made his whole chest ache.

"All I can think about is how that must have felt for Bardo. I don't ever want to be a disappointment to you, Dad."

"There's no way," Arthur said. He placed his hands on her shoulders and shook her gently for emphasis. "Not even if you were an ugly chalk-eating goat. You're my beautiful daughter, and I know who you really are. I see your beautiful soul, Rosie Hart. I'd still love everything about you."

"I'm sorry. I'm so sorry I didn't tell you. I love you too, Dad. So, so, so much."

Rosie squeezed him back. He was struck by the strength in her arms. She accepted another tissue from Will and blew her nose, gently this time. "I'll try not to set the van on fire." The corner of her mouth tucked itself into a wry twist.

"I'd been talking to Bardo about getting out of Nocturnaturals. Since his Ah Ma died, there was no reason he couldn't go back to school and learn a trade."

Arthur held his tongue. It was a moot point now, but the odds of recovering from the languor, once a magical was addicted to synthetic magic, were slim.

"He spoke with his supervisor and they agreed to release him from his contract. He had to return all his equipment and samples. They agreed not to make him pay back what he still owed them if he showed them his Ah Ma's grimoire."

"How did they even know about the grimoire?" Arthur asked.

"Bardo bragged about it during his interview. That's mostly why they hired him, I think. He said he would bring magical assets to the company."

"Son of a troll," Will uttered wearily.

"But it wasn't his book to share," Arthur filled in the next bit. "So he needed you to bring it."

"To be fair," Rosie repeated, "he didn't even really know what was in the book. Ah Ma never showed it to him. He thought he'd borrow it and just let them copy down some of her stinky old chicken soup recipes and we'd be on our merry way," Rosie explained.

"And what did you think?" Arthur tilted his head, and raised his brows. He knew full well his daughter wasn't that kind of pushover.

"I thought that book's not going anywhere without me." Rosie sat up straighter. "But I let him take it. I knew there was no way they'd be able to open it up without me. I'm the only one who can open it now."

"So you had a plan?" Arthur asked this question as gently as possible, tamping down any urge to reprimand his daughter. This was no small task, as every cell in his body was pulsing with four more judgmental words.

What were you thinking?

"Sort of," Rosie said. "I figured it couldn't hurt Bardo to have a live dragon there as backup, if they got too pushy about the book. I figured I could change their minds if it came to that." Her lower lip trembled, and she bit down on it. She hugged herself tightly, gripping her own elbows. "That might not have been the best idea. I take full responsibility for that."

"Okay." Arthur took a shallow breath in. "So, how did it go down?"

"This man was waiting for us in the alley outside the passage. We gave him back the samples, and Bardo handed him the book. For a minute, it seemed like everything was going to be okay. Like he was cool about it," Rosie said. "But then he tried to force open the book, and it burst into flames. He didn't like that."

"What'd he do?" Will was wide-eyed.

"He grabbed me and threatened to kill me if Bardo didn't make the book open for him."

"What did Bardo do?" Arthur's hand was cramping where it gripped the leather bench seat.

"Bardo laughed." Rosie's face crumpled. "He said he didn't care what the guy wanted to do with me or the dumb book. Then he grabbed a bunch of the samples and started eating them. He shifted and started running for the bridge."

"What in the?" Will was at a loss for words.

"Such craven recklessness!" Arthur groaned. He was surprised this hadn't already made the newspapers.

"I think he was trying to buy some time for me." Rosie's breathing was shallow. "The man—his boss, rep, or whatever—

wasn't expecting me to be a dragon. He seemed shocked when I shifted. Ran for cover. It wasn't too hard for me to get away from him." Rosie rocked in her seat, her face contorted now with pain. "I tried to catch up with Bardo. I knew he wouldn't be in his right mind. He was moving so fast, and he just kept saying he was going to be like me, that Nocturnaturals were setting him free. That the world would finally see his fire." She wiped her eyes with her sleeve. "He actually managed to breathe a little green fire, right before I caught up to him at the middle of the bridge. 'Who's a disappointment now?' he said."

"Have some water." Arthur pulled a bottle of cold water from the armrest, and waited as Rosie took a few sips and collected herself.

"Where was his sales manager when all this was happening?" Will asked. "Did he run away too?"

"No." She set the water bottled down. "He followed us. Chased us all the way to the center of the bridge. I wasn't particularly worried about him, though. Not until he took out the wand."

"A wand?" Arthur asked. "As in a wizard's wand?"

"Yes, but not like any wand I've ever seen before," Rosie said. She waved this question away, eager to finish the story. "He was still furious. He told Bardo the deal was off. He wasn't interested in a drug addled yak like him. Then he pointed the wand at me."

Arthur placed an arm around Rosie again. Her whole body was shaking with the stress of telling this story, but she had to get it out. She shook him off and stood up, using her hands to illustrate as she finished the story.

"The next thing I knew, Bardo was charging at the guy. He was running full force at him, a million miles an hour, headed directly toward the railings."

"What happened!?" Will flinched.

"He went right through the man and over the edge," Rosie said. "I felt a tap on my shoulder and spun around. The wizard was standing right behind me. 'Simple sleight of hand,' he said. He called Bardo a halfwit. Then he introduced himself to me and offered me a candy bar." She shuddered. "I didn't stick around to see what flavor it was. I got the hex out of there. I flew—faster than I've ever flown."

"Thank the stars. Good girl." Arthur stood and gathered her again, kissing the top of her head. "Good girl, Rosie."

"I hid in a belfry for four hours. The only reason I didn't come right home is because I was afraid he was still following me. And then I had to go back and check on Bardo. I had to see if he was okay."

"I'm so sorry, Rosie. There was no way anyone could have survived that fall." Arthur rubbed his daughter's back.

"No, I know. I don't know what I was thinking. Maybe I was just in shock. I mean, I think I'm still in shock. That man, he seemed so normal at first. He was handsome, well dressed." Rosie shuddered. "Do you think it's because of the synthetic magic? I'm usually much better at reading people. Cormac seemed so reasonable and nice. Until he...wasn't."

"Cormac?" Arthur froze. Had he heard that correctly? Did she say Cormac? He met Will's eye. "Wasn't that the name of the man who dropped off Rosie's book?"

"Yes, and he's also the founder of Nocturnaturals." Will swallowed.

"Small detail! Whatever was he doing in Primrose Court?" Arthur thundered.

"Product research?" Will shrugged. "Maida said he seemed concerned about Bardo and committed to safeguarding the magical community." Will raised a hand to his forehead and shook his head. "You know, come to think of it, he was in Los Angeles just before Maida's apartment was broken into, too."

"I'd like to know the last time he was in Primrose Court," Arthur growled.

"You think it was around the time the Mudpuddle vanished?" Rosie asked breathlessly.

"Oh. My. Goddess." Will was already on his feet, drawing a circle on the wall of the car. "I've got to warn Maida."

"Are you sure?" Arthur asked. "You've already ported four times today. And you haven't had a chance to recover." He knew that there was a limit to the number of times Will could travel in a day. He suspected that whatever it was, Will was already testing it.

"I can't take you with me." Will was already stepping into the light. "But we're not too far from the passage. Maybe ten minutes at this hour. I'll meet you there."

Ten minutes to the passage! That meant close to twenty before he could possibly get back to the Mudpuddle.

Arthur slammed his fist against the wall of the van just as the portal snapped shut. "I knew there was a link to those blasted Ordinary products. When will folk ever learn not to mess with synthetic magic?"

Rosie blanched.

"So we're talking about the same guy? You really think that Cormac was responsible for the Mudpuddle disappearing. And Zephyr?"

"Yes." Arthur opened and closed his palm, still feeling the impact of the metal on his knuckles. He didn't mind the thrum.

"If Cormac was at the Mudpuddle this afternoon," Arthur spoke quietly, both in an effort not to alarm his daughter, and to calm his own nerves. "I'm guessing that he's come back to finish whatever he started."

Rosie turned back to her father. "Do you think Maida's in danger?"

Arthur nodded stiffly, unable to disguise his worry. "I do. We never should have left her alone in the shop."

"What about Granny?" Rosie banged the partition again. "Where is she?"

"She went to fetch the doctor. In case you needed treatment when we came home," Arthur said.

"Stop the van!" Rosie pounded on the partition with the driver. "Just pull into an alley. Right there, up ahead!"

"But we're almost there," Arthur protested.

"Nevermind, I can get us there faster," Rosie said. She reached for the handle on the door and threw it open before the van had even come to a complete stop.

"Hang on, Dad, I've got you."

A moment later, the biggest, most spectacular dragon that he could ever have imagined gripped him by the shoulders, tucking its talons under his armpits and lifting him into the night air.

FORTY-FOUR

THE MAGIC MIRROR'S TALE

While it is natural for a pure-blooded witch or wizard to take pride in their appearance and accomplishments, one must never succumb to the siren call of vanity. Superiority requires no gaudy displays or excessive preening. Those of noble lineage are recognized by their inherent grace and power.

Narcissism is the indulgence of lesser beings, whose diluted bloodlines compel them to seek validation through superficial means. A pure-blooded witch's confidence should rest firmly in her heritage and abilities. Admiration is not something to be chased, but something rightfully bestowed upon those of distinction.

-EXCERPT FROM THE ARCANE ELITE: UPHOLDING THE SANCTITY OF WITCH BLOODLINES

A map of the Arcane Archives was etched in Minerva's memory. After all, she was the one who had been curating the collection for the better part of a century. She had come up with the intake system, meticulously cataloging and classifying every item brought in.

Once an item was received and logged into the system, the item would be cleaned and prepped for storage.

Storage of enchanted items required careful consideration. One could not simply toss items onto a shelf and be done with it. Many of the items stored in the Archives were dangerous. Vials of obscure poisons and hexed manuscripts required special handling. Many of the storage systems were bespoke. One glass display case full of bottles was submerged in a seven foot long aquarium. The tank was a necessary precaution, as all the bottles in the case contained volatile Djinn.

The aquarium was also quite aesthetically pleasing when the light streamed down through the basement windows. Minerva loved the shadows it cast.

Even with her mental map, navigating the Archives from such a diminished perspective was going to be challenging. Minerva was grateful that she would not have to retrieve anything from the underwater case today.

"This should only take a minute," Minerva spoke to Gemini, who was still as a statue, waiting and watching the open door at the top of the stairs.

Minerva took off running, her sense of purpose renewed.

Although she'd like to claim that she recalled every single item she'd checked into the Archives over the years, she did not. But she most certainly recalled the mirror that Zephyr brought to her, years and years ago, when they were first courting. Zephyr had made a special visit to bring it to her for safekeeping. It was such a minor item. It seemed quite harmless, a mere trifle when compared to most of the items in her care. Wishful thinking convinced her he might have been using it as an excuse to see her.

Zephyr's mirror was one of a handful of items proudly displayed in a large glass curio cabinet on the back wall. The cabinet sat beneath a circular celestial-themed stained glass window that bathed the chamber in colorful light on sunny days.

On nights the moon was full, like tonight, the moonbeams poured in as well. This was where she kept her favorite items—the ones that were safe for public viewing, anyway.

Of course, the mirror had a story and nobody told a story like Zephyr Nightshade.

Zephyr had owned it since he was a child, or so he claimed. He'd picked it up at a flea market in Belfort, France, while on holiday with his parents. She'd loved the fable that he'd shared when he handed over the mirror, almost as much as the charming object.

Minerva wasn't so sure that the story was true, but it didn't really matter. She'd simply been so flattered to see him she hadn't even examined the mirror with her special glasses to check if it truly was enchanted. She'd taken his word for it.

Minerva recalled glimpsing Zephyr's reflection in the hand mirror. His cerulean eyes had sparkled even more brightly as he'd handed it to her. Once or twice as he told her the item's story she let her mind wander. She'd still been listening but also dreaming about a trousseau, and how strange it might be to share the blue turret room with this man.

Veronica's Mirror

Once upon a time, at a bustling flea market in northeastern France, a humble vendor sat impatiently at his stall, waiting for a buyer to trick. He was hoping to offload a peculiar hand mirror. He had no idea the little mirror was enchanted—he only knew it was old, tarnished, and might fetch a higher price if he played his cards right.

"A rare gem! A magical mirror!" he called out to everyone who passed by, though in truth, he had no clue about the item's value. He'd found it in a box of junk, discarded by the roadside.

Along came a series of eager shoppers, each with a common objective. They hoped to get something for nothing and sought to swindle the vendor. The first was a wealthy businessman, his pockets heavy with cash he hated to part with. He saw this as a great opportunity to invest, but only if he could turn a fast profit.

"I'll give you half of what you're asking," the businessman said with a sly grin, certain the vendor was too foolish to know better.

The businessman gazed into the mirror, fully expecting to see his handsome, well-groomed reflection. Instead, staring back was a twisted, miserly wraith, with cold eyes and bony hands clutching at his wallet. He recoiled from the vision and set the mirror down without saying a word, lest the vendor notice.

Next came a haughty society maven. She was pampered, powdered, and rouged like a puppet. Her fingers were adorned with large and colorful stones that sparkled in the sunlight. She examined the mirror with a superior air. "Where are the gems? This looks like a cheap piece of tin," she scoffed, offering a pitiful sum. She lifted the mirror to admire her own face. But she did not find the timeless beauty she'd imagined reflected there. Instead she was facing a sneering, bloated monstrosity, with jewels as dull as her hollow eyes.

One by one, more shoppers came, each trying to con the vendor, and each shamed by what they saw in the mirror. They all sped away hastily, unable to face the truth.

At last, a curious child approached, his pockets empty. He gazed at the mirror with wide eyes. "How much?" he asked softly.

The vendor was weary. It was now the end of the day. He had begun to pack up his wares, and only wished to lighten his load. "For you," he sighed, "just a smile."

The child grinned and lifted the mirror. In it, he saw his reflection bright and true, big blue eyes full of wonder.

The vendor scratched his head, finally noticing how the mirror seemed to change with each potential buyer. "Strange," he muttered. "Perhaps it was worth more than I thought."

But the deal had already been struck, and the mirror was bartered to the little boy with the sunny disposition.

"And you'd have me believe that little boy was you, Zippy?" Minerva had rolled her eyes. "It's a wonderful story, though. It seems like just the sort of item that would end up at an Ordinary flea market. I'll keep it safe for you."

Now she wished she'd recorded Zephyr's voice telling the tale, not just the words, via a transcription charm.

Zephyr had encouraged her to look in the mirror back then too —teased her about it even. But Minerva was superstitious. She didn't dare tinker with any of the items in her care. It was strictly forbidden. More than that, she'd been scared. Scared of seeing a mousy old spinster, who would end up dying alone.

Now she had nothing to lose.

Finally Minerva reached the glass fronted case. She examined the twisted wooden columns on either side. These columns, resembling those on the mantel, were hand carved and sat on clawed feet with dragon scaled talons wrapped around wooden balls. It only took her a moment to locate the opening, hidden in a knothole that was positioned against the back wall. Minerva smiled. She would not have to climb the curtains after all.

She raced up the spiral staircase, past the entrances to the first shelf, and the second shelf. When she reached the third, she turned left and exited onto the velvet lined shelf where the mirror was resting, face down.

It was solid sterling and at least three hundred years old. The ornate tooling on the back contained some unusual markings that also suggested the item was enchanted. By the size, she'd guessed it was a child's hand mirror. Too small for an adult human. But far too big she thought, as she struggled with it now, for a mouse.

Minerva lifted the side of the mirror, attempting to flip it. Try as she might, she could not raise it high enough. Perhaps if she had a lever? She scanned the other items on the shelf, seeking something suitable.

Her eyes landed on the Chalice of Bravery—a silver goblet famous for imparting courage to those who drank from it. Unfortunately, the Chalice was also known to suppress common sense, leading to an increased likelihood of bufoonery, and possible death.

This was the case with most enchanted items. They'd been created to solve a particular problem. But like all inventions, there were bound to be problems when users strayed from the intended use.

Other unhelpful items on this shelf included the Ring of Lost Love, a bit of jewelry that provided relief to the broken-hearted, and the Hourglass of Awkward Pauses.

She'd been tempted to try the ring on, numerous times. But loss of trivial items was a notorious side effect. Even if her ethics had allowed it, she wasn't sure she wanted to trade temporary relief from heartache for the ability to remember where her keys and glasses were.

The Hourglass of Awkward Pauses was shoved into the corner. She'd almost forgotten the modest-looking glass contraption filled with pale gray sand was there. It was a simple device that allowed one to freeze time for up to six seconds. A time-stopping artifact seemed quite powerful in theory, but The Hourglass of Awkward Pauses only worked in specific social situations. It was perfect for creating uncomfortable silences in the midst of important conversations, and delaying laughter immediately following the punchline of a terrible joke. It was a great tool for pulling pranks, but served no other grand purpose that she knew of.

If only she had the Quill of Relentless Creativity, or the Spoon of Good Taste at her disposal. Either one of those mysterious items could have been well put to use as a lever.

Suddenly, a shadow crossed the window and Minerva felt a

chill. She heard footsteps outside the window and heard a familiar voice.

"Of course," the woman said. "I'm happy to help you out. You know I'm one of your biggest fans."

Minerva recognized Lucretia's voice immediately. Hearing it unexpectedly thrilled her. Although her niece could be difficult, she was still family. Minerva longed to speak with her and to share her recent discoveries about their lineage. Lucretia wouldn't like it, but perhaps it would soften her a bit towards Maida.

She wondered if Lucretia might recognize her in this form, as had Granny Luna.

Minerva glanced back at the mirror, forcing her mind to remain on task. She tried once again to heave it up. This time she got it as high as her waist. She glimpsed the flash of silver on the underside and shoved till her arms started to shake. It wasn't working. She needed to get her shoulder under the handle.

Out of the corner of her eye she saw Gemini spring to her feet. There were noises coming from upstairs. More footsteps and in the distance she heard the shop bell. It was late for Lucretia to be calling, but perhaps one of the others had asked her to stop by.

"It's just my niece, Lucretia," Minerva called to the cat.

Gemini wasn't listening to Minerva. Her whiskers fanned out and her ears swiveled. She crouched and sniffed the air. Suddenly the hair on her back stood up on end. She growled a low scratchy warning. Then Gemini took off running toward the stairs.

"Hey! Don't leave me here alone!" Minerva cried out. Her plans really only went so far as gazing into the mirror. She hadn't quite worked out an exit strategy.

She could hear Lucretia's heavy footfall as she made her way down the hallway. Good. Her niece was coming this way.

"Nonsense. Just leave it to me. Maida will be happy to help you with your request." Lucretia's tone was so obsequious and pandering, Minerva wanted to slap her. "I just don't think she understood how important you are to our family. You absolutely need to get hold of that missing grimoire from your grandmother. Where did you say she was from, Cormac?"

Minerva felt her insides turn to jelly at the sound of the mage's name. Her worst fears were coming true.

"That depends who you ask," the silky voice purred. "But she liked to tell people that she was from the same parts as your family."

"Why am I not surprised?" Lucretia laughed. "We purebloods really have to stick together."

FORTY-FIVE

IT'S NOT THE PLANT'S FAULT

Unclaimed fruit still left on the tree when the freezing rains come are an invitation for Ghost Apples to form. They are clear glasslike replicas of the bounty that was left behind.

Trapped inside an icy prison, the once sweet fruits shrivel, rot, and surrender their form. Only the briefest moment of sunshine is required for them to make their escape, slipping silently out of their frozen shells and returning to the earth below.

Ghost Apples are beautiful but hollow. They are a symbol of sadness and loss. They may be pleasant to look at, but provide no sustenance.

– EXCERPT FROM THE MUDPUDDLE MANUAL OF NATURAL MAGIC

While in the mudroom searching for matches, Maida heard a knock on the front door of the Mudpuddle.

Thanks to the full moon, she could see Lucretia Lathrop's pinched face pressed up against the glass. Her aunt rattled the doorknob.

"Hello?" she called out. "Maida?"

"I'm coming!" Maida shouted back. "Just a minute."

She was quite surprised, and not at all delighted to see her aunt, but at the very least, she hoped Lucretia might be helpful. She could use her magic to light a candle.

Maida made her way to the door, navigating around a sleeping Hildegarde, and dodging tables and chairs. There were still embers glowing in the fireplace in the foyer. As she passed by, the mantel clock chimed yet again. She hoped Arthur and Will would be home with Rosie soon. In fact, she wished they were already home. She didn't relish the thought of being alone with Lucretia. She undid the lock and was about to open the door, but there was no need. The shop bells clanged and clattered as Lucretia imperiously pushed her way in.

"Did you change the locks? My key didn't work." Lucretia frowned. "What's with the candle?"

"Come in." Maida waved her aunt into the room she'd already invaded. "And no, I have not changed the locks. The candle is because there's a blackout. I was just searching for matches. Maybe there's some on the mantel?" She felt along the ledge for a box.

"I told you she was useless!" Maida was surprised to see Lucretia looking over her shoulder, back out towards the porch. Lucretia pointed a finger at the candle, closed her eyes, whispered a short incantation and instantly, the candle's wick bloomed with a flickering flame.

"She can't even do the simplest, most basic spell that any four-year-old witch could master." Lucretia clucked her tongue.

Now that the candle was lit, Maida could see the figure stepping out of the shadows.

"I wouldn't put it that way." Cormac stepped into the doorway, smiling at her with his charming, compelling smile. His words were velvety as he came to her defense. "I think that Maida can do anything she puts her mind to, with the right incentive."

"Pfft." Lucretia rolled her eyes and ran a finger along the

mantel, checking for dust. "We'll see about that." She strode into the bookshop.

"I just want you to know this wasn't my idea," Cormac whispered to Maida. "I told Lucretia I could wait till tomorrow. She wasn't having any of it."

"Any of what?" Maida asked, suspiciously.

"Waiting till tomorrow to retrieve my great grandmother's grimoire." Cormac shrugged. "She also wanted to see that book I dropped off earlier. She thinks it might be a dragon grimoire. Do you still have it?"

"I do," Maida said.

"Well, where is it?" Lucretia suddenly reappeared. "I'd like to have a look at it. It's awfully strange that someone would have dropped it in the passage, don't you think? A banned text like that?"

"Dragon grimoires are not banned, Lucretia," Cormac corrected Lucretia. "They haven't been for some time. They're just restricted."

"Well, they should be banned, if you ask me." Lucretia huffed. "It's an insult to our kind to even call them grimoires."

Maida saw Cormac roll his eyes behind her aunt's head, and she bit back her own smile. Perhaps it wasn't such an awful thing that he was here.

"What did you do with it? I hope you took it right down to the Archives!" Lucretia strode to the center of the bookshop and cafe and snapped her fingers, lighting all the candles in the wall sconces and on the bistro tables. She looked disdainfully at the sleeping customer. "Is that Hildegarde Fish? Are you taking boarders here now too?"

"She was sleeping so peacefully." Maida shrugged. "We didn't want to disturb her."

"I see." Lucretia sniffed. "So, where's that dragon book now?"

"It's in the mudroom, actually," Maida admitted.

"The mudroom?" Lucretia gasped. "You left something that dangerous just sitting out on a shelf in the mudroom?"

"I was actually taking it down to the Archives when the lights went out." Maida could hear the defensive tone in her voice, and she didn't like it. She didn't have to explain herself to Lucretia. Cormac caught her eye and shrugged his shoulders. She appreciated his show of support.

"Well by all means let's go do that now, immediately before another moment passes and this whole place goes up in smoke." Lucretia bustled towards the hallway. "And while you're down there, you can help my friend Cormac here. I couldn't believe you were so rude to him earlier when he brought that dreadful book in for you. The least you could have done was offer to check the Archives for his grandmother's grimoire. He has as much of a right to that book as you have to this place!" Lucretia railed. "Possibly more." She strode towards the hallway, still mumbling officiously under her breath. "I certainly think there might have been other, better, more obvious candidates to run this place."

"Maida had quite a bit going on here earlier." Cormac came to her aid yet again.

"That's still no excuse." Lucretia snorted. "I run a busy apothecary. You run a multi-million dollar international business with thousands of employees. Sometimes it's necessary to compartmentalize!"

"I was fine coming back tomorrow," Cormac soothed.

"Well, that won't be necessary now, will it?" Lucretia's heels clacked against the floorboards as she strode down the darkened hallway, flicking her fingers at sconces to light her way.

"I'm so sorry." Cormac's hand rested gently on the small of her back, bolstering her as she followed her aunt. "She really is the worst. I can come back tomorrow. I certainly don't mean to disturb you."

"What else does Maida have to do, right now?" Lucretia asked.

"Actually, I was about to feed the cat," Maida answered, remembering that she had not yet fed Gemini.

"The *cat*?" Lucretia was horrified. "You brought a cat into this household?"

"Why not?" Maida couldn't help but laugh. "Aren't witches supposed to like cats?"

"Not our kind," Lucretia froze in place. "Lathrops do not take familiars, and we certainly don't condone bringing a vile feline into our personal sanctuaries."

"Enough already!" Maida stopped in her tracks. "I understand that you have your way of doing things, but if you wanted me to do things your way, you could have reached out at any point during my childhood. You didn't. And now this place is mine. With all due respect to you and the Lathrop line, I'm going to do things my way."

"Well done!" Cormac whispered in her ear.

"Hmmmph. I guess she does have some of her mother in her after all," Lucretia mumbled.

"I'll be right back," Maida said, ducking into the mudroom to retrieve the dragon book. She looked around for Gemini and called the cat a few times with no luck.

"Perhaps I should come back tomorrow," Cormac was saying to Lucretia, as she emerged.

"Nonsense. Just leave it to me. Maida will be happy to help you with your request." Lucretia was practically simpering over Cormac. Maida was embarrassed for her aunt. "I just don't think she understood how important you are to our family. You absolutely need to get hold of that missing grimoire. Where did you say she was from, Cormac?"

"That depends on who you ask," Cormac drawled. "But she liked to tell people she was from the same parts as your family."

"Why am I not surprised?" Lucretia laughed and batted her lashes at him. "We pure bloods really have to stick together."

"I can't find the cat," Maida said. "So we may as well take this book down now." She held up Rosie's book. "Just for safekeeping till its owner turns up," she added. "I guess we can have a look for your missing grimoire at the same time."

"That's more like it!" Lucretia cooed triumphantly, leading the way to the large ironclad door at the end of the hallway. But when she reached it, she stopped again, gasping in horror.

"Maida Westabrook, is this how you care for things?" She gestured to the open door. "Do you simply leave the Archives open and unguarded?!"

"What do you mean?" Maida leaned forward to see. She was certain that as long as she'd been there, the door had never been opened.

"Fangs and claws!" Lucretia jumped and screamed out loud as Gemini raced out from the door full speed and tore down the hallway hissing. She reached into her wand pocket.

"Stop! It's just the cat!" Maida said.

"Just the cat? You allow that thing into the Archives?" Lucretia sputtered in disbelief.

"Her name is Gemini," Maida said. "She was chasing something earlier, a mouse, I think. She must have followed it down there somehow."

"And now you're suggesting that we have a vermin problem?" Lucretia was in a full lather now. "I'm sorry, but this is the final straw, Maida. I'm going to have to make a formal appeal to the Society. You are not fit—"

"I'm sure it's just some kind of minor glitch. Weren't you just telling me the house is temperamental, Lucretia?" Cormac interrupted, speaking in soothing tones. "Let's just go down and make sure nothing's been disturbed." He looked to Maida for permission and when she tentatively gave him the thumbs-up, he held the door open wider for Lucretia.

"You're not hiding any more cats down there, are you?" Lucretia peered down the stairs, suspiciously.

"It's an archive full of ancient texts, charmed and cursed objects, and you're worried about a house cat?" Maida questioned her aunt.

"Of course I'm not scared. I grew up in this house!" Lucretia blustered, touching her hair and smoothing a hand over her skirt. She placed a hand on the banister and started down the staircase. "I can't recall the last time I was down here with Minerva. Still smells the same, though. Peppermint, mugwort, and brimstone." She inhaled deeply.

"After you." Cormac waved Maida ahead.

The lights were not on in the Archives, but the space was well lit by the full moonlight. It hung perfectly framed by a high, round clerestory window, as if the window were crafted for this particular moment.

"Wow." Maida stopped to marvel at the space. Part cozy library, part underground lab. It somehow managed to be both cozy and clinical at the same time. A long leather sofa sat facing a giant aquarium on the wall beside the stairs. To the left were rows and rows of glass-fronted bookcases with rare books stacked in storage cases. Still more storage cases were made of metal, and there were several refrigerated cases as well. Maida saw shelves full of test tubes and Petri dishes, plant pots and potting material, several saws, chisels, and drills, and at least five fire extinguishers spread throughout the stacks. She glanced around for a safe place to set Rosie's book.

Against the back wall, beneath the round window, was a single glass-fronted display case full of interesting looking items. Long copper-topped work tables sat to either side of the case. Maida set the book down on one of them.

"I'll just check the card catalog for your family's grimoire." Lucretia sat down on a wheeled stool by the tables, then rolled herself towards the tall filing chest in the corner. "What was the name again?"

Maida thought she saw a flash of movement in the case, but when she looked again, it was gone.

"Vorador," said Cormac. He stopped to admire something floating in a jar.

"No. Not your name," Lucretia tittered. "Obviously I know that. I mean your grandmother's name. We're looking for the maternal line."

"Of course." Cormac looked up from the jar and smiled. He smacked his forehead. "What was I thinking? Try Delombre."

"Delombre, Delombre...Is that French?" Lucretia asked as she thumbed through the cards. "I'm not seeing any entries. Do you know when your people came over? New Orleans or—"

"Oh shut up already, you boring old mire maven," Cormac barked.

Out of the corner of her eye, Maida saw a flash of light. Not just one flash, but several blinding lights danced across her field of vision.

"Mmmph! Mnughff!" Lucretia grunted.

Maida swiveled back to face Cormac. He was still standing on the bottom step. Only now he was grinning. Not the charismatic grin she was used to. His smile had somehow slipped, and twisted. It was ominous and off.

"What's going on?" Maida asked.

Cormac reached in his pocket and pulled out a hairy, malodorous black bloom, fashioned into a corsage.

Stapelia grandiflora.

"Did you like my housewarming gift? I made sure to line the pot with some tracking stones when I left it on your doorstep in California, but you didn't take it with you. Thank goodness Addy got your friend to bring it back for you. The blooms have a strong sedative effect on house spirits. Knocks them right out. All the better for exploring the Archives uninterrupted. We can't have this place disappearing again, can we?" Cormac strode across the room and slipped the blossom on her wrist. "The flower looks lovely on you, Maida. You should wear it well."

It's not the plants fault it smells like that.

Compassion, she found, was a very effective way to calm her gag reflex.

A cloud of slithering purple vines surrounded Cormac. They sprang from his pockets and slipped from beneath his sleeves, tangling and untangling as they floated silently around him. She noticed he was holding an odd, ball shaped, mirrored wand aloft. He waved it like a conductor, conducting a symphony, bringing the swirling mass to a crescendo and then flinging it at Lucretia.

"She really talks too much and I can only go along with her antiquated ideas for so long. Pure bloods this, sacred traditions that, you know what I mean? You must. You've always been an outcast too, right?"

Maida watched with horror as the vines bound her aunt more tightly to her chair. They moved and behaved exactly like the branches of the willow tree.

"One hundred percent organic, made from seaweed and upcycled plant matter," Cormac bragged, watching the way she was looking at the deadly plants. "As long as they're powered on, they'll do whatever I tell them to do, and when I'm done with them, I can put them in the green waste bin. Think of how this will revolutionize the security industry!"

He tipped his wand towards the stairs, sending another squadron of the snake-like plants to patrol the perimeter of the Archives.

"What are you doing, Cormac?" Maida tried to speak calmly and evenly as she attempted to calculate her escape route. She didn't think she could outrun him. And she didn't like the look of those vines blocking the stairs. She could still recall what they felt like wrapped around her neck in her father's garden.

"The old ways are over. I've democratized magic and made it available to everyone." Cormac walked over to Lucretia and slipped her wand out of her pocket and into his. "Thank you for supporting the cause." He tipped his head to her.

"The only thing is, I constantly need to harvest more magical items to grow my brand." Cormac sighed. "It's tedious, and I don't really think it's the best use of my time." He used his wand to blast open the case. "So rather than scouring flea markets for magical items piecemeal, I thought I'd come shop at a superstore."

Cormac pulled a small pouch out of his pocket and with

another wave of his wand he transformed it into a full-sized suitcase, and began tossing items in.

"Cormac, stop. Please!" Maida cried out. "Aren't you worried about the effect Nocturnaturals is having on the magical community?"

"Seriously, Maida?" He blasted open another locked case. "When has the magical community ever been worried about the Ordinary community? You know exactly what I mean, don't you? How many times do you think the Director wiped your memory?"

He turned his head and caught her eye. Maida refused to look away. Even when Lucretia yelped and strained against her leafy prison. Even when a pair of vines floated around her, brushing at her knees and fingertips like a curious dog that wished to sniff her. Maida stood straight, kept her gaze level, her breathing even.

"You really think magic solves everyone's problems?" she asked.

"I think having access to magic makes it a lot easier for everyone to solve their own problems." Cormac's answer was immediate. "You can't argue with that, can you, Maida?"

She didn't answer. "So that's your plan, then? Steal from the magical community in order to synthesize products for the Ordinary masses?"

Cormac was nodding along enthusiastically, as if she were praising him. He seemed utterly unaware that she was horrified.

"Yes! Yes, Maida. I'm so glad you get it."

"I don't get it, Cormac. You're not saving lives. You're destroying valuable and important items to make stickers and candies that make women look prettier and men feel smarter. There's not an endless supply of the resources that you're using."

"Exactly!" He gazed at her with so much pride it chilled her. He gestured at the suitcase full of looted treasure. "This stuff is helpful, don't get me wrong, but it's finite. Eventually I'm going to run out of gadgets, gizmos, and grimoires. What I really need is a magic *generator*. Someone who can manifest something from nothing."

He started stepping towards her as he spoke, holding out his free hand, making his intentions and the invitation clear. As he stepped, new vines sprung up from the ground and spiraled around his limbs, creating the impression of a tree walking.

"I don't want to do battle with you, Maida. In fact, that's the furthest thing from my mind. I want us to—"

A whirring sound interrupted Cormac. There was a buzzing of bees and then the brightness of oblivion as a portal began to materialize the wall opposite the display case. Maida turned away from Cormac just long enough to see the way the center of the opening melted and the outer edges turned to static. She saw a hand. Then an arm, clothed in colorful brocade. Someone was trying to come through, but the appendage wasn't quite solid. The colors were off, like an overexposed film negative.

"Will!" she cried out.

"Mayday! You gotta get out of there. It's not safe. That man, he's—"

She could hear Will's voice and she could see his arm flailing, but it was like he was trying to reach the room from too great a distance. The more he struggled, the farther back he shrank. Cormac aimed his wand at the portal and the opening grew smaller. The vines circled the edges of the opening, weaving in and out of the fabric of ether, stitching it up and gathering it like a drawstring purse.

Maida reached towards Will, holding out both her arms.

"Let him go, Maida. We don't need a porter. And if we do, you can just make another," Cormac said.

"It doesn't work like that!" she snapped, turning back to face him.

"Then show me. Show me how it works." Cormac lowered his wand. The stitches went slack and for a moment allowed her to glimpse Will's faded face. He looked utterly bereft. "I can't take you with me, Mayday. I'm not sure I even have the energy to get back," he shouted. But his words came through as a flicker and a whisper. She thought about Will's helplessness and how he must feel. The sadness nearly overwhelmed her.

"What a pity," Cormac said, without pity. "There's nothing to be done though, is there?" He used his wand to scratch his head.

"Come thru, Will!" Maida cried. "Please, Will. You can do it. I believe in you." She clutched her locket, wishing she could save him, do something, anything, to help her friend.

Lucretia grunted loudly and tipped her chin towards the floor. Maida stared down at her own feet and saw the goblet. She picked it up and threw it at Cormac's face. He caught it easily, though, and laughed.

"I'm still waiting, Maida. Show me what you can do to save your friend."

She clutched her locket, praying for a miracle.

There was another flicker of light, movement of some sort from the display cabinet, like the flash of a mirror sending a signal from a mountaintop. Maida could hardly believe her eyes, but a child's hand mirror was moving around inside the display case. She could only conclude that it was an enchanted mirror that had somehow sprung to life. It positioned itself to face Cormac. He caught a glimpse of himself, but quickly turned away, refusing to look.

"You think I don't know what I am?!" Cormac flicked his wand at the mirror, breaking the glass. "It doesn't matter what you show me. You cannot trap me. I have the power to be anyone I want to be. And so will everyone, someday."

"Maida!" Will called. The buzzing sound was back and the portal was shrinking again, this time without Cormac's help. She knew they wouldn't have long.

"I love you, Mayday," Will called. She could feel his very essence, reaching out to her from the oblivion.

I love you too, Will Porter.

Maida held Will close in her heart as she fiddled with the locket's clasp. Then she popped it open, set her intention and whispered the magic word she prayed would save him.

"Gearheart."

The portal contracted and vanished with a pop. Only a haze remained, and this too faded quickly.

Surreptitiously, while Cormac was still distracted by the mirror, she snapped the locket shut in her hand.

FORTY-SIX

CROSSING THE DIVIDE

A pure-blooded home must be vigilantly warded against magical misfortune, for there are envious folk who would seek to hex or curse us. Be cautious when accepting unfamiliar gifts, second-hand items, or objects of unknown origin, as they may carry ill will or dark enchantments designed to undermine the purity of your household.

To recognize a cursed item, look for sudden changes in temperature, appearance, or moisture levels. Objects may emit unsettling sounds, peculiar odors, or even reappear in places where they were not left. If any of these signs are detected, the object should be swiftly and carefully disposed of using proper banishment spells, ensuring your home remains free from harmful influences and malicious intent.

-EXCERPT FROM THE ARCANE ELITE: UPHOLDING THE SANCTITY OF WITCH BLOODLINES

This was an unmitigated disaster.

Minerva crouched behind the goblet, gathering her courage. If only she had some elderberry wine to pour in the magical cup, she might even take a sip.

At the moment, she would have to settle for the righteous indignation that was flowing through her like an electric current. How dare this muddled Ordinary mage appropriate her heritage? What right did he have to come in here and raid the Archives? And for what? Whiter teeth and fresher breath?

She was positively crackling with outrage. Enough was enough. Someone needed to teach Cormac Vorador a lesson. He couldn't be allowed to leave the Archives with the items he was looting. She just needed a moment to take stock, and come up with a plan.

"Cormac, stop. Please!" Maida cried out. "Aren't you worried about the effect Nocturnaturals is having on the magical community?"

"Seriously, Maida? When has the magical community ever worried about the Ordinary community?"

Reflexively, Minerva thrust her paw into her wand pocket. Finding it empty, yet again, her hand now sought her tail. The entitlement of this idiot! How she'd like to teach him a lesson—both literally and figuratively. Cormac didn't know half of what the magical community took care of. If it weren't for the Society's intervention, Ordinaries would have destroyed the entire planet several times over.

"Magic cannot be packaged like cereal," Minerva wanted to shout.

Was everything that came out of that mage's mouth a lie?

Nocturnaturals were all poisonous smoke and funhouse mirrors. Superficial and short-lived. Even Cormac's claims about his horrible botanical minions were false. Synthetic magic had the effect of salting the earth. There was no way those...things...could be composted!

She stood still as a statue and glared at the vines creeping like eels as they passed by the case. Surely there was an enchanted weed whacker hiding in one of these drawers? Even if there were, she wouldn't have the strength to wield it. In the distance, she heard the chime of Papa Lathrop's reliable mantel clock. It seemed to be speaking to her.

Bide your time...

Lucretia was starting to freak out. She looked absolutely terrified, Minerva thought, and who could blame her for that? But although she was bound and gagged, she didn't seem to be in mortal danger. She was still able to breathe and grunt. Her eyes were not covered. She risked waving at her niece, in the hopes that Lucretia might know her and find it comforting. If a fairy could figure out who she really was, surely her own flesh and blood would recognize her?

Minerva hopped up and down. "Lucretia," she squeaked. "It's me! Auntie M!"

But she may as well have been invisible. Lucretia, wild-eyed and terrified, turned back to Cormac, who was ransacking yet another cabinet. This one contained a multitude of poppets and figurines. Lucretia looked on as he piled them into his seemingly bottomless case.

Minerva felt disappointed in her niece.

Watching Maida bravely arguing with this madman, however, filled Minerva's heart with equal measures of pride and regret. She could see why the house had chosen and reached out to the girl. She should have done the same. At the very least, she should have made an attempt to get to know Maida.

She waited till Cormac's back was turned and he was busying himself with his loot, and returned to the task of flipping the mirror over.

She lifted the mirror's handle enough to wiggle her body beneath, lining it up with her spine. Then she nudged her head beneath the base of the mirror. This way, she could use her whole body to accomplish the task. She pushed up on all fours, attempting to balance the mirror, but it slipped, crashing into the stand holding the goblet.

From there, it was a domino effect. The stand fell over, causing the goblet to topple against the glass door to the side of the case. When the door opened from the weight of the goblet, the oversized chalice toppled out and rolled across the floor.

Minerva was sure she'd been spotted. But Cormac and Maida's attention was elsewhere. She heard the buzz of strong, incoming magic a few seconds before she saw the portal appear.

Maida and Cormac were arguing more now, and he used that obscene wand of his to try to close the portal. There was no time to waste.

Minerva got down on her belly and crawled back under the mirror, redoubling her efforts. This time she used her entire body, as well as her tail, to stabilize herself and stayed upright.

She wasn't sure how she was going to safely set the mirror down again, with the glass side up. Her best bet, she decided, would be to back up and lean the mirror against the back of the case. Slowly, she spun around, teetering left and right. She finally stopped when she and the mirror were both facing out towards the room in front of her.

This meant she was staring directly at Cormac. She was terrified that the manic mage would notice her, that he would turn that foul wand on her once again, making her feel even smaller.

But Cormac didn't seem to notice her at all. He was too busy staring at himself.

"Do you think I don't know what I am?" Cormac snarled at his own reflection. Then he lifted his wand and took aim at the mirror.

Minerva was blown back. She heard the sharp crack of glass breaking. The force of the blow separated her from the unwieldy mirror. She simply couldn't hang on. The mirror toppled backwards, landing face up on the shelf.

"No!" Minerva squeaked, seeing the jagged fissure up the middle of the now-broken mirror. She fell to her knees, hovering above it for a moment before breaking all the rules to peer down into the enchanted mirror at herself.

She wasn't quite sure if it would work. She didn't know who or what she would see. She would have to force herself to look, though, really look. It had been decades since she'd studied her own image for more than a passing moment or two. Just long enough to make sure she had nothing in her teeth.

Grasping her tail for luck, she leaned forward and looked down.

There were two Minervas in the mirror, standing opposite each other, their heads almost touching.

Outside the case, she could still hear Maida arguing with Cormac.

"What have you done?" Maida cried.

"Nothing much. I just sealed the porthole. Don't worry, he'll be out of there and running around with his fairy friends in a few days." Cormac wiggled his fingers at her, attempting to wave her feelings away.

"Don't worry? Will's my friend! He can't 'just stay in there' for a few days!" Maida sputtered. "Nobody can survive that long in oblivion. Not even a porter."

"It might not be that long, actually." Cormac shrugged. "Synthetic magic is very potent but also fleeting. One of the kinks we're still trying to work out."

Minerva stared down at the version of herself on the left. She looked almost exactly as she had in the mouse library. The sight of herself as a mouse no longer shocked her. Her light gray fur was fluffy, and she admired the fact that her delicate whiskers were fine and straight. She recognized a wisdom in her own eyes that she didn't think had ever been there before.

On the right side of the mirror, though, she saw her old self, almost exactly the same as she was before her home was attacked and her world was turned upside down. She was a proud witch again—a spry woman with long braids and decent eyesight, even in her old age.

Both images moved in synchronicity. When Minerva stood up straighter, both reflections did the same. When she leaned closer, so did they. She spun to the right and the two images turned to face one another. Both reflections acted in perfect unison with her and each other. When she took a deep breath, they breathed. When she blinked, they blinked.

She leaned in and noticed something even more peculiar.

In the reflection on the right she was holding up her wand hand, as if to cast. But there was no wand, nothing to cast with. In the reflection on the left she was holding her tail aloft in her wand hand, a familiar gesture that felt completely natural. It had become more and more comfortable to her over the past few weeks.

Minerva looked away from the mirror and turned her head to study her own tail.

From the first moments of becoming a mouse, she had appreciated it for its utility. It had helped her to balance, and made so many tasks easier. She had used it to gain entry into the Archives and to help summon her broom. It had comforted her occasionally too, this extra appendage that gave her an edge. To be sure it was no thing of beauty—it didn't sparkle or shine or radiate an ethereal beauty. But neither had her beloved ash wand. Her wand had been small, simple and perfectly functional, like it was made for her own hand.

Synthetic magic is fleeting.

She gripped her tail tighter and pointed it at the lantern on the table close to Lucretia. Quickly, and with her eyes shut tight, she whispered an illumination charm. This time, the magic moved confidently through her like a warm, welcoming stream. It washed away all fear and uncertainty, leaving understanding in its place.

Minerva didn't even have to open her eyes to know the lantern was now lit. She could feel the glow of her own magic radiating back at her from a distance. She wasn't the only one. Lucretia was staring at the glass case. At her. Her eyes were wide with shock, confusion, and recognition. Lucretia saw her.

It felt like the first time that Minerva had been seen, truly and completely. She held a finger in front of her mouth and Lucretia nodded slightly, showing that she understood and would keep Minerva's presence a secret.

Minerva looked back at Cormac, who was still rummaging

through cabinets, packing some things and leaving others on the floor. There seemed to be no method to his madness. Many of the items he threw away were powerful. And others that he kept, were gaudy and decorative at best.

He had not noticed the lantern being lit. He'd been too busy devouring yet another Nocturnaturals bar. The wrappers lay on the floor with the discarded items.

At present, he was wrestling with a fiddle that refused to stop playing. When his own magic failed to silence it for more than a few moments, he resorted to breaking it in half. Still it played on. It was a fairy object. Their charms were some of the most persistent. Not so easy to do away with. Minerva felt a renewed appreciation of and respect for the fae folk.

Maida slipped into the chair beside Lucretia. "It's going to be okay," Minerva heard Maida whisper. "We'll figure something out. We won't let him get away with it."

"No we won't," Minerva agreed. She took one last look at the mirror, and nodded at both her selves. Then she raised her tail to repair the broken mirror and watched as the two images came together quite beautifully.

FORTY-SEVEN

VERY IMPORTANT SOCIETY BUSINESS

A true gentleman understands that even the most capable among us must sometimes ask for help. Recognizing the need for assistance is not a sign of weakness, but of wisdom. When requesting help, do so with humility and clarity—state your needs plainly, without embellishment or fuss.

Equally important is how you accept help. A simple, heartfelt "thank you" and sincere acknowledgment of the aid given are essential. Never diminish the support you've received, nor should you feel compelled to repay it at once. True grace lies in accepting help as easily as offering it.

-EXCERPT FROM THE METAMORPHIC MAN: A GENTLEMAN SHAPESHIFTER'S GUIDE TO CULTURED CONDUCT

"Just this once, Dad, will you let me have your back?" Rosie landed gracefully and set her father down in the alley outside the passage to Primrose Court. She shifted so seamlessly there was barely a break in the conversation. "You don't have to do everything yourself."

Arthur took off running, with Rosie close beside him. They raced through the alley on two legs, but with the preternatural speed of their shifted selves. Arthur held his tongue till they reached the brick lined passage. It was easier to say what he had to say without looking at her.

Rosie ducked behind the billboard first and Arthur followed close behind.

"I want you to promise you won't come in," Arthur said. "No matter what happens. Say it back to me. I need you to promise, or I'm going to worry."

"Please, Dad." Rosie was tearful again. When she exhaled, a purple plume of fire lit up the tunnel for a brief moment. It exposed a litany of wishes, complaints, poems, love letters, and secrets carved into the wall. All those words tumbling all over each other. But Arthur couldn't find the right ones.

"You know you aren't the only one who worries about the people they love," Rosie entreated. "Let me help."

She was right, of course. He could start by acknowledging that.

"You're right," Arthur said. "But even if we both go in, it might not be enough. We've already seen what Cormac is capable of. I need you to call in Amrita, Buffalo, Granny Luna, and the doctor. Call the entire town council if need be. And use your T-watch."

"So you're cutting me out again?" Rosie groaned in disbelief. "I'm not a helpless little goat shifter, Dad. I have every reason to go after Cormac, too. Bardo wasn't an angel, but he was still like family to me."

"I'm not cutting you out, Rosie. I'm counting on your help. I can't do this alone, which is why I need you to go. I need you to fly as fast as you can and bring reinforcements."

A few months ago, it would have broken him to ask his daughter for any kind of help. But now it was a comfort. He knew she was capable, and more than that, he felt relieved to know that when push came to shove she was someone he could rely on.

"Can you do this for me? Please, Rosie. I need you," he said as they emerged into the square.

"Okay." Rosie nodded. She took a deep breath and stood tall. "I'll do as you ask, but I don't like it. I hate the idea of you going in there alone."

"Not alone. You've got my back." Arthur smiled and gave his daughter one last hug.

"About time someone came," Arthur heard a disgruntled voice coming from the street in front of the Mudpuddle. He was surprised to see three very sleepy squirrels in pajamas sitting on the fenceposts by the gate. One of them was wearing a sleeping cap. Another was holding a candle in a metal candle holder.

"That Ordinary chap is down in the basement with Lucretia and Maida. They're making a racket. We can't sleep, and we really need to get some rest. Tomorrow night is our book club."

Rosie turned to the three squirrels. "You three should get back to bed. Would you mind if I used your house phone, though?"

"Is it a local call?" the largest squirrel eyed her warily.

"It's several calls," Rosie whispered conspiratorially. "Highly confidential stuff. Very important Society business." She winked at her father. "Can we trust you three to keep a secret? I'd be happy to deliver some extra cookies for your book club meeting tomorrow."

"Official business? Like in our books? Of course, of course, we won't tell a soul!" The squirrels were already chattering amongst themselves, nodding quite excitedly and calling out to their friends in the trees.

Rosie was a genius.

"Go." Rosie waved at Arthur. "Quickly. And be careful. I'll get help."

"Give our regards to Minerva!" Arthur heard one of the squirrels call out as he opened the front door.

It was quiet inside the bookshop. Too quiet. The power appeared to be off, but there were candles burning on all the cafe tables and in sconces down the hall. He was surprised to find the malodorous plant from California sitting on the mantel.

Arthur heard Gemini before he saw her. There was a clattering sound as she knocked a tin of runestones from a shelf in her haste to reach him.

"Rosie's fine," Arthur spoke softly, reassuring his daughter's familiar. "She's okay. I promise."

At the end of the hallway, the door to the Archives stood open. He could hear voices coming from below. The stench of synthetic magic coming up from the basement was cloying—a thousand times worse than that smelly plant. He had to stifle a gag.

"Go hide, Gemini! Go somewhere safe. Hide and wait for Rosie," Arthur quietly urged the cat.

Slipping off his shoes, Arthur crept quietly down the hall. When he reached the end, he slipped silently through the ironclad doorway. From the top of the stairs, he could see Maida. She was sitting at a table towards the back wall of the Archives. She wasn't alone. Lucretia Lathrop was seated next to her. At least he thought it was her. It was hard to tell under all those vines.

Will was nowhere to be seen.

Cormac was partially concealed, standing beside a rack full of musical instruments. He seemed to be wrestling with a broken violin.

"Someone needs to put you out of your misery!" he snarled, bashing the fiddle against the cabinet.

"The same could be said for you," Arthur snorted.

By the time he reached the bottom of the stairs, which was no time at all, Arthur was in full stag form. His shoulders had broadened to twice their human width and his limbs had lengthened. Thick brown fur covered his sinewy, muscled form. Above his head, a massive crown of antlers sprawled skywards, like the branches of a mighty tree. Cormac was barely half his height.

The element of surprise was very much in his favor. He pawed at the ground, feeling his natural adrenaline surge. He was more surefooted on his hooves, and much faster as well.

"Arthur, look out, he has a wand!!" Maida cried out, jumping to her feet. Lucretia strained against her binding and grunted.

Out of the corner of his eye, Arthur saw Cormac brandishing

the wand, and it gave him pause, especially since he wasn't pointing the wand at Arthur. It was pointed at Maida.

"Seriously, Maida?" Cormac hissed. "What do you see in this guy? He's an *animal*. Literally. Lucretia will back me on this."

Her eyes filled with tears.

Arthur's heart skipped a beat.

Cormac took advantage of this hesitation, smiling a canny smile.

"I could change her mind about you, Hart." Cormac circled around Maida, waving his wand rhythmically and speaking in a sultry tone. "You know I'm a much better choice for you, Maida. Why don't you just tell Arthur to go away..."

If the smell of Cormac's magic wasn't already making him sick, this performance would. He watched as Maida shuddered, and blinked confusedly, trying to shake it off.

"Always trying to play the hero, Hart," he drawled. "Doesn't it get tedious trying to save all the creatures?"

Doesn't it get tedious being such a cliché?

Arthur pawed at the ground.

"Right, I forgot you can't speak in your present form. Must be challenging for a solicitor. Your type is always full of so many words, words, words. I think I prefer you in this form."

I think I'd prefer to release you from yours.

He knew Cormac was baiting him, trying to get him to shift to a more vulnerable form. Arthur couldn't waste a single precious second. Not while the mage had his wand pointed at Maida.

The things Cormac was saying made Arthur's blood boil.

"You and I are going to be so good together..."

When he looked at Maida, he saw the vines creeping closer.

Arthur lowered his head, preparing to charge. His nostrils flared and he snorted and pawed the ground again. If he was fast enough, Cormac wouldn't have time to cast.

"Ah, Ah, Ah..." Cormac waved his wand back and forth like a finger, warning Arthur off.

Don't you touch a single hair on her head.

"No," she shook her head, "no, no, no..."

"No, what? No, we shouldn't let him go? I agree." Cormac laughed and turned back to Arthur. "Your timing is impeccable, Hart."

"Arthur, no!" Maida pleaded. "Just go. Rosie needs you. You shouldn't be here."

He lowered his head again, and Cormac spun to face him, eyes full of mad, unhinged glee.

"You know what, Hart? I forgot that synthetic magic doesn't work so well on half-breed manifesters like Maida. But it sure works wonders on simple shifters like you." Cormac held the wand between his palms and started to spin it back and forth rapidly.

"I'm not normally this much of a carnivore," Cormac said. "But I'll make an exception for you. I've heard consuming a shifter in their altered state can impart the eater with the creature's powers." He took a step forward.

Arthur's ears rang and his vision became blurry. He lunged forward to charge, but it was as if, all of a sudden, his limbs were stuffed with cotton wool. He wasn't getting anywhere. He couldn't move.

All around him, the swimming vines began to fall to the ground. That was good, at least. Had Maida managed to make that happen?

He couldn't see her but he had the sense she was near, moving her hands like she was sketching something. She was swaying back and forth, waving her arms as if she were painting with her whole body.

"Get out of here, Mr. Pants!" Maida shouted. Her voice was muffled, like she was far away. Or perhaps it was all the stuffing that made it sound that way.

It's happening again, he worried. He was being discarded. The more he struggled to get closer to Maida, the farther away he flew. This was nothing like flying with Rosie. He caromed off walls and tumbled over tables. He hit the floor hard and immediately ricocheted back off the ceiling.

It should have been quite painful, this abuse. But he was surprised to find he was completely numb. He couldn't feel his limbs at all as he was bounced and rolled back up the stairs and out the door.

It was only his pride and his heart that ached as he lay there alone, desperately wishing he could have done more.

FORTY-EIGHT

GO FISH

In the realm of Magical Naturalism, spontaneous generation is the theory that life or matter can seemingly appear from nowhere, though we know that all magic, like energy, is finite and ever-circulating in the universe.

One argument for this theory is the well documented existence of star jelly—an ethereal substance believed to fall from the sky without origin.

Though it feels as though it materializes from nothing, it is simply a manifestation of energy, transformed and given shape by forces we do not yet fully understand. In nature, nothing truly comes from nothing; it is all part of a greater magical cycle of energy.

-EXCERPT FROM THE MUDPUDDLE MANUAL OF NATURAL MAGIC

The last thing Maida wanted to do was call Cormac's attention to the magical item around her neck, inside of which she prayed her friend was safe.

She was pretty sure her plan to save Will had worked. The

gearheart locket felt heavier. It whirred and buzzed contentedly against her chest. The warmth of it was very welcome in the damp chill of the cellar. Maida tucked it into her shirt and continued to chastise Cormac for leaving Will inside the portal.

The trick was standing up to him, without pushing him over the edge.

Cormac's greed was making him reckless. He plowed through cabinets and tore down carefully organized displays, all the while devouring more of his magic bars. He seemed voracious, manic, and unpredictable. He was getting frustrated by the simplest items, flinging them to the floor at the first sign of resistance.

She did not know how long he planned to spend down here, but they both knew that he couldn't stay forever. The clock was ticking. Eventually, it would be morning. Arthur and Granny and Rosie would return. The bells would chime and there would be customers in the shop above. She couldn't bear to think about what Cormac might do to any of them.

"Cursed chords!" Cormac shook the enchanted fiddle that was screeching an ear-splitting dirge. "Stop that wretched warbling! Silencio!" He pointed his wand at it and spoke officiously, but the instrument refused to obey. It seemed to get louder. Cormac kicked at the case and cast again, trying spells in other languages and dialects, to no avail. The cacophony continued.

Maida took advantage of Cormac's distraction to creep over and sit beside Lucretia. If only she could release her aunt's bindings, Lucretia might help.

Tears were streaming from Lucretia's eyes as she looked at Maida, imploringly.

"It's going to be okay," Maida whispered to Lucretia. "We'll figure something out. We won't let him get away with it. I know you didn't know before. But you do now. And you've got to help me. There's got to be something we can do."

Lucretia nodded, but she wasn't looking at Maida. She was staring over Maida's shoulder at the display case. The same case that Maida had noticed flashes of movement in. Another single tear fell from the corner of Lucretia's eye.

Maida turned her head and spied the motion again. Squinting her eyes, she struggled to make out the tiny figure that was responsible. At first she thought she was imagining it, that it was a trick of the light. But as the lantern on the table in front of them suddenly lit, as if by magic, she realized her eyes did not deceive her.

There was a tiny mouse inside the display case, casting spells with her tail. A moment later, a message appeared on the lantern's glass, as if it were written with a finger.

Welcome to the Archives, Maida. You'll do just fine.

Maida sat up straighter, and felt her whole self lifted, as understanding dawned on her. The mouse that she'd been seeing all over the house, in the mudroom, the bookshop, and the cafe—that wasn't any ordinary mouse.

She looked at Lucretia.

"Is that?"

She'd been about to say "Minerva", but the question was interrupted when she noticed a familiar figure standing at the top of the stairs, silently assessing the situation.

"Urrrrghhhh! Someone needs to put you out of your misery!" Cormac was so busy bashing the fiddle against the cabinet that it took him several seconds longer than it should have to notice Arthur's entrance.

"The same could be said for you," Arthur retorted.

Before she could blink, Arthur was at the bottom of the stairs.

Even in his animal form, there was no mistaking the Arthurness of him. His flaming eyes were wise and understanding. His massive, muscular form was strong, capable, and steady. His entire body glowed with the glossy brown warmth of fine, polished wood. And of course, his crowning glory, a thorny forest of horns, stretched over six feet high towards the ceiling. He wasn't just magical. He was majestic. It was such an impressive sight, to see him like this, that it made her forget the situation, and all the danger they were in, for a moment.

But she was quickly reminded of the threat. Cormac was holding his wand over his head, staring cagily at them both, deciding what to do.

Maida leapt to her feet.

"Arthur, look out, he has a wand!" she shouted.

"Seriously, Maida?" Cormac hissed. He spun to point his wand at her. He stood straighter and cracked his neck. "What do you see in this guy? He's an *animal*. Literally. Lucretia will back me on this." Cormac jerked his head toward her aunt, in a broken bid for support.

Arthur, who had been about to charge, lifted his head slightly. He watched with feverish eyes as Cormac shook the wand at her.

With a whistle Cormac called the circulating vines. They swarmed closer to her. Not close enough for contact, but enough to menace her, surrounding her like airborne leeches.

Lucretia closed her eyes, and Maida could see she was shaking.

"I could change her mind about you, Hart." Cormac turned the full force of his false charm on Maida now. He smiled that falsely charismatic smile and shook his wand back and forth like a metronome, then touched it gently to her cheek. "You know I'm a much better choice for you, Maida. Why don't you just tell Arthur to go away..."

Cormac rolled the wand impatiently between his fingers and flipped it showily.

She could feel the waves of his spell breaking over and rolling off her like a toxic oil spill. What tried to cling was revolting.

Arthur met her eye again, his nostrils flaring. He pawed the ground again, gazing from Maida to the wand, and back again.

The vines edged in closer, distracting her as they tickled her forearms and kissed her calves. The spell hadn't stuck, but it had still dazed her. She couldn't make sense of what Cormac was saying.

"No," she shook her head, "no, no, no..."

"No, what? No, we shouldn't let him go? I agree." Cormac laughed and turned back to Arthur. "Your timing is impeccable, Hart."

"Arthur, no!" Maida pleaded. "Just go. Rosie needs you. You shouldn't be here."

She saw the look in his eye, the flash of pain and hurt, followed by sheer determination and resolve. Suddenly she was feeling everything he was feeling; how desperate he was to save her, how he was willing to risk everything. For her.

She felt the same way about him.

"You know what, Hart? I forgot that synthetic magic doesn't work so well to hypnotize half-breed manifesters like Maida." Cormac pivoted back to face Arthur. "But it works on shifters like you."

Cormac lowered his wand and placed it between his palms. He rolled it slowly back and forth, shooting sparks of prismatic white light that crackled and crystalized, taking the form of razor-sharp teeth. Row after row clicked together, like beads on a string. They spiraled around Cormac, creating an insatiable vortex with him at the center.

"I'm not normally much of a carnivore," Cormac said. "But I'll make an exception for you. I've heard consuming a shifter in their altered state can impart the eater with the creature's powers." He took a step forward.

Maida was horrified as she watched Arthur struggle against Cormac's mesmerizing spell. His eyes were wild with fear, pain, and sadness. She could sense his emotions as if they were her own.

What is the point of empathy if you are powerless to change things?

"Such a pity, Hart." Cormac laughed in anticipation of his own punchline. "Here you came to get the girl, but instead you're going out stag!"

Maida caught the glint of something glass moving in the display case again.

Time froze. Cormac, Lucretia, and Arthur froze. The vines that bound her aunt, and all the ones surrounding Maida, withered. They fell in limp coils to the ground. Even the corsage on her wrist went limp, making her feel sad for the plant once again.

It's not just about bees and butterflies, Maida. It's about hopes and dreams. You have the ability to create change in impossible ways.

Arthur's words echoed in her mind. He'd had such faith in her. He'd trusted that she'd find her way.

He'd been right.

All at once, Maida understood. Her magic wasn't about synthesis. It was about emphasis. Cormac couldn't make something from nothing and neither could she. No one could. Energy didn't exist in a void. That wasn't how manifestation magic worked.

What Maida could do, she realized, was harness her capacity for empathy to direct energy and emotions toward a different outcome. Arthur was right to trust that everything flowed from intention. She knew exactly what she had to do to harness her power.

Maida closed her eyes tight and threw out her arms. She pictured Arthur somewhere else. Somewhere safe and comforting. This part wasn't any more difficult than holding a candle and shielding it from the wind. Instead of cupping her hand to protect the flame, she opened herself to Arthur's essence, offering it temporary shelter in the safety of her heart. She felt her chest contract, growing warm as his energy filled her.

She didn't have time to properly enjoy the sensation.

Time was moving forward once again, and Cormac's spectral teeth were gnashing.

"It isn't true about eating shifters! That's an old charlatan's tale!" Lucretia shouted, now freed from her bonds.

"It's still worth a shot." Cormac's eyes were all pupil. They bulged with ravenous desire, and she could see the tip of his tongue poking out from between his parted lips.

"Talk about your deer in the headlights." Cormac smirked, advancing another step towards Arthur.

And there it was again. The glint in the cabinet. Time standing still.

Cormac froze, but Maida did not. She began to sway and wave her arms as she sketched out a vision in the air. She pictured the bookshop, the cafe and the twinkling of stars in her turret bedroom. She imagined Granny's afghans and mugs of cocoa, and sitting in front of a warm, cozy fire. She thought of feelings first. Then she imagined physical things. And then finally, as she drew them in the air, she said the words aloud. One by one, Maida conjured all the creature-comforts that made her feel most safe, finally focusing most intently on the one that she and Arthur had in common.

Mr. Pants.

"Abracadabra," she said. "I create as I speak."

How long did it take? Five seconds? Maybe six?

When she opened her eyes again, Maida was still standing in the chilly basement Archives. But she was no longer cold now that she had magic to warm her. She was delighted to discover that she was also wearing Granny's afghan like a cape. Mr. Pants was safely tucked under her arm.

"What have you done with him?" Cormac roared in frustration as he came back to life. "Where is he?" He whirled around in a circle before turning his famished, snarling tornado of teeth in her direction.

"Get out of here Mr. Pants!" Maida flung the toy away from herself, aiming for the stairs.

Cormac swiveled and lunged at the toy, missing it by mere inches. The cyclone of teeth retracted back into his wand as he gave up and gave chase on foot. But he couldn't keep up with Mr. Pants. The toy moved more quickly than him, eluding him as it bounced through the Archives, up the stairs, and out the door.

Lucretia clapped her hands. "Well done!" she whispered to Maida.

"Enough with these distractions!" Cormac stood at the top of the stairs, glaring down at them. He reached into his pocket for yet another snack, only to find he was out. He grimaced. "Not to be a bane bard, ladies, but it looks like it's about time for me to hit the road."

Outside the high windows, the first rosy tendrils of dawn were streaking the horizon. Cormac eyed the overstuffed suitcase still on the floor below and raced back down the stairs.

"I don't know what you did with the shifter, but this is not over," Cormac said, waving his wand at everything and everyone in the room.

He gathered the suitcase under one arm and turned towards the stairs. Almost as an afterthought, he reached out to rip the afghan off Maida's back as he strode by.

It was a terrible mistake.

All the carnivorous flowers crocheted into the design sprang to life at once, rearing their hideous hissing heads. One of the largest blooms, an oversized black blossom that was surely a cousin of the unfortunate corsage on her wrist, thrust its feral face forward and struck. It tore a chunk of flesh from Cormac's outstretched arm, causing him to drop his wand.

"Pernicious plant!!" Cormac howled, dropping the suitcase to grip his damaged limb. "That was my wand arm, you slobbering shrub!"

"Excuse me?" A timid voice rang out from the hallway above. "Hello? Is anybody here? Is everything alright?" Maida heard the unmistakable sound of sturdy, sensible shoes trudging down the hallway.

"My goodness, what time is it? I must have drifted off," Hildegarde mused. "Hello?" She tapped at the light switch by the entry to the Archives with her wand.

And then the poor, discombobulated witch came clomping down the stairs.

"Look out! Hildegarde!"

"Stay where you are. Don't come down here!"

Maida and Lucretia both called out, trying to warn the bumbling witch away.

Cormac lunged forward to retrieve his fallen wand, but it jumped away from him every time he tried to grab it. He scrabbled on the floor frantically, reaching mistakenly for empty wrappers, as he grew increasingly more agitated and weak.

"It was right here a second ago! What is this trickery? Where did it go?!"

"Looking for something?" An elderly witch materialized before their eyes. She had her hand in a paper baggie, as if she meant to scoop animal refuse. The stem of Cormac's wand poked out of the open end. Now that he was no longer waving it around, it looked shabby and pathetic. Several pieces of mirror were missing from the mosaic on the handle.

"I think it's time we did away with this, don't you?" The elderly witch opened a drawer marked Magical Waste Disposal, and dropped it in. When she slammed it shut, they heard the whir of machinery, followed by a crunching sound and suction.

"Oh good. Is that you Minerva, dear? Are you back, then? Do you know whose toy this might be? I found it in the cafe."

Hildegarde reached the bottom of the stairs just in time to see Cormac lunge.

"Oh heavens, no!" she cried. "You stop that at once!" And with a flick of her wand, Hildegarde turned Cormac into a tiny flopping fish.

FORTY-NINE

A FAMILY BRUNCH

Perhaps there is much we could stand to learn from the humble sea otter. To this keystone species, family is everything.

In order to stay close in the ever-shifting ocean currents, these playful creatures form a "raft" by holding hands, linking themselves together in a web of love and protection. It's a magical sight—otters floating in perfect harmony, bound not only by their paws, but by the invisible threads of connection.

Otters remind us that even in the vastness of life's currents, family holds us together, keeping us anchored in the most unexpected ways.

-EXCERPT FROM THE MUDPUDDLE MANUAL OF NATURAL MAGIC

"Who's up for some fresh baked scones and herring?" Granny Luna and the doctor breezed back into the cafe where Maida, Arthur, Rosie, Buffalo, and Will were already assembled.

"It's about time," Will said, reaching into the bag of pastries. "I thought you'd never get back here."

"Where's Hildegarde?" Granny Luna asked.

"She left as soon as Rosie got back with Amrita and Buffalo," Maida answered. "She seemed in a hurry to get home."

"She should have stuck around for tea," Granny said. "Although I don't think we can charge her for tea ever again after what she did this morning."

"Agreed." Lucretia sipped from her cup, pinky extended. "It might be the first time in Primrose Court history that 'wrong-spell-Hilly' got it right."

"Are you just going to leave him there?" Buffalo looked askance at the beta fish flouncing around inside the mirrored glass orb on the bookshop counter. Every time the fish spied itself, which was often, it fanned out its fins.

"Why not?" Maida shrugged. "Hildegarde helped to put him inside that habitat and Minerva reinforced it. He can't hurt anybody now and he gets to spend his days looking at himself, which was always one of his favorite activities."

"What will happen to his company?" Lucretia asked, a worried frown playing upon her brow.

"I think that's for the Society to decide." Arthur cast a stern look at Maida's aunt. "But I imagine it's not long for this world."

Lucretia folded her hands piously in front of herself and stared down at them, nodding as she processed this. "Good," she said. "I just hope the products are destroyed before anyone else gets harmed. I...I had no idea." Her voice faltered. Finally, she looked back up at Arthur and Will. "And I'm so sorry to both of you."

"We know." Will grinned. "And that apothecary discount you offered us for life is still a thing. You'll honor that, right? I'm almost out of OPF cream."

"Absolutely." Lucretia crossed her heart. She used her wand to stir her tea. The wand had not left her hand since the moment she'd retrieved it from Cormac's bag.

"Then no harm, no foul, right, Arthur?" Will prodded Arthur

in the arm. "It was nice of Lucretia to help Maida restore us, wasn't it?"

"I appreciate your efforts to make things right," Arthur agreed. "As well as the discount." He was still picking stray fluff off his clothing, meticulously gathering the bits into a tiny pile, so that they could stuff them back inside the original Mr. Pants. Now that he and Maida had finally found each other, he felt more whole than he ever had in his entire life. Perhaps he was just being superstitious, but he didn't want to risk losing any more bits of himself.

"Goodness, I'm famished!" Will popped an entire scone into his mouth.

"I thought you said there were donuts inside the gearhart locket?" Arthur asked.

"Mmph..." Will chewed and swallowed. "There *were* donuts, but I was operating on a deficit. I really appreciated them though! Such a thoughtful touch sticking The Bunny Hole in the locket with me." He beamed at the group. "Maida thinks of everything."

"It wasn't fully intentional," Maida confessed. "I just wanted you to be somewhere you found comfortable. The Bunny Hole was the first place that came to my mind."

"Didn't anyone notice the donut shop went missing?" Arthur poured some cream into his coffee.

"Not really." Will helped himself to a second scone. "It was still the middle of the night in LA. Business hasn't been so great there lately. Ever since The Greatest Crepe opened up down the street. They're targeting a more international porting clientele but the Ordinaries can't get enough of their food. That coastal crowd is notoriously fickle."

"The struggle between sweet and savory is hardly a regional phenomenon," Rosie noted. "Do you think we should put crepes on our menu?"

"I think it's an excellent idea. But only if they include cheese," Minerva chimed in. She and Amrita had finally returned from their debriefing down in the Archives.

Buffalo stood to hold a chair for each of them, then settled himself back down beside Amrita. He placed a scone on her plate and poured her a cup of tea from his own teapot. Maida didn't think she'd ever seen her father so solicitous, and it amused her to see this unexpected side of him. He seemed younger and somehow softer around the Director. She couldn't help noticing the way they kept catching each other's eyes, either. It was as if they were wordlessly sharing secrets. She supposed they had quite a bit to catch up on.

Under the table, Arthur laced his fingers through hers. Taking advantage of a lull in the conversation, he leaned forward to whisper in her ear. "You know, when I said I trusted you to take care of Mr. Pants, that scenario wasn't exactly what I had in mind."

"I know." She blushed. The feel of his skin against her own had her imagining other scenarios. She longed to be alone with him. She wanted to see him transform again, to sketch him as he was in both states. She wanted to map his every sinew with her fingertips, and revel in the miracle that he was. Their togetherness seemed inevitable now, written as it was in the stars.

"You're really something," she whispered. "Thank you for coming to my rescue again."

"Always," he replied. "But it turned out this time that you were the one meant to save me." He held her gaze. "Not just me. All of us, apparently. So thank *you*. Thank the moon and the stars, the gods and the goddesses and all of nature in her infinite wisdom, for you." He held her hand more tightly now, and looked away, gazing at his feet. "I hope you weren't too disturbed, seeing me shift like that."

"Arthur?" Maida looked into his eyes, the eyes that had come to feel as much like home as the house around her. "I loved what I saw."

She also loved the shy smile that bloomed on his face at her words. It reminded her of the boy he had once been. She'd only seen that smile once, over her shoulder, but it had imprinted on her soul, a negative image waiting to develop into something more.

"Does this make me your toy?" His lips grazed her earlobe, and she shivered in the nicest way.

"I sure hope so," she murmured.

"Good," he whispered back. "Because I don't think either of us should play alone anymore."

The clunk of wood and the clink of china as Granny set a heavily laden tray on the table interrupted their interlude. The tray contained fresh plates of cookies, toast, savory cheeses and vegetables, and the aforementioned herring, as well as a fresh pot of tea in a floral pot.

Granny passed the herring plate first.

"No herring for me, Beryl!" The doctor waved away Granny Luna's offer. "You know I'm vegan."

"I'll take some. You know this was Zephyr's favorite." Minerva helped herself to a piece. "I wish he could have been here today."

Will helped himself to one of Rosie's freshly baked cookies. He closed his eyes in rapturous pleasure as he crunched. "You know Rosie, have you considered the concept of a brûlée bar for a pop-up bakery?"

"Don't go giving her ideas. First, she has to finish high school," Arthur admonished.

"This tea is for you, Minerva." Granny set the pot down in front of the senior witch. "Don't let it get too cold."

"Thank you, Beryl," Minerva replied. "And thank you for helping to put the Archives back to rights. I don't know how you did it so quickly. Some items will still need repair, but there's nary a sign of the mayhem that took place."

"Well that's what house fairies are for." Granny smiled. "We do come in handy occasionally."

"She even got rid of that stubborn synthetic magic smell," Will commended.

"I hope you have fun with the hourglass, Beryl." Minerva winked at the fairy. "A small token of my appreciation. At our age, sometimes you just need to freeze time and have a laugh."

"Oh I've got plans..." Granny Luna's eyes glittered mischievously.

"Just go easy on the customers! Have you decided yet whether you're going to stay here at the Mudpuddle?" Minerva asked Granny Luna. A pointed look passed between the two.

"I suppose I'll go back to Buffalo's when I'm no longer needed here. The Westabrook estate is where I'm bound."

"You know you're free to go wherever you wish, Beryl," Buffalo said gently. "I released you years ago."

"Don't encourage her, Buffalo." Will washed down his cookie with a glass of milk. "I need to regain my strength before she asks me to take her to Marrakech to shop the souks."

"You're both welcome to stay here as long as you like, you know," Maida felt as though she should say something.

"Thank you, Maida. I can't speak for Beryl, but I think it's time I found a place of my own," Minerva said. "I have some savings and a few ideas." She smiled at Lucretia. "There's an empty storefront between the apothecary and the pet shop. I'm thinking I should open a small fromagerie."

"I just can't believe you were here the whole time," Lucretia marveled. "Right under our noses. And nobody noticed."

"Almost nobody." Minerva exchanged another quick glance with Granny Luna. "But to tell you the truth, I hardly recognized myself."

"What changed?" Lucretia asked. "Was it the hex wearing off?"

"Cormac never cursed me." Minerva smiled sweetly at her niece. "In fact I think he blessed me."

"What are you talking about, Auntie M?" Lucretia's brow wrinkled. "That cretin turned you into a mouse!"

"No, my dear, I was always a mouse." Minerva disappeared for a moment, and reappeared on the edge of the table, a mouse once more. Just as fast, she shifted back and lifted her cup of tea.

"But...that's impossible! It goes against the code of purity! It's wrong. It's...it's...." Lucretia stammered.

"It's who I am, dear. You too. All of us Lathrops. We're all the products of a mixed marriage." Minerva took a sip as she gave Lucretia time to process. Then she pulled her great great grandmother's journal from her apron pocket and pressed it into Lucretia's hands.

"I know this is probably coming as a shock to you, Lucretia, but it's true. And it's the only thing I can thank that muddled mage for. I never expected to learn something new about myself at my age. And now that I have..." Minerva stared off into the distance for a moment, gathering her thoughts. "Well, it's important not to dwell on regrets, but I won't lie. I have quite a few. I thought I knew who I was, but I wasn't seeing the whole picture. I don't intend to spend the years I have left living a half-life."

Minerva turned to Maida next.

"Maida Lathrop Westabrook." Minerva placed a soft dry hand on Maida's cheek and beamed at her. "Meeting you at last brings such delight. But I'm afraid I owe you an apology. I should have reached out sooner. Even if you had turned out to be an Ordinary, you're still kin." Minerva leaned forward and reached across the table to grasp Buffalo's hand now. "You did a fine job with her."

"I did my best." Buffalo bowed his head. He met Maida's eye and held it for a moment, both of them acknowledging the emotional sea of storms they'd traveled through together. Throughout it all, her father's love for her was one thing that had never wavered, never faltered. It would take time to rebuild their relationship, but she didn't doubt it would happen. There were still so many truths to reveal, and stories yet to be told. She looked forward to it even.

Beside her, Arthur gave her a comforting squeeze and Rosie beamed.

"Your Mama was hardly the first Lathrop to test the old traditions," Minerva told Maida. "In fact, none of us would be here in Primrose Court, and there wouldn't have been a Primrose Court at all, if Papa Lathrop hadn't married a mouse." She looked around at everyone assembled, gauging their reactions.

"To Papa Lathrop and knowing, and embracing, one's true self." Amrita raised her teacup. Maida was surprised to see that Amrita's beautiful raven colored hair had rearranged itself into a wreath of cascading feathers. Amrita patted it unself-consciously and clinked her glass against the others. "I think there may have been a drop of absolute truth in the mist last night. It seems to have settled on us all."

As if to punctuate the toast, the clock in the foyer chimed out the hour.

"We'll need to open soon," Maida said. She stood to help Granny and Rosie clear the table.

"Sit down, Maida," Rosie commanded. "Enjoy your company. We've got this handled."

"I see you have, indeed," Minerva agreed, smiling wistfully. She sipped her tea, draining the last dregs from the cup. "I cannot thank you all enough for what you have done for me and this place." She looked around the table, making eye contact with every one of the assembled group, and finally settling on Amrita. The Director of the Society nodded sympathetically at Minerva and patted her hand.

"Finish your tea please," Minerva continued, "but as soon as you're done, I think I should like to pay my last respects to Zephyr. He deserves his peace."

FIFTY

FAIRY TALE NONSENSE

Let it be known: no sacrifice is too great to preserve the purity of one's bloodline. Better to spend your final days alone in a crumbling tower, with only the whispers of your ancestors for company, than to tarnish your heritage by mingling with shifters, fairies, or—perish the thought—Ordinaries.

Should the grand halls of your home fall silent and your name fade from memory, rest assured that you, at least, remained unsullied. The fleeting comforts of friendship, love, and family pale in comparison to the eternal triumph of an untainted lineage.

-EXCERPT FROM THE ARCANE ELITE: UPHOLDING THE SANCTITY OF WITCH BLOODLINES

On the morning of Minerva Lathrop's return to Mudpuddle Bookshop and Cafe, the Primrose Court Town Council met to decide the fate of Zephyr Nightshade's remains. As the esteemed witch made her way past the picturesque shops that lined the central square in Primrose Court, she was surprised to see the shopkeepers coming to their windows to wave and welcome her home. At least a couple of them clapped, and several, still in their pajamas, leaned out their windows to shout a greeting, telling her how much they had missed her. She was deeply touched by the display, but she did not slow her pace.

She needed to get to the morgue.

Three people walked alongside Minerva that morning. She was accompanied by her great niece, Maida Westabrook, her niece's solicitor, Arthur Hart—though anyone could see their relationship was closer than that—and Amrita Berman, the Director of the Society for the Protection of Natural Magic.

The sun was shining, and the air was clean and crisply cool with the coppery edge that told her more snow was coming. Minerva set the pace at a fast clip. She was anxious to get there and see what she might find. She reached her right hand into her empty pocket as she walked. Then she pulled her hand out again, not sure what to do with it. Her hand had no place to go, and nothing to do without a wand or a tail.

She shifted the basket she was carrying on her other arm and rested her free hand inside atop the contents. There was a fresh batch of her lemon biscuits, bundled up and still warm from the oven. All respect to Rosie and her snickerdoodles, but the lemon drizzles had always been Zephyr's favorite. A herring sandwich garnished with petite cornichon pickles was wrapped in plain brown paper and tied with a bit of twine. She'd included today's newspaper, and of course, Zephyr's mirror. If he was to be buried in his earthly form, it was Minerva's wish that he might be buried with it. Inside that basket, she had everything she needed to prepare an altar. The only thing missing was a bit of Zephyr's dust.

"There's been no deterioration," Amrita assured her. "His body is just as we found it."

At first when Amrita had told Minerva about Zephyr's strange state, Minerva had been quite upset. She didn't want to think about the way Zephyr had looked when she last saw him. She preferred to remember him as he was in her visions. But if she was being honest, she didn't care all that much. She was simply grateful for the chance to see him one last time. She wanted to lay her hand on his brow and apologize for the way she'd tossed him out of the shop so unceremoniously. What a terrible last impression that was.

Minerva couldn't think of a single reason his body had not moved on. And what about his soul? Was it trapped here as well? Was that the reason he'd been able to come to her in dreams?

"We're here now." Arthur held the door open for Minerva. The coroner didn't waste any time showing them back to the private chamber where Zephyr's body was still being held.

It was just as they'd said. He was perfectly intact, stretched out so peacefully on the marble slab that he might have been sleeping. But of course he wasn't sleeping. He wasn't snoring. He wasn't even breathing.

She laid her hand on his cheek.

"Stubborn old pishogue," Minerva said. "You just refused to leave, didn't you? Were you waiting for someone to chase you out?"

"Perhaps we should give you some privacy?" Amrita suggested.

"I would appreciate that." Minerva nodded. "I'd like a few moments alone with him. Zephyr was quite special to me."

"I'm sure he felt the same way about you," Maida said, placing a hand on her aunt's shoulder. "I'm so sorry, Aunt Minerva."

"Thank you." Minerva nodded. "I appreciate that." She placed the basket down on the slab beside him. She bit the inside of her cheek to stave off the tears. "Now leave me, please."

"Of course," Maida said, and began backing towards the door. Amrita took her hand and Arthur held the door for them.

Minerva waited at the center of the freezing cold room, until the door clicked shut, then she kicked off her shoes and unbound her braids. She removed her hat, her glasses, and her overcoat, and climbed up on the slab next to Zephyr.

"I've got your favorite biscuits here, Zippy, still warm from the oven." She removed the plate of biscuits and placed them to his far side.

"You should probably save them till after the sandwich,

though. Don't worry—I didn't forget the pickle. Granny Luna picked up the herring fresh this morning."

One by one, she unpacked the items she'd brought, narrating it like a story as she passed the items before his unseeing eyes.

She smoothed out the newspaper and laid it beside his open hand. The lead headline read *Mudpuddle Mystery Solved, Missing Witch Returns!* There was even a photograph of Minerva and the Mudpuddle bookstore. The photo was taken a few years ago, but she didn't think her appearance had changed much.

"There's so much more to the story that they left out." Minerva laid herself down and curled up beside Zephyr. She draped her arm across him. "I'm sure you would have figured it all out so much faster. You suspected something was different about me all along, didn't you? Is that why you didn't want to marry me?"

But, of course, Zephyr did not answer. Minerva inhaled, still smelling Zephyr's pipe tobacco. He still smelled like himself, but his body was cold. She shivered a bit and pushed herself up on her elbow to study his face. It was just so strange, seeing him like this. Like visiting a familiar figure in a wax museum.

"You were right about Nocturnaturals, and that boy as well." Minerva brushed the hair out of his eyes. "I should have listened to you. That mage was bad news. And poor, poor Bardo Chan. I don't know if he could have been saved, but if anyone could have found a way, it would have been you. I know you certainly would have tried."

There was so much she wanted to tell him now. About Maida and Arthur, and about Rosie too.

"You were right about dragons, Zephyr. They aren't extinct. I'm sorry I argued with you about that."

Minerva sighed and rolled onto her back. "I was wrong about so many things, and so full of pride. Honestly, Zephyr, I was insufferable. How could you even stand me?" She swallowed and continued. "I'm sorry. So sorry. Sorry, I was so stubborn. Sorry, I kicked you out like that. Sorry, I was such a stick in the mud." She stared up at the chamber's ceiling, which was enchanted to display a starry night view. In the blur of her tears, the stars grew streaky, wavering and running together like watercolors.

"At least your view's not too bad," she commented. "Though I imagine it would get boring after a few weeks. I can imagine wanting to get out and about for a bit."

She gathered herself for a moment, then stood up and walked away from him. She wasn't sure what she expected, but this was not going so great. It was nothing like speaking to the real Zephyr. It wasn't even like speaking to the one who came to her in her visions. This was like speaking to a shell. Perhaps she was just being foolish. She considered shifting and showing him what she could do. But what was the point? He couldn't see her now, and perhaps he never really had. She would never know. Just like she would never know if his tale about the mirror was true.

Frustrated, Minerva paced around the space.

"Was that really you there with me, Zephyr? I'd like to believe it was. I'd like to believe you led me to the mirror, because you knew something. But perhaps I'm nothing more than an old fool."

Kneeling beside him now on the narrow plinth at the base of the slab, she reached into the basket one more time and pulled out the mirror. It was so much easier to lift now that she was her old size again. Old size, but not old self.

She placed the mirror beside him, face up, reflecting the stars. She could still recall the days when Ordinaries used a mirror to check for signs of life. Witches were more sensitive. They didn't need tools to detect the absence of life. But still she noted that the mirror sitting beside her dearly departed's face, remained crystal clear.

"You know, I used to be afraid that one day I'd be discovered. That nobody would love a mousy old shopkeeper. And that would be the reason I'd end up alone. Always alone. But somehow I still hoped."

A single tear fell from her eye and landed on Zephyr's hand. She watched the trail as it slid down towards his thumb and into the crevice formed by his tightly clenched fist. It was then she remembered what Amrita had asked her this morning.

"Do you have any idea how Zephyr might have come to possess your wand?"

She thought back to the last time she'd seen him—the morning the Mudpuddle disappeared. How shocked she'd been to see him like that. She hadn't been prepared for Cormac's attack. And she'd lost her wand. Had she dropped it? And had he caught it?

She'd assumed he was dead. But what if he had still been clinging to life at that point, and instead of saving him, she'd run away? She wrapped her hand around his now, calling her wand home. Instantly, his hand relaxed, and the wand slipped itself back into her pocket.

"Oh, Zippy." She crumpled across his chest. "I'm so sorry. I didn't know. Maybe that's why you're still here?" She pulled out her wand and brandished it. "Because you were keeping this safe for me? You dear, dear old wizard."

Leaning forward once more, she caught a glimpse of his reflection in the mirror, and was not at all surprised to see a mischievous little blue-eyed boy waving back at her. He even went so far as to wag his eyebrows and blow her a kiss before disappearing again.

"Well, that's one mystery solved, you imp," Minerva said. Impulsively, she threw his arms around him. She placed her warm cheek against his cool one. It may not have been meant to be in this lifetime, and there were no guarantees for the next. She wanted to kiss him. Just one last time before he turned back to dust.

It wasn't like her to take such liberties. She'd always been far too timid to do anything so bold. But who was here to judge her now? The pull was so strong it was nearly magnetic. And so she simply turned her head, parted her lips and did it.

It didn't happen immediately.

The first thing she noticed was how soft his lips were.

And the second was how warm.

By the time she realized he was kissing her back, she had lost her senses. It wasn't till he wrapped his arms around her and pulled her up onto the slab with him, kissing her more passionately, that she recalled where she was and pushed herself away. She flew to her feet, staring at the formerly dead man in disbelief. He sat up and brushed himself off.

"How?" she exclaimed, followed by, "What?" "Why?" and "When?"

"You forgot 'where' and 'who.'" Zephyr winked. For the first time in her life, Minerva was speechless.

"Don't tell me you're speechless," Zephyr teased. "I still have a few tricks up my sleeve, Minnie."

"Clearly!" Minerva said. "But raising yourself from the dead? That seems a bit dark, no?" She stepped back now, concerned about the effects of dark magic that might be taking hold. Thankfully, she had her wand back, and was already holding it.

"Technically, it was you that brought me back." Zephyr hopped off the slab. He continued to speak as he performed a series of small stretches. "But don't fear, I wasn't really dead. I was only *mostly* dead."

"Mostly dead?" Minerva could feel the wrinkle in her brow. "What does that even mean?"

"It means that while my body was dead, my spirit was quite alive and well." Zephyr took a step towards her and held out his hand.

"It was?" Minerva replied skeptically.

"Indeed. Remember when I said there were still sparks in the old fireplace?" His eyes sparked when he said that. "Why else did you think I chose to visit you that way?"

"So that *was* you?" Minerva whispered.

"Of course it was." Zephyr took her hand.

"And the mirror?" She glanced back at the mirror on the table.

"You needed to see yourself properly, Minnie. The way I have always seen you. The whole beautiful package. I've been trying to tell you for years. You just wouldn't listen."

"And you don't mind?" she squeaked.

"Mind? I think it's spectacular!" Zephyr exclaimed. "I wish I had a tail for a backup wand!" He pulled her closer and twirled her into his arms. "I've always thought you were too good for me, Minnie. Not the other way around. Let's not waste any more time?"

And then he kissed her again. More tentatively this time. His lips were tender. They moved gently and slowly, giving her time to reconcile the very fact that they were kissing.

"Wait!" Minerva pushed him away. "You still haven't told me how you did it? I thought Cormac killed you!"

"Well he certainly tried." Zephyr nodded. "But I spelled myself first. Hit myself with a True Love's Kiss Hex."

"A what?"

"True Love's Kiss Hex."

"You're kidding me." She wrinkled her face skeptically. "That's just some fairy tale nonsense."

"Just like dragons?" Zephyr's eyes crinkled as he bit his lip trying not to smile. "I'd like to hear more about that, when you have a chance. What changed your mind?"

"Nevermind about that!" Minerva snapped. "You're telling me you risked permanent death if I didn't kiss you? What if I hadn't been able to shift back!?"

"I had faith you would."

"But what if I didn't?"

"It was a chance I was willing to take. I'm an old man. I don't plan to live forever. And I don't want to live without the love of my life any longer." He paused, speaking more tentatively, "I just hope I didn't judge the situation wrong?"

"Oh, Zippy." She threw her arms around him. "I'm so sorry. I haven't even said it yet. Of course, I love you too. You have to know, I always have."

Now it was Minerva's turn to kiss him. Besides his mouth, she peppered kisses on his cheeks, forehead, and eyelids. "I love you so much! I can't believe what a fool I've been!"

"You're no more fool than me," Zephyr corrected. "Although I must say, I've heard you admit you were wrong more times in the last hour than I have in the entire last hundred years."

"Well, don't get used to it." Minerva sniffed.

"Oh, I won't." Zephyr grinned. "But you know how you could make it up to me?"

"How?" she asked.

"You could hand me those delicious lemon drizzle biscuits. It's been an absolute age since I had a bite to eat."

A LETTER FROM THE AUTHOR

Dear reader,

I hope you've enjoyed your visit to the world of Natural Magic and I look forward to meeting you back at the Mudpuddle Bookshop and Cafe for the next books in this series. If you want to join other readers in hearing all about my new releases, you can sign up here:

www.stormpublishing.co/ciara-blume

For bonus material, writing updates and anecdotes about my adorable furry familiars:

linktr.ee/ciarablumeauthor

Most of all I hope this book has brought a little magic, delight and joy into your life. If you've enjoyed this book, please leave a review on Amazon in order to help other magical folk find their way to Primrose Court.

I was inspired to write *The Mudpuddle Manual of Natural Magic* by the delight I felt as a child upon discovering a new "*Maida*" book by Inez Haynes Irwin at a used bookshop or estate sale. These books were hard to come by as they were penned in the early 1900s. They'd been a favorite of my mother's when she was a little girl too. I still have her original copies. I can perfectly recall the excitement of spying a particular shade of orange cover on the bookshelf in some dusty attic or corner. Oh, the anticipation when it was a story I had yet to read! Treasure! I think that adults deserve this same joy. I've named several of the characters in my series after characters from Irwin's stories. They already felt like friends and I am happy to greet grown up, magical versions of them again in my own pages.

Fondly,

Ciara Blume

www.ciarablume.com

instagram.com/ciarablumeauthor
facebook.com/ciarablumeauthor
tiktok.com/@ciarablumeauthor

www.ingramcontent.com/pod-product-compliance
Lightning Source LLC
Chambersburg PA
CBHW011923050726
47591CB00009B/2310

* 9 7 8 1 8 3 7 0 0 6 0 4 5 *